Christmas Spirits

Gideon felt chills go down his spine. He peered back down the stairs into the darkened entryway. It wouldn't have surprised him in the least to have seen someone standing there.

But the entryway was empty.

Gideon straightened. He was hearing things... He'd had a very long day and the wind was playing tricks on him. Either that or he'd spent far too much time looking at Megan McKinnon. She unsettled him more than the wind...

—from "The Three Wise Ghosts" by Lynn Kurland,
national bestselling author of *Stardust of Yesterday,*
A Dance Through Time, and *This Is All I Ask*

CHRISTMAS SPIRITS

Lynn Kurland
Casey Claybourne
Elizabeth Bevarly
Jenny Lykins

JOVE BOOKS, NEW YORK

"The Three Wise Ghosts" by Lynn Kurland copyright © 1997
by Lynn Curland.
"Keeping Faith" by Casey Claybourne copyright © 1997
by Casey Mickle.
"Only Fifteen Shopping Days Left . . ." by Elizabeth Bevarly copyright
© 1997 by Elizabeth Bevarly.
"The Ghost of Christmas Present" by Jenny Lykins copyright © 1997
by Jenny Lykins.

CHRISTMAS SPIRITS

A Jove Book / published by arrangement with
the authors

PRINTING HISTORY
Jove edition / November 1997

All rights reserved.
Copyright © 1997 by Jove Publications, Inc.
Book design by Casey Hampton.
This book may not be reproduced in whole
or in part, by mimeograph or any other means,
without permission. For information address:
The Berkley Publishing Group, a member of Penguin Putnam Inc.,
200 Madison Avenue, New York, New York 10016.

The Putnam Berkley World Wide Web site address is
http://www.berkley.com

ISBN: 0-515-12174-6

A JOVE BOOK®
Jove Books are published by The Berkley Publishing Group,
a member of Penguin Putnam Inc.,
200 Madison Avenue, New York, New York 10016.
JOVE and the "J" design are trademarks
belonging to Jove Publications, Inc.

PRINTED IN THE UNITED STATES OF AMERICA

10 9 8 7 6 5 4 3 2 1

CONTENTS

THE THREE
WISE GHOSTS

Lynn Kurland

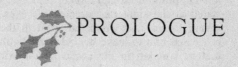

PROLOGUE

The inn sat back well off of the main road, nestled cozily on the hillside amongst rosebushes, hollyhocks, and delphiniums which had long since turned their minds to sleep for the winter. It was a comfortable abode fashioned of sturdy stone walls and a heavy, timbered roof. Well-wrought leaded windows found themselves surrounded by thick branches of climbing roses and wisteria. Light spilled out from the windows, beckoning to the weary traveler to enter and join in a companionable quaff or two of ale before retiring to the comfort of one of several guest chambers. At the moment a thin stream of smoke wafted up into the darkened sky from one of the fireplaces, as if to indicate that the innkeeper was indeed at home with something tasty on the fire.

At the sight of the smoke, a tall, elderly man quickened his pace up the way. His feet skimmed heedlessly over the finely laid brick pathway that wound through the slumbering garden. He hardly noticed the richly appointed entryway with its heavy beamed ceiling. He paid no attention whatsoever to the long hallway with its walls covered by pictures of famous (and infamous) former guests. His crisply pleated kilt flowed gracefully around him and his great sword slapped against his thigh as he strode down the passageway.

There was trouble afoot. He could smell it from a hundred paces.

He came to an abrupt halt at the kitchen entrance. And then Ambrose MacLeod, Laird of the Clan MacLeod during the glorious sixteenth century, statesman of the most diplomatic proportions and thinker of deep, profound thoughts, stared at the sight that greeted his eyes, frowned a most severe frown, and wondered what in the blazes had ever possessed him to leave his beloved Highlands. Never mind that he had kin in the castle up the way who warranted looking after now and then. Never mind that the Boar's Head Inn boasted the most reputable and thorough hauntings on the isle—a distinction Ambrose had personally seen to at every opportunity. Those were things that could have sorted themselves out without him.

Nay, he decided as he observed the occupants of the kitchen, 'twas these two who had held him so long away from home. And damn the lads both if they weren't assorted family, making it just that much harder to leave them to peaceably killing each other!

"And *I* say," the first said, "he spends far too much time fiddling over those infernal gadgets of his."

"Better that than flitting from place to place, never staying more than a few months," the second retorted. "As *she* does."

"At least she has the imagination to do so."

"She's flighty," the second grumbled. "Changeable."

"At least she hazards a risk now and again. Unlike that stuffy, pebble-counting lad of yers!"

That final insult was delivered by the man on Ambrose's left. Ambrose looked at the ruddy-complected, red-haired former Laird of the Clan McKinnon (and Ambrose's cousin by way of several intermarriages), Hugh McKinnon. Hugh was done up handsomely in full dress, his kilt swinging about his knees as he bounced from one foot to the other, obviously anxious to inflict bodily harm on the man he faced.

And that man was Fulbert de Piaget, second son of the fourteenth Earl of Artane, and to Ambrose's continued astonishment, his own beloved sister's husband. Second son though he might have been, Fulbert carried himself with the complete arrogance of an Artane lad. Ambrose couldn't help but feel a faint admiration for that, especially considering the murkiness of Fulbert's claim to several other titles. Fulbert's finely embroidered doublet flapped about his legs as he gestured with his mug as he might have a sword.

"Pebble-counting!" Fulbert thundered, ale sloshing madly over the edge of his cup onto the floor. "I'll have you know me nevvy does a proper day's work!"

"As does she!"

"When she can remember her place of employment!"

The two glared at each other furiously for a long, highly charged moment, then they lunged, bellowing clan mottos and other such slogans appropriate to the moment.

"Oh, by the saints," Ambrose exclaimed, striding out into the chamber and interrupting the fisticuffs. "Now's not the time for quibbling over tiny faults. We've serious work to do!" He turned a dark look on his cousin. "Hugh, cease with this meaningless bickering."

Hugh wanted to do anything but that—that much was apparent by the white-knuckled grip he had on the hilt of his still-sheathed sword.

"Hugh," Ambrose warned.

Hugh scowled, then ducked his head and gave his polished boots a closer look. "As ye will, Ambrose," he muttered.

Ambrose turned to his brother-in-law. "Fulbert?"

Fulbert looked to be chewing on a word or two, but finally nodded briefly and sought comfort in his cup.

"Then 'tis settled," Ambrose said, pulling up a chair and settling into it. "Sit, lads, and let us speak one last time of our plans. The pair's set to arrive on the morrow."

"Ha," said Fulbert, pursing his lips. "We'll be fortunate indeed if she manages to find her way—"

Ambrose held out his hand to stop Hugh from throwing his chair rather ungently in Fulbert's direction.

"Actually, Fulbert," Ambrose said, turning to him, "your brother's son—albeit many times removed—was the

one I was most concerned about. He was particularly difficult to convince."

"And how would you know?" Fulbert demanded.
" 'Twere me own sweet self that saw to getting him here.
And I can't say as I blames him not wanting to come, what
with all the important work he does." He cast a pointed
look at Hugh. "Unlike that girl—"

"There's naught a thing wrong with me wee granddaughter," Hugh declared. He paused, looked faintly puzzled,
then frowned. "I suppose I could consider her such."

"Indeed, you could, Cousin," Ambrose said, with a nod.
"And, to be sure, there is naught amiss with her." He ignored Fulbert's snort. "Now, lads, let us turn our minds
back to the good work set before us." He looked at his
kinsman. "You saw to the other establishment, did you
not?"

"Aye," Hugh said, with a smile. "No room at the inn,
as it were. Not that it was all that difficult, it being the
season and all."

Ambrose nodded in approval. "I've seen to it that there
will be none but the two reservations available here for the
holidays and given instructions to Mrs. Pruitt on who shall
receive them. All we must do is wait for the morrow and
then lend a hand where needed."

"I still say we should have planned something in particular," Fulbert grumbled. "Perhaps a reprise of my performance for that Dickens fellow."

Hugh snorted. " 'Twere bad fish he ate that gave him
those foul dreams."

"Dreams? He bloody immortalized me Christmas visit in
print!"

Ambrose suppressed the urge to throw his hands up in
despair; it was a wonder he saw anything accomplished with
these two underfoot. Even though the telling of tall tales
went hand in hand with proper haunting, there was no time
for such happy recollections now. If he allowed Fulbert any
more room for speaking, they'd be listening to him boast
till dawn.

"We're best served by seeking our rest," he said, rising. "We've a full fortnight ahead of us."

"But, wait, Ambrose," Hugh said, holding up his hand. "Ye never told us where ye went to find me wee one."

Those were memories Ambrose didn't care to discuss. After all, they had been surely the most traumatic events of his afterlife. He, Ambrose MacLeod, powerful laird of an even more powerful and noble clan, had taken his pride and courage in hand to do what no other laird (alive or otherwise) had done before him. His sires and grandsires who had passed on before him had no doubt held their collective breaths until his task had been accomplished.

"Aye," Fulbert said, suddenly perking up. "Just where was it you went to fetch that fidgety, harebrained—"

Ambrose cut him off by suddenly sitting back down. Why his sweet sister had chosen to marry an irascible Englishman, Ambrose would never know, but there it was. He took the mug Hugh handed him, and had a long swallow of ale, just to shore up his strength.

"Well," he began slowly, "it was a tad more difficult to track her down than I'd thought it would be."

Fulbert smirked. Hugh looked primed to say something nasty in return, so Ambrose quickly told the worst of it to distract them.

"I began in a Colonial fast-food establishment," he announced.

Both Fulbert and Hugh gaped at him, stunned into silence. Ambrose took a firmer grip on his cup. "Indeed, I was forced to venture into more than one."

Gasps echoed in the kitchen.

"Failing to find her there, I searched further and learned that she had taken other employment." He paused. "In a theme park."

Fulbert tossed back the remaining contents of his cup and lunged for the jug. Hugh went quite pale in the face.

"Is there more?" Hugh asked, in trembling tones. "I beg ye, Ambrose, say us nay!"

Indeed, there *was* more, and Ambrose was loath to give

voice to the telling of it. He looked about the chamber, just to avoid the eyes of his companions.

"I discovered," he admitted, his voice barely audible, "that she had been dressing up as a mouse."

"By the saints, nay!" Hugh gasped.

Fulbert made gurgling noises as he struggled to express himself. Finally he managed a word or two.

"You!" he exclaimed, pointing an accusing finger at Ambrose. "After all these years of proper haunting . . . consorting with cartoon characters! By the saints, Ambrose, what were you thinking!"

"I did what was required," Ambrose said stiffly. "And once she was found, I paid a short visit to her brother. He was quite willing to send her off on an errand here and more than happy to believe a healthy case of indigestion had given him the idea."

"Och, but the indignity of it all," Hugh breathed. "Traveling all the way to—" his voice trailed off meaningfully.

No one could voice the word.

California.

And, worse yet, the southern region of it! Aye, 'twas enough to give any sensible shade the shakes.

" 'Tis just that," Fulbert said darkly, "which leads me to believe that perhaps the lass is not quite—"

"The lass?" Hugh interrupted indignantly. "No matter where she's been—" He swallowed audibly and then pressed on. "At least she possesses some spark of creativity. *I'm* less than certain about that lad of yers—"

Fulbert leaped to his feet, cast aside his cup and drew his sword. "I'll not have me nevvy slandered by a man in skirts!"

"Skirts?" Hugh gasped, hopping up from his chair and flinging aside his goblet also. He drew his sword with relish. "Outside, ye blasted Brit. I'll need room fer me swingin'."

Ambrose gave one last fleeting thought to the peace and comfort of his ancestral home in the Highlands before he thundered a command for the lads to cease. He shook his head in disgust. "By the saints," he said, "have you nothing better to do than fight with each other?"

Fulbert looked faintly surprised. "Actually Ambrose, 'tis fine enough sport for me—"

"Aye," Hugh agreed. "Passes the time most pleasantly—"

Ambrose thrust out his arm and pointed to the door. "Be-gone, the both of you and leave me to my ale."

Fulbert opened his mouth to protest. Ambrose gave him the quelling look he'd given to more than one adversary over the course of his long and successful career. Fulbert shut his mouth with a snap and vanished from the kitchen. Hugh made Ambrose a quick bow and bolted as well.

Ambrose leaned back in his chair and sighed. Now that he finally had peace for thinking, he turned over in his mind the events of the past pair of months, gingerly avoiding the memories of his trip to the Colonies. Perhaps he shouldn't have meddled, but how could he have helped himself? Young Megan was his granddaughter—never mind how many generations separated them. Despite the personal in-dignities he'd suffered already in this venture, how could he not feel a certain responsibility to her and her happiness? And he had to admit Fulbert's lad was a good one, despite his preoccupation with modern inventions.

Aye, he would simply do all he could for them, then pray they had the good sense to finish falling in love by them-selves.

Though, considering the pair due to arrive on the morrow, the only good sense to be found in the inn would be his own.

ONE

Megan MacLeod McKinnon stood on the side of the dirt road, stared at her surroundings, and wondered why in the world she'd ever agreed to any of this. She'd known the British Isles could be damp, but she'd never suspected they would be *this* damp. And what happened to that dry rain that supposedly fell strictly for atmosphere? Maybe she'd taken a wrong turn somewhere, like at Kennedy. She should have boarded that plane bound for Italy. How rainy could it be in Italy this time of year?

Of course, if things had gone according to plan, she would have been ensconced in a cozy inn, reading Dickens and sipping tea while toasting her toes against a cheery fire.

Instead she found herself trudging up a muddy road on the Scottish border in the middle of what had to be the worst storm in two hundred years. In December, no less. With only the clothes on her back.

This was not exactly a Currier and Ives kind of Christmas vacation.

She turned her face into the wind, picked her way around a puddle and kept walking. She wouldn't go home until she'd done what she came to do. She'd bungled every other job she'd ever had, but she wouldn't bungle this one. No matter how awful things got.

Rain began to leak past her collar. As her back grew increasingly damp, her thoughts turned to her brother. This was, of course, entirely his fault. If he hadn't been bitten by that search-for-your-ancestors bug, he never would have bought a castle and all that went with it, and he never would have sent her to look it over. Surely he should have known what would befall her on this ill-fated trip.

Hadn't he had an inkling that her row-mate on the flight over might be a screaming two-year-old? Shouldn't he have warned her that her luggage might vanish as she stood innocently in line to buy a train ticket north? Should there not have been some doubt in his overused brain that the weather in December might be a tad bit on the wet side? Hadn't he felt the slightest desire to rethink his plans for her as he booked her a room in a no-stoplight town at an inn that would subsequently lose her reservation?

Megan hopped over another pothole and gave her missing reservation more thought. Had it been merely missing or deliberately mislaid? Had the desk clerk taken one look at her bedraggled, luggageless self and come to a hasty decision about her desirability as a guest?

After making certain she understood there was no room for her at his inn, he had offered to make her a reservation at the only other hotel within miles. *A quiet place, just a wee bit up the road—conveniently near the castle,* he'd said. Megan had been overjoyed that there was actually another bed waiting for her within walking distance, especially since she hadn't seen anything resembling a taxi since the train had paused long enough for her to jump down onto the platform. Maybe Thorpewold didn't see all that many visitors.

She lurched to a stop, braced herself against the wind and peered into the mist. She frowned. Had she taken a wrong turn somewhere? Just how far was ''wee'' anyway?

Then she froze. Either the wind was revving up for a new round of buffeting, or that was a car approaching. She listened carefully. Yes, that was a car, and it sounded like it was heading her way. Megan stood up straighter and dragged a hand through her hair. No sense in not looking her best for a potential ride. The car came closer. She put on her best smile and started to wave. It was the Cinderella parade wave she'd perfected but never had the chance to use.

Even the headlights were now visible. Good. At least she wouldn't get run over before she could beg a ride.

"Hey," she shouted as the car materialized from the mist, "can I have a—"

She barely had time to close her mouth before the tidal wave struck. The car whizzed by, drenching her from head to toe. Megan looked down at her mud-splattered self, then blinked and looked up. The taillights faded into the drizzle.

She hadn't been seen. That was it. No one was in such a hurry that they would drive past a dripping maiden in distress and not offer so much as a "keep a stiff upper lip" in passing. Well, at least the car seemed to be going somewhere. That was reassuring. Megan wiped her face and continued on her way.

Fortunately it took her only minutes to reach civilization. The mist lifted far enough for her to see a sturdy, comfortable-looking inn. The lights were on and smoke was pouring from the chimneys; these were very good signs. Maybe she would actually be able to hold on to her reservation this time.

Her eyes narrowed at the sight of her errant would-be rescuer's car parked so tidily next to the inn. A tall figure headed toward the door and a horrible thought occurred to her. What if her room was the last one and this person sweet-talked his way into it?

She bolted for the steps. The man entered before her, but Megan didn't let that deter her. She grabbed the door behind him, then elbowed her way past him and sprinted to the little desk in the alcove under the stairs. She plopped her shoulder bag onto the counter then smiled triumphantly at the woman behind the desk. In fact, the thrill of victory was making her light-headed. She clutched the edge of the desk as she felt herself begin to sway.

And then, quite suddenly, her feet were no longer under her. She squeaked as she felt herself being lifted up by what seemed to be remarkably strong arms. She threw her arms around very broad shoulders—just in case her rescuer decided she was damp enough to warrant dropping. She let go with one hand to push her soggy hair back out of her eyes. She opened her mouth to tell him his actions would have been more timely had they occurred fifteen minutes earlier, then completely lost track of what she'd intended to say.

Maybe all that water had seeped into her brain. Or maybe she'd just never seen anyone quite this handsome before. *This* was the kind of man she wouldn't mind finding under the Christmas tree with a bow on his head.

His face was ruggedly chiseled, with only the fullness in his mouth to soften his features. His dark blond hair was, irritatingly enough, perfectly dry and casually styled, as if he'd just shaken it out that morning and it had behaved simply because he'd wanted it to. Megan stared into his bluish-green eyes and found that she was fanning herself. There was something so blatantly, ruthlessly handsome about the man that she felt a bit weak in the knees. All right, so his driving habits left a lot to be desired. The man had saved her from a possible faint and, considering how he looked up close, she thought she might be able to forgive him.

"Thanks," she managed, surreptitiously wiping a bit of drool from the corner of her mouth.

He only frowned back at her.

Even his frown was beautiful. Megan smiled her best smile. "Thanks," she repeated, wondering if it would sink in this time, "but I wasn't going to faint."

He pursed his lips and set her down well away from where she'd been standing.

"You were dripping on my laptop," he said, reaching down to give his computer bag a quick swipe. He looked back at her. "And you're also dripping on the carpet," he noted.

Megan blinked. That certainly didn't sound like an undying declaration of love, nor an offer to stuff himself in her stocking. Perhaps her current state of drowned-ratdom was getting in the way of his falling at her feet and pledging eternal devotion. She flipped her wet hair to the other side of her face, hoping to achieve a more windblown, ruffled look.

The man looked down at the new drops of water on his computer bag, then scowled at her.

"How did you manage to get so wet?" he demanded.

Megan frowned. Maybe hers wasn't the only brain that had taken on too much water. "You would know," she said.

He blinked. "I would?"

"You splashed me," she reminded him.

"I did?"

"With your car!"

"Hmmm," he said, then glanced down at his computer. Something must have caught his attention because he knelt down and started unzipping the bag. Megan watched as he pulled out a cell phone and fired it up.

Megan gritted her teeth. Somehow his manly good looks had distracted her, but she was feeling much better now. This was not the kind of man for her, no sir. No matter how finely made he was, if he couldn't remember his moments of unchivalry and apologize properly for them, she wanted nothing further to do with him.

She turned her back on him and his bad manners and planted herself resolutely in front of the little desk that seemed to serve as the check-in point. When he could tear himself away from work long enough to apologize, then she would think about forgiving him. Until then, he could suffer. She would ignore him until he begged her to stop.

That resolved neatly, she gave her attention to the matter at hand: throwing herself upon the mercy of the innkeeper. She took in the sight of the sad attempts at making the reception area seem dressed for the holidays, hoping to find something there she could gush over. A little buttering up of the proprietress couldn't go wrong. The desk was decorated with a few sprigs of holly and a ribbon or two. Megan looked up. Garlic hung in great bunches above the desk area, draped liberally on the overhang made by the stairs.

"Expecting vampires any time soon?" she asked the woman behind the counter.

The white-haired woman leaped to her feet as if she'd been catapulted out of her chair.

"Ye've no idea," she whispered frantically. Her eyes darted from side to side and she kept looking over her shoulder as if she expected to be attacked from behind at any moment.

Megan opened her mouth to suggest that perhaps the garlic might do the woman more good if she wore it around her neck, then thought better of it. The innkeeper looked as if one good push would topple her right over the edge as it was.

"Yer name, lass?" the woman asked, leaning forward as if to keep the walls from overhearing.

"Megan," Megan began slowly. "Megan McKinnon."

The woman's hand flew to her throat and she gasped. "A McKinnon in the house! The saints preserve us all!"

"This isn't good," Megan said, biting her lip. This was all she needed, to be kicked out on account of her ancestry. "My mother was a MacLeod," she offered.

"Even worse!" the woman exclaimed.

"I'm from America," Megan said quickly. "Does that help? No, wait, don't say anything else. I don't want to know. Let's just get down to business and forget all the rest. Ye Olde Tudor Inn called over and made a reservation for me. You did get the call, didn't you, Mrs. . . . ?"

"Pruitt," the woman moaned. "And, aye, I've got yer roo—" her voice cracked, then she cleared her throat. "Room," she managed. "If ye're sure ye want it."

"Oh, I want it," Megan assured her.

"Ye've a private bath, too," Mrs. Pruitt added. "Up the stairs, down the hallway on yer left. If ye're certain here is where ye truly want to stay—"

A pen suddenly slapped itself down next to Megan's hand. Mrs. Pruitt screeched and leaped back, making Megan jump. Megan took a deep breath to calm her suddenly racing heart. Then she remembered the splashing one who'd been kneeling beside her, dusting off his precious computer. He'd obviously decided to interrupt Mrs. Pruitt's tirade by throwing his pen at her. Maybe he was antsy to get checked in.

Megan turned toward him, ready to give him a lecture on not frightening potential hostesses.

Only he wasn't standing next to her anymore. He was talking on his cell phone, looking for a plug for the laptop he'd already unearthed from its case.

Odd. Megan looked back at Mrs. Pruitt. Maybe this quaking creature had produced the pen with a clever sleight of hand trick. But if she'd been the one to do it, why had she screeched like a banshee? Megan decided it was best not to give that any more thought. Mrs. Pruitt owned a hotel possessing a room with a private bath. At this point, that was all that mattered.

She signed her name and held out the pen. Mrs. Pruitt looked at it in horror.

"Okay," Megan said, setting the pen down carefully. "You don't seem to want this. I'm not sure why, but I'm certain I don't want to know. What I do want to know is if I can get dinner here."

"In an hour," Mrs. Pruitt blurted out. "In the dining room. The saints preserve us through it!"

"Okay," Megan agreed. "I'm sure it will be just lovely. Now, where do I go—"

"Up the stairs. Last door on the left." The woman practically flung the key at her.

Megan caught it neatly and gathered up her shoulder bag.

"Do ye need yer other bags carried up?" Mrs. Pruitt asked.

Megan paused. Her lack of luggage certainly hadn't aided her cause previously, but at least this time she had the key already in hand.

"My luggage was stolen," Megan admitted.

"Oh merciful saints above!" the woman exclaimed. "What'll happen next to ye?"

"It wasn't all that bad—"

"Ach, but ye've no idea," the woman interrupted, her eyes practically rolling back in her head. "No idea—"

"BY THE SAINTS, MRS. PRUITT, QUIT YER BABBLING. AND YOU, MEGAN, GO UP TO YER BLOODY BEDCHAMBER!"

Mrs. Pruitt gave vent to another screech and ducked down

behind the desk. Megan whirled around with a gasp, incensed that a perfect stranger should speak to her so rudely.

"What did you say?" she demanded of the delectable hunk of manliness with no manners.

He didn't look up.

"Hey," she said, coming to stand next to him, "I asked you a question." She dripped on him for good measure.

He looked up and blinked at her. "Yes?" he asked, tipping his phone away from his mouth.

Megan looked at him with narrowed eyes. "Who said you could order us around like that?"

"I beg your pardon?"

"Hey," Megan said, wagging her finger at him, "don't give me that changing your voice routine either. Where'd that obnoxious accent go?"

There was a groan and a thump. Megan looked over to find that Mrs. Pruitt had fallen to the floor in a dead faint.

"I haven't the foggiest notion of what you're going on about," the man said, looking very perplexed. Then he turned back to his computer and said no more.

Megan looked from him to their fallen proprietress and then back to him. He was already entrenched in his business again. Obviously good looks and good manners did not necessarily come in the same package. She sighed. So much for a handsome stocking stuffer this year.

She turned and walked back across the foyer. It took only a touch on the arm to have Mrs. Pruitt roused from her swoon and screeching again.

"It's just me," Megan said, flinching. "I think you fainted."

"I'm f-fine," Mrs. Pruitt said, her teeth chattering like castanets. She accepted Megan's help in getting back to her feet. "Just go up to yer room, miss, quick as may be."

"But I think you might need help. Is there somewhere you could lie down? I'll fix you a cup of—"

"OH, BY ALL THE BLOODY SAINTS . . ."

Megan froze. She met Mrs. Pruitt's terrified eyes and swallowed, hard. Then she looked over her shoulder. The Corporate One was still gabbing into his cell phone, completely ignoring them. Megan turned back to Mrs. Pruitt.

"The wind?" she offered.

Mrs. Pruitt turned her around and pointed her toward the stairs. "I'll bring ye some dry clothes as quick as may be," she said, pushing Megan across the entryway. "Just go on up, lass. *Please.*"

Megan hesitated at the bottom of the staircase. What sort of loony bin had she signed herself into? Men doing business in entry halls, innkeepers begging their guests to move along, voices coming from nowhere?

"I'm beginning to wonder if I should even stay," Megan said slowly.

The front door flew open and slammed back against the wall. The next gust of wind blew Megan up half a dozen stairs. Mrs. Pruitt fled around the desk and hid behind it. Megan saw the rude one rise, shut the door and then return to his hunched down position near the wall.

She shook her head, then turned and climbed slowly up the remaining steps. It was either stay here or head back out into the storm, and the latter was a very unappealing alternative. So what if everyone else in the house was bonkers? With any luck, her room would have a heavy-duty lock on it and she could bolt herself inside except for meals.

The front door must not have closed very well because the wind seemed to howl in spite of it. Megan shivered. Mrs. Pruitt's jumpiness was starting to rub off on her.

She let herself into her room and closed the door behind her. A hot bath awaited. She smiled for the first time in hours. Yes, indeedy, things were certainly looking up.

Maybe the trip would be worth it after all.

Ambrose MacLeod sighed as he stepped into the fray and forcibly removed Hugh's fingers from about Fulbert's throat.

"Dinnae order me gel about!" Hugh thundered.

"She wasn't moving bloody fast enough to suit me," Fulbert threw back, rubbing his offended neck. "And she called me accent obnoxious!"

"Which it is, especially since we agreed not to converse

with them unless absolutely necessary!'' Ambrose exclaimed, glaring at Fulbert. ''And you needn't have spoken to the child in such a coarse manner.''

Fulbert scowled. ''She should have gone straight up to her chamber instead of chattering on with that blasted Mrs. Pruitt. Besides, she kept adrippin' all over his confounded . . . ah . . . confounded scribbling machine,'' he finished, looking less than sure of his terminology.

''That's computer, dolt,'' Hugh snarled. ''Any fool knows that—argghh!''

Ambrose applied himself this time to removing Fulbert's beefy fingers from about Hugh's throat.

''By the saints, cease!'' Ambrose put one hand on Fulbert's shoulder and the other on Hugh's and held them apart. ''How are we to do any proper matchmaking when all you two can do is go at each other? I'm of a mind to banish you both outside until the deed's done.''

Fulbert folded his arms over his chest and clenched his jaw. Hugh scrunched up his face in what Ambrose readily recognized as his determined expression.

''I'm beginning to think neither of you wants to see this come about.''

There was more clenching and scrunching. Ambrose knew it was time for drastic measures. He'd never see anything finished if he had to spend all his time reprimanding the troops.

''Very well,'' he said, with his sternest look, ''I've come to a decision. Since Fulbert has had his turn urging young Megan along the proper path, 'tis only fair Hugh should have his turn with Gideon. I daresay he'll know what needs to be done first.''

Hugh eyed the laptop with barely restrained glee. Fulbert huffed in outrage.

''He'll damage the boy's livelihood! The saints only know what'll happen to his person!''

Ambrose clapped Hugh on the shoulder. ''He'll only do what he must. Perhaps you'll have a bit more care with Megan the next time.''

Fulbert harrumphed and vanished. Ambrose smiled pleasantly at his cousin.

"I'm off for a stroll, Hugh. I'll expect a report on your progress before nightfall."

"Aye," Hugh said, advancing on Gideon.

Ambrose walked through walls and such until he came to the overgrown garden. He clucked his tongue at the sight. He'd have to have another chat with Mrs. Pruitt about her care of the inn. If she'd only stop screaming long enough for him to give her his list of instructions.

Truly, women could be so confounded irrational at times.

TWO

The Honourable Gideon de Piaget, president and CEO of Artane Enterprises, suppressed the urge to take his cellular phone and smash it through the wall.

"Put the fool on the phone, Humphreys," Gideon growled.

"I fear, my lord Gideon, that your brother is engrossed in a medieval text at the moment."

"I don't doubt it!" Gideon shouted. "Interrupt him!"

Humphreys tsk-tsked. "Really, my lord. Such displays of temper do not become you."

"I'll have you sacked!" Gideon roared.

"I believe Lord Stephen retains that privilege. Have a pleasant holiday, my lord," Humphreys said.

Gideon listened to the line go dead. Damn Stephen! As if this bloody holiday was actually going to relax him! He had mergers to contemplate, acquisitions to make, huge sums of money to move about. The entire company would go under in two weeks with Stephen at the helm. If he held true to form, he'd stay buried in some blighted old manuscript while billions of pounds floated merrily off down the Thames!

Gideon closed up his laptop and jerked the plug from the wall. He'd check in and then get down to some serious work in spite of his entire staff. And once this enforced holiday was over, he'd return and sack every one of them. Starting with his personal secretary.

Gideon ground his teeth at the thought of her. Alice had taken Stephen's suggestion that she go on holiday without so much as a by-your-leave from him personally. And this only after passing on to the rest of the employees Stephen's instructions for the entire company to refuse Gideon's calls. Gideon scowled. They could refuse to talk to him, but they couldn't control what he did four hours away from London. He would hook up his modem and pretend he was at the office. Stephen would never be the wiser.

Go on holiday or I'll sack you.

Gideon grunted as he gathered up his gear. His brother had walked into his office two days ago and said those words, as if Gideon would actually take them seriously! Stephen had been inspired, he'd said, to send Gideon off to his own favorite retreat. It would do him a world of good, or so Stephen had claimed. Gideon had thrown his brother out of his office bodily.

Of course the board meeting the next day had been a little unsettling, what with Stephen having led a unanimous vote for Gideon's holiday on pain of termination. Protests had gotten him a signed motion requiring him to leave that day and hole up in some deserted inn on the Scottish border for a fortnight. Alice had been smirking as she'd taken notes. The old harridan had probably instigated the entire affair.

Gideon strode purposefully toward the reception desk. The woman behind the desk stood, looking quite frankly unsettled. Perhaps she wasn't used to her guests assaulting outlets in her entryway. Or, more likely, she was used to Stephen who retreated here once a year to do nothing more than ensconce himself in the blasted library and bury his nose in yet another book. Gideon looked at the proprietress.

"Mrs. Pruitt, I presume?" he said, dropping his suitcase with a thud. "I'm Gideon de Piaget."

"Aye, Lord Blythwood," she said, in shaky voice. "Your b-brother said you'd be arriving today."

"No doubt," Gideon said curtly. "And it was against my will, as it happens."

Mrs. Pruitt held out the key. Her expression was such that Gideon couldn't help but feel a faint fondness for her. She looked as if she were sentencing him to certain death.

"I couldn't agree more," he said, taking the key from her trembling fingers. "My room?"

"Up the stairs," she said, her very essence seeming to become more frantic. "First door on the right."

Gideon frowned. "You do have a phone in the room, don't you?" he asked. "And an outlet?"

"Aye, my lord."

What else did he need? Gideon attributed her actions to far too much inclement weather and not enough hustle and bustle. After all, what sort of mental stimulation could a sleepy old inn in the midst of nowhere provide a person? It was no wonder Stephen loved the place. He could read in peace.

Gideon started up the stairs, eager to finally get settled in and down to work.

He frowned as he fought to reach the upper floor. His bags weren't that heavy. He looked quickly behind him, but no one was there. He could have sworn someone was tugging on his laptop. Taking a firmer grip on his things, he leaned forward and applied himself to just getting up the steps.

And then, quite suddenly, he lost his grip. He made a frantic grab for the computer, deciding in a split second that his suitcase would better survive the trip back down to the entryway. The phone had flown upward and Gideon quickly positioned himself to catch it when it came back down.

And then he watched in complete astonishment as it flew past his outstretched hand, back down the stairs and smashed into the front door. Mrs. Pruitt screeched and fled. Gideon looked at the pieces of his phone scattered in the entry.

It just hadn't been his day.

He sighed deeply as he descended and retrieved his suitcase. He turned his back on the wreckage and climbed the steps. What good was his cell phone anyway? It wasn't as if anyone would talk to him.

He entered his room, tossed his suitcase on the bed and looked about for a desk. Espying a choice antique vanity, he removed all the paraphernalia and set up his machine. Miracle of all miracles, there was a phone nearby. He unplugged it and secured the modem cable. Finding an outlet wasn't as convenient, but he'd purchased an extra long cord for just such a situation.

He shrugged out of his mac, stripped off his stifling sweater and sat down to work in his shirtsleeves. He turned the computer on, then called in to his company server. He drummed his fingers impatiently against the wood of the vanity. Remote access was irritatingly slow, but he'd make do.

He typed in his password and held his breath.

And then he smiled for the first time in seventy-two hours. Stephen obviously hadn't been thinking clearly, else he would have locked Gideon out of the system. Gideon opened up his favorite spreadsheet program and pulled up a list of the week's transactions, already feeling his pulse quicken. This was what he was meant to do. Just looking at the columns and knowing he was responsible for their contents sent a rush of adrenaline through him. The sheer power of controlling these kinds of—

The room was suddenly plunged into darkness.

Gideon swore in frustration. Damned old inn. He heaved himself up from the chair, strode across the room, and threw open the door. To his surprise, there was a light coming from the end of the corridor. Perhaps only his room was acting up. He gathered up his gear and tromped down the hallway toward the light.

He opened the door and entered without knocking. A woman gasped and Gideon pulled up short. He recognized her as the one who had dripped all over his computer downstairs. He frowned at her.

"I need your outlet."

"What?"

"Your outlet," he said impatiently. "The power's out in my room."

"I'm trying to get dressed here," she said curtly.

Gideon wrestled his attention away from his outlet search long enough to verify that she was indeed standing there in only a towel.

The sight was enough to make him pause a little longer. He started at her toes, skimmed over nicely turned ankles and continued up. Then he stopped. She had freckles on her knees. For some odd reason, it made him want to smile. It was like seeing sunshine after endless days of rain. She obviously didn't use much sunblock, or she wouldn't have had so many sun spots. And what a shame that would have been.

Sunblock. He frowned. What was the status of that cosmetic company acquisition? He'd been on the verge of closing the deal when he'd been interrupted by that disconcerting board mutiny.

"I said, I'm trying to get dressed here."

"I won't watch," he said, scanning the room.

"I don't care if you won't watch!"

He flashed her a brief smile. "Then we're settled. You don't care and I won't watch. Lovely."

She took a menacing step toward him. Gideon fell back, instinctively clutching his computer to his chest. The woman pointed toward the door.

"Get out," she commanded.

Gideon followed her long, slender arm back over to her seemingly annoyed self.

"*Hey,*" she snapped.

He blinked and looked up at her. She seemed to have an abundance of rather reddish hair, which at the moment was piled on top of her head. And then he looked at her face and he wanted to smile all over again. It was the sunshine effect, but this was even more potent than her knees. It wasn't that he'd never seen a more beautiful woman. Indeed, he had. But he'd never seen a woman whose beauty made him think of sundrenched meadows and armfuls of wildflowers. He was certain he'd never loitered in a meadow, but looking at this woman made him want to.

He dropped his eyes and studied her figure. She certainly knew how to wear a towel to its best advantage. A model, perhaps? No, too friendly-looking. An executive? He took a quick look around her room but saw no executive trappings. Oddly enough, he suspected she actually might be on holiday to have a holiday. But why, when she looked so well-rested as it was?

"Do I have to call the cops?" she demanded.

Ah, an American. He nodded to himself over that. Maybe that was why she looked so relaxed. Perhaps she was from one of those big middle states where they farmed a great deal and avoided the city rush.

The thought of Americans brought to mind a clothing company acquisition his executive VP had been working on. Adam MacClure had a knack for the American market. Gideon made himself a mental note to double-check how the numbers were running on that as soon as he was back online.

He strode purposefully to the desk, plugged himself in and began the logging-in process all over again. He heard a door slam behind him. Maybe his befreckled American neighbor had decided to dress in the bathroom.

Gideon sighed in relief once he'd accessed the server. Now maybe he could get some work done. He pulled up the file on Totally Rad Clothing and flexed his fingers. He'd missed his modem during the past few hours.

The computer beeped, then the screen went blank.

"Damn!" he exclaimed.

And then he realized the bedroom light was still on.

All right, perhaps just the outlets were on the blink. No wonder Mrs. Pruitt had wished him well. Had Stephen known? Was that why he'd been banished here? Gideon cursed his brother thoroughly as he retrieved his computer case from his room and hastened back to what appeared to be the only lighted bedroom in the entire place. He would just have to use up his spare batteries.

The woman with red hair was coming out of the bathroom. She was dressed this time, but Gideon wondered where she'd gotten her clothes. Her gown looked like something from a costume shop. Early medieval. Pity she hadn't tried it on before she rented it. The hem hit her well above her ankles, and she was positively swimming in the rest of it. Perhaps it had been fashioned for a much shorter, much plumper customer.

"Not exactly a perfect fit," he noted.

She looked down at herself, then back at him. "I lost my luggage," she said defensively.

"Nothing in your size?"

"Mrs. Pruitt brought it to me," she retorted. "What else was I supposed to do—run around naked?"

"Hmmm," he said, tempted to give that more thought.

Then he caught sight of the desk and remembered what his primary task was. He sat back down and slipped a newly charged battery into the computer. Then he crossed his fingers and plugged his battery charger, with its spare battery, into the outlet. He blinked in surprise as the charging light began to flicker. Now the outlet was functioning? The inn was a disaster. He was surprised the place hadn't burned to the ground long ago.

Gideon turned the computer back on and it sprang to life. He sat back and heaved a huge sigh of relief. He would run on battery power for awhile, just to be safe. It wasn't his preferred way—

"Would you mind telling me how long you're going to be using my outlet?"

Gideon turned. "I beg your pardon?"

"My bedroom," she said, with a wave of her arm. "My bathroom. My outlet. The space I've paid for for the next two weeks. How long are you going to be camping out in here? Dare I hope it won't be for long?"

Gideon frowned at her, then turned back to his laptop. "I don't know how long I'll be. I've important things to—"

The charger made an unwholesome sound. Gideon looked at it in alarm as smoke began to curl up from its sides. He blew on it, but smoke only began to pour forth more rapidly.

He dove under the desk for the outlet and unplugged the charger, but not before he'd heard an ominous pop, followed by a crackling sound. He whipped back up, smacking his head loudly against the front edge of the desk. He lurched to his feet, clutching the top of his head.

He stared down in horror at his laptop.

It was on fire.

Gideon stood rooted to the spot, unable to believe his eyes. His last link with civilization was going up in smoke right in front of him.

"Here."

He felt something wrap itself around his head. He unwrapped and found himself holding a sweatshirt. He used it liberally, smothering and beating until he was sweating and rather cross. Finally, he stood back and looked at the ruins of his working tools. He fanned his hand sadly over the smoking remains. It was a tragedy, really. He'd planned to put this fortnight to good use.

He looked at the sweatshirt in his hands, then unwadded it to see what was left.

"So sorry about Mickey's ears," he said, casting the woman an apologetic look.

She waved her hand dismissively. "Don't worry."

"I'll have another purchased."

"You can't. They gave it to me at the Kingdom when they canned me. In lieu of severance pay."

"The Kingdom?"

"Disneyland."

"You were sacked from Disneyland?"

She scowled. "I kept stepping on Dumbo's ears, all right? Can we move on to less painful topics? Your computer, for instance."

Gideon sat down heavily. It was just more than he could talk about.

"Can I make a suggestion?"

Gideon nodded.

"Take a vacation."

"You sound like my brother." He gave her a cross look. "He's the reason I'm stranded here. Told me he'd sack me if I didn't come."

"Hmmm," she said, "a workaholic, then."

"I have many responsibilities. I run the family business."

"Really? I'd hazard a guess the family business runs you."

He looked at her narrowly. "You Americans are very outspoken."

She shrugged. "I call 'em as I see 'em. And I'd say you needed a vacation."

"It doesn't look as if I'll have much say in the matter. Unless," he said, an idea springing to mind, "unless I might find a computer for let somewhere here about."

She laughed. "Where, here in the boonies? You'd be better off with pencil and paper."

He shook his head and rose. "No, I fear a search will have to be made. I'm already behind on the Far East markets today."

"And I'm behind in my meal schedule, so if you'll go back to where you came from, I'll be going to the dining room." She looked at the sweatshirt in his hands. "You can keep that if you like. So you can carry your mess away," she added.

Gideon was recovered enough to take the hint. He gathered up the smoldering remains and nodded at his unwilling hostess.

"Thank you . . ."

"Megan," she finished for him. "Megan McKinnon."

He balanced his computer on one arm and thrust out his hand. "Gideon de Piaget. I run Artane Enterprises."

She took his hand and smiled politely. "What a pleasure to finally learn your name after all we've shared so far."

"You've heard of me?"

"No," she said slowly, "we just met, remember? Maybe you should get some distance from your computer. The fumes aren't doing you any good."

He shook her hand some more. "You've never heard of Artane Enterprises?"

"Sorry."

"We're an international company."

"How nice for you."

Gideon found, oddly enough, that he couldn't let go of her. He wondered if it might be because of something sticky from his battery charger, but nothing seemed to be burning his skin.

Except the touch of her hand, of course.

He looked at her searchingly. ''The name doesn't ring any bells for you?''

She put her free hand to her ear, listened, then shook her head. ''Nary a jingle.''

''I'm the president of the company.''

''Ah.''

''A powerful CEO.''

''I see,'' she said. Her gaze slid down to his ravaged computer, then back up. ''Believe me, I'm impressed. I would have rushed to let you into my room if I'd only known.''

''I don't think you're nearly as impressed as you should be.''

She pulled her hand out of his and walked over to the door. ''Beat it, business boy. I'm starving.''

''Scores of people know who I am,'' he said, as she pushed him out into the hall.

''I'd take a shower if I were you. That scorched computer smell is starting to rub off on you.''

The door closed behind him with a firm click.

Gideon stopped, sniffed and then began to cough. She had a point about the last.

He made his way unsteadily down the hallway to his room, the smell of burning components beginning to make him rather ill. He entered his room, shut the door behind him and set his burden down on the floor. He'd have to take it out to the trash. By the smell of things, his hard drive hadn't survived the fire.

Then he pulled up short. The lights were back on in his room. Gideon shook his head. Perhaps one of Stephen's henchmen had been at the fuse box, flipping things on and off on Stephen's direct orders. Gideon snorted. That he could believe.

So Megan McKinnon had no idea who he was. Gideon scowled to himself over that thought as he pulled his suit-case off the bed, opened it on the floor and rummaged inside for his kit. Maybe he was looking a bit on the unkempt side. A shave might be just the thing to restore him to proper form and jar Megan's memory. Perhaps he'd drop a hint or two about his title. He rarely made mention of it, preferring to impress and intimidate with his wits alone, but she looked to be a particularly difficult case. His was a small barony, and one he rarely had the time to visit, but it was a bit of prestige all the same. Short of clouting her over the head with a copy of *Burke's Peerage,* it was the best he could do.

And once she was properly impressed, he would turn his thoughts to procuring some other kind of machinery. If there was a laptop within a hundred miles, he would find it.

He shaved quickly, then showered, hoping a good scrub would leave him smelling less like char. He tied a towel about his hips and dragged his hands through his hair, surprised at how much better he felt. Perhaps that was what he'd needed all along. He wiped off the fog from the mirror and stared at himself. A bit of holiday now and then wasn't such a bad thing. Snatching the occasional half hour every few months for a bit of rejuvenation might improve his disposition.

He stepped out of the bathroom, humming cheerfully. Then he came to a teetering halt.

His suitcase was on fire.

Or, more to the point, the clothes in his suitcase were on fire.

"Damn it!" he exclaimed.

He whipped off the towel and leaped across the room to beat out the flames. It took more doing than he'd expected, almost as if the fire was determined to burn through every last article of clothing he'd brought with him.

By the time all that was left was a bit of smoke wafting lazily toward the ceiling, Gideon was sweating and swearing with equal intensity.

He stared down at the ruins of his clothes, ashes which of course contained the clothes he'd been wearing earlier, and wondered at which end of his more colorful vocabulary to start. He had the pair of boxers he'd worn into the bathroom. Period.

He waved away more smoke. It was becoming a bad habit. He waved a bit more and considered.

"Hell," he said, finally, unable to find anything else that properly expressed the depths of his disgust. He folded his arms over his still damp chest and glared at no one in particular.

"Would anyone care to tell me what I'm supposed to wear now?" he demanded. "The bed linens?"

There was a small squeak from the wardrobe to his right. His gaze snapped immediately to it and he looked at it narrowly. Wonderful. No clothes, but likely a very large rodent. He strode over to the wardrobe and jerked the door open.

There was nothing inside but a pair of baggy yellow tights and a long green tunic.

Gideon stared, agog. Tights? There was no way in hell he was going to put on a pair of yellow—

The tights shook themselves.

Gideon frowned. There had to be some kind of hole in the back of the bloody armoire. With that kind of draft, Heaven only knew what sorts of things were making their nests inside.

The tights wiggled again, brushing the tunic and sending it dancing as well.

Well, it was either wear the blasted things or go naked. Perhaps Mrs. Pruitt could be persuaded to go out in the morning and procure him something suitable.

Gideon donned his boxer shorts, then retrieved the tights from the closet. He stuck his feet into the legs and drew them up. It wasn't a pretty sight. He took an experimental step or two, finding the way the tights scrunched up between his toes to be highly irritating. He swore and hitched the tights up forcefully.

Then he coughed and abruptly hitched them back down.

He put on the tunic. It felt more comfortable than he'd dared hope. He looked into the wardrobe again, wondering if by chance there might be something to put on his feet.

Oh, but there was.

He pulled out a pair of bright purple elf shoes. Indeed, they could be nothing but elf shoes. The toes curled up several times. Gideon looked at them askance. Just watching him walk would probably put any rational person into a trance. Perhaps he could use them to hypnotize Miss McKinnon, aiding her in recovering what memories she had to have of him.

Gideon put on the shoes, cursing over the renewed scrunching of tights between his toes. But he didn't hitch; he'd learned his lesson about that.

He jerked open his bedroom door.

"The court jester arrives," he groused. "Dinner can begin."

 THREE

Megan walked down the hallway, feeling completely ridiculous in the King Arthur-era dress that made her look as if she expected the deluge to turn into a flood at any moment—and boy would she be prepared with her hemline halfway to her knees! If her own clothes hadn't been wringing wet, she would have put them back on and taken her chances with pneumonia.

Well, it wasn't as if she was out to impress anyone. And not that anyone in the vicinity would have forgotten about business long enough to be impressed. Gideon de Piaget was a man who needed to learn to relax. She could have taught him a thing or two about leaving work behind. Considering the times she'd done just that involuntarily, she could have written a book on the subject.

Megan descended the last of the stairs only to find that Mrs. P. was no longer at her post. Megan took that as a sign: either the woman had flipped out and left the inn for good or she had retreated to the kitchen to whip up something for dinner. Megan sincerely hoped for the latter. The taste of airline food still lingered in her mouth.

Not knowing where to go, Megan began opening doors. She found a sitting room boasting the same kind of comfortable clutter her own bedroom did. It was tempting to

37

curl up in one of the overstuffed chairs and do her best to forget the last twenty-four hours. On the other side of the hall was a beautiful library with shelves stocked full of books, and a cheery fire burning in the hearth.

After searching through several more rooms, she opened up a double door and hit the jackpot. This room contained a long, elegant dinner table, chairs, a side buffet, and several other chairs sitting against the walls seemingly waiting for their turn to be needed. Megan took it all in, delighted by the atmosphere. Then she realized what had nagged at her from the start.

There were no places set. No fine linens, no silverware, no candles in silver candelabras. Maybe Mrs. P. had driven off all her helpers.

Or maybe she'd driven herself off and Megan would be left to fend for herself.

The thought was terrifying.

All of a sudden there was a terrible clang. Megan ran to the door at the back of the dining room, then stopped short. What if intruders had come in? She looked around, snatched a handy ornamental dagger from the wall and put her hand on the doorknob. Maybe those fencing lessons would finally be of some use.

She opened the door a crack and looked into the kitchen.

Mrs. Pruitt was doing battle with thin air. She held a lid up as a shield and waved a cleaver in front of herself, frantically fighting off something Megan couldn't for the life of her see.

"Nay, I'll not listen to reason!" Mrs. Pruitt shouted. "Ye bloody Scot, I'm sick to death of ye and all yer undead cohorts! I'll sign the bloody deed and be done with ye all!"

And then, quite suddenly, Mrs. Pruitt dropped her pot lid and her blade and clapped her hands over her ears. With a screech she turned and ran straight toward Megan. Megan jumped out of the way, then turned and watched, open-mouthed, as the woman ran the length of the dining room. Gideon stood at the far doorway, wearing a similar look of disbelief.

"Out of my way," Mrs. Pruitt said, giving him a healthy

shove. "I'll not stay here another minute with these bloody old ghosts ahounding me!"

Megan watched Mrs. Pruitt disappear out into the hallway, then looked at Gideon, wondering what he thought it all meant.

Then she did a double take. Gideon was dressed in bright yellow tights and an apple green tunic that barely covered, well, all the important parts. His sandy hair was mussed. His aqua eyes were blazing. And his tights were sagging at the knees. That didn't even begin to address his shoes.

Megan set down her dagger and clapped her hand over her mouth. She didn't clap fast enough: an errant giggle escaped before she could stop it.

Gideon's expression darkened considerably.

"Oh my gosh," she gasped, doubling over and wheezing. "If your board of directors could see you now!"

"Ah ha!" he said, striding forward and wagging his finger at her. "You *do* know who I am! I knew it would come to you soon enough. Perhaps you've seen me gracing the cover of *Fortune,* or clawing my way up the *Forbes 4—*"

Megan put her hand over his mouth. "Be quiet," she said, straining her ears. "I think a door just slammed."

"Wovwee," Gideon said. He took her hand away. "Lovely," he repeated crisply. "We likely have other guests arriving and here I am, impersonating Robin Hood."

Megan did her best to put on a sober expression. "I don't think Robin Hood would have been caught dead dressed like that."

Gideon looked at her archly. "At least what I'm wearing reaches where it's supposed—"

"Sshh," she said, "listen."

They stood, silently, listening.

"I don't hear anything," he whispered.

"Neither do I . . ." she began, then realized he hadn't let go of her hand.

It occurred to her, strangely enough, that she didn't mind. His hand was very warm. It was a comfortable sort of hand, the kind you would reach for across a dinner table or as you walked down a country road. Megan looked at her hand surrounded by his and was struck by the perfect picture it made.

She looked up at him to find a most thoughtful look resting on his face. In fact, for possibly the first time since he'd drenched her, he was looking at her and truly seeing her. Completely. Intensely.

It was enough to make her start fanning herself again.

Then she paused. Other than her own heavy breathing, there was no noise.

"Mrs. Pruitt," she whispered. "Oh, no, Mrs. Pruitt!"

"Wait—"

"She's not screeching anymore," Megan said, pulling Gideon toward the hallway. "We can't let her leave!"

Gideon seemed to be struggling to keep up with her. She spared him a brief glance. The toes of his shoes were flapping wildly as he dashed alongside her.

And then the unthinkable happened.

His curly toes curled together.

He went down like a rock.

Megan left him behind without a second thought. She fled into the hallway just in time to see Mrs. Pruitt come dashing out from the library. The woman bolted for the front door, her apron strings fluttering furiously behind her.

The front door closed behind her with a resounding bang.

"Help!" Gideon called.

Megan ignored him. She leaped the remaining few steps to the door like a champion long jumper and jerked it open. She clutched the door frame.

"Oh, no!" she exclaimed.

She heard Gideon thumping behind her. He lurched to a teetering halt on his knees at the threshold.

"Oh, no!" Megan repeated, pointing frantically outside.

"Oh, yes," Gideon corrected grimly. "There she goes, pedaling her bicycle off into the gloom."

"No other helpers?" she asked, looking down at him as he knelt beside her, staring off morosely after their former hostess.

Gideon shook his head. "My brother favors this inn for precisely that reason. Mrs. Pruitt is a widow and only hires in help from the village. There'll be someone in during the week to clean, but she does everything else. The place'll be dead as nails until then."

Megan looked off at the increasingly small figure of their innkeeper. "Think she just ran to the store for an egg?"

He shook his head slowly.

Megan looked out into the twilight and sighed. "We're stuck, then."

"It looks that way."

"Doomed."

"Very likely."

"We'll starve before they find us." She looked down at him. "I can't cook."

A faint look of panic descended onto his features. "You can't?"

"Hot chocolate is the extent of my skills," she admitted. "How about you?"

"I'm a powerful executive. I have a chef."

"Ah," she said, with a nod. "I was afraid of that. You know, I got a job a few months ago to try to learn, but . . ." she shrugged. "It didn't work out."

"It didn't? Not even for an edible few dishes?"

"Nope. Fast food is unhealthy. I couldn't cook it in good conscience."

"Sacked?" he asked kindly.

"As usual," she sighed.

He laughed softly. "Oh, Megan," he said, shaking his head.

Megan was so surprised by the sound that she had to look at him again, just to make sure he'd been the one to make it. And the sight of him smiling was so overwhelming, she had to lean back against the door frame for support.

"Wow," she breathed.

The smile didn't fade. "Wow?"

"You have a great laugh."

His smile was immediately replaced by a look of faint puzzlement. "Do I? No one's ever told me that before."

"They must have been distracted by your powerful and awe-inspiring corporate self."

"Ah *ha*," he said triumphantly, "you really *do* recognize me this time."

Megan rolled her eyes, pushed away from the door and started back to the kitchen. "Let's go see if Mrs. P. left us a cookbook."

"Wait," he said, maneuvering himself onto his backside. "I seem to have tangled my toes."

Megan watched him fumble with the spirals for a moment before she knelt, pushed his hands away and did the honors herself.

"Nicely done," he said, sounding genuinely impressed.

"I subbed for Snow White once. You'd be amazed what trouble dwarf toes can get into."

"Hmmm," he said, looking down at his feet.

Megan looked at him and felt something in the vicinity of her heart crumble. Just the sight of this intense and (by his own admission) powerful man sitting there with his sandy hair mussed, his tights bagging now around his ankles, playing with the toes of his purple elf shoes—well, it was enough to make a girl want to throw her arms around him and hug him until he couldn't breathe. That any man should look so ridiculous and so adorable at the same time was just a crime.

"Too much time in ears," she said, rising and shaking her head.

Gideon looked up at her. "I beg your pardon?"

"I spent too much time at Disneyland," she said. "It warped me. My judgment is clouded. My taste in shoes is skewed."

"Don't tell me you're acquiring a liking for fairy footwear."

And drooping yellow tights and aqua eyes and a smile that transforms your face into something even more breathtaking than usual.

"Nah, give me Keds every time," she said, making a grab for her self-control and common sense before they both hit the same high road her luggage had. "Let's storm the ~~hen~~."

~~on~~ rose, keeping his feet a safe distance apart.

"Might I regale you with stories of my latest business coups whilst we prepare our meal?" he asked, reaching for her hand.

Megan found her hand in his and her common sense/self-control nowhere to be seen.

"Business coups?" she echoed, frowning up at him in an effort to distract herself. "I don't think so."

"Tales of exciting market trends and investment plans?"

She looked at him in horror. "You've got to be kidding. It'll ruin my appetite!"

"You sound annoyingly like my brother."

"He sounds like my kind of guy. Maybe he's the one who booby-trapped your computer."

"I'm beginning to suspect that might be the case."

"Well, then take your vacation. Getting fired is highly unpleasant."

"You seem to know of what you speak."

"Honey, you don't know the half of it."

And she had no intentions of telling him the full extent of it. A few amusing anecdotes might make him smile, but he'd flip if he knew just how many times she had been canned.

But that wasn't going to happen anymore. She nodded to herself as she led him back to the kitchen. Thomas had given her a chance to be successful at something. After all, how hard could it be to get up to the castle, take a look around and tell him what he'd bought? It was a little chance, but one she had been desperate enough to take. She wouldn't fail. She *couldn't* fail. If she couldn't even do something this simple, there was no way she could show her face at home again. They all thought she was flaky as it was. She would head up to the castle first thing tomorrow. It couldn't be that far and it couldn't be that hard to find. She'd send home a report, then settle back and enjoy a well-deserved recuperation.

But first, dinner had to be made.

"Heaven help us," she muttered, as she and Gideon walked hand-in-hand into the kitchen.

She stood surveying the various pots and pans Mrs. Pruitt

had left simmering on the stove, then looked at Gideon. He returned her stare, looking just as perplexed as she felt.

"Would you rather find a cookbook and read, or would you rather . . . *stir*?" she said, hoping a little subliminal suggestion might work on him.

"I'm a fabulous reader," he said promptly, commencing a search for a cookbook.

Megan stared back at the stove. Well, at least this would distract her from the deafening clamor her hand had set up at being parted from Gideon's.

"Bad hand," she said, frowning down at it sternly.

"I beg your pardon?"

Megan shoved her hand behind her back and smiled at Gideon. "Just giving it a pep talk in preparation for cooking. Find anything useful?"

Gideon held up a fistful of scribbled notes. "I think this might be it."

Megan sighed.

It was going to be a long night.

FOUR

Gideon sat at the table, plowing manfully through his meal. The potatoes were scorched, the meat both raw and burned depending on what side of it faced up on one's plate, and the vegetables were unrecognizable in their mushiness. Somehow, his deciphering of Mrs. Pruitt's notes and Megan's stirring hadn't turned out the way it should have. At this point, Gideon didn't care. He was starved enough to eat about anything.

Once his nutrient-starved brain could function properly again, he looked over at his dinner companion. She was currently toying with her carrots, as if she thought they might provide the answers to life's mysteries. Gideon leaned over and looked at them.

"Don't see any answers there," he said, then met her eyes. "Do you?"

"Nope," she said. "Just overcooked vegetables."

"We'll do better next time."

"We'll starve to death," she said gloomily. "Surrounded by raw ingredients we can't put together to save our lives."

Gideon watched Megan's downcast face and wondered what troubled her. She couldn't think the disaster before them was her fault. He was as much responsible as she. Perhaps she was merely fatigued from her journey to the

45

inn. While they'd cooked, she had told him of her harrowing experience with the thieves in London. Add that to her long walk from the village and it was no wonder she looked a bit on the peaked side.

Gideon couldn't deny that no matter how she looked, she still made him pull up short. There was something just so open and artless about her. He couldn't remember the last time he'd encountered another human being who didn't have some sort of agenda where he was concerned. Even his father, useless bit of fluff though he was, managed to tear himself from the races long enough to give Gideon a lofty earlish order or two. The only person who called him anymore without wanting something was his mother.

Megan didn't seem to have any expectations of him. She had no idea who he was and, distressing though it was to him, seemingly couldn't have cared less what he did. Not even blatant boasting about his title and manor hall at Blythwood had fazed her. She did, however, like his laugh.

He was beginning to wish some of her nonchalance would rub off on him. Just the sight of her left him with his head spinning. Having her undivided attention was almost more than he could take. Though he certainly wasn't having any of the latter presently. Her vegetables were enjoying far too much of her scrutiny.

Perhaps she was still put out with him? He'd apologized thoroughly for having splashed her. Secretly, he was relieved he hadn't plowed her over. He'd been trying to fix the blasted fax machine in his car. Another one of Stephen's insidious little assaults, no doubt.

Perhaps, then, she wasn't looking at him because she found the company dull. He frowned. He could be entertaining. Perhaps he should try out some of those skills he'd learned in that Don't Alienate Your Partner seminar his mother had coerced him into taking the year before. He'd done it to please her, because she asked so little of him, though he hadn't seen the point in it. He never alienated anyone unintentionally. Yes, he would trot out his hard-won skills and see if they were worth the sterling he'd paid for them.

"Tell me more about your family," he said. There, he was off to a smashing start. People loved to talk about their families. And there he was, fully prepared to listen to her. It was a foolproof plan. "You mentioned a brother? The one who sent you over here?"

"Thomas," she said. "He bought the castle up the way. He wanted something that had originally belonged to a McKinnon. He's always been big on the ancestral stuff."

"And he sent you here to study the terrain, as it were?"

She sighed and stuck her fork into a mound of carrots. "It was a charity gig. You know, after the mouse debacle."

"Poor Dumbo and his ever-lengthening ears."

"He kept pinching my tail. He deserved every bit of whiplash he got."

"Oh, Megan," he said, unable to do anything but shake his head and smile. Megan McKinnon was a business disaster.

"The rest of them are just like Thomas: all successful, all the brightest of stars, all settled into their careers and forging ahead, the obstacles be damned."

Everyone except me. Gideon didn't have to hear her say it to know it was exactly what she was thinking. He had no frame of reference for that. Everything he'd put his hand to had turned to gold. Schooling, sports, business. He'd never once been sacked, never once been told he wasn't good enough, never once questioned his direction or his purpose. He could hardly believe such things had happened regularly to the woman across from him. Surely there was something she'd done that was noteworthy.

"How did you fare at university?" he asked.

"I quit. I didn't like them telling me what to study."

Gideon mulled that one for a moment before turning to another possibility. "Your mother's clothing business—"

"Baby clothes are cute, but not for a life's work."

"The theater?" he ventured.

"I've done it all. Sewn costumes, painted scenery, worked lights, acted, danced, forgotten my lines. All in my sister's theater troupe."

Gideon looked at her in horror. "She didn't sack you, did she?"

"I did the honors myself."

Gideon reached over and took her hand before he knew what he was doing. And once he had ahold of it, he found he didn't want to let go.

"You just haven't found your niche," he stated firmly. "Something will turn up."

She looked at him and her eyes were bright. Gideon suspected it might have been from the tears she was blinking away.

"Do you think so?" she whispered.

"I'm certain of it," he said, giving her hand a squeeze.

And then he understood what had been troubling her, why she'd said half a dozen times while stirring supper that she hoped the weather changed so she could pop up to the castle first thing. She needed a success.

And then a perfectly brilliant idea occurred to him. He would help her fix her career. His Don't Alienate instructor had specifically listed the fixing of partners on his list of Don'ts, but Gideon was certain that didn't apply to him. If anyone could fix Megan McKinnon's life, it would be him. And he would, just as soon as he had pried her away from her veggies so he could have her full attention.

"Let's escape to a tidier room," he suggested, rising. "We can talk more comfortably there."

"I can't leave the kitchen like this—"

"It will keep," he said, pulling her up from the table. "Maybe you can tell me a little about your career interests." He knew he was pushing, but he could hardly help himself. Business was his forte, after all.

"I don't have any career interests."

Gideon froze. "You don't?"

"Not in the sense you probably mean. I hate dressing up for work."

"You hate dressing up for work," he repeated slowly. "Yet . . ."

"I hate the corporate thing. Don't own panty hose. Don't want to own panty hose."

He lifted one eyebrow. "But wearing mouse ears and a tail didn't bother you."

"I didn't have to wear panty hose."

"I see."

"I think you do."

Gideon smiled at the way she looked down her nose at him. She was so adorable, it was all he could do not to pull her into his arms and kiss the freckles right from that nose.

Almost before he knew what had happened, he found himself doing just that.

She pulled away and laughed. And that was when he felt himself falling. It was the first time he'd heard her laugh, and he'd been the one to bring in out in her. He was so taken aback by it, he couldn't stop smiling.

She was smiling back at him.

Gideon realized then that there was much more to it than just a smile. For the first time in his thirty-two years, he found the thought of standing right where he was and staring into green eyes to be the most important thing he could possibly do with his time.

Alarms went off in his head.

Gideon ignored them.

They sounded again, but with words this time. *Just what the devil are you thinking to stare at a woman's knees, then watch her destroy dinner, then want to kiss her?*

Gideon blinked.

Good heavens, he was losing it. He was supposed to be taking her in hand and repairing her life. He was not supposed to be feeling his knees grow unsteady beneath him. He was not supposed to be gaping at a woman he hardly knew and finding himself so charmed by her that he had to remind himself to breathe. It was all he could do not to haul her up into his arms and stalk off with her like one of those blasted barbarians from one of Stephen's medieval texts.

But the stalking sounded so appealing if it meant having Megan McKinnon in his arms.

He looked down at her again, considered his alternatives, then gave his common sense the old heave-ho. He took her face in his hands, stared down into her fiery green eyes, smiled at the silky touch of her riotous hair flowing over his fingers, then lowered his mouth and covered hers.

And for a blissful moment, the earth moved.

And then, just as quickly, Megan had moved—but not too far away because somehow his watch had gotten caught in her hair.

"Ow, ow, ow," she said, grabbing her hair with her hand.

"Wait," he said, following her with his arm.

She gingerly pulled strands of hair from his watchband. "I don't kiss on the first date," she said, staring intently at her hair.

"This isn't a first date."

"Then I *really* don't kiss, especially on the first non-date."

Half a dozen pot lids suddenly crashed to the floor. Megan screeched, a sound reminiscent of the recently departed Mrs. Pruitt, and threw herself into his arms. Gideon contemplated the positive aspects of this turn of events. He put his free arm around her and pulled her close. She clutched his shirt.

"Do you think . . ." she began, "I mean, do you think we might have a few—"

"Absolutely not."

"Mrs. Pruitt said the inn had them."

"Mrs. Pruitt left her sacred post at the stove without a backward glance. Her character and stamina speak for themselves."

"Maybe it's just the wind," Megan said, pulling out of his arms and working more frantically at her hair. "After all, there aren't any such things as gho—"

The lights went out in the kitchen and several more lids crashed to the floor.

Gideon found himself again with an armful of Megan McKinnon.

"I don't hug on the first non-date either," she squeaked.

"You might make an exception for this," Gideon offered. "The storm seems to have picked up again."

It was dark as pitch inside the kitchen, so he wasn't sure

what her expression was, but he could tell she was mulling
it over. She relaxed a bit in his arms.

"It *is* a pretty bad storm," she agreed. "What with all
the wind howling and everything."

"Yes, indeed. Dreadful."

She released her death grip on him, but not by much.
Gideon reached around her head, released his watchband
and gingerly eased it from her hair.

Megan didn't move a muscle. "Should we find a candle
or something? Or light a fire?"

"Smashing thought," he agreed. He released her, only
after promising himself he'd find a way to have her back in
his arms as soon as possible.

It took some doing, but after rummaging about for several
minutes, he and Megan both were proud owners of lit candles.

Now it was time to get down to business. Perhaps he
could find a way to put his arm back around her while distracting her with chatter about her choice of occupations.

"Shall we go talk about your career possibilities?" he
asked brightly.

She looked at him and blinked. "My career possibilities?"

Damn. The proverbial cat was out of the bag now.
Though he'd intended it to be a pleasant surprise, there was
no sense in hiding his agenda now. They could fix her career, then move on to other things, such as getting the first
date over with so the second could occur and she could see
her way clear to kissing him again.

"I'd wanted to broach the subject more gently, of
course," he began, steering her toward the door.

"Career possibilities?" she repeated.

"I'm the perfect one to help you, don't you think?" he
asked. "After all, my résumé is quite impressive. I have
hundreds of contacts and could likely find you any sort of
employment you want."

"You want to talk to me about my *career possibilities?*"
she demanded.

"Well, of course," he said.

She looked like she was going to hit him. Indeed, it was only by sheer instinct that he managed to duck in time to avoid her swing.

"You jerk!" she exclaimed.

He straightened and looked at her with wide eyes. "Me?"

She swung again.

Gideon jerked back. "Good heavens, Megan, have you lost your mind? I'm *helping* you!"

"I don't *want* your help, you big idiot!"

"But why ever not—"

She advanced and he retreated. Amazing how one could still see murder in another's eyes by candlelight.

"I can't believe you!" she exclaimed. "What in the world makes you think I need to be *fixed?*"

"Fixed? How did you—"

He ducked instinctively, prepared for another blow, but this one came at him from a different angle. Her foot connected solidly with his shin.

"Ouch, damn it," he said, jerking his candle. He wasn't sure what hurt worse, her shoe in his shin or the hot wax on his fingers. "Megan, I don't think you realize what you're turning down."

"I realize exactly what I'm turning down," she said, poking him in the chest. "You're just like the rest of them. I don't need to be worked on, I don't need to be a project and I don't need any damned career advice! If I want to keep getting fired from now until doomsday, that's my business!"

"But—"

"But nothing! Good night!"

And with that, she slammed out of the kitchen. Gideon heard her stomp across the dining room, then heard the far door slam.

Well, that hadn't gone off well at all. Gideon stood there with the wind making an enormous racket as it came through the cracks under the door and shutters, and wondered why he felt so flat. He'd only been trying to help. And who better to fix her career than him? The countless people he knew, the businesses he owned—why he was a veritable gold mine of corporate acumen and resources! Her reaction to his generous offer was insulting, to say the very least.

He studiously ignored the thought that he'd just made an ass of himself and bruised Megan's feelings in the process.

Well, it was a sure sign that he'd put his foot to the wrong path. It was time he took hold of his priorities and wrested his destiny back onto its original course.

"I don't have time to worry about this," he announced to the kitchen. "I have work to do. I don't need any of these feminine distractions. My life is full of important tasks."

The wind continued to howl.

What about love?

Gideon turned a jaundiced look on the door. "I'm certain," he said crisply, "when the wind starts blathering on about love that it's far past the time when I should be back at work."

He turned to the dining room door and held his candle aloft purposefully.

"Tomorrow," he said, taking a smart step forward, "I'll be on my way tomorrow!"

His candle flame went out. Another collection of pots crashed to the floor behind him.

"How many bloody pots does this inn have?" he demanded of the darkness.

The wind only growled an answer.

Gideon left the kitchen with all due haste.

"Holidays are useless wastes of time," he said as he made his way up the stairs. "I'll find myself a proper set of clothes in the village, then search for another laptop. I've already lost a day."

He paused on the landing as a most unsettling thought struck him. He tried to push it aside, but it came back to him, as if someone had whispered it to him.

I think, my lad, that you stand to lose much more than just a day.

Gideon felt chills go down his spine. He peered back down the stairs into the darkened entryway. It wouldn't have surprised him in the least to have seen someone standing there.

But the entryway was empty.

Gideon straightened. He was hearing things. He nodded to himself and opened the door to his room. He'd had a very long day and the wind was playing tricks on him. Either that or he'd spent far too much time looking at Megan McKinnon. She unsettled him more than the wind.

Freckles, he decided as he closed his bedroom door behind him, were hazardous to a man's good sense.

FIVE

"Nay, you'll not do it!"

"Out of me way, ye bloody Brit, and leave me to me work!"

" 'Tis a brand new Sterling! This horseless cart cost me nevvy a bleedin' fortune!"

Ambrose put his head beneath the bonnet of Gideon's car and glared at his companions.

"Will you two cease with this confounded bickering!" he snapped. "We're here to pull the spark plug wires, not argue over who'll do it!"

Fulbert leaned heavily against the fender. "I don't think I can lend my aid. That pot banging last eve took all my strength."

"Ha," said Hugh, casting him a derisive sneer. "I flung a far sight more than ye, and look at me in the bloom o' health this morn."

"We're all under a great amount of physical strain," Ambrose said sternly, "but we'll have time enough to rest once the deed is done. Now, we've eight of these slim little cords to pull and precious little time to argue over the pulling of them."

"Eight's too many," Fulbert groused.

"I want no chance that the automobile will spring to

life," Ambrose countered. "I've done a goodly amount of reading on the subject and know of what I speak. Now, we'll start from this end."

It took a great amount of effort, and there was much grunting and swearing given forth, as well as several bouts of condemning modern man for his ridiculous inventions that required more than oats and a good rubdown, but finally the deed was done. Ambrose stood back from the car and admired their handiwork.

"There," he said, with satisfaction. "Gideon will not be off today. As the rain seems eager to aid us in our task of keeping him here, I daresay he won't be venturing out on foot any time soon, either." He reached up to close the bonnet.

"I'll see to it," Fulbert said, suddenly. He did a little leap in the air. "I feel quite the thing suddenly."

Ambrose was quite frankly surprised at Fulbert's change of heart, but wasn't about to challenge him on it. Lifting things from the physical world was, as always, exhausting. There were but few hours before dawn. He would do well to rest before Gideon rose and gave them any more trouble.

"As you will, Fulbert. Come, Hugh. Let us seek our rest while we may."

Ambrose took a final look at the engine, then, satisfied his work was done properly, entered the house and sought his bed for a well deserved nap.

Fulbert waited until Hugh and Ambrose passed through the door before he peered back down into the engine.

"They plucked too bleedin' many of these things," he muttered to himself. "I'll just put a few back. The saints only know what kind of damage could be done to the beast otherwise."

It was an intense struggle and he had to admit he couldn't quite remember how the rubber cords had been attached at the start, but he plugged five of them back in, crossing the cords here and there and stretching them when they didn't wish to go where he decided they should.

Calling upon the very last reserves of his considerable strength, he pulled the bonnet down home.

He made his way slowly inside and took up his post at the end of the upstairs passageway. It didn't take long before he'd sat, then stretched his legs out, then fallen asleep.

It had been a most tiring night's work.

The house was silent as Gideon trudged down the stairs, elf shoes well apart to avoid toe tangleage, dragging his heavy suitcase with him. It contained, of course nothing useful. He'd decided, though, that he just couldn't leave his ruined computer and the ashes of his clothes lying about in the bedroom. The least he could do was find a rubbish bin somewhere and add to it.

He set his burden down and walked back to the kitchen. There were pots strewn all over the floor and the remains of last night's meal still on the table. Gideon looked down at Megan's fork still standing in her now congealed vegetables. The sight of that brought other, disturbingly distracting memories to mind: Megan in his arms; Megan's lips under his.

Megan mad as hell over him wanting to fix her.

He'd given her response to his innocent suggestion quite a bit of thought over the past sleepless night. He'd given even more thought to her successful family, and he could see where she might feel as if she didn't quite fit in. He wondered if they made it a point to point out her failures to her. The thought of that set his blood to boiling.

Actually, just the thought of Megan set his blood to boiling. He felt himself becoming distracted all over again.

"Work, work, work," he said, chanting his favorite mantra.

Damn. All he could think about was freckles.

"Price/earning ratios," he said, letting the seductive words roll off his tongue with a silky purr.

Freckled knees.

No, no, this just wouldn't do. Gideon planted his feet well apart, put his hands on his hips and smiled his favorite pirate's smile.

''Corporate takeovers!'' he said, trying to infuse the term with its customary gleeful overtones.

Freckled nose. Flaming red hair. Sweet, kissable lips.

''Spreadsheets, annual reports, chats with my broker!'' he cried out in desperation.

Megan.

Gideon clapped his hands over his ears, spun around and bolted from the kitchen. Maybe Megan's vegetables were starting to put thoughts in his head. It was best he escaped the whole place before he lost his mind.

He grabbed his suitcase on his way to the door. Perhaps if he got some distance from the inn, his sanity would return. Yes, a little jaunt to Edinburgh would be just the thing. His first stop, however, would have to be to a tailor's shop. No one would take him seriously in his current dress.

He threw his suitcase into the boot, then got into the car. His footwear didn't fit all that well under the wheel, but he made do. He pumped the gas pedal once and turned the key. The car made a hideous, thunderous bang, then smoke began to pour forth from the engine.

Gideon could hardly believe his eyes. ''Not again!'' he exclaimed. He released the latch, bolted from the car and jerked open the bonnet.

His engine was on fire.

Why he was surprised, he didn't know.

The rain started up again with renewed vigor. Gideon looked up into the heavens with narrowed eyes. There was something afoot in the world and it seemed either bent on burning up everything he owned or soaking him to the skin.

The front door wrenched open and Megan appeared. Gideon looked at her helplessly. Her eyes bulged, then she disappeared. Gideon looked back up into the sky and wished for a stronger downpour than the one that drenched him at present. But no matter how large a downpour, it likely wouldn't put out the inferno beneath the bonnet of his brand-new Sterling.

The next thing he knew, Megan was wielding a fire extinguisher. When the dust settled, there were no flames, and hardly any smoke. And no serviceable motor.

"Hell," Gideon said.

Megan looked up at him. "Do these kinds of things happen to you normally, or are you just having an off week?"

"The elements are combining against me."

"Maybe somebody's trying to tell you something."

"Go on holiday?"

"That'd be my guess."

Gideon looked at her and considered. His car was ruined. He'd already tried the inn phone that morning and found it unresponsive. There he was, loitering in backwoods Scotland with no computer, no modem, and no cell phone.

And Megan McKinnon.

"Ah *ha*," he said, feeling the force of the moment reverberate through him.

What could it hurt to take a day or two and put work aside? It wasn't as if he could do much about it anyway, short of walking to the village and hiring a car. It would just be time wasted. Stephen might not be interested in the company, but Adam MacClure was. He could hold down the fort for a day or so.

Besides, Christmas was right around the corner. People all over the world were contemplating holidays with their families. There was food to be prepared, gifts to be wrapped, carols to be sung. He hadn't done any of that in years. Christmas had always seemed a perfect time to catch up on things at the office. Stephen had always thrown a lord-of-the-manor type of affair, doing his damndest to revive old customs. Gideon had thought it politic to just stay in London and not spoil Stephen's party.

But now he was, for all intents and purposes, prisoner on the Scottish border with only time on his hands and Megan McKinnon to admire.

Damn, but the holidays were shaping up brilliantly.

"I think," he said, reaching out and relieving Megan of the fire extinguisher, "that a holiday is just the thing for me."

She blinked. "You do?"

He shrugged and smiled. "I hear they're quite therapeutic. Perhaps you'd care to show me how they're done?"

He watched her look at him, then her eyes narrowed. "Why?" she demanded. "So you can sneak in some fixing?"

Gideon shook his head. "I was wrong to even bring it up. I apologize."

"Well," she said, looking quite off balance. Gideon suspected she'd been bracing herself to really let him have it.

"Well," she repeated, "I just don't need to be fixed."

"No, you don't."

She looked at him suspiciously. "What's the deal with your new angle here?"

"No angle. No agenda. I've just come to realize rather suddenly that I'm the one who needs some fixing. I work too much."

She reached up and felt his forehead. "You're a little warm. Maybe you caught a bug from being out in the rain."

Gideon took her hand and pulled her back into the house. He'd caught a malady and it had red hair and green eyes. He set the fire extinguisher down and shut the front door.

"I'm officially on holiday. What should we do first? Decorate the place?" He looked about the entryway. "We could investigate the nooks and crannies of the inn, or learn how to cook. Sing a carol or two in front of the fire." The more he thought about it, the more appealing it sounded. Perhaps he would stretch his holiday into three days instead of two. After all, Christmas was in three days and he certainly wouldn't get any work done then. "Read Dickens before the fire," he said, his head filling with ideas. "That Ghost of Christmas Past is one of my all time favorite characters. Why, I'm starting to think this will be brilliant fun," he said, beaming down at her.

"Can't."

He blinked. "I beg your pardon."

She smiled up at him. "I have to work. See ya."

And she turned and walked back to the stairs.

"Work?" he asked, aghast. "*Now?*"

She looked over her shoulder. "I'm here to work, Gideon. Remember? My brother's castle? I have to go take a look at it."

"But, surely that can wait . . ."

"Nope, I've got to get right on it."

"But—"

She waved at him over her shoulder as she mounted the steps. Gideon stared after her in shock.

"But it's Christmas!" he called after her.

She didn't stop.

Well, this just wouldn't do. Gideon watched her disappear upstairs and frowned. He tapped his foot impatiently, which generally provided him with stunning solutions. All it did now was make him dizzy. He shook his head. How could she be so consumed with work this close to Christmas?

"Work can wait," he said, trying the words out on his tongue. They felt, surprisingly enough, quite good.

"It isn't everything," he added.

That felt even better.

"Why, holidays are a *good* thing," he said, with enthusiasm.

It occurred to him, suddenly, that he was possibly responsible for Megan's desire to work through the holidays. Good heavens, had he been the one to drive her to this madness?

Well, he would rectify that. He had just recently seen the light and burned with the enthusiasm of the freshly converted. Holidays were good for a body. Too much work was hazardous to one's health.

And he would know.

 SIX

Megan tugged on her leather jacket and shoved her feet back into her still-damp boots. It was raining outside anyway and she would get soaked within minutes, but it didn't matter. She had work to do. A little rain wasn't going to stop her because she'd be damned before she would fail at this job. She would show them all that she could follow through, do what she said she would, make things happen. Her family would finally think she was a success.

As would Gideon.

Not that she cared what he thought. No sir.

She stepped out into the hallway and shut the door firmly. No time like the present to start down the road to success. She put her shoulders back and marched smartly down the hallway.

"Damn the gel if she hasn't ruined him for decent labor."

Megan froze. Then she put her fingers in her ears and gave them a good wiggling. Surely there was no one else in the hallway. She was just hearing things.

"She may as well have gelded the poor lad!"

Megan whirled around. She would have squeaked, but she had no breath for it.

There, standing not fifteen feet from her was a man. A big man. A man wearing a sword. In fact, he looked to be wearing chain mail too, what she could see of it under his folded arms and knightly overcoat-like tunic. He might have looked like something out of an historical wax museum collection if it hadn't been for the disapproving look he was giving her.

Megan gulped. "Help," she whispered.

"Doin' a full day's work's no sin," the man grumbled.

"Help," Megan squeaked. "Help, help!"

"You're fillin' me boy's head with womanly notions!" the man exclaimed. He unfolded his arms and shook his finger at her. "I'd take it more kindly if you'd stop with it!"

"Gideon, help!" Megan screamed, backing up rapidly.

"Megan, good heavens!" Gideon called from a distance.

Megan heard him thumping up the stairs behind her, but she didn't dare take her eyes off the knight to look at him. She backed up into him and pointed down the hallway.

"Look," she whispered.

"Look at what?"

"There's someone in the hallway. Look, down there!"

"I can't see a thing," Gideon said.

"He's standing right there!"

"Who?"

Megan spun around, grabbed him by the tunic front and shook him. "There's a man at the end of the hallway wearing chain mail and a sword, you idiot!" she said. "Open your eyes and look!"

Gideon put his hands on her shoulders to steady himself. "Megan, you're thinking too much about work—"

"See?" the man behind her complained. "Look at what you've done to him, gel!"

Megan pointed back behind her. "He's talking to me. There at the end of the hall."

Gideon put his arms around her. "Now, Megan—"

"Don't you 'Now, Megan' me," she warned. "Mrs. Pruitt said there were ghosts and I'm telling you there's one standing at the end of the hallway!"

Gideon gave her a squeeze. "If it will make you feel any better, I'll go have a look."

Megan looked over her shoulder and squeaked at the new addition to the troops.

"Damn ye, Fulbert, dinnae scare me wee granddaughter like that!" a red-haired man in a kilt exclaimed in tones of thunder.

"I was only tellin' her—"

"I heard what ye said—"

"Wait," Megan said frantically as Gideon tried to move past her. "Now there are two of them!"

Gideon frowned at her. "I think you've been working too hard." He sidestepped her and started down the hallway.

Megan watched in horror as the kilted one drew a sword and waved it menacingly at the first.

"They're going to kill each other!" She leaped toward Gideon. "Duck," she said, jerking on his arm. "You're going to get your head chopped off!"

Gideon pushed her gently back into the doorway of his bedroom. "Megan," he said calmly, "there's nothing in the hallway. I'm going to go have a look in your room. You stay here until I get back."

Megan watched him turn and walk straight into the path of a swinging sword.

"Oh my gosh!" she exclaimed, clapping her hands over her eyes so she wouldn't have to watch him be decapitated.

"Megan?"

Megan paused, then peeked at him from between her fingers.

Gideon was standing in the middle of the hallway, unhurt. But the two swordsmen were going at each other with murder in their eyes, neatly fighting right around him.

"Don't you see them?" Megan asked incredulously.

"See who?"

"Those two men fighting? Right in front of your nose, Gideon!"

Gideon put out his hand, waved it up and down, side to side, then shook his head.

"Nothing."

Megan rolled her eyes. "I can hear them calling each

other names." She paused. "And not very nice names, either."

"Enough!" a voice roared from her left.

Megan fell back against the door with a gasp. A man strode angrily up the stairs. He was wearing a kilt as well, along with a very long broadsword. His cap was tilted at a jaunty angle; the feather flapped madly as he leaped up the remaining steps. He advanced on the two fighters.

"By the saints, you lads are trying the limits of my patience today! You, Fulbert, leave young Megan be. She has enough to think on without you tormenting her."

"But look what she's done to me nevvy—"

"She's done nothing that didn't need doing. Now, be off with you!"

The first man shoved his sword back into its scabbard, threw Megan a disgruntled look, then vanished.

"And you, Hugh," the one seemingly in charge scolded. "I'm ashamed of you! Brawling in the passageway thusly!"

The red-haired one ducked his head. "I was just defendin' me wee one's honor."

"Well, I can't say as how I blame you," the other said, with a nod, "but it isn't seemly to hack at the blighter in front of her."

"Aye, Ambrose. Ye're right, of course."

"Then off with you, Hugh."

The other put away his sword, then vanished.

Then Megan watched in astonishment as the commanding one turned and made her a deep bow.

"My deepest apologies for the disturbance, granddaughter. Please carry on with your day."

And then he walked through Gideon and disappeared into the closet at the end of the hallway.

Megan bolted after him and jerked open the closet door, fully expecting to see someone hiding inside. Instead she came face-to-face with stacks of bed linens. She clutched the door frame and came to a quick conclusion.

"I'm losing it," she announced.

"I think I agree," Gideon said, coming up behind her. "You need a holiday."

"What I need is some fresh air." She turned, pushed past him, and walked down the passageway. "Maybe I should go get some work done. That would probably snap me right back into reality."

"I've been a bad influence on you," Gideon said, trailing after her.

"No, I think you've been just the opposite," Megan said, thumping down the stairs. She reached the entryway well ahead of him and strode to the front door purposefully. A nice walk to the castle would be just the thing to clear her head of the surreal experience she had just had.

She opened the door and peeked out—into a hurricane.

"It's just a little rain," she said. She turned the collar up on her coat and steeled herself for the worst.

A large hand caught the door before she could open it any further.

"Megan, it's raining too hard to go out."

"I don't care," she said, putting her shoulders back. "I have work to do."

Gideon eased her back from the door and shut it. He turned her around and looked down at her gravely.

"There's more to life than work," he said.

"But," she said, gesturing toward the door, "I need to look at the castle—"

"It's been there for centuries. It will be there for another day or two."

She looked up at him with a scowl. "Why the sudden change of heart?"

He smiled and shrugged. "I've come to realize quite suddenly that there is more to life than work."

"You've got to be kidding."

"I've been distracted by freckles."

"Freckles?"

"Yours."

"Oh," she said. Then she froze and felt a blush creep up her cheeks. "Mine?"

"Oh, yes," he said, with a nod. "Enough to make a man rethink his priorities."

"Oh, really," she squeaked. She cleared her throat and

dredged up the most uninterested expression she could. "Well," she said, her nose in the air, "there is more to me than my freckles. Attractive though they might be."

"You have my full attention."

"Hmmm, well," she said, quite at a loss for words. This about-face by a dyed-in-the-wool CEO was very hard to believe. "I would elaborate on my other desirable qualities if I had the time," she said finally.

"You have the time. It's too wet to go out right now."

She wanted to argue, but couldn't. It was just as nasty outside today as it had been when she'd walked to the inn and she had very vivid memories of that soggy trip. "I suppose it is a little on the rainy side," she said reluctantly.

"You can go after Christmas. The castle will keep until then."

He had a point. "All right," she conceded. "I'll wait until then."

"Good," he said. "Interested in breakfast?"

"If you stir."

"Done."

And then Megan watched as he took her by his comfortable, companionable hand and led her toward the kitchen. And she went with him, partly because it was too wet to go to the castle and partly because she had to see more of the Gideon-on-vacation side he seemed to be showing. And, lastly, she went with him because there was something about a man with bouncing purple curly cues on his toes that was just too much to resist.

Gideon stopped at the entrance to the kitchen and looked around, seemingly perplexed.

"I must admit, I haven't the vaguest idea where to start," he said, scanning the area.

"Clean-up first, then cooking," Megan said. "Here, I'll show you what to do."

Organizing was definitely one of her strong points and she used it to its best advantage. Once the kitchen was tidied, she turned to Mrs. Pruitt's notes. She flipped through until she found something she thought they might manage.

"Ever had bannocks?" she asked.

"They're tasty enough. I think we could manage."

"All right, here goes."

Megan did her best to decipher Mrs. Pruitt's scrawl while Gideon sifted and stirred to her specifications. Megan looked into the bowl.

"I think they're supposed to look like pancakes," she said, tipping the bowl this way and that. "This is too runny."

Gideon looked at her helplessly. "Should I stir more?"

"It says not to stir them too much." She looked at the bowl and rubbed her chin thoughtfully. "I think maybe we should add . . . um . . ."

"A wee bit more flour."

Megan squeaked and whirled around. The red-haired, kilted ghost from upstairs was standing directly behind her. He took off his bonnet with the feather stuck under the badge and clutched it in his hands. He made her a small bow and then straightened and smiled shyly.

"Hugh McKinnon, at yer service," he said, with another bow.

Megan backed into Gideon, hard.

"Megan?" he asked, putting his arm around her waist.

Megan shook her head with a jerk. "I'm okay."

Hugh scrunched his cap all the more. "I was quite the cook in me day," he offered.

Megan gulped and nodded, then turned and looked at Gideon. "A little more flour," she said.

Gideon added more, then stirred. "Well," he said, looking astonished, "that did the trick." He looked at her and smiled. "I'd say that time at McDonald's wasn't wasted at all."

"If you only knew," Megan said, under her breath.

"Well, now all we have to do is cook them," Gideon said, firing up the stove.

"Heaven help us," Megan said. She stole a look at Hugh, who had moved to stand behind Gideon. He leaned up on his toes to peer over Gideon's shoulder.

Gideon shivered and brushed off his right shoulder, as if

trying to rid himself of an annoying fly. Hugh didn't seem to notice; he only peered more intently.

"Och, but he'll burn 'em with the fire up so high," Hugh said, casting Megan a look of concern.

"Maybe you should turn the heat down," Megan suggested quickly.

Gideon did so, then poured some of the batter into the pan. He waited, studying it intently. Then he eased his spatula under the flat cake and flipped it. The cooked side was a beautiful, golden brown. Megan peeked over Gideon's left shoulder. She exchanged a quick look with Hugh, who was leaning over Gideon's right shoulder, and received a nod of encouragement.

"I think it's done," she announced.

Gideon flipped it onto a plate.

"Perfect," Hugh said, beaming his approval on her. "I always ate them with a wee bit o' butter and a smackerel o' jam." He smiled crookedly. "Always had a sweet tooth, did I—"

"HUGH!"

Hugh gulped, plopped his cap on his head, made her a very quick bow and then turned and fled through the pantry door. Megan didn't even bother to go after him to see if he was lurking inside with the tins of vegetables. She had the feeling he wasn't.

She took a deep breath and smiled up at Gideon.

"I hear butter and jam are good with these."

"Sounds delightful," Gideon said, holding out the plate. "Shall we share the first fruits of our labors?"

The bannock was very tasty and Megan put her newfound kitchen skill to good use by overseeing Gideon while he cooked more. Megan stole looks around the kitchen as she did so, but saw nothing else out of the ordinary. Hugh must have been able to escape the watchful eye of that distinguished ghost for only a few minutes.

"Megan, what are you looking at?"

She looked at Gideon and put on her most innocent smile. "Nothing."

"You're supposed to say," he said, plopping another bannock on her plate, "that you can't tear your eyes from me. You aren't thinking business thoughts, are you?" He looked at her closely.

"Not a one."

"A day or two's holiday won't hurt you."

"My, how the leopard has changed his spots."

Gideon smiled ruefully as he sat down with her at the table. "I like to believe I'm intelligent enough to recognize a better course when it comes along."

"And that better course would be?"

"The holidays spent with you, of course."

Megan rested her elbows on the table and propped her chin on her fists. "So," she said, "what do you have in mind, since we're stranded together in this haunted inn in the middle of nowhere?"

He smiled dryly. "I don't believe in ghosts."

A pot lid went sailing across the room and landed at the back door.

Gideon sat bolt upright in his chair.

Megan only smiled serenely. Maybe Hugh McKinnon had taken exception to that last remark.

"Just the wind," she said soothingly.

"Of course." Gideon jumped to his feet. "How about a fire in the library?"

"No talk of work? No fixing?"

He shook his head as he pulled her to her feet. "You don't need to be fixed." He cupped her cheek with his hand, leaned down and brushed his lips across hers. "I won't talk about my work either. We'll sit and gaze dreamily into each other's eyes."

Megan suppressed the urge to tell him he was starting to make her crazy. She'd come to the U.K. to be a success, not to find herself captured in the arms of some renegade CEO who for some unfathomable reason had decided that a couple of days' vacation really would be good for him. What would happen when he snapped back to reality?

She would never see him again, that's what would happen. He would go on his merry way accompanied by his business toys and she would be left with her heart in shreds.

Too many more looks into those aqua eyes would just do her in.

"Megan?" He looped his arms around her waist.

It was too much. What could he possibly want with her? He was probably used to dating very successful, very rich women who could keep up with him at parties and things. She couldn't even keep a job for more than three months. How would he introduce her, "this is my wife, the queen of pick-up-your-paycheck-on-your-way-out-the-door?"

As if he'd even stick around long enough to decide he wanted her for a wife!

"I need to clean up the kitchen," she said, pulling away from him. "I can't look at this mess any longer. You go on ahead."

She turned to the table and started stacking plates, bowls, and utensils.

Gideon didn't say anything. Instead, he merely worked beside her as she scraped and washed and dried and put away. And when all she had left to do was twist a dishtowel into unrecognizable shapes, he took the cloth away from her, then pulled her into his arms.

It was the last place she wanted to be.

Unfortunately, it was suddenly the only place she wanted to be.

She closed her eyes and hoped she wouldn't make a fool out of herself by either crying or blurting out that she wasn't the kind of girl for a fling.

"I'm scared," she whispered instead.

She felt him swallow.

"So am I," he said, just as softly.

She jerked her head back so fast, it almost gave her whiplash. "You are?" she asked incredulously.

He looked as helpless as she felt. "Of course I am. You weren't exactly on my agenda."

"I didn't have an agenda. But," she added, "if I'd had one, you wouldn't have been on mine either."

"I see." He paused and looked at her solemnly. "I don't date, you know," he said, finally.

"Really? Me neither."

He continued simply to stare down at her. Well, maybe he'd said all he was going to say and it was her turn.

"I don't fling," she announced. She watched him closely for his reaction.

"Neither do I," he stated. He frowned suddenly. "If you don't date and you don't fling, when do you kiss?"

He asked it so earnestly, Megan couldn't help but smile.

"I like you," she said.

"I like you too," he replied. "And I feel certain a small kiss would be entirely appropriate at this point, but you seem to have a schedule about these things."

Megan slipped out of his arms. "Actually, I think there's an application involved."

Gideon blinked. "What?"

"And a résumé," she added, heading toward the dining room door.

"You can't mean that."

"And I'll have to check your references," she said, pushing open the door.

"You've got to be joking!" he exclaimed, hurrying after her. "You've applied for too bloody many jobs; it's ruined you for romance!"

Megan only smiled. She wasn't sure what his intentions were, but he didn't date and he didn't fling. As for anything else, she would just wait and see. At least they were on the same shaky footing. Time would sort out the rest.

She was halfway through the dining room when she heard an *oof,* then a substantial *whump* behind her. She turned to find Gideon flat on his face.

"Damned shoes!"

Heavens, how could she resist such a man?

 SEVEN

The next morning Gideon sat in an enormously comfortable overstuffed chair in the library and watched Megan do marvelous things with the pitiful decorations Mrs. Pruitt had left behind. And as he sat there, he came to two conclusions: Stephen didn't read because he liked books, he read because he was basically a hedonistic blighter who liked overstuffed chairs; and, Megan MacLeod McKinnon was a magical creature who had completely stolen his heart.

After his abrupt reunion with the floor after breakfast the day before, she had tied his toes into little knots so they wouldn't tangle anymore. She had drawn from him his innermost secrets and dreams during a rousing game of Truth or Dare, then she had taken those words in her hands and crossed her heart as she vowed not to repeat them to anyone—especially Stephen, who might poke fun at him. She'd beaten him at chess, exacting a kiss for every man she took—and he hadn't even had to fill out an application or cite references.

They had explored most of the inn the previous afternoon. Gideon had watched in amazement as Megan had identified obscure works of art, styles of furniture and patterns of lace and china. Her employments might have been short-lived, but they hadn't been failures.

And when he'd walked her to her door very late in the evening, he had been completely surprised by how wrong it seemed to have her go inside alone and shut the door, leaving him outside. He'd stood there with his arms around her, gazing down into her lovely, befreckled face and wondered what she would do if he proposed on the spot.

Likely have dashed off for the thermometer.

So he'd kissed her sweetly, then retreated to the library to read for most of the night.

No wonder Stephen buried himself in books.

"Well, I've taken this about as far as I can. We'll have to go to town if I want to do more."

Gideon blinked at Megan. Those were almost his exact thoughts. Though whilst she no doubt spoke of Christmas decorations, his thoughts were more along the lines of procuring a marriage license.

"Hey, look at this."

Gideon wanted to get out of the chair, but it seemed reluctant to let him go. "I fear I'm trapped."

Megan walked over to him, her eyes glued to a document she'd picked up from off the desk in the corner. She held out her hand and hauled Gideon to his feet.

And then she started to shake. She looked up at him. "I can't believe this."

Gideon looked at her blanched face and immediately threw his arms around her. It seemed like the proper precaution to take when your beloved looked as if she might fall down in a dead faint.

"Read it!" Megan exclaimed, shoving it in his face.

Gideon read. And then he reread. And then he shook his head in wonder.

"I'll be damned."

"This can't be legal!"

"It certainly looks as if it is. All you need do is sign. I can witness it for you."

"Gideon, Mrs. P. left me the entire inn! What am I going to do with a haunted inn? I don't know the first thing about cooking, or cleaning, or advertising—"

Gideon pulled her close and rubbed his hand soothingly

over her back as she continued to list in great detail all the things she could not do. He smiled into her hair as he scanned the rest of the deed. It was all quite legal and quite binding. And he knew without a doubt that Megan would do a positively smashing job at all of it.

"I'll be stuck out here all by myself for the rest of my life with the rain and the ghosts—"

Gideon paused, then stroked her back more thoughtfully. That was a problem. After they married, she wouldn't be able to be here full time. In fact, he didn't know how she could spend more than a week or two here during the year. His business was in London. AE, Inc. would collapse without him overseeing it every day. Good heavens, his vice presidents couldn't tie their shoelaces without Gideon giving them a memo on it!

Well, there had to be a solution to the dilemma. Gideon was known for his creative solutions to impossible tangles. He'd fixed other things, he could fix this too.

"—probably doesn't even have a washing machine. I'll be washing things on a rock in the river. All right, so my nails aren't in great shape anyway. Can you imagine what they'd look like after a few months of that?" She pulled back and looked at him. "Well? Can you imagine?"

Gideon took her by the hand and led her over to the desk. He put the deed down, found a pen and handed it to her.

"Sign," he commanded.

"Oh, I just don't know—"

"Sign, Megan. It will all work out for the best."

She leaned over the document, then looked at him from under her eyebrows. "Will you," she paused, then cleared her throat and looked away, "will you come visit me now and then? When you take another vacation?"

"Oh, Megan," he said, surrendering his heart to her all over again. "Of course I will."

She started to cry. She dragged her sleeve across her eyes and looked at the deed. "You know, I'll probably end up just as batty as Mrs. Pruitt. At least she was a Mrs. She hadn't been stuck here alone her entire life."

"Megan, sign the deed," Gideon said, forcing himself not

to blurt out his intentions. He wanted his proposal to have the proper romantic setting; popping the question while his bride-to-be sniffled liberally into her sleeve was not it.

Megan signed, then buried her face in her hands and wept. Gideon witnessed her signature, then pulled her into his arms and held her.

"Megan, you just acquired a lovely little getaway. These should be tears of joy."

"Oh, I'm just thrilled!"

"The place could stand a little sprucing up, of course."

"I'm broke!"

"You're forgetting whom you're drenching. I'm the extremely powerful CEO, remember?"

She froze, then looked up at him. "But, I don't want your money."

"I'm not going to give you any money." *You'll just take it out of our joint account,* he added silently. "I'll just help you get a business loan," he lied.

She worried a loose thread on his tunic. "And you'll show up now and then?"

"Probably more than you'll want," he said, fishing heavily for a compliment.

"I could use help with the cooking," she said, looking no further up than his chin. "And maybe the decorating. You know, British input and all that."

He laughed softly and tipped her face up to kiss her. "Of course, Madame Proprietress. My proper British tastes are at your disposal." He smiled down at her. "Well, shall we go ransack Mrs. Pruitt's room and see what other surprises she left for you? Then perhaps we should head down to the village and stock up for the Christmas feast."

"It will be a quick trip," Megan said as he pulled her toward the library door. "My savings account isn't exactly padded."

"I'll buy—"

"No, you won't," she said, digging in her heels.

Gideon frowned down at her. "Megan—"

"No, Gideon. I don't want your money."

"Ah, but seeing my hands prune up from too much dish washing appeals to you."

She smiled up at him so brightly, he almost flinched.

"Exactly," she said.

"Are you going to be this stubborn for the rest of our lives?"

She blinked. "The rest of our—"

The front door slammed, making them both jump. Gideon pulled her behind him. "Let me go first."

"Oh, brother. It's not a burglar."

"Humor me."

"Maybe it's another guest," Megan said suddenly. "Hurry, Gideon. Maybe he'll pay in cash up front."

Gideon stumbled out into the entryway, thanks to Megan's hearty push. It was a good thing his toes were tamed, or he would have embarrassed himself.

A young man stood there, soaked to the skin. His jaw dropped.

"We're in costume," Gideon said, gritting his teeth. No sense in pummeling any of Megan's potential customers.

"I was sent for Lord Blythwood. Is he—?"

"I am he," Gideon said, swallowing a feeling of dread. "What is it?"

"An urgent message from a Mr. MacClure. The phone's out up here so I was sent to give it to you. Lord Blythwood," he added in a tone that said volumes about his opinion of Gideon's manner of dress.

"What was it?" Gideon demanded. Heaven only knew what kind of disaster Adam had landed them in. Gideon cursed himself thoroughly. He never should have given up so easily on staying connected with the company.

"He said it was something of an emergency, and a long, expensive one at that. They need you in London as soon as you can get there."

"I knew it, damn it," Gideon said, dragging his hand through his hair. This was what he deserved for thinking to take a holiday. And when the company collapsed, Gideon would personally hold Stephen responsible.

"All right," Gideon said, striding to the door, "let's go.

Are there any cars for hire in the village? I suppose the train might be just as fast. Or maybe a flight from Edinburgh. Well, come on, lad. Don't just stand there.''

Gideon strode out the front door into the pouring rain and swore. The boy had come up on a motorbike. Well, perhaps it was fitting to end his ill-fated holiday soaked to the skin, since it was how he'd begun it once his car had caught fire. The car likely would have exploded if Megan hadn't been so quick with the fire extinguisher.

Megan.

Gideon froze in mid step, then turned around. Megan was standing in the doorway.

Gideon strode back to her and put his hands on her shoulders. "I'll ring you soon.''

"Sure.''

"I will,'' he promised. "And I'll arrange for some help to come up. I'm sure there is someone in the village who'll hire out for the holidays.''

"It's okay,'' she said, pulling away.

"I'll send a decorator too. Maybe a chef to get things rolling. We have an advertising division at AE. I'll have someone ring you after Christmas with some ideas—''

"Gideon?''

He closed his mouth on the rest of his plans. "Yes?''

"I'll be okay on my own. Really.''

"But I can help,'' he said.

She shook her head. "I don't want your money.''

"But—''

She backed away. "Just go do your business thing.''

"Megan—''

"It was fun.'' She smiled, but her eyes were too bright. "I'll see you around.''

And with that, she shut the door in his face.

Gideon stood there on the porch and felt worse than he'd ever felt in his entire life. Not even blowing the entire U.K. telecommunications market had left such a sinking feeling in his gut.

"My lord?''

Gideon turned. It was all he could do to put one foot in front of the other.

He climbed onto the back of the motorbike. It was an unpleasant ride to the village, but it was probably just what he needed to bring himself back to his senses.

He would straighten things out in London and ring Megan the first chance he got. He would fly her down and they could resume their relationship in town. He could come home earlier at night, in time for a late supper, perhaps. Maybe he would give thought to taking a few hours off on Sundays to devote to her. Things could work out remarkably well.

He had Adam on the line within moments of arriving in civilization.

"What?" he barked. "Were we robbed? Scooped in the Far East? Did the infrastructure of the company collapse?"

"No," Adam said, sounding confused, "but the stock was off ten points today in New York."

"And?"

"What do you mean 'and'?" Adam exclaimed. "It was off *ten* points, Gideon!"

"Stocks dip."

"What?" Adam gasped. "The last time it dipped *two* you dragged us all out of bed for an emergency board meeting!"

"It will bounce back."

"It will bounce back," Adam echoed, disbelief plain in his voice. "Gideon, have you lost your mind? This is a disaster!"

"Adam, relax—"

"Relax?" Adam bellowed. "I'm sprinting through the halls, bloody frantic about this and all you can say is 're-lax'?"

Gideon whistled softly. "I think you need a holiday."

"What did they *do* to you up there?" Adam yelled.

Gideon paused, wondering where to begin. Normally he would have gone on about equipment failures and the time it had cost him, but now he saw clearly that business went on in spite of him. Even the few hours he had spent fretting and stewing had been nothing but a waste of time.

And then quite suddenly a most amazing thought occurred to him.

"Adam, I think I understand."

"Understand what?"

"What she wants."

"Oh, no," Adam moaned. "Tell me there isn't a she involved!"

"I'll call you in a few days. Maybe after the new year."

"Gideon, wait—"

"Go home, Adam. It's Christmas Eve. You need a holiday."

"What I'm going to need is a trip to hospital—thanks to the chest pains you're causing—"

Gideon hung up the phone and lowered himself onto a handy bench. Realizations of this magnitude were better digested while sitting. Yes, it was all becoming clear. He wondered why he hadn't seen it before.

He looked up at his dripping chauffeur. "Are there any shops still open? I need ingredients for a modest Christmas dinner and a few of the trimmings."

The boy nodded, his eyes wide.

"Then let's be off, shall we? I won't spend much. That isn't what's important."

And now he knew what was.

 EIGHT

Megan looked at the rain beating incessantly against the window. She'd been watching it from the same position for most of the day. Part of it was she couldn't seem to get out of Gideon's chair, and part of it was she just didn't have the heart to move.

It being shattered and lying all around her in pieces as it was.

Well, it was getting close to dark now. Probably time to go and see what was in her kitchen. Somehow, she just couldn't get enthusiastic about the thought of it being hers. She would never go into it that she didn't see Gideon standing over the stove, coaxing his bannocks to cook properly and not scorch themselves.

"Get over it, McKinnon," she commanded herself sternly.

She clawed her way out of the overstuffed chair and dragged herself through the entryway and down the hallway to the dining room. She walked over the place where Gideon had planted his face more than once. Then she gave herself a good shake. She couldn't walk through the house and see him at every turn. He'd made his decision and it was blindingly clear that his priorities didn't include her, despite his brief about-face. He was a workaholic. There was no changing him.

She put her hand on the door, then froze. There was someone in the kitchen. More than one someone, if her ears weren't deceiving her. She grabbed her trusty ornamental dagger from off the buffet and eased the door open the slightest bit.

"I'll go after him," a voice said, in less than friendly tones. "I'll teach him to break me wee granddaughter's heart!"

"Leave him be, ye blighted Scot! He's regained his senses and gone off to do his manly labors!"

"Och, and what more manly a labor is there than having a wife and bairns?" the first voice demanded. "Pebble countin' ain't the way to happiness!"

There was a sudden ruckus and a great deal of gurgling. Megan feared murder, so she shoved open the door and leaped into the kitchen, her dagger bared and ready.

"Eek!" the ghost dressed in knightly garb said, leaping back and tripping over his chair. He landed ungracefully on his backside.

Megan froze, her eyes glued to the scene before her. There were three men in her kitchen, two of whom were dressed in kilts, one in chain mail. And she recognized all of them.

"Ah," she said, lowering her dagger and straightening up from her lunging position, "um, hello."

Hugh smiled and waved. The knight heaved himself to his feet with a grunt and frowned at her. Megan looked at the third ghost, the one with the commanding presence and very fancy kilt. A huge brooch of emeralds and silver fastened a scarf-like bit of cloth to his shoulder. Megan felt completely frumpy in her dress that was six inches too short. She gave the chief ghost a little wave.

"Hi," she said, whipping her hands behind her back to hide her dagger, "I'm Megan." She wished she had a pocket to stash the knife in. It looked ridiculous compared to the swords the ghosts were packing.

The head ghost made her a low bow. "Ambrose MacLeod, Laird of the Clan MacLeod, at your service."

"Okay," Megan said slowly, giving in to the urge to drop a little curtsey.

"He's your granddaddy," Hugh said, "on yer mama's side."

"A bit removed," Ambrose said modestly.

"I see," Megan said, wondering if her eyes were bulging as far out of her head as she thought they might be.

"And I'd be your granddaddy on your papa's side," Hugh added proudly. "A wee bit removed," he added, darting a glance at Ambrose.

Ambrose nodded to Hugh, then turned and nodded to the knight who had plunked himself down into a chair. "This is Fulbert de Piaget. He's Gideon's uncle."

"Several times removed," Megan surmised.

"Aye," Fulbert grumbled.

Megan leaned back against the door frame. "Well, he's off to do his business. Aren't you happy about that?"

"Of course I am," Fulbert retorted, scowling. "He does mighty important work, missy!"

"And he misses out on life because of it," Ambrose said, sitting down heavily. "Come, Megan, and join us. We've puzzled our heads sore trying to understand the lad and I've no more mind to speak of him. We'll speak instead of your plans for the inn."

Megan soon found herself sitting in a circle with three hale and hearty ghosts, listening to them discuss what could be done with the inn now that a member of the family finally had it back in her possession.

"Then you don't mind?" she asked Ambrose.

"Mind?" Fulbert snorted. "Missy, we saw to the deed ourselves!"

"And *you* don't mind?" she asked, turning to Gideon's grumbly ancestor.

Fulbert looked at her from under his bushy eyebrows. "I'm wed to your blasted aunt, gel. I'll learn to put up with you soon enough."

Hugh whipped out his sword. "Keep a civil tongue, ye blighted—"

"It's okay," Megan said, holding up her hand. "He doesn't have to like me. Maybe it runs in the family."

Hugh looked at her and his bright blue eyes filled with tears. "I think Gideon liked ye fine, Megan lass. He's just a bit off in the head."

Even Fulbert seemed to have nothing to say to that.

"Plans for the inn," Ambrose broke in. "What do you think, my dear, about this modern fascination with the past? I daresay we could make use of it. After all, we're quite conversant with many decades of traditions."

"I don't doubt it," she said, feeling the faintest glimmer of enthusiasm. "You mean, period costumes and traditional holiday celebrations?"

Hugh elbowed Fulbert. "She's a quick one, she is. That's *me* wee granddaughter, ye stubborn Brit."

Megan smiled at him, then turned back to Ambrose. "It would have to be small scale, until I have more money to invest in it."

And with that, they were off and running. Megan listened to ideas fly between her ancestors and wished she'd had a tape recorder. She hardly had time to wonder if they could *be* recorded before she found herself swept into a maelstrom of ideas. And if she only put into practice a fraction of them, she would be busy for the rest of her days.

Which was a good thing, since she would have all that time on her hands.

She refused to think about Gideon. And about how much she would have loved to share this with him. And about how adorable he would have looked in a kilt.

And just before she was tired enough to lean her head back against the chair, she looked at Ambrose and decided, based on the twinkle in his eye, that he had been the one to rustle up the purple elf shoes.

And that was almost enough to make her fall asleep with a smile on her face.

She woke later, stiff and sore. The kitchen was lit with a single candle burning low on the table. There was no sign of the chairs that had been occupied by three spirits earlier, nor was there any sign of their silver mugs or the keg Fulbert seemed to have produced from thin air. Megan blinked. She was tempted to think she'd dreamed it all, but the memories were too fresh in her mind. At least her relatives cleaned up after themselves.

She stretched, then froze. Was that a noise?

"Hugh? Ambrose?" She looked over her shoulder. "Fulbert?"

There it was again. And it wasn't coming from the kitchen.

Megan took her dagger in hand and went out into the dining room.

"Anyone here?" she asked.

The noise stopped abruptly.

That was enough to spook her. She peeked out into the dimly lit hallway. There, over the McKinnon coat of arms was a sword reminiscent of Hugh's. It would be a far sight more protection than the little unsharpened dagger she held. She slipped out into the hallway, laid the dagger on the reception desk and tiptoed over to the sword.

She eased it down. And the point immediately made a whumping noise as it fell against the carpet. It was, however, not as heavy as she feared. She hoisted it, took up the stance she'd seen Hugh and Fulbert take when they'd been trying to decapitate each other upstairs, then walked softly to the library.

Something was shuffling inside.

Megan didn't give herself time to think. She flung open the door and jumped inside, brandishing her blade.

Gideon whirled around in surprise, stumbled backward, and went down heavily into a Christmas tree.

"Ouch, damn it! I'm being poked everywhere!"

Megan tossed the blade onto the couch and ran to help him. She pulled him up, then turned him around and picked out the bits of ornament and tree parts that had somehow found their way into his backside.

"You scared me to death," he exclaimed. "You could have cut my head off with that thing!"

"Nice to see you too," she said, with a scowl. "How

was I supposed to know you weren't a burglar?''

''Decorating?''

Megan tried to resurrect the tree Gideon had sat on. It had been a rather small one to start with and Gideon hadn't done it any favors. She let it flop back to the ground, then stared down at it.

''It was a nice thought,'' she said quietly.

''It took me a long time to find the right one,'' he said, taking her hand. ''A very long *time*.''

She met his gaze. ''It did?''

''It did.'' He led her over to the chair of no return, snagging a shopping bag on his way. He sat and pulled her onto his lap. ''Here. These things will explain it better than I could.'' He reached for his bag and dumped its contents into her arms. He held up an unwrapped umbrella, then set it aside. ''You didn't need to open that. It's just to get you up to the castle, so you can put that job behind you before we start on the inn.''

Before we start on the inn. Megan was just certain she'd heard him wrong. She frowned.

''What about your emergency?'' she demanded.

''I took care of it.''

She frowned some more, just to let him know where she stood. ''Did it take all afternoon?''

''It took about five minutes. The rest of the time I was looking for things for you.''

''Well,'' she said, feeling rather at a loss. There she'd been griping about him to her ancestors, and he'd been hunting up presents. ''That sheds a different light on things.''

''I thought it might.'' He smiled. ''Aren't you interested in what I got you? And the humiliation I went through whilst shopping in yellow tights and purple shoes?''

Megan felt her heart soften even more. Gideon had tried to spruce up the library with his little tree and he had left his dignity behind to shop for something to put under it for her. It merited at least a second glance at what was piled in her lap.

There were four packages of various sizes. She immediately zeroed in on the very small, very ring-like looking box, then forced herself to look at something else. It couldn't be what its size screamed it might be. Megan looked at Gideon from under her eyebrows and saw a twinkle in his eyes, as if he had an impressive secret he couldn't wait to share.

Taking a deep breath, she opened up a long, slender package—and held up a paintbrush.

"To use in our redecorating," he said.

"*Our* redecorating?" she asked.

"I told you I'd offer my humble services, didn't I?"

That was before he'd hiked right on out of there—but then he'd hiked right back in again. Megan held up the brush and considered.

"It's a really small brush, Gideon."

"Then I guess it will take a long *time*, won't it?"

"Hmmm," she said. On the surface that looked good, but what was his definition of time spent? Would he be there for two or three days, consider his decorating contribution fulfilled, then toddle off merrily to London? She set the paintbrush aside. No sense jumping to any conclusions quite yet.

She chose another hastily wrapped gift, convinced Gideon had done the wrapping honors himself.

"Interesting," she said, holding up rubber gloves.

"So I don't get dishpan hands while I'm washing up after supper," Gideon said, with a smile.

"Well," she said. A man didn't buy yellow rubber gloves if he didn't plan on using them, did he? And these weren't the wimpy kind that supermarkets sold; these were heavy-duty, dabble-in-toxic-waste-and-not-ruin-your-fingernail-polish kind of gloves. These were gloves meant for more than just a handful of dips into sudsy water. Did he plan on doing dishes for more than just the weekend?

"And this is a cookbook," Gideon said, relieving her of the gloves and handing her a heavy package instead. "I perused the index already and I think there are several things we could actually succeed in making. I was somewhat alarmed by the quantity of raw ingredients required, but I decided that together we might have a go at it. What do you think?"

"Ah," Megan said, stunned, "um, well." She unwrapped in a daze. Based on their previous forays into the kitchen, the gift of a cookbook was not something to be taken lightly. Especially one that required them to make things from scratch. "It sounds pretty time-consuming," she said. "Not exactly a single weekend project."

"I know," he said, smiling widely. "It will be brilliant fun, don't you think? All that time together in the kitchen, bonding over bouillabaisse?"

Megan clutched the cookbook, looked at her errant business mogul and wondered if one too many equipment disasters had finally forced him to relinquish his tenuous grasp on sanity.

"Gideon," she said slowly, wanting to make sure he understood each word, "when in the world are you going to have time for all of this?"

"I'll make time."

"You can't. You're the president of an international company."

"I'll manage it."

"You hobnob with billionaires!"

"I know."

Megan gritted her teeth. He was wearing a cheesy grin, and that annoying twinkle was still stuck in his eyes.

"You don't have time to cook," Megan said. "That's why you have a chef."

"We'll send him on holiday."

It was time for the killing blow. He would have to admit his true intentions sooner or later, and this was guaranteed to force him to face reality.

"You wouldn't last a week up here," she said. "You can't live without your laptop."

Gideon calmly took her face in his hands, leaned up and kissed her softly.

"Yes, I can," he said, his smile sweet and gentle. "I realized when I left that what I was heading toward was far less important than what I'd left behind."

It started to sink in. He was serious. Megan felt her eyes begin to water.

"I can live without the company, Megan, but I can't live without you."

He proceeded to hand her the little box she'd been so carefully avoiding. Megan clutched it. She didn't dare open in.

"A new marble for my collection?" she asked, trying to smile.

Gideon only laughed. "Hardly."

Megan looked at him and saw nothing but love in his eyes and tenderness in his expression. He covered her hand with his own comfortable, companionable hand and gave her a reassuring squeeze.

"Open it, please," he said softly. "Quickly, so I'll know if I've just made a great fool of myself."

Megan opened the box to reveal a slim gold band. At least she thought it was a slim gold band. She could hardly see it for her tears.

"Oh, Gideon."

"It's just a placeholder," he said. "Thorpewold isn't exactly a buzzing metropolis."

"No, it's beautiful."

He ducked to catch her gaze. "I can't guarantee I'll be perfect," he admitted, "but you've seen quite a bit of me at my worst. I'll still have to work, but I'll work less. Much less." He put his hand under her chin and lifted her face up. "I know you won't marry me for my money or my title, and that will confuse my father greatly, but," he said, with a smile, "will you marry me for my time? I'll make it worth your while."

"Somehow, I imagine you will," she said, returning his smile. "And yes," she added, "I will marry you."

And then she learned just how much time he planned on lavishing on her as he took many, many minutes to kiss her breathless.

"If we could get out of this damned chair," he said, when he came up for air a very long while later, "we could adjourn to another room and see how much more time we could spend at this. I mean, after all, we're engaged now, and there really isn't any reason . . ."

"Why, there'll be none of that!" Hugh gasped. He appeared behind the chair and looked down at Gideon with marked disapproval. "Imagine that! The thought of visitin' me wee one's marriage bed 'afore the ceremony!"

Gideon blinked. "What did you say?"

Megan shook her head. "I didn't say anything."

Gideon scratched his head, then shrugged. "Well, what do you think—ouch, damn it!"

Hugh had given Gideon what Megan could only term a thorough boxing of the ears.

Gideon looked down at her hands that were captured handily enough in his own, then raised his gaze to hers slowly.

"You didn't do that," he stated.

" 'Fraid not."

He lifted one eyebrow. "I don't suppose you would know who had, would you?"

"I suppose I would."

Gideon shivered. "All right," he said, to the middle of the room. "I take the hint."

Hugh harrumphed and disappeared. Gideon looked at her and laughed uneasily.

"I don't suppose we'll have any privacy on our wedding night either."

"I think they know where to draw the line." Or so she hoped.

"Will I pass muster if I limit myself to kissing you? After all, it is Christmas Eve. I think it's tradition."

"And we wouldn't want to break with tradition," she said, the moment before she found much more interesting things to do with her lips besides form words.

And between kisses, Gideon briefly described the makings for Christmas dinner he'd found. He polled her opinions on what other holiday traditions she thought they could indulge in to distract themselves until they could arrange a wedding.

"Yule log," he offered, then kissed her thoroughly.

"Bing Crosby on the stereo," she managed when he let her breathe again. "Counts as Christmas caroling."

"Wassail and other trappings," he said, winding his fingers through her hair.

"*It's a Wonderful Life,*" she suggested.

He smiled. "It certainly is."

Megan started to tell him that he didn't understand what she meant. Then she saw the look in his eye and realized he understood completely.

And it certainly was.

It was very late when the fire had burned down and Megan woke, only to realize she'd fallen asleep in Gideon's arms. He was sound asleep, still fully trapped in the chair's embrace. Megan blinked as she saw Fulbert come up behind the chair. He gave her a scowl that wasn't as scowly as his former expressions, then plopped a red bow on top of Gideon's head. He huffed something under his breath, then turned and went to join Hugh and Ambrose who were standing next to the fireplace. Hugh was beaming. Ambrose looked perfectly satisfied with his work.

"Stocking stuffer," Ambrose clarified.

"Thank you," Megan said, with a smile.

"Hmmm?" Gideon said, stirring.

Megan kissed him softly. "Nothing. Go back to sleep."

Once he had drifted off again, Megan looked at the small collection of gifts on the floor next to the fallen tree, gifts that represented the time Gideon intended to commit to their relationship. The last glowing embers from the fire sparkled against the thin gold band on her hand, a symbol of love found in the most unexpected of places.

Then she looked at Gideon and decided that he was by far the best Christmas gift of all—even if he was too big to fit into her stocking.

She tucked her head into the crook of his neck and closed her eyes, content.

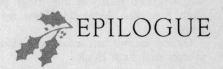

EPILOGUE

Ambrose MacLeod, grandfather several generations removed, escorted his granddaughter down the aisle. Her sire walked on the other side, preoccupied with not tripping over his daughter's flowing medieval gown.

"Good grief, Megan, where did you come up with all this medieval hoopla?" her father muttered.

"Oh, Dad," Megan said, with a little laugh, "the inn just seems to inspire it."

Ambrose looked down at her and felt pride stir in his breast. Of all the places he could have been, this was the best. Of all the posterity he could have matchmade for, this lass was the sweetest. She looked up at him and smiled brilliantly. Ambrose returned the smile proudly.

He turned his gaze to the front of the chapel. Gideon stood there already, resplendent in his medieval finery. Fulbert stood to one side, his hand on his sword, Artane pride etched into his very bearing. Fulbert had made his peace completely with Megan over the past month, once he'd realized she actually increased Gideon's capacity for proper labor. The office Gideon had installed in the inn had satisfied them both. Ambrose knew he would miss Megan when she and her love made for London, but Gideon had given his word they wouldn't stay overlong. Of course, Gideon had been looking in the wrong direction when he'd said as much, but Ambrose had accepted the gesture just the same. The lad's vision would clear up soon enough.

Hugh stood next to Megan's sisters Jennifer and Victoria, clutching a beribboned nosegay of conservatory flowers. Megan smiled fondly at him. Hugh pulled a snowy linen cloth from his sleeve and blew his nose into it with a honk.

Gideon jumped half a foot and whipped his head around to stare straight at Hugh.

Then he seemingly caught sight of Fulbert's blade and jerked around to stare at him.

"Uh oh," Megan said, looking up at Ambrose. "The jig's up."

Ambrose felt Gideon's eyes on him and he returned the lad's startled look.

"Come on, Dad. Gideon's going to faint if we don't hurry up."

Ambrose stood back and let her hasten to her blanched groom's side. It was rather touch-and-go until Fulbert barked for the lad to stand up straight. At that, the boy stiffened as if he'd been skewered up the spine.

Ambrose didn't relax truly until the vows had been spoken, the rings exchanged and the kiss given. Then he sat down wearily next to Megan's father and his own kinswoman.

"Where does she come up with these things?" the man asked, shaking his head. "All this medieval hocus pocus. Look at me, Helen, I'm in a kilt!"

"Yes, dear."

"It's that damn MacLeod blood, Helen."

"Of course it is, dear. It's a family trait."

Ambrose smiled at his daughter, many times removed, then blinked in surprise as she looked straight at him and winked.

"Well, I'll be damned," he whispered.

It was several hours later that Megan and Gideon were sent off on their honeymoon, the guests were all put to bed and

Ambrose could finally relax in the kitchen. Even Hugh and Fulbert seemed at peace. They were only hurling mild insults at each other. No blades were bared.

"I say we turn our sights to those two sisters of hers," Hugh said, clutching his cup. "I'm thinkin' they'll be a far sight easier to see settled."

Fulbert snorted. "Didn't you mark that Victoria? By the saints, Hugh, she's a bleedin' garrison captain!" He shivered. "I wouldn't cross her if me life depended on it."

"Ambrose?" Hugh prodded. "What think ye?"

"I'm leaving it up to you two for a bit," Ambrose said, rising and stretching.

Hugh and Fulbert gaped at him.

"Where're ye off to?" Hugh asked.

Ambrose stared off into the distance thoughtfully. "The Highlands, I believe."

"But ye can't," Hugh gasped.

"We've more matches to make," Fulbert spluttered.

Ambrose smiled fondly at his two compatriots. "They'll keep well enough until I return."

"But—"

"How can you—"

"Lads, lads," Ambrose said, shaking his head. "A well-earned rest is nothing to take lightly."

"A holiday?" Hugh's ears perked up.

Fulbert tossed his mug aside. "I'm for France." And he vanished.

"The Colonies," Hugh announced, standing and tilting his cap at a jaunty angle. "I'm feeling quite the risk-taker at the moment." He made Ambrose a quick bow and disappeared.

"And I'm for the Highlands," Ambrose said, feeling his pulse quicken at the very thought.

Home.

And, of course, the precise area Megan and Gideon had chosen for their getaway.

After all, a grandfather's work was never done.

Ambrose smiled, set his mug on the table and made his way from the kitchen, turning out the lights behind him.

KEEPING FAITH

Casey Claybourne

ONE

London 1813

Blimey, she was tired. The sad kind of tired that made you feel like crying until you plumb ran out of tears. The dizzy kind of tired that ached in your back and your bones and your belly. Especially your belly. Wrapping her arms around that grumbling hole in her middle, Faith tucked her chin into her chest as a blast of wind swept down the alley, whistling its icy song.

She shivered and drew the scrap of blanket tighter around her neck. Beneath her rag-wrapped feet, the last leaves of the season crackled like the satisfying crunch of a crisp green apple or a toasty-brown bread crust.

Mmm-mm, bread . . .

She shook her head, her two scraggly braids thumping against the thinness of her back. *It sure ain't goin' to do no good to start thinkin' on that,* she scolded herself. Not when she didn't know when or where she might be finding her next meal. So rather than daydream of tart apples or soft bread, she focused instead on the familiar rattle of distant carriage wheels and the call of the lamplighter men.

Wiping her nose with the back of her hand, she sniffed the air—tentatively. In this part of town, London didn't smell so awful. Even the alleys, narrow and close, smelled better than where she'd been living in Cheapside.

Suddenly, at the end of the alley, a back door slammed. She ducked and darted to the shadowed side of the lane.

Her empty stomach groaned and twisted, telling her that she ought not to have moved quite so fast. Nausea made her head spin, her knees start to buckle. Sweat popped out on her forehead. Blinking hard, she leaned her palms against the cool bricks, struggling to stay on her feet.

Just a wee bit of a rest, she told herself. That was all she needed. If she could only find a stable with an unlatched window or a covered peddler's wagon out of the wind . . .

Faith. Oh, Fai-i-th.

She cocked her head to the side. Was someone calling her? She listened. Nothing. Nothing but the busy hum from the streets beyond. It must have been her imagination, the wind playing tricks on her.

Another bone-chilling draft hunched her over, warning her not to linger, exposed to the freezing onset of night. With an effort she shoved away from the wall, wishing her belly would stop its mad churning. She managed to stumble a dozen more steps down the alley before she saw it—a haven. A stack of willow crates, like the ones they kept chickens in at the Smithfield market.

Relief made her forget to stoop low as she hurried toward them. Dizziness tangled her feet, but she kept her sights fixed on that wonderful, wonderful refuge. *Just a little rest,* she kept telling herself. Then, she'd be all right.

She scrambled into the bottommost crate, scraping her knees over the alley's rough cobblestones. A stray chicken feather tickled her nose and she brushed it away, curling into the far corner where the wind could not reach her. Sighing, she tucked her thumb into her mouth and gazed out into the alley.

Against the silvery light of dusk, a lacy white snowflake floated by, soon followed by another and then another.

A weary smile curved her chapped lips. Snowflakes. Grandpa used to say they were angel tears. As she drifted off to sleep, Faith wondered if the angels might not be crying for her.

Lady Alice Stratford sat alone in the intense quiet of her parlor, staring at a chair. A rather ordinary yellow-and-white striped chair, it was one of a matched set in the style of Sheraton, a companion to the one she occupied. But the chair sat empty. It had for many months.

Dusk had begun its stealthy descent, shadows like ghostly gray thieves stealing into the corners of the room. Across the carpet they crept in a slow and steady rhythm that seemed to keep pace with the doleful ticking of the mantel clock.

Tick. Tock. Tick. Tock.

Alice bit into her lip as her gaze lifted to the clock's crystal face. This time of day was indeed the hardest: the sleepy hour before sunset, meant for sharing confidences and mugs of warm milk, a time meant to celebrate the passing of another day. But Alice did not celebrate. Alone with her shadows, she felt the profound solitude weigh upon her, dragging at the edges of her sanity. So quiet. So alone. Day after day, always the same.

Alone. Alone. Alone.

The word echoed through her thoughts, until her breath started to come fast, her fingers digging fitfully into the chair's linen fabric. She could not bear it. She simply could not tolerate even one more minute.

She lurched to her feet, kicking at the twisted hem of her black skirts. *The kitchen.* Yes, she'd go downstairs to the kitchen. At this hour, preparations for the evening meal would be well under way. Mrs. Imes and Betsy would be peeling potatoes and laughing over Timmons's new hair tonic. The kitchen would be odorous and hot and suffused with smoke, and she, praise God, would not be alone with her shadows.

As she approached from the servants' stairs, she heard a pot clatter to the floor. A high-pitched giggle answered. The insignificant yet comforting sounds brought a smile to Alice's lips as she pushed open the kitchen door.

The chatter and activity instantly ceased. Alice's smile grew stiff.

Betsy, her sturdy arms elbow-deep in dough, stopped her kneading as she looked up from the porcelain mixing bowl. Mrs. Imes, caught in the act of stirring the kettle, stood before the stove with a sticky wooden spoon suspended half-way over her mobcapped head.

Silence, self-conscious and heavy, fell upon the room. The only sound came from the kettle popping and bubbling.

"Can I get you somethin', Lady Stratford?" Mrs. Imes asked kindly. Too kindly.

And in a sudden and painful realization, Alice saw how she must look to them. Poor Lady Stratford, she could hear them thinking. Poor, sad, lonely Lady Stratford.

Alice cleared her throat, searching for a reasonable explanation for her intrusion, anything that might dispel the pity so plain to see in Mrs. Imes's aged gray eyes.

"No, Mrs. Imes. I—" She could not think what to say. "I thought to . . . take a walk."

"A walk?" young Betsy queried, sending a disbelieving glance toward the kitchen's steam-blanketed window. "Why, it's startin' to snow!"

"Yes. Well . . ." Alice felt her color rise, but continued toward the back door as if she had not, only a second earlier, paused so hopefully in their midst. As if, in actuality, she had planned to stroll along the wintry back streets of Mayfair.

"Walkin' in the *alley* without even her cloak?" Alice heard Betsy whisper behind her.

"Hush, and run fetch Mr. Timmons," came the cook's hissed response.

At the door, Alice stopped and turned, valiantly attempting to preserve her dignity. "Really, that's not necessary, Mrs. Imes. I'm only getting a breath of fresh air. A quick breath of . . . fresh air."

Determinedly she opened the door and stepped outside, where the unwelcoming December evening greeted her with a furious explosion of cold. Her lips quivering—not from the weather, but from humiliation—Alice tilted her face to the sky, cooling her fiery cheeks beneath a flurry of moist, ivory snowflakes.

Never could she recall being so ashamed. She'd become a figure of pity in her own home, for heaven's sake. A pathetic creature whom even the servants felt sorry for. Dear Lord, how had her life come to this?

Alice wandered but a few steps down the alley before her thin satin slippers were damp from the gathering snow, her teeth chattering with cold. Chagrined by her foolishness, she was about to turn back to the house when the wind suddenly gave her what felt like a tremendous shove in the center of her back. Surprised by the force of the gust, she grabbed hold of a tower of crates.

And for a moment a stillness fell, a strange unearthly quiet that hushed even the moaning wind.

Then . . . the crate whimpered.

Alice drew back in silent startlement. An animal? An abandoned dog perhaps? She hesitated only briefly before dropping to a crouch beside the crates, her conscience not permitting her to leave even the sorriest mongrel out in this intolerable cold.

She narrowed her eyes as the wind whipped her face, stinging bitterly. *There.* In the corner of the crate, a small gray bundle stirred and whimpered again. Alice reached out—

Her breath lodged like an icy lump in her chest, her hand hovering just above the . . . *child.*

A child. Panic and elation flooded her in a giddy, mind-whirling rush. A child. Dear God, He had heard her prayers after all.

Alice jerked her gaze away as the kitchen door flew open and a flushed, harried-looking Timmons appeared in the doorway. His angular face wore a troubled frown.

"Timmons, thank goodness." Alice waved him closer. "Come, give me a hand."

The frown grew even darker yet as the butler approached. "My lady, what have you found? I do not believe his lordship will care to have another dog running about—"

"Sshh!"

He silenced. Following her cue, he hunkered down beside her in the snow, heedless of the damage to his resplendent scarlet livery. A strangled, choking sound drew Alice's attention and she found him gazing wide-eyed toward the back of the crate.

"My lady . . ."

"What, Timmons? What would you have me do?" she demanded in an impatient whisper. "Leave the infant here?" But she knew what the servant had to be thinking. She was thinking the same.

"I—I . . ." Timmons's anxious gaze shifted to her and Alice saw how his brown eyes softened in instant understanding. Without another word, he reached forward and cautiously pulled the blanket-shrouded child into his arms.

Alice steadied him as he labored to his feet, for Timmons was no longer a young man. Then, unable to contain her curiosity, Alice gently tugged aside the filthy and tattered blanket that shielded the child's face.

"It's a girl, Timmons," she whispered in awe. "It's a girl."

"Yes, my lady," he said, and Alice rather thought his voice sounded as teary as her own.

She rushed ahead to pull open the kitchen door. Waiting just inside were Betsy and Mrs. Imes, wearing matching expressions of concern.

Alice laughed softly. "No, it's quite all right," she said, wanting to reassure them, yet still giddy with her discovery. "I have not taken leave of my senses. Look." She turned triumphantly to Timmons as he stepped inside, his arms full. "Look what I have found in the alley."

The child's blanket had fallen away to reveal a brilliant red head of hair.

"Oh, dear," Mrs. Imes murmured, clucking her tongue as she craned forward. "The little thing must be half-frozen. Betsy, fetch a warming pan while I put on another pot of water."

Alice's gaze swept protectively over the girl. "Come, Timmons, let us get her into bed."

Using the servants' staircase, which was significantly

chillier than the kitchen had been, Alice led the way upstairs. Timmons seemed to be managing well enough with
his charge, his steps ringing out steady and strong on the
wooden planks. Halfway down the second floor corridor,
Alice hesitated in front of a door.

"Lady Stratford," Timmons said at her back. "Don't you
think another chamber . . . ?"

Alice shook her head. "No, Timmons. *This* room." With
a deep breath, she pushed open the door.

A cheery rose-and-green apartment, decorated with dainty
lace curtains and matching bedhangings, the room smelled
freshly of lemon, as if it had been recently cleaned. Not
everyone would have noticed the hint of lilac laced through
the lemony aroma, but Alice did, for lilac had been the fa-
vored scent of the room's last occupant.

After an almost undetectable pause on the threshold, she
strode to the bed and pulled down the lace-and-satin counterpane. Timmons followed her into the room and tenderly
laid the child, still curled up like a newborn kitten, upon the
bed.

Alice's heart contracted. Goodness, how very small the
poor darling looked. Smaller than Alice had at first imagined. Six years old or perhaps even younger, though it was
difficult to determine due to her unnatural slenderness. Carefully Alice rolled her onto her side so that she could remove
the soiled gray blanket the girl had been using as a cape.
The child did not so much as stir.

As Alice passed the blanket to Timmons, a pungent, most
unpleasant aroma wafted forth from both the blanket and
the bed. Alice wrinkled her nose, while the butler's brows
lifted.

"A bath might be in order," he said, stretching the of-
fensive quilt to a full arm's distance. "I'll summon Constance."

Alice was about to say that she would bathe the child
when Betsy walked in with the warming pan, accompanied
by Constance, the upstairs maid, hefting a steaming basin
of water.

Alice dismissed Timmons and Betsy, but Constance remained to assist her.

"Oh, ain't she a runty li'l thing?" the maid commented as the two of them peeled away the girl's soiled pinafore. "And her skin's like ice, it is. How long do you reckon she's been out in the cold?"

Alice chewed thoughtfully at her lower lip. She hated to conjecture. Judging from the child's appearance, she would have to believe that the girl had been living on the streets for some time. Her face was browned and freckled from the sun; dozens of gingery spots spattered her turned-up nose. She had no shoes; mere rags covered her blistered, dirt-encrusted feet. And her hair and clothes, heavily infested with vermin, could not have seen the better side of a bar of soap in God only knew how many weeks.

"I don't know, Constance. I fear it's been a very long while."

"Well, I don't see no bruises on her," the maid remarked, stripping off a shift made up of more holes than fabric. "So she must not have run away from an apprenticeship."

Alice shot the servant a sharp glance, not caring for the maid's implication. She refused to believe that anyone could be so vile as to subject a child—especially one so young and frail—to physical abuse.

"But the little miss sure must be fagged out to be dozin' right through all this," Constance said, waddling her bulky frame over to the fire and tossing in the last bit of the girl's clothing.

Worry furrowed Alice's brow. The child *was* sleeping deeply, reminding her uneasily of another time—

She shunted aside the abhorrent comparison and dipped a cloth into the bowl of hot water. Gently she mopped the child's chilled brow.

"Oh, milady, you shouldn't be botherin' yourself with that," Constance said, reaching for the cloth. "I'll wash her up. Besides, once she wakes, she's still goin' to need a real good scrubbin' with Mrs. Imes's camphor mix to rid herself of them vermin."

Alice pulled the washcloth out of her reach. "No, Con-

stance, I want to do it.'' The longing in her words made her
drop her gaze self-consciously to the bowl. ''Not to mention,'' she added, ''that it will go much more quickly with
two of us working. I . . . I'd like for her to be made pre-
sentable before Lord Stratford returns.''

The maid's black eyes widened with comprehension. Alice went back to mopping the child's face, and then moved
on to her reed-thin arms and narrow chest. The prominence
of the girl's ribs brought a painful tightness to Alice's throat.

''Constance, would you please fetch a clean nightrail
from the wardrobe?'' After all this time, Alice still hadn't
found the courage to pack away any clothes or toys. ''I think
I have managed to remove the topmost layer of grime, but
you are right in that she's going to require a good soak to
come truly clean.''

The maid rummaged for a moment, then produced a
snow-white nightrail lavishly embroidered at the neck with
twining roses. Alice's own needle had worked the intricate
design. Constance carried the gown over to the bed, then
tilted her head assessingly.

''She's not precisely what you'd call a beauty, is she,
your ladyship?''

Alice's fingertips lingered on the girl's cheek, now warm
and flushed a pretty shade of pink. ''Perhaps not in the con-
ventional sense, but there is something charming in the com-
position of her features, don't you think?''

''If you say so,'' the maid murmured, evidently not convinced.

With one last wash of button-sized toes, Alice dropped
the cloth back into the bowl, where the water had changed
to a dark brown. ''Constance, take this out and I'll slip the
nightrail on. The poor darling looks like she might be asleep
for some time yet.''

The maid left with the basin, and Alice cautiously wedged
her arm under the child's back, lifting so that she could slide
the gown on over her lolling head. She weighed almost
nothing. Again, Alice was struck by her gauntness. By her
features, sharp and sunken, which lacked the pleasant round-
ness of youth.

Yet, she did not think the child could have been more perfect. Freckled face, shell-shaped ears, cracked petal-pink lips that parted with each shallow breath. *Perfect.* A perfect miracle.

For, in the space of a few minutes, this small, bedraggled waif had restored Alice's faith in God. God had not forsaken her; He had not forgotten her or her loss. He had just taken His time, searching for just the right child to send to her. And He had sent her this child. This perfect little girl.

Alice could not have said how long she sat there on the side of the bed, staring at the sleeping youngster. It might have been three minutes or perhaps as long as thirty. But the unmistakable slam of the town house's front door roused her from her study as no other sound could have done.

"Timmons!" came the subsequent roar. Footsteps scurried down below.

Lord Stratford was home.

Piers knew he'd had too many and, somewhere at the back of his mind, he regretted it. It reflected poorly on a fellow to stumble home in his cups so early in the evening like this. It was neither gentlemanly nor proper, and certainly his lady wife deserved better. Far better.

But tonight Piers needed the fortification of spirits if he were going to present Alice with his decision. He rather suspected that she was going to take it badly, and he regretted that as well. He truly did. But what else could he do? What choice did he have?

He knew that he could not go on like this. He could not go on living in this house, pretending that he was actually living. He couldn't.

No, the Continent was the only answer. He and Alice would go away for a while, get as far away from England as they could. Far, far away from the memories.

But what would Alice say? *Sweet, sad Alice.* Stronger than he was, she would weather it through. She would. He would simply have to tell it to her straight-out: After the new year, he was closing up the house and they were leaving for Italy. He could not pretend any longer. He simply was not man enough.

Stumbling into the brightly lit foyer of his home, Piers staggered to a stop, blinking. What in blazes was going on here?

His questioning, suspicious look to the footman went unanswered, for the servant was too intent on all the activity taking place in the front hall. Constance, plump and perspiring, was dashing down the staircase as if her skirts were afire. Betsy, on her hands and knees, was busily mopping up a spill on the red Oriental carpet Piers had long despised. And, through the open doors of the salon, a wildly gesticulating Mrs. Imes was apparently arguing with a disheveled and muddied Timmons. No one was paying Piers the least mind.

Piers rubbed uncertainly at the side of his face. Damn it all, he had not seen such a commotion in this house since—

"Timmons!"

His angry bellow produced the desired results, sending everyone scuttling off to their proper province. The butler, looking appropriately chagrined, hustled forward to claim Piers's cape.

"What the hell have you been doing, Timmons? Rolling about in the snow?" Making no effort to hide either his disgruntlement or his inebriated state, Piers did not wait for an answer, but demanded, "And what's going on here? Where's Lady Stratford?"

"Good evening, my lord. Her ladyship is above stairs. Shall I ring for"—he appraised Piers frankly—"a strong pot of tea?"

Frowning, Piers marched past him. "I'm not as far gone as that," he lied. "Just a glass of max at White's." He headed toward the staircase, Timmons dogging his heels. "Where is Alice?" he muttered aloud. "I have to speak with her."

Somehow the aged Timmons managed to dart around him, blocking his path. "Ah . . . my lord. There's a fire in the library; shall I send her ladyship to you there?"

Piers almost acquiesced. A warm fire on a blustery

night— But something, some emotion, in the butler's tense posture provoked him to say, "No. I'll find her myself."

For a second, Piers thought Timmons was not going to let him pass—which was, in and of itself, ludicrous in the extreme. Not merely the fact that the servant would bar him from seeking out his wife, but that the frail Timmons could prevent him from doing anything at all. While at Eton, Piers had earned the nickname "The Bear" because of his deep growl of a voice and remarkable height and breadth. In truth, Lord Stratford figured he must have been nearly thrice the size of his octogenarian butler.

"Is something amiss, Timmons?" he asked, the gin allowing him to find a measure of amusement in the situation.

"No, my lord. No." Yet it was with evident reluctance that the butler stepped aside.

As Timmons persisted in trailing him up to the second floor, the humor Piers had enjoyed a moment earlier began to fade. Something *was* afoot, something that made the fine hairs on Piers's forearms bristle. For almost a year, the Stratford home had been as quiet and solemn and cheerless as a graveyard. Tonight the air was fair to crackling with the most peculiar sense of apprehension.

Then again, his gin-muddled brain countered, perhaps the foreboding he felt originated within him, from his recent decision to leave England and this house. And, hopefully, the memories.

Turning in the direction of Alice's suite, Piers felt his feet go suddenly leaden. At the other end of the hall—the opposite end from Alice's chambers—his wife was emerging from a bedroom. One that had not been occupied in ten long months.

Pain exploded in Piers's chest.

"What were you doing in there?"

Although he hadn't meant to shout, he could hear his words booming down the length of the corridor.

Alice went absolutely still, her large blue eyes growing even larger. In an oddly protective gesture, she pulled the door to the bedroom nearly closed, leaving it open a crack.

Then she clasped her arms around her waist and came toward him, her silk skirts rustling.

In the honeyed light of the beeswax candles, she looked to Piers almost as she had the day he had first met her. Her hair the color of sunshine, her figure still as slender as a girl's, she could have been that same Alice Mayton he had fallen in love with fifteen years ago. God, he could never forget the first time he'd laid eyes on her, when she'd been newly arrived to the London social scene. A being of infinite loveliness, she had seemed out of his reach, a porcelain doll he dared not even hope for or desire. When she had accepted his suit, he had honestly thought himself the luckiest man alive. This woman so precious and fragile and . . .

And yet Alice was the one who had proven to be the strong one. Not him.

"What were you doing?" he demanded again, his voice less loud but still gruff with pain.

Alice gestured toward the bedroom she'd just exited. "I— I have something to show you, Piers."

Hackles rose along his nape and he instinctively took a step back. He did *not* want to go into that room. Why, for the love of God, would she believe that he would?

Then, to his surprise, Alice reached out and took hold of his hand. Her touch, unfamiliar after all these many months, acted on him more powerfully than the gin, reminding him once again of their early courting days and the poignant first flush of love.

He did feel flushed, caught off guard by Alice's unexpected overture. In his vision's periphery, Piers could see Timmons hovering anxiously in the background like a mother hen or overzealous duenna.

She tugged. He resisted. She tugged again, her smile taking on a tinge of pleading. Piers relented, although he genuinely, sincerely, did not want to enter that room.

Perspiration made his fingers slick in hers as she led him by the hand down the hall. She turned to him just outside the door, her expression now radiant, all uncertainty gone. She looked for all the world as if she were about to share a closely guarded secret—a wondrous one.

Alice pushed open the door. Piers swallowed. His gaze darted from the shelves of dolls to the flower-strewn wallpaper to the rocking chair he'd commissioned so many years ago. In another lifetime. God, he'd not forgotten a single detail. Not one.

He half pivoted on his heel, ready to go, but Alice drew him farther into the room. To the bed. To the bed that was not empty. . . .

Piers jerked his hand out of Alice's so fast, she made a soft sound of surprise. Lurching backward, he felt his way to the door, afraid even to turn his back on what he had seen. A thousand different emotions surged through him at lightning speed, anger taking precedence over them all.

Somehow he made it as far as the hall before he lost control.

"Blast it, Alice!" He felt her come up behind him and he whirled around, battling his fury. "How could you? How *dare* you?"

Confusion shone in her face and she reached out to him.

"Don't!" He raised his splayed hands to his sides, warding her away.

Good God, had she no understanding of what she had done, of how she had betrayed him? To bring another child into this house, into Laura's room—

"Piers, I found her in the alley. She would have frozen to death if—"

"*No!*"

Never had Piers used his size to dominate his wife, but he did so now, looming over her, his expression dark with foreboding. He knew he was behaving like the veriest brute, but he recognized his limitations and, to his dismay, those limitations were vast. "I will not stand for it, Alice. I want her *out.*"

"What are you suggesting, Piers? That I throw her back onto the street?"

"It makes no difference to me what you do with her. I do not want another child in my house!"

Alice's blond brows knit together, and her small chin trembled. She crossed her arms over her chest, as if to hug herself, while her eyes began to fill. "Do you mean in your house, Piers?" she asked quietly. "Or in your heart?"

The question hit him in his most sensitive spot, like a blow to a bruise still tender and swollen.

"You should see her, Piers, really see her. She is so thin it frightens me, and I fear she's taken a chill. Please don't ask me to send her away, for I do not believe that I can."

And I do not believe that I can do this, Piers argued with himself. To know that another little girl was sleeping in Laura's bed and playing with her toys and wearing her nightgowns— *No.* He could not bear it. It would surely drive him mad.

But in his mind's eye, he saw again a cheek hollowed by hunger, a comforting thumb tucked between cracked lips.

He squeezed his eyes shut, angered and hurting.

"Very well, Alice, the child can stay for a few days until she recovers her health. But as soon as she is strong enough, I want her *gone.* And I do not want to see her or hear her or have the slightest indication that she is in this house, do you understand?"

"I understand, Piers."

As their gazes met, his hostile and defensive, hers tender and grateful, Piers felt as vulnerable as a newborn babe. Alice understood, all right. She understood far too well.

TWO

Faith sank back against the down-filled pillows, a sigh of relief puffing out her cheeks.

They were going to keep her.

The man with the deep rumbling voice didn't sound too jolly about it but, from what she'd been able to hear, they were going to allow her to stay. For a few days at least.

When she'd first been awakened by the row outside, Faith had thought that she'd died and gone off to heaven. Surrounded by billowing white lace and lying on what felt like a soft puffy cloud, she'd told herself that maybe dying weren't such a bad thing, after all.

But, after shaking off her groggies, she had recognized that instead of heaven, she had awakened in a house. A home. The home of the grumble-bear man and the lady with the kind voice. The lady who'd been arguing to let her stay.

Faith yawned—a long, sleepy, stretchy yawn that had her toes curling contentedly. She burrowed back beneath the blankets, comforted by the knowledge that she was not likely to be tossed out any time soon. She was still awful tired. Her eyelids fluttered shut, and her favorite thumb found its usual resting place.

Tired. Awful . . . tired.

"Hullo."

Just a hair's breadth away from drifting asleep, Faith pretended she hadn't heard. She made a show of snuggling her face into the pillow and feigning a light snore. Maybe the person would sneak out as quietly as they had snuck in.

"I said 'hullo there.' "

Oh, criminy. Faith peeked open one begrudging eye. A girl, about her own age, sat in the rocking chair next to the bed. Perched on the seat's edge, the girl was swinging her feet back and forth. Her small hands clasped to the rocking chair's arms.

Tied up in thick sausage curls and pink satin ribbons, she had hair the handsomest yellow color Faith had ever laid eyes on. Her dress was pink and frothy, her eyes a pale green. She was uncommonly bonny, as Grandpa would say.

"Hullo," Faith answered in a sleep-muffled voice. "How do ye do?"

The girl giggled delightedly as if Faith had made some terrific joke. "You cannot determine that for yourself?" she teased.

Faith frowned, wondering what on earth she could mean. "What ye talkin' ab—" And then she noticed. The girl was not altogether there. That is to say, she wasn't precisely solid or real. She was like a wisp of fog off the Thames or like the curtain of lace hanging from the bed. . . . Faith could see straight through her.

Now, after living on the streets of London for nearly two months, Faith had seen some devilishly scary sights, so she wasn't about to get herself into too terrible of a pucker over this. Or so she told herself, while goosebumps popped up all over her skin. Very cautiously, her movements slow, she sat up in the bed.

The girl's smile widened. "So you *can* tell?"

"Tell what?" Faith questioned belligerently. One thing she'd learned on the streets was to play the slowtop when you found yourself backed into a corner.

The girl stopped her rocking. "Why, that I'm a ghost, of course!"

Faith's quavering breath took forever to leave her lungs. "Aye. I noticed."

Obviously pleased, the ghost-girl beamed and set the rocker in motion again, her pink slippers swinging playfully. "I am glad, since you're the first person to see me, you know."

She acted as if Faith should be flattered by that bit of news; Faith wasn't at all certain that she was.

"I am?"

"Oh, yes." The girl tossed her blond curls in a coquettish display. "You see, when I saw you in the alley, I just knew that you would be perfect."

Saw me in the alley? Faith pressed her palm against her forehead, checking for fever. She was but tolerably warm.

"Well . . ." A tiny woebegone moue curled the ghostly mouth. "Well, perhaps not perfect. I mean, it is a pity that you aren't, you know, prettier."

Since the ghost appeared to be in genuine sympathy with her lack of beauty, Faith saw no reason to argue with her or to get her back up about it.

"But you do seem as if you might be nice," the ghost-girl offered generously. "And Mama always said that an unselfish nature is much more important than one's appearance."

"Mama?"

"Hmm-mm. Lady Alice Stratford. She saved you."

Ah, the music-voice lady. Faith's brow creased. "Then who might ye be?"

Folding her hands together as if she was reciting a lesson, the ghost primly answered, "I am—or was—Laura Elizabeth Stratford. I died on March 8th of this year."

"Oh. I'm sorry."

Laura shrugged. "It came quickly, if unexpectedly. We hadn't known it, but my heart was weak."

Faith's fingers coiled around the blanket, and she glanced uncomfortably from the toy box bearing the initials *LES* to the thick flower-festooned carpet. "Blimey, so this was yer room?"

"Yes, though you needn't get the willies or anything. I didn't die in my bed."

Faith wrinkled her nose, but couldn't help asking, "Where did ye . . . ye know—?"

"Breathe my last?" Laura matter-of-factly patted the rocker, although her expression assumed a pained wistfulness. "I died in Mama's arms," she said softly. "Right here."

Faith had to look away from the hurtful yearning in Laura's face. She had already seen enough of dying to last her a lifetime. Mother and Da. Grandpa. And now this Laura Stratford girl.

But weren't they all supposed to have gone to heaven?

"How come ye ain't up there?" Faith asked curiously, pointing skyward.

Laura made a face, revealing a dimple in her left cheek. "It's my parents. Mama and Papa won't let me go and I can't leave them while they're so unhappy." She dipped her head to the side, summoning a smile. "But that's where you come in."

"Me?" Faith recoiled. Though she saw no reason to fear this particular ghost—after all, as spooks went, Laura was rather pleasant and not at all frightening—Faith still did not much care for the notion that a dead soul was making plans for her. "What do ye be wantin' *me* for?"

Laura tipped forward in the rocker. "Faith," she announced most seriously. "I want you to reunite my parents."

Faith blinked.

"It honestly is quite perfect," Laura explained in a rush. "You need a family and a home. Mama and Papa need you to remember what it is to love again. Not that Mama has necessarily forgotten, but I daresay she's having a thoroughly rotten time of it with Papa. He's always been on the gruff side, you know. I call him my Grumblygus. But, you see, my death was more than he could cope with. He's a very successful businessman—do you know we own five houses?—so he simply cannot tolerate not being in charge. The fact that he wasn't able to prevent my death was a terrible, terrible blow for him."

Nodding absently, Faith recalled the angry voice in the corridor. "But how—"

Laura fluttered her dainty fingers in a dismissive motion. Faith resisted glancing to her own dirty, chipped nails.

"You needn't worry about how," Laura assured, "since I'll be here to help you."

"I dunno." Faith rubbed her nose with the heel of her hand, trying to sort her thoughts. "A body would have to be all about in the head not to want to live in a swell place like this, but . . . ain't there no other way to go 'bout it? I mean, can't ye just talk to yer Mum and Da like ye're doin' with me?"

Laura shook her head of curls. "They can't see me," she sighed. "I'm not certain why, but I've begun to suspect that it has to do with the fact that they are so very sad."

"Oh." Faith thought again of the man's angry voice and the unmistakable despair that had threaded the woman's. Of course, she realized, anyone would be sad to lose a lovely little girl like Laura. She glanced at the ghost all glowing and golden.

"Laura, I don't want to be hateful or nothin', but I don't think this idea of yers'll fadge. I mean, just look at the two of us. We're as different as chalk from cheese. I ain't special like ye are. Or pretty. Or smart. Lord and Lady Stratford ain't never goin' to think of me the way they did you."

"Oh, Faith, I don't expect you to take *my* place. Of course you can't. Just as I never could have taken your place in the hearts of your parents. But that isn't to say that Mama and Papa cannot learn to love and care for you as much as they ever did for me. It only means that it will be different. Just as you and I are different."

Faith considered for a moment. "Were ye this clever when ye was alive?"

"Well . . ." Laura pertly wiggled her brows up and down. "One does learn a lot after dying, you know."

Faith grinned. She was starting to like this Laura-The-Ghost. She really was.

"So, now that we've settled that." Laura smoothed out

her translucent skirts, assuming an expectant pose. "Are you going to help me?"

Faith screwed up her face, thinking. Thinking hard. She had not yet actually met Laura's parents, so she couldn't rightly say if this plan would work. And if it didn't work— What was the worst thing that could happen?

Faith tugged pensively at her lower lip. 'Cause if she couldn't convince the Stratfords to keep her, they would probably ship her off to a foundling home or the parish workhouse. Either of which would be a far sight worse than living on the streets.

And yet . . . what if? What if she could convince them to keep her?

A tiny spark of hope flared inside her and she heard herself answer, "All right. I guess I can give it a go."

Laura clapped her hands delightedly. "I was certain that you were the right one. I just knew it. Mark my words, Faith Burns, you and Mama and Papa are going to make a wonderfully happy family. Now, you have a good sleep and we shall talk again tomorrow. Oh, I am so pleased; it is simply perfect. Good night, Faith. Sleep well."

"Good night, Laura."

With a waggle of her fingers, the ghost began to fade away, her edges softening, as if the mellowed candlelight were absorbing her, taking her into its golden glow.

It was all so strange and dreamlike that Faith, her mind filled to overflowing, did not know how she would ever be able to fall asleep. But she did. Before the fire crackled even once more in the grate, Faith had drifted off to dream. To dream of a world where little girls had mothers and fathers and cloudlike gowns and all the bread they could eat.

In the distance a night owl asked "who, who?" as Alice slipped quietly into the violet-shrouded room an hour or so before sunrise.

After a dozen visits throughout the long night, Alice had at last succumbed to the realization that she could not stay away. Constance had reported earlier in the evening that the child was resting easily, but Alice had not been content with that. She had to assure herself that the banked fire sufficiently warmed the room; she had to make certain that the child had not kicked off the bedclothes with the onset of fever; she had to see for herself the miracle that had been deposited on her back stoop.

So with a woolen shawl across her shoulders and an indescribable joy in her heart, Alice sat down in the padded rocking chair and reveled in her miracle.

Resting with one hand tucked beneath her cheek, and the other turned palm up and trustingly open, the girl slept with her lips slightly parted, her breath even and rapid in the natural rhythm of a child. Her color had improved, her dark russet lashes falling on cheeks neither too pallid nor too rosy. Across her forehead tumbled soft auburn curls.

Alice smiled wistfully, unable to recall the last time she had felt even half so peaceful. *If only Piers—*

Her contentment ebbed as her thoughts turned to her husband. Following their argument in the hall, Piers had stormed off to his study, his animosity swirling about him like an ominous storm cloud. Alice had understood that he was angry and hurt and threatened. She'd seen it in the way he'd carried himself, stiff and straight as if he were up against a wall. She would have liked to have gone to him, to have done something that might have eased his burden. But she hadn't. In this case, she knew that she had to be selfish. Not only for the girl's sake, but for her own.

As she stared in wonder at the slumbering child, Alice felt her arms start to ache with the desire to hold her. Literally ache. More than once since Laura's death, Alice had experienced this phantom weight in her arms, a heaviness that mimicked the remembered presence and feel of a child. When she had tried to explain this phenomenon to Piers, he had curtly cut her off. He had been incapable of hearing or sharing her pain when his was already so great.

Not that she had suffered less than he had. God, no. The agony of those early months had left its mark upon her, just as a wound healed still leaves its scar. But even in her grief, Alice had refused to diminish her daughter's legacy—her light, her laughter, her love. To not acknowledge Laura's exuberance and zest for life was to not acknowledge Laura. Yes, Piers was outraged that she had brought this bedraggled little street urchin into Laura's chambers, but wasn't that precisely what Laura would have wanted had she been alive?

And in truth, here—right now, with another child resting in Laura's bed—Alice felt closer to her daughter than she had since the day they'd buried her. It wasn't that the tiny redhead reminded her so much of Laura. They were most dissimilar in appearance. But Alice *sensed* Laura in a way she had not done during these past ten months. She sensed her in a magical, spiritual way that had nothing to do with common sense or reality, and that had everything to do with the unseverable bond between mother and child.

The girl shifted and groaned, her outstretched hand curling like the petals of a morning glory responding to dawn's first light.

Alice glanced to the windows. The sun's rays had begun to filter around the curtains, coloring the room's shadows a dusty mauve. Daybreak approached.

From the bed came a faint hiccuping sound, followed by a languorous stretch. The girl's eyelashes fluttered a few times, and slowly swept up to reveal a pair of enormous brown eyes. Not ordinary brown, but a rich cinnamon that seemed to echo the luminous red hue of her hair, and matched the color of her numerous freckles.

Their gazes met and Alice's pulse quickened.

"Good morning," she greeted.

The girl blinked a few times in succession, obviously unsure of her whereabouts.

"Don't be distressed. You are safe here. I am Lady Stratford."

Suddenly the girl's eyes rounded as if in panicked recollection, and she bolted upright against the pillows.

Alice laid her hand on the girl's slight arm.

"Please do not be frightened," she said. "You will come to no harm here, I assure you. Tell me, what is your name?"

The child turned back to her, lips trembling, and Alice felt that single look chisel away a corner of her heart. The fear and confusion were gone, replaced by an expression of infinite trust. More trust than anyone had the right to expect from a homeless, half-starved urchin.

"Faith," the girl answered in a voice much too large for her size. "Faith Burns."

Alice gave her a reassuring smile. "It's a pleasure to meet you, Faith. How are you feeling this morning?"

Alice noticed that instead of looking directly at her, the girl fixed her attention on the rocking chair. "Well 'nough, I suppose, mum."

"Won't you please call me Lady Alice? It sounds nicer than 'mum,' wouldn't you agree?"

Faith nodded, then made a show of giving her nose a thorough polishing with the heel of her palm. Above the small hand, two big brown eyes watched Alice carefully.

"You know," Alice said, with a gently teasing smile, "you cannot rub them off that way."

The small hand stopped its gyrations. "What?"

"Your freckles. You cannot scour them off like that."

A moment's bewilderment preceded a bashful grin and Faith dropped her hand to the counterpane.

"Faith . . . do you have family? Anyone I should contact?"

Though she had to ask, Alice was reluctant to hear the answer. Already, in her heart, she knew that this little girl, this precious gift from Heaven, must belong with her. That God had sent her to Alice for a reason. The only reason. To be loved.

"Not no more."

Relief and regret mingled in Alice's frown. "Have you been recently orphaned then?"

"Well . . ." Tucking her chin into her chest, Faith shrugged, studying the fine lawn nightrail she wore, then rotating her wrist to examine the embroidery at the cuff. "Depends how you look at it, I guess. I was still in leadin' strings when my mother and da died, so I don't remember 'em none. I went to live with Grandpa who brung me to London when I was four."

"How old are you, then? Six, seven?"

"Eight last month. Though I reckon I'm small for my age."

A pang shot through Alice. Laura had been eight. Could it be only coincidence?

"At any rate, Grandpa drove a hack, you see, and then 'bout six weeks ago, he was trampled by a runaway horse— Mr. Cheeps was the one that told me."

How simply the child told her tale, without the luxury of self-pity.

"And who is Mr. Cheeps?"

Faith's sour-lemon face nearly made Alice grin. "He was our landlord on Boyle Street. I didn't like him none. He smelled of onions all the time and sweat more than was natural. Even Mrs. Cheeps said so."

Alice was going to inquire about Mrs. Cheeps when Constance, after a cursory knock, pushed open the door and bustled in with a covered breakfast tray.

"Thought I heard voices in here," the maid explained, "and figured the little miss would be hankerin' for her breakfast right soon."

Faith sat up straighter, her nose twitching in anticipation, like a hound on the scent.

"I daresay you figured accurately," Alice said. "Faith, this is Constance, our upstairs maid. She'll be tending to you."

Constance set the tray on the side table with an exaggerated flourish. "How do ye do, Miss Faith?" She placed her hands on her broad hips, smiling down at the girl. "I suppose you'll be needin' a bath after your breakfast, hmm? I'll just be seein' to the water then." She trundled out.

A loud grumble from Faith's stomach caused her to turn away to hide her blush. Alice acted as if she had not heard it, while hoping that the maid had been lavish with the breakfast portions. She had no need to worry. Upon removing the cover, she found the plate piled high with ham, coddled eggs, fried trout, and toast. A small pitcher of chocolate completed the feast.

"Gor," Faith breathed. "Is that all for me?"

Alice bit her lips. When had the child last eaten a proper

meal? She didn't dare ask for the sake of Faith's dignity. But, as her gaze swept over the child's frail shoulders and sunken cheeks, she could not help but wonder if Faith had ever once in her short life sat down to a meal such as this.

Alice spread out the linen napkin, and set the tray gingerly across Faith's lap. The girl grabbed the fork and was poised to dive in when abruptly she stilled. She lifted her face to Alice, her eyes huge and pleading. And embarrassed. Alice understood.

She rose from the bed with a bright smile, tugging at the edges of her shawl. ''Well, the day is getting on, isn't it? I shall leave you to enjoy your meal. Then after breakfast, Constance and I can help with your bath and perhaps find something suitable for you to wear.''

Faith gazed up at her and, with a solemnity that seemed misplaced on an eight-year-old child, said simply, ''Thank you, Lady Alice.''

Alice felt her throat thicken. ''No, Faith. It is I who thank *you*.''

THREE

Passing the night in a Chesterfield chair had done little to improve Piers's disposition. The ache in his back, coupled with the aftereffects of excessive drink, left him with a taste in his mouth—and a temper—indescribably foul.

Closing his gritty eyes, he leaned his head back until his neck muscles creaked. The hour approached noon. He was half surprised that Timmons had not yet materialized with coffee and *The Morning Post* but, upon recalling his conduct of yesterday evening, Piers found himself less surprised.

His fists spasmed as he thought back to the previous night's events. How could she have done it? How could Alice have brought a strange child into his home?

Yet . . . now that the initial shock had faded, and now that he'd had time to calmly reflect on their conversation, he could almost sympathize with his wife's reasoning. Almost. Once, not so many years ago, both he and Alice had yearned for parenthood above all else—prayed for it even. How then could he fail to appreciate her wish for another child? He couldn't. 'Twas only that he could not share in that wish any longer.

His gaze wandered to the miniature portrait of Alice at the corner of his desk, the one he'd commissioned as a gift to himself on their fifth wedding anniversary. She was so lovely, his Alice. But even in the portrait, he could detect the melancholy, the hopelessness. It had been five long years, and they had both begun to despair of ever conceiving a child. And then quite miraculously, before another year had passed, they had been blessed with Laura.

Laura, child of their dreams. With her buoyant blond curls and delicate bones, she had been a breathtaking reproduction of Alice. Only the famous Stratford green eyes had evidenced any contribution of his to his daughter's design. And, like everything else about Laura, her peridot-colored eyes had been the prettiest and the most vivid produced by the Stratford family in decades.

Laura.

Piers dropped his head into his hands, pressing his fingers into his temples as if he could physically propel the memories from his mind. They were a double-edged sword, those remembrances so sweet and so torturous. He wished he could be rid of them forever; he wished he might never forget.

"Are . . . are ye all right?"

Piers jerked up his head. A pint-sized, flame-haired urchin stood boldly studying him from the other side of the desk. Disbelief immobilized him for a long moment.

"What?"

She tilted her chin, as if trying to get a better look at him. "I asked if you was sick. You was kind of moaning like."

The cords in Piers's neck grew taut, a strange panic spreading through his limbs. Alice had promised to keep the child away from him, blast it.

"Where is Lady Stratford?" he demanded, his voice choked and gruff.

Blithely the child skipped around the desk and lifted her nightrail to reveal a pair of bare feet. "Lady Alice went 'round to the shops for shoes," she explained. "There was some frocks in the wardrobe that ought to fit me well 'nough, but hang it all if my feet aren't just too fat for the slippers."

She made an inelegant swipe at her nose, before leaning forward to add in a confidential whisper, "I suppose she meant for me to stay in bed and all, but I was feelin' better and thought I'd like to have a look-see 'round.''

Piers swallowed. A dozen different emotions seemed to be holding his tongue captive. His gaze swerved to the velvet bellpull. By Jove, he wished he had the nerve to cross the room and ring for Timmons. He wanted to order the child out. Out of his sight and out of his life.

"I'm Faith," she offered.

Vaguely he identified the accent behind the cockney as being from Manchester.

"Are ye Lord Stratford then?" she asked with friendly perseverance.

The panicky feeling welled up even stronger, and Piers felt like a man asea, completely lost. All he could do was stare at her. Skinny, bran-faced, and sun-browned, the girl was as far from his precious Laura as any child could be.

"What happened to your hair?" he asked abruptly, with no notion from whence the question came.

"Oh." She threaded her fingers through the back of her closely cropped curls. "Lady Alice and Mrs. Imes said they had to cut it 'cause of the bugs." Her lips turned down at the corners. "Lady Alice said it weren't too very awful, but don't gammon me none—do I look a fright?"

Piers recoiled slightly in his chair. The truth was poised to burst from his lips when he noticed the nervous movement of her tiny hands, the way she was pleating her fingers into her nightrail.

His brows veed together. "It suits you," he stiffly replied.

She smiled, and for Piers that smile was like the sun suddenly bursting from behind the clouds. It was blinding and brilliant, a smile of childish innocence and joy, that pierced straight into his chest as an honest-to-God physical pain.

"Do ye really think so?" she asked, leaning closer.

Piers involuntarily pushed back into his chair, the pain growing sharper, more acute. Lilac, a scent he'd not encountered in many months, wafted toward him, cloaking him in memories unbidden. Lilac was the smell of hugs and piggy-back rides. It was bedtime kisses and a favorite blanket. It was Laura.

The girl's smile teetered in confusion. "I asked if—"

"Go." He jerked his chin in the direction of the door, afraid to point for fear that his hand was shaking. "Go on, get out," he ordered curtly. "Can't you see that I'm a busy man?"

Her eyes clouded but she obediently turned away. Piers began to breathe more easily as she shuffled across the room, scuffing her bare feet over the Axminster carpet. With her hand on the door latch, she swung around, awarding him a look of childish reprimand, her lower lip pushed out well past the upper.

"Ye could have just asked, ye know. Ye didn't have to be such a Grumblygus about it."

The door shut with a firm *clunk* and Piers thought it must have been the sound of his jaw hitting the desk.

"My God," he breathed. "Did she call me a Grumblygus?"

Alice was smiling as she removed her gloves, inordinately pleased with the boxes and packages the footmen were carrying in by the dozen from the Stratford carriage. As she watched Timmons trudge upstairs to her suite, his arms piled high, Alice wondered for a moment if perhaps she had been indiscriminate during her enthusiastic whirl through Bond Street. It had been so long since she'd been able to coo over a child's frock or admire a little girl's bonnet that she might have been immoderate in her many purchases. But then again, she told herself, Faith had nothing. Absolutely nothing.

"*What* is all this?"

Alice swung around, her heart in her throat. In the open doorway of the study stood Piers, his arms folded across his chest. Dark stubble shadowed his jaw and his hair fell untidily about his head. At the back of her mind, Alice recognized that he wore the same clothes he'd been wearing the previous evening.

She squeezed her fur-lined gloves into a ball, her gaze colliding with Timmons's. "A few necessities . . ."

Piers's black brows snapped together. "Alice. A word if you please."

She bit gently at the inside of her cheek. Though eager to see how Faith had fared during her absence, she knew that she dared not ignore her husband's summons. Not after last night's confrontation. With a reassuring nod to the butler, she crossed the foyer and followed Piers into his study, closing the door behind her.

Piers stood staring out the window, his fingers clasped behind his broad back, his posture poker-stiff. Silhouetted against the gray light of winter's afternoon, he looked somehow proud, yet defeated, like a war-weary soldier who knows he still has many battles yet to fight. A rush of longing washed through Alice, and she wished that she could go to him and wrap her arms about his waist, and offer him solace. But she also knew, from these past months, that he would reject her comfort. That he would turn away from her, unable to accept what she offered.

"You ventured out in this cold?" he asked brusquely, if unnecessarily.

Alice flicked her tongue over her dry lips. "The child had need of a gown. Stockings. A coat."

"Shoes?"

"Y-yes. And shoes."

Piers shifted his weight onto his heels, still staring fixedly out onto the snowy streets. "I have something to tell you, Alice. I had meant to tell you last night, but . . . well . . ." He rocked forward onto his toes, his manner uncharacteristically diffident. A breath worked its way up his body, expanding his broad shoulders. He unclasped his fingers, then clenched them at his sides. "I am going to close up the house, Alice. Leave England. I think that it's time that we . . . we got away."

The words held no meaning for her, as if he had spoken them in a foreign tongue. She tried to make sense of them, but could not. To leave their home, their friends, their country . . . everything?

"I am sorry," he said. "I know that I haven't been able to handle this at all well, but I cannot maintain this charade.

I cannot go on living in this house and acting as if our lives will ever be normal again. It's . . . it's beyond me.''

Nothing. Alice neither felt nor understood any of it. She was only aware of a ringing in her ears that grew progressively louder.

"I thought perhaps Italy," Piers was saying. "We can leave in a few days. I've already begun to—"

"Christmas is but a week away," she whispered.

Very slowly Piers pivoted away from the window, his handsome face wreathed in frowns. "Christmas?"

Yes, she had nearly forgotten about the holidays herself until yesterday. Until she'd discovered Faith.

Alice swallowed and nodded.

Piers appeared confused, then made a vague dismissive motion. "About the child."

"Yes, the child," she echoed hopefully.

"I understand, Alice, I honestly do. I should have realized earlier. . . ." Puffing out his breath, he raked his fingers through the coal-black hair at his temples. "I think it all the more reason we should leave as soon as possible. Three or four days to put our affairs in order and—"

"No."

Piers froze, his hand cradling the back of his neck.

"No," Alice repeated staunchly, though her stomach lurched with fear. "I am not leaving."

His gaze flickered. "What?"

"I won't do it, Piers. If you decide to go, you go alone. I will not leave with you. I won't. We can run halfway across the world and back, but we cannot run from the memories, from the pain. There is no place to hide from it, surely you must realize that."

"You won't go with me?"

"No."

No. And she would not let Piers go either. Already she had lost Laura; her daughter was never coming back. Never. But Piers—

Granted, he'd been moving farther and farther away from her these past months. But if she let him leave now, he, too, would be lost to her forever. . . .

Images flashed before her eyes, fleeting vignettes of their years together. Piers asking for her hand in the gardens at Ranelagh; that terrible quarrel following his brother's Bath wedding; walking the beach together the summer they conceived Laura. They had survived the heartache of the childless years, and come out of it stronger than before. They had shared the times of happiness, the times of misery. They had shared everything . . . but the pain of losing their daughter.

Alice drew herself together, gathering her strength for a fight. She would not give up. She would fight for her marriage with her very last breath. She could not let Piers leave her, now that there was hope at last. Now that there was Faith.

A few halting steps carried her over to her husband. Outside the snow blanketed the sky in clouds of swirling white. Inside the fire spat and hissed like an angry cat.

"Please, Piers." Her voice quavered. "Give us a little more time. Just through Christmas. Let us celebrate Christmas together as a family."

His eyes narrowed, darkening to a deep forest green. "Without Laura, we can't—"

"But we have Faith, Piers. The child upstairs. If only you would meet with her, talk to her, you would see she's a darling girl. She has had so little joy in her short life—she's never experienced a real Christmas, I'm sure of it. Cannot we find it in our hearts to provide her just this one? This one happy memory?"

Hurt flared in his gaze, dilating his pupils. Alice knew that she was asking a lot of him. Perhaps more than he was capable of giving. But she knew if she had just a little more time . . .

"I—"

She forestalled him by laying her hand on his bare forearm, his body heat skittling goose bumps along her spine. Good God, how she missed the feel of him. "Please, Piers. For me."

She had asked so little of him these past months. Surely he could grant her this. This one final request.

"I will leave after the new year," he gruffly conceded.

It was a compromise, a small one, but one she would gladly accept for now.

With reluctance, she let her hand slip from his arm, hoping against hope that he might clasp it in his. After so long without, she found it difficult to surrender the simple pleasure of her husband's touch.

"Thank you, Piers."

He did not answer her but turned away to stare blindly into the fire.

Alice began to pray for another miracle.

"Blimey, let me see if I can recollect it all."

Faith screwed up her face and repeated back what she had learned so far that afternoon. "Lord and Lady Stratford met at a ball, given by Lady Stratford's cousin. They married quick, less than a month. Both like dancin' and ridin' and Lord Stratford has a special fondness for sweets. He likes poetry—especially the old borin' stuff, er, classics. And Lady Stratford don't know it but he keeps in his desk a scrap of a poem she wrote him for his birthday nine years ago. His only brother, Frederick, lives in India with a wife, Sophia, and one son—um, don't tell me . . . Harry.

"Lady Stratford don't have no brothers or sisters, and she was borned and raised in Shropshire. Her favorite color is yellow. She had a habit of callin' Lord Stratford 'darling' and givin' him kisses on the end of his nose. One of her happiest memories is when the three of ye baked cookies two Christmases past and burnt 'em all and fed 'em to the dog. And let's see . . . oh, yeah, she hums when she's happy."

"Splendid, Faith. Splendid." Laura's smiling praise brought a blush to Faith's cheeks. "You make an excellent student. Mrs. Anderson would have been most satisfied. I say, I wonder if Mama will find you a governess soon?"

Faith shrugged lightly, uncomfortable with Laura's unflagging certainty that she would be allowed to stay. After her earlier interview with Lord Stratford, Faith was less convinced than her ghostly friend that she wouldn't be shipped off to the nearest foundling home before the week was out.

"My stars, just look at the hour." Laura stopped her rocking as the mantel clock chimed eight. "Time for you to go down to dinner."

Faith wiggled her toes inside her new kid slippers, tugging at the apricot-colored sash of her gown. Through her too-short curls Constance had threaded a matching apricot riband that Faith secretly thought the most beautiful little piece of frippery she'd ever seen.

"All right then, wish me luck."

"You won't need luck," Laura answered confidently. "It's meant to be, you know."

It's meant to be, Faith chanted to herself. *It's meant to be.* But she began to question that as soon as she stepped into the dining room and found only two places set with the Stratford blue-and-white crested china. Timmons was lighting the candles in the silver epergne at the center of the massive cherrywood table, and he glanced up as she entered.

She nodded, then surreptitiously scanned the room, searching for another table—perhaps one closer to her size. But aside from a pair of matching marble sideboards and some vases big enough to sleep in, there was nothing that looked to provide a place for Faith.

Hesitantly, she asked, "Um, Mr. Timmons, am I s'pposed to eat somewhere else? In another room?"

The butler straightened, his spine as linear and rigid as the shipmasts she'd viewed from London Bridge.

"On the contrary. Lady Stratford informed me this afternoon that you would be dining with her."

"Oh." Faith wrinkled her nose. "And what 'bout his lordship? Don't he eat?"

Timmons bestowed on her a look that said little street orphans should tend to their own affairs. "When Lord Stratford dines at home, he chooses to take his meals in his study."

Bother, thought Faith. *That will never do.* And as the butler returned to lighting the sconces, Faith slipped out of the room. She hurried along the corridor, afraid that if she slowed down to think about what she was going to say, she might lose her nerve.

Outside the study, she paused a second before pushing open the heavy oak door. The room, dark and deeply shadowed, smelled of pipe tobacco and cedar smoke and old leather.

"Did no one ever teach you to knock?"

There was no mistaking that bearlike grumble. It originated from a tufted chair in front of the screened hearth. With the curtains drawn, and only the guttering light of the fire playing across his features, Lord Stratford looked even more forbidding and more intimidating than he had earlier that afternoon.

Faith was about to reconsider her plan when a ball of black-and-white fur emerged from the shadows and came trotting toward her, whimpering excitedly.

"Hullo there," Faith greeted, forgetting all about the frowning lord as she hunkered down and offered the spaniel a friendly scratch behind the ears. "What a pretty dog ye are, Missy. Such a pretty li'l—"

"How do you know her name is Missy?"

The curt question gave Faith a start. "Ye know, the burnt—" *Oh, criminy.* She fairly bit off her tongue, at the last minute recalling that it was Laura who had told her about the charred cookies Missy had feasted on. Laura, the *ghost*.

"I, um . . ." She stood, rubbing uncertainly at the tip of her nose. "I reckon maybe I heard Constance talkin' 'bout it . . . perhaps."

The dog's muzzle nudged at her hand, demanding another scratch while the stubby tail wagged away furiously.

"She acts as if she knows you," Lord Stratford commented, and Faith rather thought his tone bordered on the suspicious.

"Yeah . . . I reckon she does." Faith edged back toward the wall. "Act that way, I mean."

Lord Stratford's gaze narrowed, traveling back and forth between her and the dog.

Uneasy, Faith studied her toes. Her new kid slippers, unsullied and white, helped restore her flagging confidence. Never before had she owned a spanking new pair of shoes—not ones that fit and hadn't been worn by at least two others ahead of her. With renewed determination, she screwed up her courage and announced all in one breath, "I came to ask ye to join us for supper."

A bushy black brow lifted. "At whose prompting?"

He did not sound too pleased to have received the invitation. "Oh, just me. I didn't talk it over with no one or nothin'." *Well, except for Laura.* "Mrs. Imes had said she was bakin' a special treat for afters and I thought, um, that maybe ye liked puddin'."

She rolled her weight nervously onto the outside of her foot. Lord Stratford was studying her beneath his brows the way Grandpa's cat—the orange one that had lost a leg—used to eye the landlady's mutt. One part challenge. One part . . . fear?

"I have already dined."

"Oh." Another fortifying peek at the slippers. "Well, um, if ye change yer mind . . ."

He made no response, merely kept that brow hoisted high. Faith shrugged weakly and sidled out of the study, leaving a bereft Missy behind.

Feeling a bit disconcerted and out of sorts, Faith reentered the dining room to discover Lady Alice waiting for her, fussing over an arrangement of lilies and . . . humming. Her eyes, so very blue, looked less sad than they had before, and Faith realized how greatly Laura had resembled her mother.

"There you are, Faith." Lady Alice's smile was brighter than the candelabra. "I was beginning to worry that you might have rushed your recovery. Are you sure that you are feeling well enough to be out of bed?"

"Oh, I'm fit as a fiddle, mum," and Faith slapped her chest as if to prove it.

"I am glad," Lady Alice said. "But we must be prudent and not allow you to overtax yourself."

Faith failed to see how she might become overtaxed napping and eating and having cream rubbed into her freckles, but she nodded her agreement nonetheless.

The first course was brought in and Timmons assisted them into their seats. As she glanced around, Faith privately thought it a wonder that the Stratfords had not all been blinded living in this house. Everything sparkled. Everything. The forks and candle stands and the big soup bowl gleamed a luminous silver; while gold glistened on the knife-box, vases and picture frames. Over their heads, the crystal chandelier twinkled like stars in a smokeless sky, and even the curtains looked all shimmery, woven with sparkling gold threads.

"Are ye *very* rich?" Faith blurted out.

Lady Alice's lips pursed. "I hadn't considered it, but yes, I imagine that we are."

Faith lifted her soup spoon, scrutinizing her reflection in its curve. "Funny, ain't it?" she said, talking more to herself than to anyone else. "I'd always figured that if ye lived in a place like this, ye just had to be one of the happiest bein's on earth."

A brief lull settled over the table.

"And what do you think now?" Lady Alice asked.

Faith, suddenly embarrassed, scratched at the side of her nose. She hadn't meant it to sound as if she didn't *like* it here. Even if Lord Stratford was somewhat cross. "Um, I dunno. But it sure is a pretty house," she offered.

Lady Alice's forehead creased thoughtfully and she turned her attention to the footman who had begun to ladle a thin green soup into their bowls. From beneath her lashes, Faith studied Lady Alice's profile. *She don't seem put out, thank goodness.* But all the same, Faith thought she'd do best to mind her wayward tongue.

Trying to follow Lady Alice's lead, Faith delicately dipped her spoon into her bowl, sipping slowly, reminding herself that she didn't have to gobble it down for fear of having it stolen by another more hungry than she. For now at least, she was safe, safe with the knowledge that another meal would follow on the morrow.

Lady Alice cast a glance to the servant who'd taken his

post by the far door leading to the kitchen. "Faith dear, if it's not too difficult for you to discuss"—her voice softened as did her gaze—"I think it important that I understand how you came to be alone. You had mentioned that your grandfather passed away . . ."

Faith nodded. "Hm-mm. Mr. Cheeps come and told me 'bout Grandpa gettin' run over, and he said I should pack up my belongings. I think he had a notion to drop me off at the foundling hospital, but I weren't goin' to have none of *that*. Billy—he worked at the chandler's—he'd told me 'bout friends of his who'd been taken to the hospital and how they'd had all their teeth pulled out to sell to the rich— Oh!" Faith clamped her hand over her mouth. "Oh, criminy, I didn't mean to say that 'cause you and Lord Stratford are plump in the pockets . . ."

Lady Alice had visibly paled two shades, but she smiled reassuringly. "It's all right, dear. Neither Lord Stratford nor I possess any teeth that are not our own, I promise you. Though how such a barbaric practice could be condoned by our government hospitals . . ." A small shudder rippled across her shoulders. "Please, continue with your story."

To Faith's way of thinking, there wasn't much story to tell, but she dutifully related how she'd run off and taken refuge first in the chandler's shop—Billy had snuck her in— and then for many weeks at the rear of a stables off St. Martin's Lane where she'd stolen lumps of sugar intended for the horses. Unfortunately after being found out at the stables, she'd been obliged to wander, sleeping one night under an abandoned vendor's cart, and three more in the bushes at Hyde Park.

". . . and then the next night, ye found me." Faith ended her tale and popped the last bite of lamb into her mouth, noticing that Lady Alice had not touched her own plate. "Are ye savin' room for Mrs. Imes's cake?"

As if released from a trance, Lady Alice shook her head and dropped her gaze to her plate. "Why . . . yes. She had said she was preparing a special treat, hadn't she?"

Faith nodded, squirming with anticipation as Mrs. Imes entered, proudly bearing on a gold-rimmed platter the most beautiful plum pudding Faith had ever laid eyes on.

"A Christmas cake?" Lady Alice asked, sounding pleasantly surprised. "A sennight early?"

The cook set down the cake, tipping her gray bonneted head in Faith's direction. "Well, I wasn't sure if Miss Faith'd be joining us Christmas Day and I thought, well, that the little one should have herself at least one of me plum puddings."

"What a lovely idea, Mrs. Imes, and most considerate of you." Lady Alice folded her hands together and turned to Faith. "Now who shall cut the cake?"

"I'd like to claim that honor if no one objects."

"Piers," Lady Alice breathed, as all eyes swerved to the doorway.

Lord Stratford, looking fresh from a bath and wearing a crisp midnight-blue jacket, bowed to his wife, then slowly approached the table. "I'd heard from a little bird that we were to have a treat tonight."

Faith caught her breath, scarcely able to believe her success. She jumped up from her chair, as jittery as the little bird Lord Stratford had called her, hopping from one foot to the other. "Yeah, don't it look just slap-up?" she said, bobbing her head toward the magnificent pudding.

"Splendid," Lord Stratford agreed.

While he continued to eye her cautiously, Faith noticed that his regard was not altogether unfriendly. Passing behind Lady Alice's chair, Lord Stratford gestured to the footman to hand him the knife.

"So." Lady Alice's fine features shone tense with surprise. "You and Faith . . . have met?"

Over the rich expanse of plummy sweet, Faith tried to plumb Lord Stratford's gaze. But he was concentrating on making the first slice into the pudding.

"We have," he answered, without looking up from his task.

Lady Alice smiled uncertainly. "I see."

Muttering something about "a bloomin' start," Mrs. Imes left the dining room, mumbling and tsking.

The first dense wedge of pudding peeled away from the

whole and was laid majestically onto a waiting plate. Lord Stratford handed it to the footman. "For our young guest."

Faith plopped herself back into her chair and grabbed up her spoon. The instant the plate landed before her, she dug in. Blimey, it was delicious. The devilish best thing she could ever remember eating in all her days.

She sighed blissfully and delved in for a second bite— Her spoon went *clink*. She frowned, squinting at her cake. Nestled amid the purplish-brown treat was something shiny and gold and round. . . .

"Oh, Faith, you've found the guinea!" Lady Alice cried, clapping her hands. "Good for you, dear, well done."

A guinea? In the puddin'? Faith had never heard of such a thing. In confusion, she glanced around the table, not sure what she was supposed to do next. Lord Stratford was still wearing his orange-cat-missing-a-leg expression while Lady Alice was beaming to high heaven. As if Faith had just done something truly amazing.

"Do I get to keep it?"

"Of course you get to keep it, dear," Lady Alice assured. "And tomorrow you shall be 'Queen for the Day.'"

"Queen for the Day?" Faith brightened. She rather liked the sound of *that*.

"Yes," Lady Alice said. "You see, it is a game we play at the holidays. Since you have found the guinea, you get to be the queen. Tomorrow we must all do your bidding, Faith. All you have to do is ask and it shall be yours."

Faith shot a peek toward the ceiling, biting her lips to hold back an impish grin.

Criminy, Laura, could it possibly be any easier?

FOUR

"Ice-skating, by Jove. *Ice-skating!*"

In the cheval looking glass, Piers's reflection stared back at him, skeptical and scornful. And scared.

Undeniably scared.

The irony of it did not fail to escape him. Here he stood, a grown man approaching his fortieth year, twice the size of most his peers, titled, wealthy, successful . . . and terrified out of his wits. Terrified of a child no bigger than a whisker.

A curse escaped him and he whirled away from the glass, feeling strangely distant from the man in the mirror—that hopeless, angry stranger he had become these past ten months. Until yesterday he hadn't acknowledged that stranger, had been incapable of recognizing, or confessing to, the changes in himself.

But last evening when that carrot-topped waif had stood before him in the study's darkness, bravely yet nervously shifting from one small foot to the next, Piers had seen himself with sudden and unpleasant clarity. He had seen how very lost he was. Lost to grief.

Good God, what had he become that small children quaked before him? He who had loved children—particularly one child—more than life itself. The question had preyed on him for a full hour until he had inexplicably found himself on his way to the dining room under the pretext of partaking of Mrs. Imes's plum pudding.

And then what? Piers rolled his eyes. The urchin finds the golden boy and has the temerity to request first a Christmas cookie party, followed by an ice-skating excursion to the frost fair on the Thames.

This morning, by keeping to one end of the kitchen, he had managed to survive the biscuit-baking well enough, except for a healthy and unavoidable dusting of flour. Idly he brushed a spot from his jacket sleeve. But ice-skating . . .

He marched to the bedroom window, then shoved aside the heavy damask window hangings to peer down upon the town house garden. Alice and the girl were frolicking about in the new-fallen snow like a pair of playful puppies. Using the garden bench as a shield, Faith crouched low and launched a snowball that missed Alice by a hair. Alice, in turn, darted behind an elm and retaliated with unerring aim, shattering a powdery ball against the child's coat front. They both exploded into giggles, their delighted laughter carrying all the way up to Piers on the second floor. He frowned, battling a niggling sense that he should be down there joining in their fun.

Still laughing, Alice tilted her head back, the sun's wintry-pale rays feathering across her delicate features. Her throat arched, and her eyes half closed, reminding him of a similar pose when she would lie beneath him at the peak of her pleasure. The image brought desire abruptly rushing through him, hot and unexpected. But the desire was tainted, tainted with regret. For Piers knew it would go unfulfilled.

She looked so very happy, he thought. Happier than he could remember seeing her. And while he envied her that happiness, another less charitable part of him came close to resenting it. Even though he knew it to be wholly irrational and unfair to Alice, he did not understand how she could *allow* herself to be happy. After losing Laura.

God only knew that he couldn't.

At his sides, his fingers curled unconsciously in a grasping motion as if trying to hold on . . . to what? To the happiness he would not permit himself? Or to Alice?

Yesterday Alice had done something she rarely accomplished with him. She'd caught him off guard, she'd shaken him. When she had announced that she would not leave with him after the holidays, Piers had been surprised—surprised by her defiance and by the fact that she would choose to remain alone in this house haunted by its past. And yet he did not honestly believe that she would remain behind. He couldn't. When he was ready to go, Alice *would* go with him. He was convinced of it. . . . Wasn't he?

His gaze sought her out, the question still lingering in his thoughts. Apparently having declared a truce, Alice and Faith had run over to a snowbank, where they flopped back with their arms spread wide, their hands joined. Despite himself, Piers felt a hint of a smile tug at the corners of his mouth. *Snow angels.* Only two winters past, he and Laura had spent an entire afternoon flat on their backs in the freezing snow, while Alice periodically brought them mugs of hot cider to keep them from turning into icicles. Laura had refused to rest until they had filled the garden with angels, creating their own "private heaven" as she had called it.

Suddenly Piers pressed closer to the glass, his breath frosting the windowpane. After imprinting her angel into the snow, Faith was leaning down and—

Dammit, could it merely be coincidence? Or a secret that only children shared? For just as Laura had always done, Faith was marking each snow angel's middle with a . . . belly button.

His narrowed eyes lingered on her flaming-red head as she dotted Alice's angel in the stomach. Against his will, his thoughts wandered back to the other day when she had called him a "grumblygus." *Grumblygus. Belly buttons on snow angels. What did it mean?*

Below in the garden, Faith was skipping around the birdbath, singing some tune he could not make out. Her short red curls bobbed and bounced, her arms swung energetically at her sides. She did seem to be a . . . cheerful child.

Then, without warning, she tripped, falling hard, plummeting face-first into the snow. Alice called out to her, but before she could reach her, Faith simply picked herself up and dusted herself off. And went back to her skipping and singing.

Reluctantly, Piers had to admit that he admired the child's spirit. Here she was laughing and playing as freely and easily as if she had not recently survived a harrowing seven weeks on the pitiless London streets. She was a scrapper, the tiny little thing. And he respected that. At one time, he had respected that same resilience in himself—until Laura's death had revealed more of his failings than he had ever wished to have had exposed.

Dropping his gaze, Piers studied his boots with a pensive frown. If he had even a lick of sense, he would send a note down to Alice this instant, begging off this outing. Devil take it, he should never have agreed to accompany them to the frost fair. To accompany them anywhere.

But Faith had trapped him, pure and simple. Her speckled face lit with joy, her brown eyes glowing more radiantly than the blasted guinea, she had issued her childish entreaty; and then Alice had joined in, turning her tremulous smile on him, leaving him with but one choice. Either crush their hopes with a refusal or swallow his fear.

Unfortunately, however, the fear was still with him. He had stood by in the kitchen, listening to the child's giggles and Alice's answering laughter, feeling the fear as an ever-increasing ache at his center, an ache that would not be gone. At least not until *he* was gone from this house.

A ragged breath shook his chest as he looked down upon the girl who stood as a constant reminder of his pain. Unaware of his scrutiny, she tossed a handful of snow into the air, smiling as it drifted down onto her upturned face. Piers squeezed shut his eyes.

Never again, he silently vowed. Never would he permit himself to be so vulnerable again. It hurt too much. It just hurt too damned much.

"O-o-o-oh!"

With a muted squeal, Alice steadied herself, grabbing hold of the first solid thing she could lay her hands on— her husband. Clutching tightly to Piers's upper arm, Alice sputtered and laughed and cursed beneath her breath, her quiet "Blast!" sending a cloudy white puff out into the frosty air.

Her feet, mutinous appendages that they were, were refusing to cooperate this afternoon, the left foot forever heading in one direction, the right in quite the opposite. And though she'd now thrice landed her abused posterior on the unforgiving ice, Alice was having the singularly most pleasant afternoon she'd known in nigh on to a year.

The day was a glorious one, crisp and clear. The smoky haze that generally enveloped the city had yielded to a brisk wind and cheerful sunshine. Patches of snow, of the purest pristine white, clung to the banks of the Thames, and far above them the sky shone bluer than a robin's egg. From the frost fair's tents, vendors were noisily hawking their wares, banners flying in each and every hue of the rainbow. Wherever Alice looked all colors seemed intensified, glowing. Magical.

Her skate-shod feet tried to slip out from under her again, and Alice let loose with another mild oath.

"Blast it all!"

Over her shoulder, she heard Piers chuckle softly—the sound of her husband's laughter all but a distant memory. She raised her startled gaze to his, encouraged to see amusement sparkling in his forest-green eyes.

"Do you mock me, sir?" she laughingly demanded.

In contrast to her own flailing and fumbling, Piers had been navigating the frozen river with remarkable ease.

"I, madam?" His lips quirked. "I daresay I have not the courage to mock you. Not after witnessing the thrashing you've given the ice this past hour."

"Thrashing! Why, you . . . you silly man." She dipped her chin, hiding a shy, hopeful smile. So hopeful, in fact, that Alice deliberately did not release Piers's arm even after she'd steadied herself on her skates. To her relief, he did not attempt to pull away.

In tandem, they began to coast across the frozen Thames, staying clear of the crowd queued up for skittles. Alice smiled proudly, thinking how very handsome Piers looked in his greatcoat and tall beaver, his dark hair glistening in the December sun. . . . How very handsome he looked when he smiled.

All around her, Alice could feel it happening—the miracle starting to occur. The mere fact that Piers had joined them today, that he was smiling, was astonishing when compared to the dour-faced and bitter man she had been living with of late. This was the Piers she remembered, the Piers with whom she had fallen desperately in love so many years ago. The same Piers whom she still loved with the same fervency, the same unchanging constancy.

Alice refused to believe that her husband was only putting on an act, a performance designed to fulfill his promise. Once Christmas came and went . . . But no, she would not allow herself to think like that. She would not wonder when or if Piers would be leaving. She would not permit herself to doubt again.

From the moment that Alice had first found Faith in that chicken crate, she had accepted that this child was a miracle. The miracle that they'd been waiting for, that she'd been praying for. There was no question in Alice's mind that the Lord had sent them Faith to heal. To heal both themselves and her.

Alice and Piers skated past ships ice-bound until the thaw, skirting around the snowdrifts mounded near the shore's edge. They avoided the groups of young men clustered together sipping at ale, and headed toward the less populated areas in the direction of London Bridge. They skated in comfortable silence, the gentle *hiss* of the blades singing along the ice.

"This is pleasant, isn't it?" Alice asked.

"Yes. It is."

"Does it remind you of . . . anything?"

Piers was quiet for a moment. "Are you perhaps referring to the Crockett's house party? What was it? Ten winters past?"

Alice smiled. So Piers did remember. She wondered how much. It had been the first time that they had ever ice-skated together, on the Crockett's frozen pond in Shropshire. When it had soon become apparent that she had no talent for it, they had snuck away from the party for a private walk through the snowy woods. There, with only the white-capped pine to bear witness, Piers had pushed her up against a tree and they had made passionate love in the frigid cold of a winter's afternoon.

Alice wondered if Piers remembered how it had been between them—the tenderness, the hunger. She missed it so much. She could not understand how he could bear giving it up when the intimacy they shared had been such a vital part of their relationship. If only he would let them be close again. If only . . .

Then—as if he had divined her thoughts—Piers reached up and covered Alice's hand with his. Not once in the past ten months had he voluntarily touched her. Until now.

Alice's mouth went dry, her heart fluttering madly like a butterfly trapped in her chest. Though afraid to attach too much significance to the gesture, she could not stop herself from privately rejoicing. It was a first step. A very important first step in her miracle. And again, whom should she thank for it? Who had granted them this wondrous gift of a day? The miracle that was Faith.

A few yards ahead, in her new periwinkle coat and matching plumed bonnet, Faith was spinning about like a figurine on a music box. She twirled and dipped as easily as a feather on the wind, her short curls a flaming beacon in the afternoon sun.

"Goodness, isn't she remarkable, Piers? Why, it's difficult to believe that she has not skated before today. She is astonishingly graceful, wouldn't you say?"

"She does seem to have—"

As he spoke, Faith suddenly caught an edge and slammed to the ice.

Piers jerked as if struck, the muscles in his arm going rigid beneath Alice's palm. She glanced up to find his features straining with unpent emotion.

"Piers?"

He did not look at her, but brusquely turned away to stare

off into the distance. Giggling, Faith scrambled back onto her feet and resumed her pirouettes.

Understanding dawned swift and sure. "Piers," Alice said softly, " 'twas only a tumble, don't you see? She is unharmed. She is fine."

He did not answer her for a long moment, his shuttered gaze remaining fixed at a point above her head. At last, he said, "She's not Laura, Alice."

Alice's chest tightened on a pang of memory.

"No, Piers. She is not Laura. And never will she be, no matter how much we might wish it. But she is a child desperately in need of love and we have much love to give."

"*You* have much to give, Alice. You do."

Still not meeting her eyes, he dropped his hand from hers, and skated off alone.

Faith couldn't figure what had gone wrong. One minute Lord and Lady Stratford had been skating together arm in arm, smiling so hard she'd thought they were like to crack open their faces. In the next minute, Lord Stratford had just up and disappeared.

Granted, she might not know a great deal about how people fall in love, but even Faith had been able to tell that something had been rekindled between the two of them. Something good and warm and nice.

"I dunno, Laura."

Faith was lying on her stomach on the rug before the fire, pretending to read a book as an excuse for her talking out loud if someone should happen to enter. Missy lay by her side, gently snoring, oblivious of the phantom of his ex-mistress.

"He's been gone three days and I think Lady Alice is afraid that he ain't never coming back. I mean, three days, Laura. That's a long time."

Laura, as always in her painted rocker, tapped a contemplative ghostly finger against her chin. "What do you think we ought to do?"

"Ye're askin' me?" Faith issued a light snort. "I'm plum

out of ideas, I am. Ye're the ghost—I was hopin' you'd come up with somethin'.''

"Come now, Faith, you cannot abandon our cause so easily. This is important to you, too, I daresay."

"Blimey, Laura, ye're not still thinkin' they're goin' to keep me, are ye? Why, frevvinsakes, I gave up on that idea pert near the minute I done laid eyes on yer papa. He ain't never going to want to keep *me,* a raggedy li'l mite who's got more pluck than brains. I just figure you and me should settle on how we're goin' to get your parents together 'fore I'm shipped off to Red Lyon Street. Lady Alice said I could stay through the holidays but I'd feel a darn sight better leavin' if I knew they was both on their way to bein' happy."

Laura's frown softened. "So you've . . . you've come to care for them?"

Faith's gaze dropped to the pages of the open book. "Well . . . sure. I mean, no one's ever treated me as nice as they have. Even when yer papa is cross, he's not mean-spirited or nothin'.''

Secrets filled Laura's smile. "No, he's not mean-spirited, you're right, Faith. Which is why he'll return. In time for Christmas."

"Gor, Laura, do ye really think so? Christmas is just tomorrow, ye know."

Laura began to nod, then tilted her curly blond head as if listening to an inner voice. "Oh dear," she said. "I must go now, but do not worry, Faith. I will be back."

Faith scrambled onto her knees. "Hold on, now. Ye can't go yet—we ain't figured out a new idea." But before her sentence was even finished, Laura had already faded into a misty vapor that vanished into nothingness.

"Bother," Faith muttered and flopped back onto her stomach, waving her legs in an irritated criss-crossing pattern. "Bother and criminy."

"I do not recall the nursery stories of my day containing such language," a deep wry voice broke in.

Faith choked back a gasp and lifted her head to find an unusually pale and puffy-eyed Lord Stratford leaning wear-

ily against the doorjamb. He looked to her as if he had
neither slept nor eaten since she had last seen him skating
on the Thames. His coat was rumpled, his soiled cravat hung
loose around his neck, and the scruffy beginnings of a beard
shadowed his face. He looked plumb awful. But Faith was
glad to see him. Very, very glad. She wondered if Lady
Alice knew yet that he was back.

He strolled into the room and sat down beside her on the
rose-trellised carpet, stretching his legs out toward the fire.
He smelled of tobacco and horses. Faith's eyes widened.

"Is that perhaps a modern version"—he tipped the book
over to examine the title—"of *Will Wander's Walk?*"

Faith tried to answer, but her tongue tripped over her
teeth. "Y—Yes. Er, no, I mean. I—I was talkin' to meself,"
she finally stammered.

He quirked one dark brow in an expression now familiar
to her, his unshaven countenance making him appear more
bearlike than ever. But rather like a nice cuddly bear, Faith
decided, instead of the snarling oversized one he usually
reminded her of. In fact, now that she pondered on it, she
realized that Lord Stratford wasn't watching her with the
orange-cat-without-a-tail expression. He seemed less . . .
wary. Less scared.

"Why don't you read to me?" he invited, indicating the
book.

A blush stole up her neck. "Well, I ain't—I mean, I'm
not much good at readin' yet. Lady Alice says I draw my
letters real nice, but the reading part is comin' kind of slow-
like. You see, I never had any schoolin' or nothin'—*anything*," she swiftly corrected.

"All the same, I could do with a good nursery rhyme.
Won't you please?"

Please? Lord Stratford was asking her "please"?

Faith mustered her courage and puffed out her cheeks on
a hefty breath. "All right, I guess I'll take a go at it."

Braced on her elbows, she leaned forward, painstakingly
studying the letters still so foreign and strange.

" 'With both his com—companions and all of their talk,

says Will to his sister, my dog here . . . pro—proposes to take a nice walk.' ''

She paused. Beneath Lord Stratford's intense regard, she had to keep herself from squirming.

''Let me understand you,'' he said slowly, frowning as he glanced from her to the book and back again. ''Is it your assertion that you could not read at all prior to one week ago?''

Faith started to rub her nose, then remembered Lady Alice's gentle counsel that it was not the most ladylike of habits. She lowered her hand, shrugging lightly.

''Like I said, I didn't have much occasion to learn 'fore Lady Alice teached me the letters and sounds. Did I say a word wrong?'' She glanced apprehensively back to the text.

''No. No, Faith, you did very well. Very well indeed. You should be extremely pleased with your progress.''

She cocked her head to the side, trying to peer into his frowning face. ''But . . . are *you* pleased?'' she asked in a small voice.

Though during their lessons Lady Alice had been generous with her praise, for some reason it was very important to Faith that Lord Stratford think that she had done well. After all, she might not be beautiful and charming and elegant like Laura, nor speak French nor play the pianoforte but, at the very least, she could now read and write. At least a little bit.

''Of course, I am pleased,'' Lord Stratford answered stiltedly. ''Education is fundamental to the human development.''

''Oh.'' Faith's lips quivered with disappointment and she had to hide behind a hasty rub of her nose, while sending a silent ''sorry'' to Lady Stratford. She didn't know why but her tummy hurt, too—not with hunger, but with something else aching and sad. If Lord Stratford hadn't been staring at her so hard, Faith would have liked to have popped her thumb into her mouth for a quick dose of comfort.

Lord Stratford cleared his throat and turned away to shuffle through the pile of books stacked at the carpet's edge.

''Would—'' He made another harrumphing noise. ''Would

you like me to read you a story?'' he offered, his deep voice even gruffer than normal.

Faith gave a cautious little nod. Her tummy felt a bit better at the prospect.

"Which one?'' he mumbled, not meeting her gaze.

"Um-m.'' Faith leaned forward, peering at the titles. "Oh, how 'bout the princess in the tower? The one with the long hair?'' she asked, brushing a wistful and self-conscious hand across her cropped curls.

"Very well.'' Lord Stratford crossed his legs beneath him and opened the gilt-edged book. The fire crackled quietly as Faith edged closer, drawn to Lord Stratford's soothing rumble, and the magical tale of witches and princesses and knights on white horses.

As Lord Stratford read, Faith noticed that he stumbled from time to time over words that even she had no difficulty deciphering.

"... and her hair was as golden as morning's light, cascading down her back—''

His voice cracked. Suddenly he slammed the pages shut and rose to his feet. He looked to be almost shaking.

Faith's face screwed up with surprised concern, as she studied the book. What had so upset him about golden hair cascading—

Laura.

"Wait!'' Faith called.

Lord Stratford was already halfway out the bedroom door but he hesitated on the threshold, unsure and guarded. Faith jumped up and dashed over to him. She faced him, eye-level to his tightly clenched fists, and swallowed. Her fingers wove in and out of her skirts. What could she say, what could she do, to take the hurt from his eyes?

She glanced up to the bit of greenery hanging above the door and found inspiration.

"Ye're standin' under the mistletoe,'' she whispered.

Then, before her resolve weakened, she grabbed his hand and pulled him down to her, tipping forward onto the points of her toes to plant a peck on the side of his jaw.

His face froze, his features going absolutely still. Faith

immediately got the feeling that maybe she'd made a big mistake, that maybe Lord Stratford didn't want any little girls besides Laura giving him mistletoe kisses. She released his hand, but he continued to stare at her from under those black bushy brows.

Faith felt her cheeks start to burn. Her eyes, too.

Laura, she silently pleaded. *Laura, help me, 'cause I think I've messed it up but good.*

And then, without even planning on it, Faith said, "Ye miss her a lot, don't ye?"

A muscle jumped at the side of his jaw.

"She misses ye, too, ye know."

After a long, long silence, where the only sound was Missy's muffled snores, Lord Stratford managed to squeeze "Who?" past his tautly stretched lips.

"Laura, of course."

He actually flinched.

"Ye see, she's been hanging 'round since she has been so awfully worried about ye and Lady Stratford but, to tell ye the truth, from what she has told me, I think she would really like to go on to heaven, if only—"

"*Don't.*" The single word reverberated through the room, bouncing off the walls and the ceiling and the floor. By the time it hit Faith, it was like a four-in-hand barrelling her over on the street. That one word, that one "don't" was packed with so much fury and so much grief that Faith figured she hadn't lived enough years to truly understand it.

Above her, Lord Stratford's eyes were glittering like shards of glass. Faith felt like she might be sick to her stomach.

"Don't . . . ever again speak her name."

Faith started to shake her head, a hundred promises of eternal silence poised on the tip of her tongue. But she did not get a chance to give them. Before she could swear on each and every one of her dead relative's graves never to utter the name "Laura" again, Lord Stratford spun sharply on his heel and strode down the hall.

Faith bit into her lip, as something wet slid down her cheek. She decided that the mistletoe must be leaking.

 FIVE

"Blasted dog."

Piers irritably rolled over onto his other side, punching his pillow into a plump round. He closed his eyes, and silently cursed spoiled animals who had no better sense than to wake their masters in the dead of night. Not that he had actually been asleep. How could he sleep when Faith's words echoed through his thoughts like hell's own torment?

Of course, he recognized that children frequently invented tall tales; Laura's favorite fantasy had held that a population of pink fairies lived in her toy box. But, for the love of God, had Faith actually been trying to say that she communicated with his daughter? Laura, who had been dead and buried these past ten months?

Piers gave his pillow another healthy jab, guilt and confusion seeping through him. He had come home tonight because he had made a promise to Alice and yet he did not feel as if he was meeting that promise. He had not spoken to his wife since his return, and, blast it, it was Christmas Eve. In truth, he had not spoken to anyone but Faith, and then all he had achieved in that conversation was frightening the wits out of the poor girl.

But, damn it, she had frightened *him*. Not just with her claims of talking to the dead, but before that. She had frightened him by making him care, by making him feel again. That point had been driven home with a vengeance when Faith had fallen during their ice-skating party. Though Alice had been right in that it had only been a harmless tumble, suddenly Piers had been thrust back in time to the single most agonizing, the single most defenseless moment of his life. He had seen himself standing over the rocking chair, shedding hot tears of frustration, as Alice hummed lullabies to their dying daughter.

God, he had felt so helpless. So powerless to stop it. A father's job was to keep his child safe, to protect her from harm. But it was an impossible task. Impossible. One moment, your daughter is climbing onto your shoulders laughing and tugging at your hair—the next moment, fate reaches out and steals her from you. Just like that. Without warning, without cause.

Piers flipped over, restless with the emotions that would not be resolved. The mournful whimpering sounded again from down the hall. But this time Piers jerked upright, his pulse racing. That was *not* Missy's cry.

He fumbled with his night robe as he headed for the bedroom door. In the hallway, he noticed vaguely that the darkness smelled wet and dank, as if it had either rained or snowed during the night. Swiftly he strode toward Faith's room, as the whimpering grew louder, more desperate. Where in God's name was Alice?

Silently he pushed open the door, not wishing to startle the child awake. A faint glow from the hearth's banked fire cast enough light for him to make out Faith's form twisting about on the bed. She appeared to be in the throes of a night terror.

He stood beside the bed, uncertain, battling that same guilt and confusion. Damn, he was probably the one responsible for giving her bad dreams, scaring her as he had done earlier in the evening.

"Faith," he called.

"No-o-o," she moaned, trapped in her nightmare. "Please don't. No-o-o."

Her little voice—so fearful, so pitiful—clutched at Piers

as surely as if she had reached out to him. He felt at a complete and utter loss as to what to do. A part of himself urged caution. The other part of him cursed his cowardice when the child was so obviously in need of comfort.

She cried out again and Piers could not stand it. His instincts took over. Pushing aside the lacy bed hangings, he pulled the still-sleeping child into his arms, then sat down in the rocker next to the bed.

"There, there now," he crooned, "it's all right. Papa's here now. It's going to be all right."

Tears glistened on her pale speckled cheeks as he rocked her tenderly, stroking her silky soft curls. His palm, already large, seemed enormous when compared to her smallness, her fragility. Slowly she began to calm.

"That's a good girl," he whispered. "You have nothing to worry about. Papa is here. He's not going anywhere."

Her tear-spiky lashes fluttered, but she did not awaken, rather nestled closer as if she intuitively sensed that here was safety. Here was home.

Crooning bits of nursery rhymes randomly pieced together, Piers continued to rock her until the last weepy hiccough had passed and her breath came low and even. Ever so gently, he laid her back on the bed, smoothing the linens and tucking the counterpane under her chin. In the burnished light of the hearth's embers, she looked to him a red-haired cherub from a Renaissance painting, perhaps a Botticelli or a Titian. He really ought to have her portrait painted, he thought, maybe for Alice's birthday—

It struck him. Like a fiery blast from an oven or an icy rush of tempest-driven wind, realization swept over him with astonishing force.

He loved this child.

By God, it had happened. Despite him. Despite the seemingly impenetrable walls he'd constructed around himself. Somehow, some way, he had come to love this odd little orphan girl as if she were his very own flesh and blood. But how? While he had been laboring to safeguard himself, Faith had gotten through his walls. She hadn't actually broken through them—she had simply climbed over. With her

optimism and her spirit and her honesty, she had reached
that part of Piers he had believed closed off forever.

Piers shut his eyes, unable to hold back the sting of tears.
Tears he had not even been able to shed beside his daughter's grave. And as they spilled silently onto his face, the
almost imperceptible scent of lilac wafted into the room. His
skin tingled and puckered with goose bumps. His eyes flew
open.

And then . . . Then, call it a miracle, but Piers saw the
entirety of the truth more clearly than he had ever seen anything in his life. Not just his acceptance of Faith into his
heart, but all of it. That loving another child was not a be-
trayal of Laura, but rather an affirmation of what he and his
daughter had shared. He had shut down, severed himself
from family and friends, for fear of being vulnerable again.
But, good Lord, had he ever been more vulnerable than he'd
been these past months?

Strength was not in the hiding, but in the sharing of yourself. Love was not an exclusive commodity, not an emotion
to be hoarded within the walls of your house. This feeling—
this love he knew again—made him feel strong, not weak.
It made him whole again. It made him a man again.

Piers wanted to laugh out loud, the rediscovery of himself
more exhilarating than he could ever describe. Lord, he had
to talk to Alice. He had to tell her what he had learned. To
set matters right between them.

After placing a hasty, grateful kiss on Faith's forehead,
he rose from the bed. He turned, then stopped. In the doorway a woman's willowy figure stood outlined against the
silvered shadows.

"Alice."

In three strides, he was across the room, folding his arms
around her. She was chilled and trembling, and smelled of
fresh pine. He led her out of the bedroom and into the corridor, where flickering candlelight from the candelabra revealed dampness streaking her countenance.

"Piers, I—I overheard. I was standing outside Faith's
door. I apologize for eavesdropping but, you see, I had gone
downstairs to fill Faith's stocking—" Alice caught her

breath, then released it shakily. "Did . . . did you mean what you said? About not leaving?"

Piers lifted his face to the ceiling. To think how close he had come to abandoning all that he had . . .

"Alice, I will never leave you, my love. Never. Not you or Faith, I promise you."

A halting sob escaped her and he drew her into his embrace. He stroked her back as she wept for a minute or two, the hushed communion more meaningful than words. After a time, Alice wiped at her eyes with the backs of her hands. When she lifted her gaze to his, Piers felt ashamed of the suffering he'd inadvertently put her through during this last year.

"Alice, I am so very sorry that I have hurt you as severely as I have. I did not mean to, I swear it. Can you ever forgive me?"

Smiling through her tears, she looped her arms around his neck, her face as luminous as the heaven's brightest star. "Oh, Piers, all that matters is that I have you back. Had I lost both you and Laura, I don't know how I would have survived. I have missed you so much, my darling."

"Lord, Alice, not as much as I have missed you."

Slowly, inch by inch, Piers lowered his head and covered her lips with his. The kiss proved as sweet and as full of promise as the first that they had shared fifteen years ago. But whereas that early embrace had been a kiss of discovery, this was a kiss of rediscovery. What began as tender and healing soon became demanding and possessive. Passions banked for far too long exploded in a flurry of fervent caresses and heated whispers.

Piers swung her up into his arms, the feel of her so right. So very right. "May I?" he asked huskily.

In answer, she drew his lips back to hers.

As the clock chimed midnight, Alice and Piers reaffirmed their love with the greatest gift of them all.

Holding her bulging stocking with both hands, Faith sprinted down the hall toward Lady Alice's room. The sun had barely risen when she had dashed downstairs to see if

Saint Nicholas had remembered her. To her amazement, Faith saw that he had. Lady Alice had told her true.

"Look, Lady Alice, look! He came, he came. How did he know I was here, I wonder? He's never known where to find me before."

Eager to share her treasures, Faith barrelled into the bedroom and skidded to an abrupt halt. Sleepy-eyed and groaning, Lord Stratford hastily dragged the sheet up and over his head while Lady Alice peeked out from a mound of tangled bed linens.

"Criminy." Stunned, Faith clamped a hand over her mouth, hiding an embarrassed, yet equally pleased, smile. "Um, I'll just—" She started backing up, clutching her stocking to her chest. "I'll just, um, be in my room. . . ."

She whirled around and dashed back out to the corridor, mashing her lips together to keep the giggles from getting loose.

It happened. Saints be praised, it had happened! Faith danced a little jig as she bounced down the hall, something tinkling mysteriously at the bottom of her stocking.

"Laura," she wanted to sing out. *"Laura, come see. Come see how wonderful this Christmas day is turnin' out."* But as she pranced along, Faith only sang the words—at the top of her voice—inside her heart.

A bit surprised not to find Laura when she returned to her room, Faith plopped down on the rug before the hearth to wait. Before she had time to admire her overflowing stocking, Lord and Lady Stratford appeared in the doorway, both looking somewhat abashed. Lady Alice's cheeks shone almost as crimson as her velvet night robe, but Lord Stratford stood tall and proud with his arm draping his wife's shoulders.

"Happy Christmas, Faith," Lady Alice said, walking over and kneeling down to wrap her up in a warm, lovely hug.

"Happy Christmas," Faith answered, hugging her back, squeezing tight, fearing that she might simply burst open with all the good feelings inside her.

Cradled cozily in Lady Alice's arms, Faith peeked around

to see that Lord Stratford had not budged from the doorway. Disappointment put an ugly wrinkle in her joy. Apparently he had not forgiven her for talking to him about Laura last night. . . .

Lord Stratford folded his arms across his chest, and tapped his foot impatiently. He turned his gaze up and away, as if unable to even bear looking at her. He sighed a deep, grumbling bearlike sigh.

"I seem to be standing under a piece of mistletoe," he announced, turning to pin her with his sharp eyes. "Faith, you would not happen to remember what that signifies, would you?"

She blinked, her mouth falling slightly open. *What—? Could he mean—?*

Then he held out his arms in entreaty, his expression silently pleading, and Faith did not need to wonder any longer as to his meaning. She leaped from Lady Alice's lap and raced across the room to fling herself into his embrace. He caught her up and swung her high, the both of them laughing uproariously, though Faith was not sure as to the reason.

When their chuckles finally subsided, Faith reached up and planted a loud kiss on Lord Stratford's cheek. "Happy Christmas," she said.

"The same to you, sweet Faith. And thank you," he added in a whisper that only she was meant to hear. Still holding her in his arms, he strolled over to the rug and sat down beside Lady Alice. "What do you think, Alice? Should we ask her?"

Lady Alice's white teeth worried gently at her lip, and Faith thought that she might be hiding a smile.

"Faith." Lord Stratford's expression became most solemn, his black brows dipping together. "Lady Stratford and I have something very important to ask you, but we do not want you to feel as if you need to give us an answer straightaway, all right?"

Matching his solemnity, Faith nodded.

"Lady Stratford and I"—his eyes sent his wife a warm, quick caress—"would like you to consider staying here with us. As our daughter. For as long as you wish."

Faith could not breathe, she could not speak. Those good feelings were bubbling up inside her, clogging her throat and her lungs so that she almost felt suffocated with emotion.

She swallowed, her gaze darting first to Lady Alice's expectant face, then back to Lord Stratford's shining emerald eyes. "Ye . . . ye want to keep me?"

Lady Alice reached out and clasped her fingers. "Faith, you have given us so much in these few short days, so much more than you could possibly begin to understand. We would like to give you a home. A family."

"Oh, my. O-o-oh, my." Faith placed a shaky hand on the top of her head, as if she could hold it all in. "I—I . . . I dunno what to say."

Lady Alice squeezed her fingers with an urgency that made Faith catch her breath—made her realize that her answer was of great importance to them. Lady Alice and Lord Stratford *wanted* her. They didn't have to take her in like Grandpa had done; she was no blood kin to them, after all. They wanted to keep her just . . . just because.

Faith hid her face in Lord Stratford's shoulder. Blimey, the last thing she wanted to do was change their minds by blubbering all over the place like a baby. So she made a small damp spot on Lord Stratford's quilted night robe instead. When she finally trusted herself to speak, she lifted her head.

"I—I don't suppose there was ever a nicer Christmas gift in the whole history of the world than the one ye just give me." She swiped her nose with the back of her wrist. "I would like to stay. Very much."

Two pairs of arms folded around her and Faith closed her eyes. Never in her life could she have imagined anything so wonderful. At least not for a skinny, freckle-faced street orphan by the name of Faith Burns.

Then, over Lord Stratford's shoulder, she saw her. Laura was smiling and waving from her rocking chair.

"Oh!" Faith gasped.

She wriggled out of their embrace, so excited that she didn't dare lift her gaze from the rocker.

"Jiminy, I've got the most special Christmas gift for the both of ye, but . . . but I'm goin' to need yer help in gettin' it."

"Dear, you shouldn't have bothered—"

Lady Alice fell silent as Faith lifted a finger to her lips, her gaze still fixed to the rocking chair.

What was it? There was something different about Laura. She seemed to be glowing even brighter, even whiter, than before. . . .

"A halo," Faith whispered. "You're an—"

Laura laced her fingers together and flattened them beneath her chin in a teasing pose. Faith actually laughed out loud.

"Faith. Dear?"

As Faith turned to look into Lady Alice's kind blue eyes, she sent up a silent prayer to the heavens.

Please, God, let them see her. Just one last time, please let them see their little girl.

By all rights, Faith didn't figure she ought to be asking any more favors of God after all He'd done for her already. But this was the only Christmas gift she could think of that was anywhere near as marvelous as the one she'd just been given.

"I know ye might think this sounds funny," she began. "But I want ye to both do me a really big favor and think about . . . Laura."

Against her back, Faith could feel Lord Stratford's muscles tighten, and she hurriedly added, "Now, don't be thinkin' sad thoughts 'cause that ain't going to help none. I want ye to think about the happy times. Think of how she giggled in that devilish way of hers and how she'd throw her head just so to make her curls all bouncy-like."

Across the room, Laura saucily tossed her blond curls.

"Think 'bout that dimple in her cheek and how very much she loved bein' yer little girl. Think of the—"

Lady Alice's faint gasp sliced cleanly through Faith's words. Staring wide-eyed at the rocking chair, Lady Alice climbed to her feet, her cheeks as pale as the snow clinging to the windowsill outside.

"Oh, dear heavens," she breathed.

Faith clambered up as Lord Stratford stood. With obvious dismay, he watched his wife drift across the room as if she were sleepwalking or in a trance.

"Alice, darling, what's wrong?"

Lady Alice stopped, half pivoting toward him. "Piers, can't you see her?" she asked. "Can't you see Laura?"

"For the love of—"

Faith tugged at his hand. "Happy thoughts," she reminded him. "Happy memories."

His frown smoothed, the tension easing from his eyes. When he turned back toward the rocker, he started so abruptly that Faith felt the shock shudder right through him. Slowly, so slowly, he walked toward Lady Alice, joining her at her side.

"Alice," he rasped.

She reached for him. Hand in hand, they approached the rocker, and together dropped to their knees beside the vision of their daughter.

"Laura. Laura, can you hear us?" Lord Stratford's voice did not sound like his own.

Laura nodded and smiled a smile at once very sad yet radiant with unearthly joy. She glanced past her parents, searching for Faith, then gestured with her palms up.

"I—I think she's leavin' now," Faith said quietly. "Ye can see that she's an angel at last, thanks to you two. I—I think she's headed for heaven."

And Laura did seem to be growing brighter and brighter, until she was like an intense white light.

"Ye should probably say good-bye now," Faith suggested.

Laura spread her arms wide as if she would gather her parents into her embrace. Lord Stratford actually leaned forward, stretching his hands out to her, but there was nothing to hold. Laura made a motion as if caressing his cheek, then blew him a kiss. Then she turned to her mother and did the same. Lady Alice returned the gesture, her slender fingers trembling as she pulled them from her lips.

"We love you, Laura," Lady Alice said.

Lord Stratford seemed to be past all words.

The light that was Laura intensified in a sudden blinding flash—so bright that Faith had to avert her eyes. When she looked back to the rocking chair, Laura was gone. And Lord and Lady Stratford were holding each other close, swaying back and forth on their knees.

Faith's heart felt so full and so heavy that she didn't know how her skinny little chest could hold it. Maybe she should slip out for a few minutes to give Lord and Lady Stratford some time alone—

"Faith."

In unison, they called her name. She glanced back and before she knew it, she was being rocked and held and petted and wept over.

"Thank you, Faith."

"Thank you. Thank you for that miracle of a gift."

And as her eyes filled with hot, happy tears, Faith lifted her gaze to heaven.

"Happy Christmas," she whispered.

ONLY FIFTEEN
SHOPPING DAYS LEFT...

Elizabeth Bevarly

For Dave and Joan Beard,
who always leave something special
under the Christmas tree

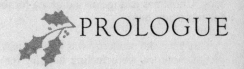 PROLOGUE

Christmas Eve 1945

Louis Krist ran a quick brush through his snowy white beard and perched his reading glasses on his cherry-red nose. He bypassed the array of rouge, wigs, fake beards, and glue that all the other part-time Santas had to use when they worked, and strode to his locker in the break room of Lauderdale's department store to don his massive, red velvet coat. Being overweight might have its health concerns, he thought, recalling his doctor's warnings about his weight, but it sure did help make him a convincing Santa Claus.

When he was all zipped up, he popped a peppermint candy into his mouth and cinched his wide, bell-laden leather belt around his ample waist with a merry jingle. Then he practiced a few perfunctory "Ho-ho-hos," an action that was simply habit by now, because Louis Krist was the epitome of Christmas spirit. He was, by far, the best Santa Claus Lauderdale's had ever employed, and everyone in Chicago knew it.

Not that Louis was one to be prideful about such a thing. He was simply so very pleased to be providing children with a bit of holiday magic, a little something special to believe in at a time when the whole world was rebuilding after a terrible war and a terrible Depression. For too long, Christmas had been celebrated in the shadow of violence and poverty. For too long, families had been forced to do without and worry about their loved ones, some not certain whether their sons and brothers and fathers were even alive. For too long, Christmas had meant indigence for too many, and loss for too many more.

But not this year.

This year, the economy was on the upswing, and the people of America were feeling hopeful for the first time in nearly two decades. Chicago was alight with holiday decorations, and snow was falling in a white, crystalline cascade, cleansing the dirt from the streets, and buffing all the rough edges from the city. "White Christmas" sounded from the store's radio speakers, and in fifteen minutes, Lauderdale's would open for the last shopping day before Christmas. And once again, Louis would experience the delight and satisfaction of hearing the breathless wishes and dreams of scores of children.

But best of all, the following evening, on Christmas Day, his namesake and favorite granddaughter Louise would be getting married to a fine young man. Louis had been looking forward to the wedding for months. He knew his family considered him to be a sentimental old fool, but the only thing that brought a warmer feeling to his heart than Christmas did was to see two young people fall in love and commit themselves to marriage. Louise had purposely chosen her grandfather's favorite holiday—Christmas Day—to exchange vows with her future husband. She'd done that for Louis. And his heart still swelled with love and joy at the knowledge.

He settled his Santa hat atop his head, the bells adorning the white fur cuff jingling as cheerily as those on his belt. Then he unwrapped another peppermint candy as he made his way toward the locker room door. Out of nowhere, another one of those annoying little pains pinched his chest, and he pressed his fingers to his breastbone in an effort to rub the sharp sensation away. He'd been suffering such pains too frequently lately. He supposed he should do as his wife insisted and go back to see his doctor. Next week, he promised himself. He'd make an appointment with Dr. Grady the day after Christmas.

The pain in his chest subsided some, but it didn't go away completely. Louis flattened his palm over his heart and pressed hard as he pushed open the locker room door. To take his mind off the pain, he thought again about Louise, about Christmas, about how there was nothing in the world more wonderful than two people falling in love during a holiday meant to celebrate just that.

And he smiled as he promised himself that nothing, nothing in the world, could ever make him miss Louise's Christmas wedding. . . .

ONE

1997

Santa's workshop was abuzz with activity, even more hectic than the elves had anticipated, with only fifteen shopping days left before Christmas. Piles and piles of gaily wrapped Christmas presents, some of them as large as appliance boxes, were scattered everywhere—even behind and around the jolly old fat man's huge, bejeweled throne. Teddy bears, dump trucks, choo-choos, and dollies littered the floor, and a rainbow assortment of oversized lollipops and peppermint sticks jutted at odd angles along the gold picket fence enclosing the workshop area. Energetic elves bedecked in red and green hustled hither and yon in an attempt to manage the chaos, some of their efforts successful, some not.

Two elves, however, had managed to slip away from the confusion, for a quick breather and an even quicker cup of cocoa, and stood observing the action from the doorway of the elves' break room nearby. The break room was only one of many concessions they were proud to have won this year, after they'd threatened to strike during the holiday season. They'd also been awarded a slight raise in salary *and* a dental plan—however meager—along with brand-, spanking new uniforms.

Okay, so the fur-trimmed, skin-tight, miniskirted uniforms were probably more suited to a Christmas centerfold than they were to Santa's workshop. The old man was getting on in years, the elves knew, and his eyesight wasn't what it used to be. And hey, if a short skirt would make St. Nick more merry, who were they to argue? With the Christmas holiday fully upon them now, there wasn't exactly time for more complaining anyway.

"Good cocoa," the first of the breaking elves muttered after she inhaled a deep drag from her unfiltered Camel. She expelled the smoke in a slow, steady stream of white and enjoyed another sip.

"Mmm," the second murmured in agreement.

"Only one thing missing from it, though," the first added after swallowing.

The second sipped carefully from the rich, sweet concoction before asking, "What's that?"

"A couple fingers of bourbon."

The second elf laughed. "Now, now. You know Santa would never approve."

"Like hell," the first countered. "Haven't you noticed the way the old guy's left boot bulges? It's because he has a fifth of rye tucked inside."

The second elf chuckled merrily. "Yeah, well, it is his busy time, after all. And with Mrs. Claus being menopausal and filing for divorce this year, it's just not quite the holiday he's used to."

Both elves trained their attention to the plump, silver-haired woman berating the man in red. As she complained loudly of his bad breath and wide girth, she tried to settle a wriggling, crying toddler in his lap. Still bemoaning Santa's many shortcomings, she moved back to the camera settled precariously on a tripod, and snapped a few pictures of the wailing child and the disgruntled St. Nick. Then, throwing back her bonneted, bespectacled head, she shouted out, "Neeeeext!"

Sophie Gift laughed at the scene as she tugged up the low-cut elf suit clinging to her like a second red skin. But to no avail. Just as it always did, the scooped neck fell right back down to hover just above her generous breasts. Along with the triangular skirt that barely covered her fanny, the little holly-spattered hat that kept dipping down over her long, black bangs, and the curly-toed, bell-dangling, red ankle boots, her outfit made her feel more ridiculous than she'd ever felt in her life.

Normally, she worked in the bridal registry of Lauderdale's, a world-renown department store located smack dab in the middle of Chicago's Magnificent Mile. But with the wedding season running idle, and the Christmas shopping season in full swing, she'd been drafted into a position as one of the department-store Santa's elves instead. The choice had been either that or housewares, she recalled now. And hawking cappuccino makers had never been her strong suit.

Not that she was much better with moody children, she thought wryly as she watched Mrs. Claus manhandle another preschooler. But Santa's workshop was infinitely more festive than stacks of toaster ovens were, and Sophie needed all the help she could get to boost her holiday spirit. This Christmas was going to be her first, in more than half her life, without Evan—and even though their marriage had been rocky toward the end, she wasn't looking forward to spending the holiday alone.

Annie McCabe, her cigarette-toking partner in elfdom, was a floater for the store, someone who worked wherever she was most needed—which, this time of year, was Santa's workshop. The slender blonde stubbed out her cigarette and downed the last of her cocoa, then turned back to Sophie. "We better get back out there before Mrs. Claus spanks someone and brings down a major lawsuit on the store."

Sophie chuckled again, enjoying one final taste of the cocoa that hadn't even had time to cool during the quick break. "The way things are going in the workshop, it'll be Santa she turns over her knee."

"She better not," Annie said indignantly. "Mr. Krist wouldn't like it."

Sophie laughed again. "Riiiiight. Mr. Krist. Oh, come on,

Annie, you don't honestly believe in that old ghost story, do you?''

Mr. Krist was, as far as Sophie was concerned, nothing more than a myth. An ingenious idea perpetuated by the Lauderdale family to generate holiday sales year after year, a direct response to the opening of a rival department store on the opposite corner of Michigan Avenue five decades ago.

As told to every employee hired for the holidays, the story went that way back in 1945, Lauderdale's hired a department store Santa named Mr. Louis Krist, who was every bit as white-haired, fat, and jolly as old St. Nick himself. He'd been the quintessential Santa, straight out of *Miracle on 34th Street,* imbued with holiday cheer, and loved and admired by all.

The good news was that he had been the most convincing store Santa in Chicago that year, one who had brought hoards of children into Lauderdale's—along with their gift-buying, money-spending parents, natch. The bad news was that, the same year, Mr. Krist went into full cardiac arrest on Christmas Eve on his way out of the locker room to work. A couple of stock boys found his body, dressed in full Santa Claus regalia and cold as a reindeer's nose, just outside the golden picket fence of the Santa's workshop display.

Fortunately, the store hadn't opened yet, so no impressionable children had stumbled upon the dead Santa and been scarred for life. *Un*fortunately, however, as the story went on, the jolly old soul hadn't quite found his way to that big Christmas tree light in the sky, and he still haunted the store to this day.

At least, that's what the Lauderdale family and a number of their employees claimed. Allegedly, Mr. Krist roused himself right at opening hours on Black Friday—the biggest shopping day of the year, the one where Santa traditionally showed up in stores and malls across the country to hear the whispered wish lists of children—and haunted Lauderdale's until closing on Christmas Eve. Allegedly, he did most of his hanging out at the Santa's workshop display on the second floor, but, from time to time, he had been known to wander as far as home furnishings on the fifth floor and fine jewelry on the first. And allegedly, at any sign of a lack of Christmas cheer, Mr. Krist manifested himself to set the offending party straight as to the true meaning of the holiday.

Sophie had heard all the stories, but she wasn't too concerned about being fingered by Santa Ghost. Not just because she didn't believe in ghosts, but because she'd seen neither hide nor hair of the alleged Mr. Krist in the two weeks that had passed since Black Friday. Besides, she was normally an extremely cheery person this time of year. To her, Christmas meant shopping uninhibitedly, donating to worthy causes extravagantly, decorating profusely, partying endlessly, and enjoying the festivities enormously. At least, that's what Christmas had always meant before.

Before she'd been exiled from her expansive Georgian house in Hinsdale to a cramped, studio apartment in Oak Park. Before her unlimited marital allowance had been cut off, and she'd had to learn to support herself with forty stress-filled hours a week—even more, now that Christmas was here. Before she'd had to take all her designer clothes to consignment and buy from discount stores instead. Before her husband—her high school sweetheart, for God's sake— had dumped her for another woman nearly half her age.

But it didn't take a lesson in gritty reality to know that there was no such fantastical thing as a ghost. Simply put, Sophie wasn't one to believe in spirits of anything other than the holiday kind, and even those were dimmer this year than usual. She was certain the only reason for Mr. Krist's continued celebrity was simply because it provided a good marketing ploy on the part of the Lauderdale family.

Annie, however, evidently didn't abide by that assessment, because she gaped at Sophie's doubt about the ghost's existence. "You bet I believe in Mr. Krist," she said adamantly. "I've seen him myself."

Sophie remained dubious. "Oh, you have not."

"I have, too. Two years ago, I was working the bath shop, and some guy came in on Christmas Eve looking for a last-minute gift for his aunt. And when he couldn't find anything he liked by closing time, he started yelling at me and insisting no one could go home until he had something for Aunt Peg.''

"Not very Christmasy of him," Sophie agreed.

Annie nodded. "Mr. Krist didn't think so, either. Before it was all over, he'd scattered an entire rack of Caswell-Massey bubble bath. Cucumber and elder flower, if memory serves. It was awesome.''

Sophie nodded. She didn't believe Annie's story for a moment, but she didn't want to appear impolite. "I still say Mr. Krist is more of an advertising instrument than a real ghost."

Annie brushed her fingers over her stubby blond ponytail and tipped her red elf hat forward. "Just make sure you stay in the holiday mood," she cautioned. "Otherwise, you'll find out soon enough that Mr. Krist won't tolerate humbugs."

Sophie opened her mouth to assure her coworker that there was little chance she'd lose the Christmas spirit, even if she would be spending the holiday alone this year, for the first time in her entire thirty-four year life span. But out in Santa's workshop, Mrs. Claus chose that moment to launch into another tirade against Santa, her face red, her knuckles white, her language blue.

So, throwing a long, black braid over her shoulder in preparation for battle, Sophie followed Annie back to the workshop posthaste. No need to rouse Mr. Krist unnecessarily, she thought, even if he didn't exist. She wasn't about to let a bitchy Mrs. Claus ruin *her* Christmas.

In fact, nothing was going to ruin her Christmas, she vowed. Not the fact that she would be alone on Christmas for the first time in her life. Not the fact that her ex-husband and his former head cashier now lived in the house she had taken such joy in decorating for the holidays every year. Not the fact that her tiny apartment barely had room for a Christmas tree. Not the fact that even with her recent raise in salary, she wouldn't be able to celebrate Christmas in the spirit she normally enjoyed.

Nope, Sophie decided, she *was* going to have a merry Christmas, dammit. If it was the last thing she did.

Inhaling deeply, she loosed the fingers she had unconsciously curled into fists, released her breath in a steady, calming stream, and went to subdue Mrs. Claus.

The little black-haired elf had potential.

In many ways, she reminded him of Louise, which in itself would have immediately endeared her to him. But there was something more that drew him to her, a sort of desolate loneliness she seemed barely capable of keeping at bay. She had always loved Christmas before—he could tell that about her. But this year was going to be different for her—he could tell that, too.

Something was making her sad, making her mad, making her forget what the holiday was truly all about. He wasn't sure yet what that might be, but he would find out, and he would fix it. He would do whatever he had to do to see that she enjoyed the merriest Christmas she'd ever had in her life. One thing was certain, though—he would have to work fast. Because she was quickly slipping away, and Christmas was just around the corner.

And one other thing was certain, too, he thought further. They sure didn't make elf costumes like they used to....

 TWO

Mitchell Lauderdale pinched the bridge of his nose with his thumb and forefinger, squeezed his eyes shut tight and tried to convince himself that he had *not* seen what he'd just seen. He had *not* seen Mrs. Claus wrap her fingers around Santa's throat in an effort to strangle the life out of him, right in front of a dozen young, impressionable children. But when he opened his eyes again, he saw a half dozen elves standing numb in gape-mouthed horror at the sight, while two other elves struggled to wrestle the rotund, silver-haired, bespectacled woman to the ground. Helplessly, Mitchell groaned out loud.

He hated Christmas. He really did. As a retailer, there was little to celebrate this time of year, except for the mountains and mountains of money that found its way into the cash drawers. But no amount of profit was worth this, he thought. Ninety-hour work weeks, ten times the usual paperwork, extra people to hire, extra payroll to count, extra benefits to figure, extra hours to schedule, extra inventory to keep track of . . .

And now Mrs. Claus had become homicidal. What next? he wondered.

"Fire Mrs. Claus immediately," he said to the woman beside him, who jotted the instruction down in her notebook.

"And get someone more even-tempered in there right away."

He shook his head hopelessly as he watched Mrs. Claus and the two elves continue with their wrestling match, and had no idea what to do. Until earlier this year, Mitchell had never made appearances in the store, his position with Lauderdale's being administrative, not managerial. Usually, he worked as a corporate vice-president, in charge of finances. Usually, he sat behind a nice, quiet, private desk in an office waaaaay up the street from the store. Usually, his assistant, Hazel Carpov, was in the next room, not right by his side. Usually, he was blissfully free of all the hands-on dirty work of retail.

Usually, he was all alone, just the way he liked to be.

But his father would be retiring as the CEO of Lauderdale's next year, and the old man wanted his son, his only son, to take the helm of the store. And Jacob Lauderdale was of the old school, meaning he wanted anyone who was going to be running the store to experience all the facets of Lauderdale's, right down to waxing the floors and working the perfume counter.

At one time or another in the last six months, Mitchell had worked in every single department—as a sales clerk, as an assistant manager, as a department manager, and as a floor manager. Now, finally, he'd worked his way up to store manager, just in time for the Christmas crunch. Which, of course, went exactly according to his father's plan. Jacob Lauderdale wanted to make sure Mitchell experienced the full arc of the holiday season—the productivity, the festivity, the velocity, the insanity.

Which brought his thoughts and attention back to the elves and Mrs. Claus. Mitchell was about to intercede in the scuffle when the two elves finally seemed to gain control of the older woman—but not before losing parts of their costumes in the battle. The blonde was missing her cap and one curly-toed elf shoe, and the dark-haired one . . .

Mitchell squeezed his eyes shut tight again. No. That was *not* a breast he had seen peeking out of the woman's low-cut costume. He opened one eye experimentally, in time to see her hastily tucking herself back inside her outfit. Then he groaned again.

"And whose asinine idea was it to dress the elves like Playboy bunnies?" he demanded of his assistant.

"Yours, Mr. Lauderdale," Hazel replied.

Mitchell turned to gape at her. "Mine? Are you sure?"

Hazel Carpov, who stood maybe four-foot-nine on a good day, tilted her head back in deference to his own six-foot-two. She gazed at him blandly over her reading glasses, then tucked her pen into the snowy white bun sitting slightly off-center atop her head. "You picked out the new costumes yourself two months ago."

"I did?"

She nodded again.

He turned his gaze back to the elves, noting the numerous curves and valleys on each and every one of them, then ran a brisk hand through his dark hair. "Man, I've got to start dating more," he muttered.

Then he noticed a number of men standing in line holding the hands of the children. Evidently, word of Lauderdale's R-rated elves had gotten around, and the fathers were turning out in droves. Oh well, Mitchell thought. At least they were spending a little quality time with their kids.

Hazel uttered a doubtful sound. "Yeah, right. Dating," she said. "You've got lots of time for that now with the holidays breathing down your neck. Besides, what woman would want a member of the Lauderdale family this time of year? You retailers don't know the meaning of Christmas."

Mitchell growled under his breath, mentally counting to ten. "Hazel," he said, striving to keep his voice level. "How long have you worked for Lauderdale's?"

"Since you were a snotty-nosed little kid in poopy diapers," she responded immediately. "I've got forty years invested in this racket. I was your grandfather's assistant, and your father's assistant, and now I'll be your assistant. *If* you survive the holidays," she added with a smirk of challenge.

Mitchell nodded. "Did you ever wonder why you never rose above the position of 'assistant'?" he asked.

"Nepotism," she replied easily.

He shook his head. "And it would have nothing to do with your attitude, would it?"

"Hell, no."

He sighed wearily, wondering why he was no more able to let the woman go than his father or grandfather had been. Must be because she was an absolute whiz at keeping his professional life in order. She would probably work wonders keeping his personal obligations in order, too, he thought. If he'd had any.

"Actually," he told her, "I, and all the other Lauderdales before me, know exactly what the meaning of Christmas is," he said.

Hazel extracted the pen from her bun and held it over her notepad, poised as if she intended to write down his definition of the holiday season. "And that would be?" she asked.

He smiled smugly. "Money."

Hazel nodded as she jammed the pen back into her hair. "Yep, you got the typical Lauderdale holiday spirit, all right. Typical."

He narrowed his eyes at her and was about to comment further, but a shout of panic stopped him. Mitchell spun around to find that Mrs. Claus had evidently decided not to be so easily subdued, and had popped one of her elves in the eye. The little black-haired one had a hand covering nearly half her face and was staggering backward, right toward a Styrofoam gingerbread boy.

Elf and cookie went sprawling, just as Mrs. Claus broke away from the blonde. Worse than that, though, the gingerbread boy's fall had created something of a domino effect, toppling candy canes, lollipops, and stacks of fake Christmas presents in its wake.

"Oh, no," Mitchell muttered as he hurried toward the workshop. As he drew nearer, he saw Mrs. Claus reaching for a toddler, presumably to use as a shield in her getaway. "Mr. Krist isn't going to like this one bit," he added under his breath.

As if his comment were responsible for rousing the ghost, a papier mâché candy cane that had started to topple over toward the long line of children, suddenly lurched backward instead. It swiveled and twirled like a cyclone before hitting Mrs. Claus square in the back of the head. The blow was enough to stun the woman for a moment, a moment the black-haired elf used to scramble up from the floor and tackle her from behind. Both women went careening forward just as Mitchell entered the workshop area, falling into a heap of tangled limbs right at his feet.

Immediately, he reached for Mrs. Claus and pulled her to standing. The woman shook her head fiercely, as if to clear it, then glared at him. When she realized the person she was attempting to stare down was none other than one of the store's owners, she backed down some. Not a lot, Mitchell noted, but some.

"Anyone care to enlighten me as to what's going on here?" he demanded through gritted teeth. He kept his voice low and level, not so much because he didn't want to alarm the children nearby, but because he was more furious than he'd ever been in his entire life.

Mrs. Claus straightened and met his gaze. "I, uh . . ." She had the decency to look sheepish. "I'm sorry, Mr. Lauderdale," she said quietly. "I've been having some personal problems lately, and I haven't been sleeping well, and I've been on medication, and—"

He nodded, suddenly not wanting to hear her explanation, deciding this was neither the time, nor the place, to sort this thing out. "Be at my office upstairs tomorrow morning at eight. We'll talk about this then."

"Yes, sir."

Reluctantly, he let the woman go, prepared to grab her again should she try anything funny. But Mrs. Claus seemed to have finally gathered herself back together, because she simply strode slowly toward the elves' break room with her head dipped toward her chest.

A movement below him caught Mitchell's attention then, and he looked down to find the elf that had corralled Mrs. Claus struggling to rise to her hands and knees. The view, he noted, was quite extraordinary. Lush breasts spilled nearly halfway from her low-cut elf suit, and the hair that had been plaited into a neat braid before now cascaded free down over one shoulder. He glanced away when he realized he was ogling the woman, but not before she looked up to catch him in the act.

Clumsily, forcing back a blush, he extended a hand toward her to help her up. Awkwardly, evidently unable to halt her own blush, she lifted her hand to take his. Then, suddenly, she froze, and for one brief, electric moment, everything around Mitchell went completely still and silent.

The elf seemed to be as affected by the odd sensation as he was, because her eyes fixed on his and widened in alarm. And when they did, Mitchell was nearly thrown backward by the clarity and liveliness of their green, green depths. He'd never seen eyes like hers before—pale at their centers, dark around their edges. And full of more emotion than he would have thought a human being could claim. Eyes that could shake a man right down to the center of his soul.

"Do you hear that?" she whispered, pulling him out of his reverie some.

All Mitchell could hear was a roaring in his ears from the blood racing through his veins. "Hear what?" he asked softly, still unable to look away from her huge, startlingly colored eyes.

She shook her head slowly, as if in confusion. "It's . . . it's like . . ." She tilted her head to the side, as if she were striving to hear better. "Jingle bells."

"Jingle bells?" he echoed, wondering if maybe the elf, too, had suffered a blow to the back of her head, one that was a bit more substantial than Mrs. Claus's had been. "I don't hear any jingle bells," he told her. Then he listened harder. "Oh, wait a minute . . . yes, I do."

"And that smell . . ." she continued, lowering her voice for some reason.

"Smell?" he repeated. "What smell?"

"Something smells like . . . like peppermint."

This time Mitchell was the one to shake his head in confusion. "I don't smell any peppermint." Then he sniffed the air surrounding him and realized that he could indeed detect the faint, clean aroma of peppermint.

For a moment, they continued to stare at each other in silence, their attentions completely focused on each other, as if everything around them had dissolved into sugarplum fairy dust. Then a soft chuckle made them both turn to the left. Mitchell saw the blond elf smiling at them, a secret little smile, as if she knew something they didn't.

"It's Mr. Krist," she said.

He nodded. Of course. The ghost. How could he have forgotten about Mr. Krist? Especially since fear for Mr. Krist's appearance had been the first thing that had jumped into his head when he'd seen the altercation between Mrs. Claus and the elves playing out? Of course, he'd only seen the jolly old soul once in his life, and that had to have been thirty years ago. He scarcely remembered the encounter now.

He glanced back down at the black-haired elf, who settled her hand in the one he still held out to her. Helplessly, he noted again the way her costume hugged her lush body, was dazzled once more by the color of her eyes when her gaze met his.

Oh, yeah, Mitchell thought. Eyes like hers and a body like that could make a man forget about a lot of things. He was suddenly grateful for his appalling lack of good taste and discretion where ordering costumes was concerned.

"Good work," he said as he continued to hold her hand, telling himself it was only because she didn't quite seem steady on her feet yet. "Miss . . . ?"

"Gift," she told him.

Well, he knew *that*, he thought. What else could such a vision be but a gift?

"Sophie Gift," she added, and only then did he realize that she had been telling him her name and not her avocation. "And it's *Ms.*, not Miss."

"Ms. Gift," he corrected himself. Damn, that could mean she was married. He glanced at her left hand, and when he saw no ring encircling the fourth finger, something warm and tingling danced around his heart. Actually danced. How very odd.

Then he wondered why he cared. It wasn't like he had

either the time or the inclination to be getting cozy with anyone, least of all a Lauderdale's employee. He'd never hear the end of it from his father if the old man found out Mitchell was lusting after the hired help. There was a strict, if unwritten, policy about employees dating other employees, especially the mingling of management and hourly workers. No telling what his father would say if he found out his choice for CEO was dallying with one of Santa's elves.

"Good work with Mrs. Claus," Mitchell continued with a smile for Ms. Sophie Gift. "Did you ever think about trying out for the Bears?"

She ducked her head shyly and said nothing in reply, but he saw her smile back. And when he did, something in his brain went *pop*, and something in his belly went *fizz*. But before he had the chance to contemplate the bizarre physical reactions his body seemed to be experiencing, her fingers tightened over his, and he realized he was still holding onto her hand. He also realized that he didn't want to let it go. Ever. How very, *very* odd.

"Um, look," he told her, shaking the strange sensation off, "I don't know how to thank you for that spectacular sack, but . . . you name it—if it's within reason, it's yours."

"How about a Christmas bonus?" she asked him when she glanced up again. Her eyes widened and her blush deepened, as if the suggestion surprised her as much as it did him. She covered her mouth with her hand. "Oh. Oh, dear. I don't know what made me say that. I'm sorry, Mr. Lauderdale. What I meant was, um . . ."

His eyebrows had shot up in surprise at her bald request, but now he found himself laughing out loud. "Don't apologize," he said. "You deserve it. And I think it could be arranged. For you, too," he added, turning to the other elf who had helped restrain Mrs. Claus. "You two are a good team. We could use more like you at Lauderdale's."

Before either of them had a chance to comment, Mitchell turned to the crowd of onlookers. "Sorry about this little episode, everyone," he told them. "But Santa and Mrs. Claus are as susceptible to holiday stress as anyone, and this is, after all, their busiest time of the year. Everything will be just fine.''

When the children in line continued to look worried, he added in a softer voice, "Don't worry about Mrs. Claus, kids. She'll be okay. We'll send her back up to the North Pole for a nice, long rest, and have one of her sisters-in-law come down and give Santa a hand.''

That appeared to appease the children some, but the adults, Mitchell noticed, still seemed a bit peeved about the whole thing. "Uh,'' he began again, scrambling for something that might improve their moods, too. "If you'd all like to go down to customer service, I'll see to it everyone gets a twenty-five dollar gift certificate for Lauderdale's, good through the end of the month. And there will be complimentary cocoa and Christmas cookies in our famous Fifth Floor Café. How about that?''

At his offer, finally, finally, everyone in line seemed to be mollified. And better yet, he thought wryly, everyone in line seemed to be leaving. Mitchell expelled a long, low sigh of relief as he watched them go.

"Santa's workshop is officially shut down for the rest of the day,'' he told the elves. "But don't worry,'' he added quickly, "you'll all be paid. Regular schedules resume tomorrow. I'll settle things with Mrs. Claus one way or the other in the morning. If we need to find a new one, then my assistant can play the role in the interim.''

"Hey!'' Hazel piped up beside him.

"Don't start, Hazel,'' Mitchell warned her. "It'll only be for a day or so. Go call customer service and arrange for those gift certificates, and then alert the café.''

She stared at him through narrowed eyes, frowning, clearly having no intention of obeying his instructions.

Mitchell sighed again. "Please,'' he muttered.

That seemed to cheer her some, but her smile was more brittle than it was bright. "All you have to do is use the magic word,'' she told him, spinning on her heel.

He shook his head as he watched her go, telling himself the only reason he didn't fire her was because he just didn't have the heart to do it right before Christmas. Hell, as it was, he would doubtless give the pugilistic Mrs. Claus a second chance.

He turned to leave, glad to have the matter fully and completely settled, when his gaze wandered involuntarily toward Sophie Gift again. Her eye and cheek were red and swelling, an indication that Mrs. Claus must have decked her harder than he'd realized.

"And could someone please take Ms. Gift to the hospital to have that eye checked out?" he asked the room at large.

"I will, Mr. Lauderdale," the blond elf volunteered. She turned to her companion with a smile. "I have something I need to warn her about."

Sophie Gift looked as confused by the announcement as Mitchell felt, but she said nothing to question it. And neither did he. There were a million other things that needed his attention more.

"Good," he told the other woman instead. Then he turned back to Ms. Gift, reaching automatically into his jacket pocket for one of his business cards. "Call me and let me know how you are," he added as he scribbled an additional phone number on the back. "If you can't reach me here at the store, try me at home." He extended the card toward her. "That's the number I wrote on the back. But do call me. I want to know that you're all right."

Which was true, he realized. He did want to know that she was all right. And not because he feared a lawsuit against the store, either. He genuinely didn't want to see this woman—this woman he scarcely knew—hurting. It made no sense, but there it was anyway. And why on earth had he given her his home phone number? That had been entirely unprecedented. He *never* gave his home phone number to store employees. He even made Hazel call his pager if she needed him after regular hours.

"Call me," he ordered her again as he turned to leave.

And without awaiting her reply, he followed the direction in which he'd just sent his assistant. But as he strode purposefully away, he wasn't thinking about the store's productivity or the new, later hours, or the clearance sales, or the fact that tomorrow morning he was going to have to deal with one moody Mrs. Claus, which were all things that should have been first and foremost at the front of his brain.

No, instead Mitchell's thoughts were consumed by a black-haired, very sexy elf with eyes the color of an endless ocean. In fact, so preoccupied was he by the visions dancing in his brain, that he scarcely noticed the scent of peppermint and the jingle of bells that followed in his wake.

Of course. Mitchell Lauderdale. Now *he'd* do nicely. He didn't know why he hadn't thought of the boy immediately. Of course, Mitchell wasn't such a boy anymore. Forty-two years old, and still too busy to have found a nice girl to settle down with. And still far too caught up in the retailer's mentality where Christmas was concerned.

Of course, not all of that had to do with this being the busiest time of the year for Lauderdale's, he knew. There was that small matter of Mitchell's having lost his mother shortly before Christmas thirty-some years ago. Still, three decades was long enough for mourning. Life went on. No one knew that better than he did himself.

He watched the little black-haired elf walk in one direction as Mitchell made his way in the other, each of them glancing unobtrusively over their shoulders at the other as they went. And he couldn't help but smile.

Oh, yes. This Christmas was looking better and better all the time. It might even be the best Christmas he'd had since, oh, say 1944. . . .

THREE

Sophie studied her reflection in her bathroom mirror and decided that all in all, being assaulted by Mrs. Claus could have been a lot worse. True, she had a black eye, but it wasn't so bad that she couldn't hide the bruise—pretty well, anyway—with some creative makeup techniques. Fortunately for her, Annie had worked all the best counters in cosmetics at some point, so she knew foundation and blush better than she knew her own name.

"See?" the other woman said as she stepped away to observe her handiwork. "I told you I could cover it up. Pretty much, at least. You look great. For the most part, anyway." After a moment's consideration, she added, "Hey, if it weren't for the slight shadow of that shiner, you'd look better than I've ever seen you."

Sophie smiled wryly. "Thanks a lot."

"I'm serious. I mean that peaches-and-cream complexion of yours is nice and all that, but you don't want to be the Ivory Girl for the rest of your life, do you?"

Sophie tilted her head to the side and swept her bangs off her forehead, considering her new, cosmetically enhanced appearance. She'd never much bothered with makeup before—she hadn't wanted the hassle. Although it was true that Annie's skill had made the best of her large eyes, sharp cheekbones, and full mouth, she wasn't sure she liked her new face better. It just didn't seem like her own somehow.

"Why not?" she asked. "What's so terrible about being wholesome?"

Annie rolled her eyes, as if praying for patience. "Because anyone in Bedford Falls would tell you that Gloria Grahame had *much* better stories to tell than Donna Reed. Mark my words. Besides," she added with a smile, "you'll want to look your best for the Christmas party next week, won't you?"

"Oh, no," Sophie groaned. She'd forgotten all about Lauderdale's Christmas party.

Tallying quickly in her head, she realized she had less than a week to buy a five-dollar gag gift for the gift exchange, and to prepare an appetizer for the pot luck, and to get rid of her black eye. She wasn't sure which bothered her most. The shiner, she realized suddenly, was actually the least of her worries. She had neither the time, nor the desire, to shop or cook. Which was very strange, because in Christmases past, she'd loved doing both.

This year, however, she was having a whole lot of trouble getting into any of it. By the time she finished her shifts at Lauderdale's, the last thing she wanted to do was shop. And cooking for strangers—which, except for Annie, was essentially what her coworkers were—was only marginally more fun than cooking for just herself.

"Don't worry—by then the bruise will barely be visible," Annie said, reading only part of Sophie's thoughts. "Whatever's left, I'll come over and fix you up. No one will even notice."

Oh, well, Sophie thought. It was one less thing to worry about, anyway. "Promise?" she asked.

"I promise."

She was about to comment further, but the ringing of the phone prevented her from voicing anything she might have wanted to say. She raced from the bathroom to answer it with a breathless hello, only to have her throat—and her brain—dry up completely at the sound of the voice that filtered from the other end of the line.

"You were supposed to call me."

Mitchell Lauderdale's softly uttered admonition sounded thunderous somehow, making Sophie's heart and breath skid to a halt as quickly as her words and thought processes had. She had been mortified by the scene that had transpired earlier in the day, and that mortification was only compounded by having to replay the whole thing in her brain once again.

There was nothing more embarrassing than looking up to find a gorgeous man sneaking a peek down your shirt, she recalled as the heat of a blush rushed from her heart to her head. Except maybe the further realization that the gorgeous man in question was your employer. And there was nothing more humiliating than being so flustered and bedazzled by the guy that you actually asked him for money. Except maybe doing it while you were dressed in an elf suit.

Sophie lifted her free hand to cover her eyes, as if in doing so, she could block out the episode once and for all. Unfortunately, she figured it was going to be a long time before she forgot about the way Mitchell Lauderdale's chocolate brown eyes had glazed over and his cheeks had turned pink when she caught him copping a look down her elf suit.

"Mr., um . . . Mr., uh . . . Mr. Lauderdale," she sputtered, her embarrassment heating up all over again when she realized she couldn't even say his name. Her voice seemed to have adopted a huskiness she'd never heard in it before, and her entire body began to tingle. "How . . . how are you, sir?"

"Don't 'sir' me," he told her. "You were supposed to call me from the hospital and let me know you were all right."

"I . . . oh, yeah," she stammered further. "I forgot."

Actually, she hadn't forgotten at all. She just hadn't wanted to bring any more attention to herself from the boss than she had already. It was bad enough that he'd seen her sprawled on all fours at his feet—not the most professional posture a person could project. Though, now that she thought about it, there were probably a lot of bosses out there who'd like to see their employees in such a position. At any rate, she wasn't about to call the man on the phone and remind him of her own unwilling prostration.

"I'm sorry, Mr. Lauderdale," she apologized. "But I just got back from the hospital a little while ago and I hadn't had dinner yet and I really needed to get out of my elf suit and—"

"Well?" he interrupted her.

She blinked, bemused, but grateful to him for cutting her off in mid-blather. "Well what?"

She heard him sigh, an exasperated sound. "Are you going to live or aren't you?"

She nodded, then realized belatedly that he couldn't see the gesture. "Yes. I'm going to live."

"How's the shiner?"

She lifted a hand to the tender skin around her eye and pressed gently, then winced a bit at the action. "It's sore, but it's just bruised. No permanent damage."

"Good. Send the hospital bill directly to the store. If workman's comp doesn't cover it, Lauderdale's will."

"Thanks."

"No, thank *you*," he countered. "You can't imagine how helpful you were."

Oh, sure, Sophie thought dryly, helpful in giving a bunch of kids a Christmas they were sure to remember for the rest of their lives. She'd wager more than one parent was having some trouble explaining the scene to his or her offspring this evening. *Well, you see, Johnny, all of Santa's elves are trained Ninjas, because you just never know when you'll need that kind of thing. And you're absolutely right—Mrs. Claus may very well have been an evil agent sent by Mr. Sinister to ruin Christmas. . . .*

But to Mitchell Lauderdale, she simply replied, "All in the line of duty."

He said nothing after that, and the silence between them drew out until it began to grow uncomfortable. Somehow, she felt as if he wanted to say something more to her, but for the life of her, she couldn't imagine why, or what that something might be. So she switched the receiver to her other ear and said, "Well, if there's nothing else . . . ?"

"No," he answered hastily. "No, nothing else. Will you

be able to work your usual shift tomorrow?''

''I'll be there.''

''Good. I'll see you then.''

Not if I see you first, she thought.

Sophie released a slow sigh as she hung up the phone, then turned to find that Annie, too, had wandered into the living room—which was basically what the entire apartment was—and now sat perched on the edge of Sophie's hide-a-bed couch, eyeing her with much speculation.

''Was that . . . Mitchell?'' the other woman asked with a wiggle of her eyebrows, her voice turning sing-songy when she spoke the name of their boss.

''No,'' Sophie told her. ''It was Mr. Lauderdale.''

''Same thing,'' Annie said.

''Not quite,'' Sophie countered.

But the other woman only arched an eyebrow doubtfully and slid from the arm of the sofa to slouch comfortably in the corner of the cushion. ''Obviously, you haven't heard the rest of the story about Mr. Krist yet,'' she said. ''And you don't know about the other things he's been responsible for over the years.''

Sophie narrowed her eyes. ''What other things? In employee training, they only told us about Mr. Krist's holiday spirit thing.''

''Yeah, but that's just because they have an unwritten rule about Lauderdale employees dating other Lauderdale employees. And they'd *really* frown on what's going on between you and Mitchell.''

Sophie shook her head at her friend and wondered why her stomach was suddenly feeling really hot. ''Annie, what are you talking about? I'm not dating *anyone* right now, least of all a Lauderdale employee, and *really* least of all Mitchell—I mean, Mr. Lauderdale.'' She remembered then her friend's cryptic announcement earlier that day. ''Does this have anything to do with what you said at the store this afternoon? That thing about needing to warn me about something?''

Annie's blue eyes fairly twinkled, rivaling the blinky lights on the itty-bitty Christmas tree that sat atop Sophie's kitchen table. "That Mr. Krist is *such* a romantic soul."

"Annie . . ." Sophie tried again.

"Okay, okay. What any Lauderdale's employee in the know will tell you—and what any Lauderdale family member will staunchly deny—is that Mr. Krist *loves* to play matchmaker with people who work for the store."

"Oh, Annie, you can't be serious."

"Of course I'm serious. When Mr. Krist died on Christmas Eve, he was planning on seeing his favorite granddaughter married the next day."

"Oh," Sophie said softly. "Oh, that's so sad."

Annie nodded. "Obviously, his granddaughter canceled the wedding. And evidently, she was so grief-stricken at losing her grandfather, that she wound up alienating her fiancé. The guy ended up breaking off with her, and in the long run, he married someone else instead."

"Oh, Annie. That's terrible. What a jerk."

The other woman nodded. "That's why Mr. Krist plays matchmaker. I think he feels responsible for his granddaughter's losing the man she loved. So he brings people together for the holidays. Just in time for, oh, say . . . a Christmas Day wedding."

"Oh, now you're just being silly," Sophie said. "I mean, even if something was going on between me and Mitchell— I mean, Mr. Lauderdale—which there's *not*," she was quick to add. "I don't think I'd be ready to marry the guy in two weeks' time."

Annie spread her arms wide. "All I know is every year, starting in 1946—the year after Mr. Krist died—someone at Lauderdale's has gotten married on Christmas Day. You can ask around."

"I think I will."

"And it's all because of Mr. Krist. He just loves to bring people together. *Especially,*" the other woman continued, "when the two people involved are badly in need of—" Annie broke off suddenly, punctuating her statement with a mysterious smile.

In spite of her disbelief in this newly added dimension to

Mr. Krist's activities, Sophie wanted to hear the rest of the story. "In need of what?"

Annie assumed an unconcerned expression and reached toward the coffee table for a *Victoria* magazine emblazoned with a dizzying Christmas cover. "Oh, what do you care?" she asked as she began to idly flip through it. "You don't believe in the ghost anyway. Oh, wow, a recipe for wassail," she added in a rush of words, sitting up straighter. "I've been looking all over for one. Can I have this?"

Sophie started to press her coworker for more details about the matchmaking Mr. Krist, but snapped her mouth shut tight. Annie was right. Sophie didn't believe in the ghost, so what was the point? Still, it was kind of a nice story. Even if it *was* just a story.

"You can have it," she said softly.

Though whether the response was to Annie's request for the magazine, or her assertion about Mr. Krist, Sophie wasn't entirely sure. What she *was* sure about was that she was going to have to go out of her way to avoid Mr. Mitchell Lauderdale tomorrow. And every day after that. In fact, it might not be a bad idea to start looking for employment elsewhere. Because she didn't know how she would be able to face him after that embarrassing display today.

Display, she repeated to herself derisively, recalling the way she'd been tumbling out of her elf suit. Yeah, that was a good word for it. She only hoped Mr. Lauderdale could find some humor in the situation. Because she sure couldn't find any herself.

She ran a hand restlessly through her long hair and sighed, her gaze roving toward the foggy dark windows of her apartment. The reflection from her minuscule Christmas tree blinked back at her in myriad distorted colors, and she couldn't help thinking that this Christmas was promising to be no fun at all. And somehow, strangely, she found herself wondering what Mitchell Lauderdale was doing right now.

Fondly recalling Sophie Gift, although a pleasant enough pastime, was getting him absolutely nowhere. In spite of that, Mitchell simply could not stop thinking about her. A week had passed since the Mrs. Claus debacle, and he hadn't seen her a single time. Even when he found himself passing Santa's workshop at some point during his workday— which, oddly enough, seemed to happen a lot more often than it used to—she was never around.

Yet her absence had done nothing to squelch his preoccupation with daydreams and fantasies about her. Even at night, he dreamed of her, and Mitchell *never* dreamed at Christmastime. He was far too busy for that.

And now, as he glanced up from his desk to find that he was already fifteen minutes late for the employee Christmas party, he was still thinking about Sophie. Wondering if she'd be at the party. And, inescapably, wondering, too, if she'd be wearing her elf suit.

Before he had a chance to ponder that further, the door to his office slammed open into the wall, and Hazel entered, looking as grumpy as ever.

"Here," she said, dropping a perfect cube wrapped in green tissue paper onto Mitchell's desk.

"What's that?" he asked.

"It's your contribution to the gift exchange at the employee Christmas party," she told him. She glanced meaningfully at her watch. "The one that started fifteen minutes ago."

He gazed first at his assistant, then at the gift he had asked her to go out and buy for him, because he hadn't had time to do it himself. "What is it?" he asked, not sure he wanted her to answer.

"That's for me to know and you to find out," she told him before turning her back on him. "Can I go now?"

The question was simply a formality, as Hazel strode carelessly out the door and slammed it shut behind her. Mitchell shook his head as he watched her go, making it through almost an entire minute without thinking about Sophie Gift.

He dropped his head into his hands and sighed. He hadn't been this besotted by a female since the second grade. Helplessly, he rose from his desk and shuffled to the tiny bathroom adjacent to his office where he started . . . oh, God, no—not that . . . primping. He straightened his wine-colored necktie, buttoned up his double-breasted charcoal suit jacket, combed his hair. And even as he told himself he was an idiot for doing so, he reached for one of the numerous men's fragrance samples that always seemed to litter his office.

Thrust, it was called, its name stamped on the little glass tube in letters that he supposed were meant to resemble steel I-beams. Could he honestly wear such a thing with a straight face? Especially since he *never* wore men's fragrances?

He popped the plastic cork and lifted the tube to his nose for an idle sniff. Not bad, he thought. Kind of nice, really, in a spicy, if somewhat sissy boy, kind of way. Still, if the skyrocketing sales at the men's fragrances counter were any indication, women must love this kind of thing. Closing his eyes, he spilled the entire contents of the container into his palm and slapped his hands against his cheeks.

Wrong move, he realized immediately. Evidently, they were making these things differently than they had in his father's day. He remembered his old man splashing on Aqua Velva as if it had streamed from the faucet. This stuff . . .

Mitchell's eyes began to water and his nose began to burn. This stuff clearly wasn't Aqua Velva.

He filled the sink, reached for a bar of soap and eyed the clock again. He was going to be a bit later than he'd anticipated for the party. He just hoped that party didn't end after he arrived smelling like he'd just fallen off the Chanel truck. And he hoped, too, that nobody struck a match while he was there.

Now he'd done it. With him smelling the way he did, the little elf wasn't going to come anywhere near Mitchell. Why did men these days insist on wearing perfume? What was wrong with Old Spice or Bay Rum, something easily found at the five-and-dime, something that lasted you years before your granddaughter gave you another bottle for Christmas?

He shook his head as he watched Mitchell wash his face for the third time. This was going to be tricky. The little elf was already upstairs in the restaurant, and the gift exchange would be starting any time now. How was a ghost supposed to get anything done around here when people were so blasted uncooperative?

Inhaling deeply, he blew open Mitchell's office door hard enough to make it bang against the wall on the other side. When he saw Mitchell turn quickly at the sound, he exhaled again and knocked the gift from the boy's desk. He watched impatiently as Mitchell grumbled and wiped his face with a towel, combed his hair, straightened his tie, smoothed a hand over his jacket, glanced up at the clock, straightened his tie once more, lifted the comb to his hair *again* . . .

With another hearty puff, he rattled the door one more time, and finally, finally, Mitchell raced toward the fallen gift. He scooped it up, finger combed his hair again, jerked at the knot in his tie, and headed out the door.

About time. If there was going to be a Christmas Day wedding this year—and there *would* be a Christmas Day wedding this year, because he hadn't missed one since 1946—then he didn't have much time. He blew the office door shut behind Mitchell, bumping the boy's backside as he did. Which was just as well. The kid needed a swift kick to set him straight. But that was about to change. Mitchell Lauderdale was going to get into the spirit of things whether he liked it or not.

And he couldn't wait to see the boy's face when he got a load of the little elf wearing something besides her elf suit. . . .

 FOUR

"Looking for someone?"

Sophie spun around at the question to find Annie gazing at her with more than a little interest. "No," she lied. "Just checking to see how the shrimp puffs are going over."

Annie smiled knowingly. "They're a hit. But don't worry. There are still enough left for Mitchell to come in and sink his teeth into one and demand out loud, 'My God— who made these incredible shrimp puffs? Bring me that woman, and I shall make her my wife.' "

Sophie frowned. "Gee, I hope not."

"Why not? Because you don't want to draw any attention to the growing attraction the two of you have for each other?"

"No, because I got the shrimp puffs at the Jewel deli, and I was hoping to foist them off as homemade." Then the import of Annie's statement hit her, and Sophie frowned again. "And Mitchell—Mr. Lauderdale—and I do *not* have an attraction for each other."

Her friend only smiled more broadly and said, "Hah."

Sophie shook her head at Annie and scanned the room again. The Fifth Floor Café was beautifully decorated for the holidays. Wide gold and silver ribbons and twinkling white lights decorated all the topiary trees, and a huge silver

wreath dotted with gold balls hung above the cash register.
There were shiny streamers cascading from the center chandelier, big silver and gold bows tying back the window
drapes, and a gleaming foil Christmas tree near the entrance.
But there was no Mitchell Lauderdale anywhere in sight.

Okay, so maybe she *had* noticed that Mitchell—Mr. Lauderdale, she corrected herself—hadn't made an appearance
yet. So what? It was only because she wanted to make sure
she stayed out of his way, that was all. Hey, she wouldn't
mind if he blew off the party entirely.

Of course, she knew he wouldn't. As the soon-to-be head
of the store, it would be bad for employee relations. Jacob
Lauderdale was already here, Sophie noted, her gaze lingering on the tall, white-haired man who was laughing as
he ladled up generous servings of bourbon-spiked punch. So
naturally it was safe to assume his son and heir would also
show up. Eventually.

"There he is."

Sophie heard Annie's announcement and cursed herself
for spinning so quickly around to see where her friend was
looking. She saw Mitchell—Mr. Lauderdale—enter the café
slowly, looking a bit self-conscious for some reason, but no
less handsome than he ever did. He hastily tossed a gift onto
the table for the gift exchange, then went to greet his father.
The elder Lauderdale smiled warmly until his son was
within arm's reach, then took a step backward. Gingerly, the
men shook hands and fell into conversation that Sophie was
too far away to hear.

"He looks awfully yummy," Annie said near her ear.

"He's okay," Sophie agreed, striving for a nonchalance
she didn't feel.

What an understatement. In his beautifully tailored suit
and white dress shirt, with his confident demeanor and dark
good looks, he could have stepped right out of the pages of
GQ. And although he carried himself with the bearing of an
executive, she recalled something a bit untamed and rebellious in his bittersweet chocolate eyes. It was something that
kept him on the wrong side of conservative, something that
indicated clearly that he may be a businessman by profes-

sion, but he was by no means businesslike in other, more personal, areas of his life.

And suddenly, the idea of getting up close and personal with Mitchell—*Mr. Lauderdale*, she reminded herself brutally—sprang first and foremost into her mind.

As if he'd read her thoughts, he jerked his head up to look around, and fixed his gaze immediately on hers. Sophie swallowed hard, helpless to look away, and watched as he began a slow approach toward her. Every time he neared someone, that person immediately glanced up and moved well out of his way, gazing after him with a wide-eyed expression Sophie could only assume was inspired by awe. After all, he was pretty awesome.

"Gotta go," she heard Annie whisper from behind her. "I promised Russell I'd help him pass out gifts from the gift exchange. See ya."

It took a moment for the announcement to register, and when it did, Sophie nearly panicked. "Annie—" she began to object, spinning around.

But the other woman was already halfway across the room before Sophie realized her intention. She kept her back turned to Mitchell—Mr. Lauderdale—and hoped like crazy that she'd only imagined the way he'd been focusing on her. Surely he must have actually been crossing the room to speak to someone else. But he never passed by her. Slowly, experimentally, she turned her head to look over her shoulder. And she saw him. About five feet away. Standing still. Staring right at her.

"Hello," he said, his voice quiet in the din of the surrounding crowd, yet reaching her nonetheless.

When she realized he was indeed speaking to her, she turned to face him fully. "Uh, hi."

He smiled, seeming buoyed by her greeting. "I almost didn't recognize you without your elf suit and the jingle bells on your boots."

Sophie smiled back, ducking her head down toward her wine-colored velvet cocktail dress, sheer black stockings, and black pumps—quite a difference from her usual attire. Thank goodness. The dress had long sleeves, and the hem dipped down below her knees. But when she'd tried it on, she'd almost skimmed it right back off again to return it to its hanger. In spite of its modesty, it fit rather snugly and seemed more revealing than it actually was.

But as she'd glimpsed her reflection in the fitting room mirror, she'd fallen in love with the dress. *And* a full one-third had been slashed off the original price, *and* it had been on a clearance rack marked, "Take an additional 30% off!" *And* with her Lauderdale's twenty-percent discount, she'd been able to buy it for almost nothing.

And when she had, she'd been hoping that Mitchell—Mr. Lauderdale . . . oh, what the hell . . . Mitchell—would see her wearing it.

"This old thing?" she asked, waving her hand airily as she looked up at him again. "It's nothing." His smile changed at her statement, to one that made something warm and gooey smoosh through her midsection.

"Oh, I wouldn't say that," he told her. He gave her a shameless once-over—which she had to admit, she'd set herself up for—then met her gaze again. "No, that dress is . . ." He sighed a little wistfully, a sound that actually curled her toes. "It's definitely something."

He took a few more steps toward her, and when he did, Sophie was nearly overcome by fumes. The smell wasn't *quite* as strong as, say, maybe nerve gas or the neutron bomb might be, but it was definitely almost as debilitating. Instinctively, she covered her nose with her hand and squeezed her eyes shut.

"That bad, huh?"

She opened her eyes and forced herself to drop her hand to her side, then breathed as shallowly as she could. But still the sharp aroma assailed her. "Oh, no," she lied in a choked voice. "Not at all. Just, um, a little, uh . . . unexpected."

He didn't look convinced. "You're sure?"

"Mm-hm." She cleared her throat against the dry, painful sensation clawing at it, then dabbed a bit at her eyes. "I'm sure. What's it called?" She hoped she only imagined the way her voice seemed to be coming out all squeaky.

He eyed her sheepishly. "It's called, um . . . Thruh . . .

uh . . ." He scrubbed a hand anxiously over his jaw, as if trying to wipe the smell away. "Actually, I can't remember what it's called. It was a sample I found in my office."

She nodded and swiped at her nose, she hoped unobtrusively. "Well, whatever it is, it's certainly, uh, memorable."

He nodded, but looked in no way convinced. "I'm sorry," he told her. "I don't usually wear this stuff, and I think I put on too much."

"Oh, no," she lied again as she dabbed once more at her eyes. "It's fine. Really."

He still didn't look like he believed her, so Sophie took a step forward to convince him. Strangely, now that she was getting used to the, ah . . . aroma, it didn't seem quite so strong. Or perhaps it had simply killed off her olfactory senses completely and she'd never be able to smell anything again. Either way, her throat didn't seem to be burning nearly as much when she swallowed. So she took another experimental step forward.

An awkward silence fell over them then, as if each of them wanted to say something, but neither of them quite knew how to proceed. So they only stared at each other without speaking, gazes locked, hands clenched together behind their backs, feet shuffling nervously against the carpet.

Finally, Mitchell cleared his throat and asked, "Did you get my Christmas card?"

Sophie smiled, remembering. Among the meager assortment of cards decorated with Christmas trees and snow scenes and nativities that were Scotch-taped to her refrigerator, one alone stood out. Embossed with a single, slender white lily on the front, the sentiment expressed inside said, "Thinking of you in this your time of sorrow, grief and hardship." And where the Bible verses in the other cards celebrated the birth of the Savior, the quotation in Mitchell's had been the one about walking through the valley in the shadow of death.

She chuckled. "Yes, I got it. Only a retailer would send out sympathy cards at Christmastime."

Mitchell laughed, too. "It's kind of a family tradition. Naturally, we only send those cards to people in the business. People who understand what the holiday is *really* all about.''

Sophie nodded. "Naturally," she agreed dryly.

Her memories of past Christmases, of the happiness and celebration and reunion she used to associate with the holiday, were fading fast. Maybe Mitchell was right. Maybe by now, in the late twentieth century, Christmas really had become nothing more than a necessity to maintain the Gross National Product. Certainly the gaggles of shoppers who assaulted Lauderdale's every day had little grasp of the festivity one normally associated with the holiday. Most of them were grabby, demanding, whiny, and resentful. Very few took the time to wish anyone a happy holiday, and none of them seemed in any way festive.

Christmas, apparently, was now less about comfort and joy, and more about discounts and toys. The only peace on earth she'd noticed lately was the few seconds of silence that inevitably fell over the store following the hourly announcements of "Attention, shoppers!"

Sophie sighed. Oh, well. At least shopping brought with it some sense of community, however dubious.

"It was nice of you to think of me," she told Mitchell genuinely. Then, before she realized how frankly she was speaking, she heard herself add, "A lot of my friends seem to have forgotten about me this year."

She cursed the slip and hoped he didn't pick up on her comment. But he took another step toward her, bringing him within hand-holding distance, and gazed down at her solemnly.

"Why would your friends forget about you?" he asked softly, clearly surprised, as if he couldn't believe such an oversight.

She shrugged a little self-consciously. "I, uh . . ." She inhaled a deep breath. Might as well just spit it out. "This time last year, I was kind of . . . married."

His eyebrows shot up at her announcement. "And this time this year?" he asked.

"I, uh . . . I'm not married," she told him. "My husband . . .

ex-husband," she quickly corrected herself, "and I divorced last February."

For some reason, he smiled at that, though Sophie herself could find nothing at all worth smiling about in her condition. But all he said was, "I see."

Right, she thought. He saw. Sure, he did. Could he see the loneliness she felt every time she entered her vacant, undecorated apartment, when before she had celebrated with Evan's extended family in a huge house decorated from floor to ceiling throughout? Could he see the sadness she experienced every time she passed by the tiny plastic tree on her kitchen table and noted the bare places beneath, where once she had enjoyed the sight of a ten-foot blue spruce in the family room towering over dozens of expensive gifts? Could he see the flat taste of store-bought Christmas cookies she'd splurged on, where before she had spent days on end in her sweet-smelling kitchen baking stöllen and cookies for everyone from the mail carrier to the family accounting firm?

Most of all, could Mitchell Lauderdale see the aching emptiness inside Sophie where once had been a vast, endless well of holiday cheer? Of course not. No one could understand how this Christmas was affecting her. Dammit, she had always loved Christmas *so much*, she remembered as an almost overwhelming melancholy settled over her. And from now on, all December twenty-fifth was going to be was a day to sleep late during a month of working longer hours than usual.

"And evidently," she added, hoping she didn't sound as angry as she felt, "when my husband divorced me, he took all our friends with him. Not only have I not received any Christmas cards from them, I haven't received any invitations, either. I guess everyone thinks it would be too awkward."

Like it wasn't going to be awkward when her ex-husband showed up at his friends' homes with a nineteen-year-old who was seven months pregnant in tow, Sophie thought further. And he was actually *proud* of the fact.

"You ask me," Mitchell said, "your absence is going to be their loss, not yours."

She smiled, feeling any anger or bitterness that had been threatening suddenly dissolve. Well, since he put it *that* way . . .

"Thanks," she mumbled, feeling that odd awkwardness settle over them again.

They were spared a prolonged silence this time by the appearance at the café's entrance of a jolly, white-bearded old figure dressed in red velvet. Russell, Sophie thought with a smile. Probably not the most sober Santa Claus in Lauderdale's history, but he would have given old Louis Krist himself a run for the money in the Christmas spirit department. The jingle bells affixed to his belt and decorating the fur trim of his cap jangled merrily with every step he took, and oddly enough, he seemed not to have been imbibing at all tonight.

"Russell!" the entire population of the café chorused in greeting at his arrival.

"Ho, ho, ho!" Russ sang out happily in response.

Sophie couldn't help but chuckle. "Looks like ol' Russ is in a good mood tonight. And he doesn't even seem to have been dipping into his flask."

Mitchell shook his head. "You know, I don't begrudge a man a drink during times of stress, but I really wish Russell would refrain on store property. He just better not let me catch him at it."

Sophie lifted a shoulder, unconcerned. "He doesn't seem to overindulge. Certainly none of the children or parents has commented. And I've never seen him drunk. Just . . . nipping."

Mitchell sighed. " 'Tis the season, I guess."

Russ strode genially through the crowd, playing his role to the hilt, asking if everyone had been a good girl or boy this year. Naturally, everyone assured the old man that she or he had been the picture of perfect behavior all year long, and then promptly demanded a reward for it. Russell scooped gifts off of the table laden with such booty and distributed them freely to everyone he encountered.

He was running low on presents when he finally made his way to Mitchell and Sophie, where he considered each of them with a secretive little smile and eyes that positively twinkled. Sophie shook her head. She'd never seen the old guy looking so spry.

"And how about you, son?" Russ asked Mitchell with a shake of his red mitten and a jingle of his belt. "What have *you* done this year that would make Santa think twice about filling your stocking with coal?"

Mitchell chuckled. "I've brought the store's sales up thirteen percent," he responded proudly. "And I've cut costs by almost nine percent." Rocking smugly back on his heels, he added, "*And* I've implemented an incentive program that should boost productivity even more."

Russ shook his head ruefully. "No, son. I meant what good *deeds* have you done? To improve life for other people? For yourself?"

Mitchell's smile fell. "Oh. Um . . . well . . ."

Russ nodded, threw out a quick, "Well, you just think on that for a minute," and then turned to Sophie. "And how about you, young lady? Have you been a good girl?"

Sophie tried to nod, but knew in all fairness that to do so would be telling a lie—to Santa Claus, no less. Because as hard as she tried, she couldn't think of a single reason why St. Nick should reward her this year. She had a crummy excuse for a Christmas tree sitting on her kitchen table, she hadn't had time to buy gifts for a soul—not that she really had anyone to buy for, anyway—she hadn't sung a single carol, hadn't baked one solitary cookie, couldn't even recall wishing a happy holiday to anyone outside the store—and she'd only offered up *those* because her job description required her to do so.

Nope, she wasn't worthy of even a broken candy cane this year. So all she said to Russ was, "Sorry, Santa, but no. I haven't been a very good girl this year."

He eyed her thoughtfully. "Aren't you the one who puts a dollar in the bell-ringer's kettle every blasted time you pass by one?" he asked. "So often, it's become an automatic reflex you don't even think about?"

She gazed back at him, stunned, and realized that what he said was true. "I guess so. But—"

"And haven't you been putting food and warm water out on your fire escape everyday for a stray cat that's been too wary to come inside, in spite of your cajoling?"

She nodded, wondering how on earth he could have known about that. "Well, yeah, but who wouldn't do something like—"

"Then you deserve a present," Russ cut her off. "Here you go." And without further ado, he stuffed a small box wrapped in bright red foil into her hand.

"And as for you," he added, turning back to Mitchell, "here's something to help jog your memory."

He withdrew another small box from his coat pocket, took Mitchell's hand in his, and deposited the little cube wrapped in green paper into the other man's palm. Mitchell eyed it warily, then returned his gaze to Russ's.

"Merry Christmas, you two," the department store Santa told them. Then he spun back around and addressed the room at large. "Happy Christmas to all!" he shouted. "And to all, a good night!" And with that, amid a jingle of bells and the fragrance of peppermint, the jolly old soul departed.

Sophie turned to Mitchell, who still stared down at the box in his hand as if he couldn't quite remember how it had come to be sitting there. Then she glanced down at the one in her own. "Well," she said, feeling oddly bemused for some reason, "that was nice of him."

Mitchell nodded, but he, too, seemed more than a little perplexed by what had just happened. "Should we open them now, or wait until Christmas?"

She glanced around. "Looks like everyone else is opening theirs."

She started to tear the shiny red paper, then felt a hand on her shoulder. When she turned, she found Annie standing behind her, out of breath and clearly worried.

"It's Russ," the other woman gasped. "You've got to help me. He's passed out cold in the locker room, and I can't get him up to hand out the presents from the gift exchange like he's supposed to."

Sophie turned to Mitchell again, who looked as confused as she felt. Then she looked back at Annie. "What are you talking about? Russ was just in here handing out the gifts."

Annie seemed to notice for the first time that everyone else in the room was in some stage of opening a package. She narrowed her eyes and shook her head. "But that's impossible. I've been trying to bring him around for the last fifteen minutes. The man absolutely *reeks*." She glanced lightly at Mitchell. "Not like *you* do," she said gingerly, "but still . . ." When Mitchell made a face at her, she turned quickly back to Sophie. "You've got to come help me."

"But he was just here," Sophie insisted.

"I'm telling you, it couldn't have been Russell. Because he's out cold."

"Then who . . . ?" Her voice trailed off as her gaze wandered toward the door through which Santa Claus—whoever he'd been—had exited. Because frankly, she was none too sure she really wanted an answer to her question.

There. That ought to get their attention. He watched as Mitchell and the little elf eyed each other in utter confusion, and then he smiled. All the best romances began with utter confusion, he thought. Why Mrs. Krist had caused him no end of puzzlement for the first few years of their marriage.

Still, those two young people weren't moving things along as quickly as he had hoped they would. Christmas Day was scarcely a week away, and they hadn't even managed their first kiss yet. He shook his head ruefully. And these nineties people thought they were just *so* progressive.

He chuckled, remembering the way wartime anxiety had made more than a few relationships move along at a more rapid pace than had been customary at that time. Maybe that was what these two needed, he thought. Not war, of course, but some other situation that would force them to reevaluate their perspectives and priorities. Something that would make them realize what was really important in life. Something that would make them see what the true meaning of Christmas—of life itself—really was.

And then he smiled. Christmas Eve was just around the

corner, he remembered. Only eight shopping days left. He had plenty to do if he wanted his plan to work properly. When he saw that Mitchell and the little elf were at least speaking, he nodded his approval and eased himself out of the café.

Forget Three Kings Day, he thought as he went. Christmas Eve was a much better time for an epiphany. . . .

FIVE

Sophie dropped her gaze to the little gift in her hand, and tucked her thumb under the paper at one end. Slowly, she peeled the red foil away, until she revealed a black velvet jeweler's box beneath. Almost afraid to open it, she hesitated before thumbing back the top. And when she did, she caught her breath at what lay nestled in white tissue paper inside.

"Oh, my God," she whispered.

"What is it?" her two companions chorused.

She lifted the diamond ring from its bed and held it up toward the chandelier. A explosion of light burst forth in a dozen shades of blue and copper, nearly blinding her. "I can't possibly accept this," she said firmly.

"Where did it come from?" Annie asked amazed.

"I have no idea. It's beautiful, but . . ." She expelled a sound of disbelief. "It's not mine."

Mitchell reached for it, and Sophie gladly released it to his care. He studied it in the light for a moment, then his eyebrows arrowed down in concern. "It belonged to my mother," he said softly.

Sophie gasped at his revelation. "*What?*"

"It was her engagement ring. I was only about eight years old when she lost it. She took it off while she was doing inventory in the store, then forgot where she put it down. It never turned up.'' His gaze met Sophie's. ''Until now.''

She didn't know what to say. ''Then, by all means, give it back to her.''

He smiled sadly. ''I wish I could. She died when I was ten years old.''

''Oh, I'm so sorry,'' Sophie said. ''I didn't know.'' When he didn't acknowledge her statement, she settled her hand gingerly on his arm. ''You keep it then,'' she told him gently. ''It belongs to your family.''

When he glanced back up at her, his eyes were filled with so much sorrow and so much loneliness, Sophie wanted to cry herself.

''But Santa gave it to you,'' he objected.

''Obviously, he switched our gifts by mistake. Here, I'll take yours.'' More out of nervousness than anything else, she plucked his gift from his hand. ''There, now we're even.''

Mitchell settled his mother's ring over his pinkie, where it stopped halfway down, at his knuckle. Then he turned to Sophie and smiled. But instead of saying a word, he only lifted his other hand to her face, cupping her jaw warmly in his palm. Before she realized what was happening, he bent toward her and touched his lips to her cheek.

Her eyelids fluttered downward as she helplessly tilted her head to the side to facilitate his kiss. And when she did, Mitchell moved, too, taking another step toward her. He skimmed his mouth along her cheek, tracing a warm, gentle path over her skin, until his lips connected with hers. For just the briefest, most exquisite moment, his mouth covered hers, long enough for her to realize that she would never again be able to kiss a man without thinking of Mitchell Lauderdale.

Then he pulled away and murmured a quick ''Thank you.'' Hastily, he added, ''For the ring, I mean.''

''No thanks necessary,'' she assured him breathlessly. ''It belonged to your mother. It should be yours. I'm just glad it turned up after all these years.''

She glanced around nervously, only to find that, thanks

to his kiss, she and Mitchell had become the center of attention in the small café—and that Jacob Lauderdale, the big man himself, seemed to be more interested in the exchange than anyone else. But before she had a chance to comment, Mitchell shifted at her side, and she turned to look at him.

He studied her intently for a moment, as if he wasn't quite sure what to make of her gesture, of the entire episode that had just transpired. Then he dropped his gaze to the other gift nestled in her hand. "Aren't you going to open your present?"

Sophie, too, eyed the little box warily. "I'm not sure I want to."

"It's okay," he told her with a smile. "That's the one I brought. Obviously Santa didn't realize that when he dropped it into my hand." He held up his crooked pinkie, where his mother's engagement ring sparkled. "But I can safely assure you there's nothing like this inside."

Sophie wasn't quite convinced, but she tore the paper off the package anyway. In her hand sat a basic, if small, standard issue, white Lauderdale's gift box. When she removed the top, she found yet another puzzling item nestled in tissue paper. A baseball. An old baseball. A really, old, really beat-up baseball.

She glanced up at Mitchell, who frowned back at her. "That's mine," he said, reaching for the box.

For some reason, Sophie pulled her hand back before he could make contact. "But you got the ring," she objected, wondering why she was making a big deal out of something she couldn't even begin to understand.

"But ... but ... that's my baseball," he told her. "Look—it has Ernie Banks's autograph on it. And if you turn it to the left a little, I bet you'll find the *nks* is smudged, just like I remember it being."

She turned the baseball in its tissue nest and found that he was correct. "Oh, and I guess you're going to tell me you lost *this* somewhere in the store thirty years ago, too, right?"

To her surprise, he nodded. "That's exactly what I'm going to tell you."

"Oh."

She extended the box toward him, and he withdrew the baseball from within, then rolled it back and forth from hand to hand. "I haven't seen this since I was . . ." He inhaled deeply, then smiled as he curved his fingers over the ball, as if to pitch it. "I guess since I was about twelve years old," he finished. "My father took it away from me one day when I brought it to the store, because I accidentally pitched it right into a Baccarat showcase. When he finally went to give it back to me at the end of the day, he couldn't find it." He shook his head and smiled. "I wonder where Hazel found it. And why she didn't tell me right off."

Sophie sighed. "Then of course, you should keep it."

Mitchell continued to palm the ball with much affection, as if he'd forgotten she was there. Then he looked up at her, alarmed. "But if I do that, you wouldn't have a present," he said.

She shrugged. "Santa originally gave it to you," she reminded him. "Obviously, he knew what he was doing, after all."

Mitchell glanced down at the ring on his little finger. "And he meant for you to have this."

She shook her head adamantly. "I couldn't possibly keep that. Don't be silly."

"But—"

He seemed so concerned that she was going to be cheated out of a present from a five-dollar gag gift exchange, she marveled. How very . . . sweet.

This time, without even thinking about what she was doing, Sophie was the one to lift a hand to cup his rough jaw in her palm. "Don't worry about it," she told him. She shrugged philosophically and forced a light chuckle. "It's no big deal. And it fits perfectly with everything else that's gone wrong this Christmas."

He opened his mouth to say something, then snapped it shut again before voicing whatever that something had been. He covered her hand with his for a moment, searched her face with eager eyes, then moved her fingers to his lips for a soft kiss. Then, without a word, he turned his back and made his way toward his father.

She watched him go with a muddle of emotion swelling up from her heart into her head, and wondered what on earth had just happened. Then she turned to Annie, who was watching her with more than a little interest in what had just happened—just like everyone else employed by the store seemed to be.

"Come on," Sophie said, before her friend had a chance to comment. "Let's go see to Russ."

Jacob Lauderdale was eyeing Mitchell warily as he approached the older man. Doubtless his father had witnessed that little kiss he'd given Sophie Gift, just as everyone else standing in the café had done. Instead of looking furious, however, Jacob Lauderdale seemed to be smiling. Sort of. In a way. Then again, the cup of punch he was holding in his hand reeked of bourbon, so it was no wonder the old man was happy. Maybe he hadn't seen him kiss Sophie, after all . . .

"Son, just what the hell do you think you're doing kissing the hired help like that?" his father asked before Mitchell could even mutter a greeting, immediately dashing his hopes.

"I wasn't kissing her, Dad," he defended himself.

"You were either kissing her," Jacob stated, "or you were tasting her. Either way, it's against store policy. Big time."

"I was saying thank you," Mitchell told him sheepishly.

"I hate to think for what."

Mitchell held up his hand, displaying the diamond ring on his pinkie. "For this," he said.

Immediately, his father's expression softened. Jacob reached for the ring, then, after a moment's hesitation, tugged it from his son's finger. "This is the ring I gave to Cathy," he said softly.

Mitchell nodded. "The one she lost about thirty-five years ago."

His father's eyes turned dreamy as he spun the ring by the diamond, looking nearly hypnotized by the play of light in the gemstone. "Even after all this time, sometimes I can hardly believe she's gone."

Mitchell said nothing, but knew exactly what his father meant. Even after the passage of three decades, there were days when he could recall his mother's laughter, her scent, her smile, as if he had seen her only hours before.

"What was that young woman doing with this?" Jacob asked him, his attention still focused on the ring.

Mitchell smiled sadly. "Santa gave it to her."

Jacob Lauderdale glanced up at his son, his eyes narrowed in puzzlement. "Russ gave this to her?"

Mitchell nodded.

"Where did *he* get it?"

"I have no idea. Maybe the same place Hazel found this." He held up the baseball for his father's inspection.

Once again, Jacob smiled wistfully. "Ernie Banks," he said. "You remember that game, Mitch?"

"The first pro game you took me to see." Mitchell smiled, too, a little more happily this time. "You remember the day you took that ball away from me?"

His father chuckled. "Hey, you took out almost two thousand dollars worth of crystal that day. You're lucky I didn't blister your behind. Hazel found this?"

Mitchell nodded.

"I wonder where." Jacob glanced up and scanned the crowd, then shouted out, "Hazel! Come over here!" when he located the object of his search.

Mitchell looked over in time to see his white-haired assistant glare at both of them. Then she took her time finishing the conversation she was having with another employee, strode off toward the ladies' room, exited about five minutes later, wandered over to the buffet to fill a plate, stopped for a cup of punch, then finally, finally, made her way to where Mitchell and his father were waiting.

"What?" she grumbled as she bit into a shrimp puff.

"Where did you find Mitch's baseball?" Jacob asked her. She ran the tip of her tongue over her upper teeth, lifted a hand to pick at a bit of spinach lodged there, then, once she had the little green sucker free, looked at Mitchell. "I didn't find your baseball."

"Then what do you call this?" he asked, holding the trophy aloft.

She eyed it carefully. "Well, now, I know this may come as a surprise to you, but where I come from, we call that particular item a baseball."

Mitchell refrained from rolling his eyes heavenward. "It was in the box you wrapped for me to bring for the gift exchange."

Hazel bit into another shrimp puff. "No, it wasn't," she denied around a mouthful of food. "Boy, have you tried these shrimp puffs? You need to find a woman who can cook like this, Mitchie."

He hated it when Hazel called him *Mitchie*. Of course, she knew that, which was why he never bothered to correct her. "I'm telling you," he insisted, "this was what was in the box you set on my desk for the exchange."

She shook her head. "And I'm telling you it wasn't. You sent me out to buy a gift for you, right?"

Mitchell nodded.

"Because you were too friggin' busy to do it yourself, right?"

He sighed in exasperation, but nodded again.

"Like *I* don't have better things to do with *my* time than shop for *you*."

"Hazel, please . . ."

Oddly enough, she relented. "The box I put on your desk had a gift certificate in it—dinner for two at Eli's."

Mitchell's eyebrows arched in surprise. "But, Hazel, that's so . . . so nice. So thoughtful." The gist of her comment finally registered. "So *expensive*. Hazel, how did you pay for it?"

"I put it on your company credit card. The way you Lauderdales skimp on the Christmas bonuses, I figured whoever got the gift could use something nice." She finished off the shrimp puff and grinned smugly. "Guess *you* won't be sending *me* out to do *your* Christmas shopping anymore, will you, Mitchie?''

She didn't wait for an answer, just spun on her heel and disappeared back into the crowd. When Mitchell turned to look at his father, Jacob was stifling his laughter.

''I should have warned you about that,'' his father said grinning. ''She did the same thing to me the first—and last—time I asked her to shop for the gift exchange for me.''

Mitchell shook his head. ''Then we still don't know where the baseball and the ring came from,'' he said softly.

His father's smile grew broader. ''Sure we do. Santa Claus brought them.''

Mitchell glanced back down at the baseball. For some reason, the explanation made sense.

''Here,'' his father said, extending the ring toward him again. ''Hang onto this. Your mother once told me that when you got engaged, she wanted to give this to you to give to your future wife.'' The older man shrugged as Mitchell took it from his hand. ''I know you're showing signs of remaining single forever, but . . . you never know.''

Without realizing he was even doing it, Mitchell turned back toward the door through which he had seen Sophie Gift disappear some moments ago. And his father's words echoed in his head. *You never know . . .*

''But, Mitch,'' the old man added.

''Hmmm?'' he asked, not turning around.

''Try to refrain from kissing—or tasting—the hourly workers. Think you can do that?''

Instead of responding, he only eyed his father contemplatively, and, without another word, turned to leave the party.

Mitchell looked at the baseball he held in one hand, and the diamond ring he held in the other and squeezed his eyes shut against the pounding in his head. He'd been sitting in his office studying both for nearly an hour, and he was no closer now to understanding where they'd come from than he had been when he'd first seen them cradled in Sophie Gift's hand.

Their sudden appearance after three decades simply defied

explanation. There was no telling where they might have been all that time. And for both of them to show up within minutes of each other, all wrapped up with a bow, gifts from Santa Claus, no less . . .

Naturally, he could only assume that Mr. Krist was responsible. He had even begun to wonder if it hadn't been old Louis himself who'd been handing out gifts at the party tonight. But this was a new dimension to the ghost. He'd never manifested himself in such a human way. Well, except for that once, Mitchell recalled now. But that had been more than thirty years ago. And the situation had been different then.

At other times in the past, whenever Mr. Krist had wanted to make himself known, he had always done so in other, less tangible ways. Knocking things over, pushing people into each other, that kind of thing. And he'd never been responsible for finding lost mementos.

Mitchell shook his head again, and realized he could no longer explain away his headache to the possibility that the overpowering aroma of Thrust had been slowly killing off his brain cells one by one all night. No, there was only one thing that could explain the throbbing in his head right now. Clearly, he was losing his mind.

As if doing so might jar his mental faculties back to normal, he dropped his head to his desk and thumped his blotter lightly with his forehead, over and over again. He was still pounding when his office door was pushed open from the outside, and, too late, he saw Sophie Gift's face peeking around from behind it. Immediately, he stopped using his forehead for a sledgehammer, and met her gaze as levelly as he could, considering the massive amount of embarrassment coursing through him.

"Hello," he said softly.

"Hi," she responded in a voice that told him she was none too sure he was safe to approach. "I knocked, but I guess you didn't hear me."

"It's okay," he assured her, straightening in his chair. "I just, uh . . . I have a headache."

She nodded. "Bashing your head against a blunt object will do that, you know."

He chewed his lip thoughtfully. "Well, then. I guess that would explain it."

She eyed him warily for a moment more, then, seeming to decide he was relatively harmless, took a step that brought her into his office. "I just wanted to give you an update on the Russell situation."

He gingerly placed the baseball and diamond ring on his desk, then tunneled the fingers of both hands through his hair in an effort to smooth it out after having clenched it in his fists for most of the past hour. Then he remembered that he had removed his jacket and tie, had kicked off his shoes, and had unbuttoned his cuffs and the top three buttons of his shirt. So any effort he made now to look halfway managerial was pretty much pointless. And then he realized further that where Sophie Gift was concerned, the last thing he wanted to appear was managerial anyway.

So he simply surrendered to his impulses and rose from his desk, moving to the front to lean back against it. He crossed his arms over his chest, crossed his feet at the ankles and quietly bid Sophie to come inside and close the door behind her.

She did as he asked, but seemed a little nervous about it once she stood there a good five feet away from him. He wanted to reassure her that he had no intention of pouncing on her, then immediately discovered that might not be the truth at all. So he said nothing, only arched an eyebrow in silent encouragement, and waited to hear what she had to say.

"Russell really was out cold," she said. "When Annie and I got back to the locker room, he was stretched out on the floor, snoring loud enough to wake Rip Van Winkle."

Mitchell nodded. Somehow, he'd known she was going to say that.

"Annie called a cab for him," Sophie continued. "Then a couple of the guys from electronics carried him downstairs and made sure he got home all right." She shrugged sheepishly. "I'm not sure he'll feel like working his shift in the morning, though."

Mitchell nodded again, this time with resignation. "I'll try to have one of the part-timers on standby, just in case."

"You, uh . . . you're not going to fire him, are you?" she asked softly. "Because if you do—"

He shook his head. "I'm not going to fire him," he interrupted her. "Like I said. I don't begrudge a man a drink in times of stress. And the two weeks before Christmas are always pretty awful. I couldn't even bring myself to fire Mrs. Claus after her attack on Santa. It just didn't seem right, firing someone this time of year."

Sophie nodded, then began to fumble for the door behind her. "Okay. I just thought you'd want to know about what happened."

When he realized she intended to leave, he quickly straightened and crossed the small office to where she stood. Without thinking, he circled her wrist with gentle fingers, and before he knew what he was doing, he blurted out, "Don't go."

She seemed as surprised to hear his petition as he felt about giving it, but she dropped her hand from the doorknob and waited.

"I just . . ." he began, not sure what had motivated his request. "I thought maybe we could talk." When she still said nothing in response, he added, "About what just happened upstairs."

Seeming resigned, she nodded. "Okay. I guess that's kind of inevitable."

He smiled, reluctantly dropped her wrist, and pulled a chair from the corner to place it in front of his desk. As she sat, he circled the desk and opened the bottom right-hand drawer, then withdrew two paper cups and a bottle of very good, thirty-four-year-old Scotch. "Interested?" he asked her, holding the spirits aloft.

She looked as if she would decline, then smiled. "Yeah, why not? I don't have anyplace I need to be."

He didn't want to dwell on how happy her comment made him feel. Instead, he splashed a couple of fingers of Scotch into each of the cups and handed one to her. "I can go up to the café for some ice, if you want."

She shook her head and sipped, rolling the liquor around in her mouth for a moment before swallowing. "This is fine," she told him after a satisfied sigh.

A Scotch-drinking woman, he marveled. Straight up, at that. Single-malt. Was there no end to this woman's appeal?

He enjoyed a generous taste himself, then asked her, "Who do you think that was tonight, handing out gifts?"

She shrugged, then stretched her legs out before her, crossing them at the ankles. Mitchell tried not to stare. Tried, and failed miserably.

"I couldn't begin to guess," she told him.

"You don't think it was . . . ?"

"Who?"

"Mr. Krist?"

She laughed, but there was a tight, anxious quality to the sound. "Of course not."

"Why not?"

She sipped her Scotch slowly, thoughtfully, as if she were considering the best response. "Because Mr. Krist is just a fabrication. He doesn't really exist."

"You don't believe in him?"

"No."

"Why not?"

She studied him as if she couldn't imagine why he was asking such a question. "Because there's no such thing as ghosts, that's why."

He wasn't convinced. "How can you be so sure?"

"I just am, that's all."

He scooped up the diamond ring and the baseball, one in each hand. Then he stood to move around to the front of his desk, perching himself on the edge. "Then how do you explain the sudden reappearance of these after three decades?"

"I can't," she admitted. "But I certainly don't think they've been in the safekeeping of a dead Santa Claus for that length of time."

He hesitated, wondering how much he should confess of

his past experiences with the ghost. Either she would come around to his way of thinking and life would become rosy for both of them—just like *It's a Wonderful Life*—or she would bolt from his office in a panic, dial 911 from the nearest pay phone, and he'd wind up spending his Christmas in a padded cell, with no other company save some lunatic behind the wire mesh across the way serenading him with carols.

What the hell, he thought, feeling reckless. Either way, it was better than spending Christmas alone.

He enjoyed a fortifying sip of his drink, then fixed his eyes on hers. "Would you change your mind," he asked her carefully, "if I told you that I've seen Mr. Krist myself?"

Oh, now this was getting good.

He settled himself into the chair behind the boy's desk and wished he could pour himself a sip of holiday spirit, too. But alas, there were some things about the afterlife that simply didn't live up to the promise of paradise. Oh, certainly he could spend eternity with his loved ones and never have to worry about losing any of them, and he could always come back to the real world for an occasional visit, whenever he started to feel a bit homesick.

And, too, there was no shortage of interesting conversation where he lived now—he had fascinating discussions with his good friends, Lao Tzu and Thomas Jefferson, every time he encountered them. Nor was there a lack of superior entertainment. He frequently went to the theater to see Sarah Bernhardt and Josephine Baker, and Shakespeare himself had recently penned a new comedy for Halloween that had left him and Mrs. Krist rolling. Even Louise had managed a smile or two.

But there was no thirty-four-year-old Scotch, nothing tangible to satisfy his more physical yearnings. Even his ability to manifest himself physically was limited—he could only do it once a year, and for no more than a few minutes' time. He didn't know why that was, nor could he quite explain how he did it. He only knew that if he wanted badly enough to cross the veil, he could—on a very temporary basis.

Whoever was in charge of the afterlife—something he had yet to find out—had made the rules and regulations eons ago. And simply put, as a citizen therein, he was obligated to obey those rules and regulations, just as he had obeyed the laws of nature and man when he had been a citizen of the physical world.

He sighed and pushed his wistful recollections away, and focused instead on the scene he had set into motion. The two young people were definitely on a roll. Now if they could just keep it going for a little while longer, he might not have to rely on the plan he had devised as a last resort. . . .

 SIX

Sophie eyed Mitchell skeptically. "You've seen Mr. Krist?"

He nodded, fully prepared for her reaction. No one else had ever believed him, either. That didn't make the experience any less real to him. "You don't believe me?"

"Forgive me for speaking bluntly, but . . . no way."

"Well, it's true. I have seen him."

She neither encouraged, nor dissuaded him to continue. So Mitchell made up his mind himself.

"It was about a year after my mother's death," he began. "I was eleven years old. Back then, my parents gave me and my sisters free reign of the store, because they were always working here. We'd come here straight from school, and we used to have the best time."

He paused for a moment, caught up in happy memories. "It was every kid's fantasy—having the run of a department store. And it was every bit as fun as you could ever imagine."

When his gaze fell on Sophie, she was smiling at him, and he knew that she, too, had indulged in such dreams as a child.

"But after my mom died," he continued, dropping his gaze to the floor, "it was never the same."

"What happened to her?" Sophie asked softly.

"She had ovarian cancer. It went undiagnosed for years. By the time they knew she had it, it was only a matter of months before she died."

"I'm so sorry, Mitchell," she said, and somehow the sound of his name on her voice eased his melancholy. "I lost my mom when I was fourteen," she added. "To pneumonia. I sort of understand."

He nodded, but even at her admission, wondered if she could fully appreciate the depth of a young boy's sorrow. "She died three weeks before Christmas," he continued. "Since then, the holiday's been pretty empty for me. People think it's because of what I do for a living, but that's not it at all." He sighed heavily. "They don't realize . . ."

He halted, wondering what had possessed him to reveal so much to her. Then he looked up to find himself lost in those gorgeous green eyes again, and decided maybe it wasn't so puzzling after all. "It was the second Christmas after her death," he went on, "that I saw Mr. Krist. I didn't realize at first that the man I was speaking to was him, but it was."

"What man?"

"A man I initially thought was the guy Lauderdale's had hired to play Santa Claus that year."

"So what happened?"

He drew in a deep sigh, remembering, then expelled it slowly. "I came in before school one morning the week before Christmas, to help stock some shelves. At one point, I was blindsided by memories about my mother, and I ran out of the stockroom so no one would see me cry."

"But someone did see you cry?"

He nodded. "A man dressed like Santa Claus found me huddled behind the throne in the Santa's workshop display, and he offered me a peppermint candy. And while I was unwrapping it, he told me not to worry—that my mom was just fine, and that she knew I missed her, but that she was never far from my side. And he said that she was looking forward to the time when she and I would be together again."

When he met Sophie's gaze after telling her the story, she

was still smiling warmly at him. "Mitchell, your history must have been common knowledge to everyone who worked for the store," she said, her voice quiet and easy. "That man was just trying to reassure a little boy about his mom, that's all. What makes you think it was Mr. Krist?"

He continued to hold her gaze as he told her, "The second I turned away from him—I mean the absolute *split second*—he was gone. And a split second after that, I saw the real department store Santa Claus come walking out of the locker-room, holding his belt and his hat in his hand."

Her eyes widened some, but she offered no other indication that she was surprised by what he'd said.

"And what's really weird," Mitchell went on, "is that after that little chat with Mr. Krist, I was suddenly okay with my mom's death. I still missed her—I still do, for that matter—and I still got sad around this time of year. But that aching void I felt for the first year after she died . . . it disappeared. Seeing Mr. Krist gave me a contentment and a certainty that I would see my mom again someday." He lifted a shoulder and chuckled lightly. "If life went on for Mr. Krist, then it must have gone on for my mom, too, you know?"

She nodded, and he was grateful that she seemed to understand.

"But you still get sad at Christmas," she pointed out. "That doesn't happen to your father. Mr. Lauderdale seems to be in a wonderfully cheery mood."

"My father remarried about fifteen years ago, to a wonderful, wonderful woman," Mitchell told her. "My stepmom is the one who brought him back to life. Me . . ." He shrugged again, but was helpless to stop his gaze from connecting with Sophie's again. "I guess I just never met that kind of woman myself."

Not until recently—not until I met you.

He had no idea what had generated the thought in his head, but once realized, he knew he couldn't deny it. There was something about Sophie Gift that wasn't like other women. Something that spoke to him in a dark, empty place where only an echo of emotion dwelled. He wasn't sure whether it was because they had both experienced such a profound loss early in life, or because they both seemed to share a feeling of emptiness at Christmas this year.

But there was definitely something there. What that something might be, and why it was coming about now, he didn't know. But it was there just the same.

He straightened himself up then, setting his drink on his desk before taking the single step forward that brought him within inches of Sophie. Then he plucked her drink from her hand to settle it next to his own, and entwined her fingers with his. She didn't protest when he pulled her up from her chair. Without hesitation, she stepped into his arms, as if it were the most natural thing in the world for her to do. And when he dipped his head to hers, she pushed herself up on tiptoe to meet him halfway. Mitchell smiled at her. She smiled back.

And then . . . she kissed him.

Her lips on his were warm and wonderful, gentle and generous, coaxing and capable. He took another step forward, bringing her body flush against his, and circled her waist with strong arms. He felt her arms move around his neck, felt her fingers tangling in his hair, felt her palms cup his nape as she pulled him down more fully into her kiss.

And then his feelings turned inward. An already compacted spring deep down in his belly slowly coiled tighter and tighter, until it lurched free in a rush of incandescent heat. He tightened his arms around her waist and pulled her closer still, lifted a hand to score his fingers through the black silk of her hair, and took their kiss to greater intimacy.

When she opened her mouth to a small gasp, he ventured deeper, trailing the tip of his tongue along her lower lip before dipping inside to taste her fully. When she arched against him, he bent her backward over his arm, settled his other hand at her waist, and dragged open-mouthed kisses along her cheek, her jaw, her throat. God, her throat. So soft, so warm, so creamy . . .

He nosed the delicate curve where her neck met her shoulder, brushing soft, butterfly kisses against her luscious skin. She uttered a quiet, almost endless murmur of longing as she dropped her head back even more, and Mitchell took full advantage of her offer.

She went limp in his arms when he returned his mouth to hers, drinking his fill of her, tasting her as deeply as he could. The hand he had curled around her waist grew restless with a desire to venture higher, and before he realized what he was doing, his fingers were tripping lightly over her rib cage. He halted at the lower curve of her breast, cradling the soft swell of flesh with his thumb and forefinger. Then, unable to help himself, he scooted his hand higher, palming the generous mound before molding his hand tightly over her.

When Sophie jerked beneath him, he hesitated, pulling his lips a millimeter from hers. Their respiration reverberated in a rapid rush of air, and her gaze fixed almost dreamily on his. Then she withdrew a hand from his hair and covered his fingers with hers. With a gentle push, she initiated a slow circular motion with both their hands, then lifted her mouth to his again.

Mitchell groaned out loud at her surrender, prepared to plunder and ravish and pillage and capture, and leave the spoils to no one but himself. But as he fastened his mouth to hers again, a quick series of raps at his office door halted him from carrying out his sensuous assault.

Before he and Sophie could spring apart, the door was thrown open wide, and the blond elf burst into the room. She blinked at the scene that greeted her, smiled broadly, then just as quickly frowned grievously. "You'd better come upstairs," she told Mitchell. "The Christmas party's getting a little out of hand."

Oh, and like things weren't getting out of hand right here, he thought. Then he realized he was still holding onto Sophie's breast. Okay, so not everything was quite out of hand, but still ...

"What's wrong?" he asked, skimming his fingers slowly back down to her waist, hoping the other woman hadn't realized just how far things had gone between him and Sophie.

But Annie's smile told him she could see *exactly* what

had been going on here. "It's not that bad," she assured him. "Just, well . . . your father seems to have had a little too much to drink, and he's giving out Christmas bonuses you wouldn't believe. If you don't get up there soon, this whole store is going to belong to Eddie Monaco."

"The guy who changes the lightbulbs?" Mitchell asked.

She nodded. "That's the one."

Mitchell nodded back. "I'll be right there."

When Annie left, he returned his attention to Sophie, who seemed to be looking at everything in the room except him, and with much reluctance, he released her. She moved quickly away from him, went to a lot of trouble straightening her dress and smoothing down her hair, and continued to avoid his gaze.

"I, uh . . ." he began eloquently.

She cleared her throat anxiously, and finally, looked at him. Immediately, her eyes widened in fear, and she dropped her gaze again. "I, uh . . ." she said, just as articulately.

"I better get up there," he told her, pointing at his office door, if not moving toward it.

She nodded quickly, but said nothing.

"I mean . . . my father . . ."

She nodded again, even more hastily. "I understand."

Instead of taking a step toward the door, he took one toward Sophie. When she tried to move away, he wrapped his fingers gently around her wrist. And when she dropped her gaze to the floor in a refusal to look at him, he curled the index finger of his other hand beneath her chin and tipped her head backward, until she had no choice but to meet his gaze.

And when she did, her eyes were filled to brimming with tears. Mitchell shook his head at the realization, unable to understand how on earth she could feel sad about what had just happened between them.

"What?" he asked. "What's wrong?"

She shook her head almost imperceptibly. "I . . . you . . . we . . . it's just that . . ." Her words trailed off before she made any sense.

"What?"

But she said nothing more. A sense of urgency overcame him, and although he knew it had nothing to do with his father's generosity upstairs, Mitchell forced himself to take steps in that direction.

"We'll pick this up where we left off later," he vowed. When she said nothing to agree with him, he quickly added, "Tomorrow. Maybe sooner."

But she only stared at him in silence, and shook her head once more in that slow, hopeless way that made him feel so helpless. Mitchell curled his fingers over the doorknob, knowing he had to leave, yet wanting so desperately to stay.

"Wait for me?" he asked her as he opened the door.

But still she remained silent. And although she hadn't said no, he knew in his heart that when he came back, Sophie would indeed be gone.

She managed to avoid him until Christmas Eve, despite his efforts to see her. But as that last shopping day before Christmas drew closer, the store was thrown into a chaotic pace that prevented Mitchell from even finding his way to the floor where she worked. There were days when he could barely remember his own name, let alone indulge in day-dreams about having Sophie Gift in his arms.

And little by little, he began to wonder if maybe the whole incident hadn't been just that—a dream.

It wasn't until closing time drew near on Christmas Eve, as the entire staff of Lauderdale's seemed to be drawing a collective sigh of relief, that he finally ran into Sophie again. Literally.

He was scanning an inventory list of holiday china that had mysteriously vanished from the stockroom, when he rushed past the elves' break room and ran right over one of the jolly little souls. So preoccupied by the list in his hand was he, however, that a muffled "oof" was the only thing that alerted him to what he had done. Well, that and the fact that he fell hard onto all fours, his ten-page inventory list scattering like oversized snowflakes, descending in a drift of white to his right.

Also to his right, he noted as he scrambled into a sitting position, was Sophie Gift, looking as fresh and dewy as . . . as . . . well . . .

Okay, so anyone who had survived the holiday retail crunch looked anything *but* fresh and dewy, he conceded. She still looked beautiful, as far as Mitchell was concerned, even with her hair spilling half out of her normally neat braid, and what appeared to be a coffee stain covering a good portion of her elf suit. And even having fallen hard onto her fanny with her hands braced behind her, her knees bent before her, and her legs spread wide. For a moment, Mitchell's gaze settled someplace that it really ought not to have settled, and just as he had the first day they'd met, he fought off a blush that threatened.

Sophie, too, seemed to realize the awkwardness of their situation and the inappropriateness of her position—not to mention the fact that, once again, he'd been noticing parts of her that no employer had any business noticing—because she slammed her legs shut so tight, so fast, he fancied he could actually hear her kneecaps clacking together. Then he heard the tinkle of the bells on her little elf boots as they shimmied, and he inhaled the aroma of peppermint that seemed to surround her. And suddenly, he forgot all about that missing china.

''We've got to stop meeting like this,'' he told her with a smile.

She smiled back a little nervously as she drew her knees up toward herself. She wrapped her arms around her legs tightly, as if she were trying to keep them from doing something she didn't want them to do. But she didn't say a word.

''I'm sorry—I didn't see you,'' he apologized. Though how he could have missed her, he had no idea. Sophie Gift wasn't the kind of woman a man overlooked.

They only stared at each other for a moment, the silence stretching out, seemingly to eternity. It was strange, because the store would be closing in less than fifteen minutes. There should have still been scores of people dashing about in a panic, and a mind-numbing Muzak version of ''Jingle Bell

Rock'' or some such thing should still be blaring from the store P.A. system.

Instead, as had seemed to be the case with all of their encounters, time grew utterly still, and Mitchell felt as if he were completely alone in the universe with Sophie Gift.

Reluctantly, he shoved himself up to standing, then offered his hand to her. She hesitated a moment before taking it to help herself up, and just as before, when she stood in front of him perfectly well balanced, Mitchell found himself hesitant to let her go. But when she tugged her hand free of his, he realized he had no choice. No matter how much he might want to bask in the glow of Sophie Gift, she evidently had other places to be.

But then, so did he, he reminded himself. It was Christmas Eve, and Lauderdale's was about to close. That meant he needed to be in a million places at once, none of them particularly inviting. And if he didn't hurry, he'd miss each and every one of them.

"Thanks," she told him breathlessly, swiping her hand over the front of her costume.

Mitchell's breath caught at the realization that the hand she used to touch herself was the one that had just held his. In a way, he was almost touching her himself, as he had that night of the Christmas party. Out of nowhere, the memory of that evening replayed itself in his head, like a Technicolor, seventy-millimeter film. He squeezed his eyes shut and banished the fantasy, reminding himself he had a long night ahead of him before he could go home.

Later, he promised himself. After New Year's, when the retail season ground to almost a halt. Then he'd have time to explore this thing with Sophie.

He muttered a quick "You're welcome," then hastily bent to gather the scattered inventory sheets. But every time he reached for one, the page seemed to slip out of his fingers or move just beyond his grasp. He took a few steps toward another, only to have an errant draft of air blow it out of range again.

"Here, let me help you," he heard Sophie say before she joined him in trying to collect the papers.

But she had no more luck with them than Mitchell had. Wherever the draft of air was coming from, it began to blow harder, until the two of them were fairly chasing down sheaves of paper in a hearty wind. He wasn't paying attention to the direction they were headed, until the inventory papers suddenly stopped blowing at the second floor freight elevator.

"Finally," he muttered as he slowed his approach. But his relief was premature, because the elevator doors chose that moment to yawn open, as if they were the jaws of a giant beast. And they must have created some weird swirling gust of air when they did, because they sucked the inventory sheets right inside.

"Oh, no," he groaned, hastening his step once more to catch up before the doors folded up and down on each other again.

"I'm afraid you're on your own!" he heard Sophie call from behind him. "I have to run if I'm going to get my things and catch my bus!"

"No problem!" he called back as he stepped into the elevator. "Thanks for trying!"

But no sooner had he scooped the pages up and begun to shuffle them into order did he feel a warm body propelled right into his from behind. Once more the papers went flying from his fingers, and Mitchell spun around erratically, hands outstretched, only to have Sophie Gift land right in his arms. And before either of them could do or say anything, the elevator doors—both inner and outer—folded closed. Tight.

There. That ought to hold them for a while. He smiled at his handiwork, at the preparation that had gone into it, at the way Mitchell and the little elf would now be forced to confront each other and themselves and the things that meant the most to them.

Tomorrow was Christmas Day, and the couple still hadn't connected. Never in his afterlife had he seen two people work harder to avoid each other. They were going to ruin his perfect record—there was no way they could arrange a wedding for tomorrow, even if they *did* manage to get together tonight.

He thought again about Louise, about how the boy he'd been convinced would be so good for her had broken her heart instead. He thought about how lonely her life had become as a result, and how her unhappiness had followed her to the other side after her recent death.

He wasn't about to see that kind of loneliness overcome someone else for all eternity, not if he could help it. Especially not at Christmastime, and especially with two people who needed and deserved so much. Then he smiled. But all that was about to change.

All Mitchell and the little elf needed was a nice, quiet place removed from the demands of their jobs, a place where they could forget about their hectic reality for a while and enjoy a little Christmas spirit instead.

Well, a place like that, he amended, and a little champagne and caviar to go with it. And maybe a little candlelight, too. And some soft music. Had to have music, after all . . .

SEVEN

For a moment, the couple only stood there in the elevator, each trying to figure out what had just happened. Sophie gazed up into Mitchell's endless espresso eyes, feeling as if she'd just staggered accidentally into the deep end of a swimming pool and couldn't quite touch bottom. She felt weightless, buoyant, giddy. As if she were going to have to learn to swim all over again.

"What . . . what happened?" he asked her.

She continued to stare at him for a moment, still not quite sure how she'd come to be enfolded in his embrace. Not that she necessarily minded the embrace, mind you, recalling how the last one had turned out. She just couldn't remember how she'd gotten there.

"I . . . I don't know," she replied honestly. "I turned around to head back to the locker room for my coat, and then suddenly, I was walking backward toward the elevator. It was weird."

It *had* been weird, she recalled. She had *felt* like she was walking forward. The motions of her arms and legs had seemed no different than they ever did when she strode from point A to point B. But as she'd watched the store inventory she was passing, she'd realized she was actually walking backward. Back to the elevator. Back to Mitchell.

245

"And then," she added, "just as I got to the elevator, it was as if someone bumped into me really hard and sent me stumbling inside. And then . . ."

"And then . . . ?" he asked her.

"And then . . . you were there."

For some reason, the recognition of that sent a warm tremor of delight buzzing through Sophie that rocked her to her very soul. After the way they had parted the night of the Christmas party, she had been convinced that whatever had erupted between them was nothing more than a physical, spontaneous combustion, the result of overactive hormones and underexercised emotions, nothing more. They barely knew each other, after all. What else could it be?

She was lonely, and he was lonely. It was a time of year when people naturally turned to each other, and the two of them had no one. They found each other attractive, and they'd acted on that attraction. Sophie was still smarting from her divorce, and Mitchell was suffering his usual seasonal melancholy, missing his mother. There was nothing more to it than that, right?

Right?

But now, finding herself in his arms again, seeing that look in his eyes that she knew must reflect the longing and need she felt herself, she could only wonder if maybe she'd been wrong. If maybe she was so lucky, so blessed, to have found someone who felt so right at a time when everything else in her life seemed to feel so wrong.

She splayed her hands open over his chest, enjoying the heat of him beneath her fingertips, reveling in the steady *thump-thump-thump* of his heart under her palm, relishing the bumps and ridges of his well-muscled body, muscles that the elegant cut of his dark suit did nothing to diminish and everything to enhance.

She inhaled a deep breath, closing her eyes at the sharp, clean scent of peppermint surrounding him, and smiled at the soft jingle of her boot bells. Then she remembered something very important, and her eyes snapped open again.

Mitchell must have heard the same thing, because he laughed out loud. "Bells seem to ring every time we get together, don't they?'' Then he glanced down at her feet, toward the jinglers in question, and saw what she had just remembered herself—that her feet were encased by green tights and nothing more.

''You're not wearing any shoes,'' he said absently.

The moment he made the statement, she covered one foot with the other, as if trying to hide from him what he had just pointed out—that she had been forced to work her entire shift in her stocking feet today. Damn, she thought. She'd almost escaped without anyone in management discovering her oversight.

When he glanced back up, she could feel the two bright spots of pink she knew were warming her cheeks. Unable to tolerate yet another embarrassing situation, she darted her gaze everywhere but on him.

''I, ah . . .'' she began softly. ''I sort of forgot them,'' she confessed. ''I wore my snow boots to work this morning, because I have to catch the bus, and I thought I had my elf boots in my bag, but when I got here, I realized I must have left—''

''No,'' he interrupted her. ''I mean, you're not wearing your elf boots. With the bells.''

''I know. That's what I've been trying to tell you. I accidentally left them at—''

''But I heard them jingle.''

''But I'm not wearing my elf boots,'' she insisted futilely.

''I know,'' he said, clearly becoming exasperated with the conversation. ''That's what I mean. If it's not your boots I'm hearing, then what . . . ?''

His voice trailed off as a realization seemed to dawn on him—dawned on him like a good, solid blow to the back of the head. But before he could say a word, Sophie cut him off.

''Oh, no you don't,'' she told him. ''You're not going to stand here and tell me Mr. Krist is behind all this.''

''Well, it would make more sense than a sudden cyclone hitting the second floor,'' he insisted. He lifted one shoulder in an idle shrug. ''This isn't tornado season.''

''It's not Halloween, either,'' she was quick to point out.

But he only smiled again. "In that case, I hope you brought enough candy for everyone."

She narrowed her eyes at him. "What are you talking about?"

"That peppermint I smell. If it's not Mr. Krist, then it must be coming from you."

"I thought it was coming from you."

He shook his head and smiled derisively. "Trust me—I don't go anywhere near men's fragrances anymore."

Sophie sniffed the air delicately, and definitely detected a soft aroma of peppermint. Then she took note of something over his left shoulder and grinned smugly.

"That," she said.

"What?"

She lifted one hand from his chest—however reluctantly— to point to what she had noticed in the corner of the elevator. But when Mitchell didn't turn around to look, she somehow got the feeling that it was because he simply did not want to let her go. Kind of like how she didn't want him to let her go. Ever. He had curved his hands around her waist and over her hips so that they fit perfectly, and the top of her head came to just the right height for her to tuck it under his chin and listen to the steady thumping of his heart.

Okay, the steady *raging* of his heart, she corrected herself when she noted the way his heart rate was skyrocketing beneath her fingertips. Whatever. The point was, Mitchell Lauderdale was an ideal fit for her. Vertically, at least. In- evitably, she wondered if the two of them would fit together horizontally, as well.

Then she dashed the thought from her brain. There was no reason to torture herself with fantasies about how Mitch- ell Lauderdale would feel—vertically, horizontally, at work or at home, dressed or undressed, outside or inside. Then she squeezed her eyes shut at her errant thoughts.

Where on earth was this coming from? she wondered, forcing herself to concentrate on the situation at hand. The store would be closing and the last bus leaving in a matter of minutes, and everyone would be going home to celebrate Christmas with their families. Everyone, but her, at least.

The last thing Sophie needed was to get caught in an elevator, with her boss and without her elf shoes, by someone in upper management on their way out. She could probably be written up for that.

In spite of her little pep talk with herself, however, it was Mitchell, not she, who ultimately broke up their embrace. With one final squeeze of his fingertips against her flesh—which she told herself immediately she must have imagined—he released her. But the stain of color on his cheeks and the spark of light in his eyes told her that his gesture had been deliberate after all. Evidently, he was no less aware of whatever hot and heavy . . . stuff . . . was burning up the air between them than she was.

She banished the thought and pointed over his shoulder again. "That," she repeated. "That's what we smell."

Mitchell turned to look in the direction she indicated, toward a haphazard stack of boxes in the corner of the freight elevator marked with logos from suppliers like Godiva, Seabear, Neuske's, Petrossian, Mondavi Vineyards and Hickory and Pepperidge Farms.

"That's where it's coming from," she insisted. "There's a whole shipment of stuff for gourmet foods over there. Doubtless something in there is mint in origin."

He turned back to her with a fond smile. "Or maybe Mr. Krist just has a more elaborate plan in store than either of us realizes yet."

"What are you talking about?"

Although he hated to do it, somehow knowing in advance what he was going to discover, Mitchell strode to the wide doors of the freight elevator, grasped the big, metal handle that would grind them open, and pushed. Hard. But what should have been a well-oiled, well-used lever, was jammed tight. He tried again, putting the entire weight of his body behind the effort. But the lever didn't budge a micron.

He turned back to Sophie, who looked very concerned. "We, uh, we seem to be stuck in the elevator."

Her whole body slumped forward as she squeezed her eyes shut in disbelief. "You're kidding."

He shook his head. "No, I'm not. I wish I was, but I'm not."

Actually, that was kind of a lie, he knew, because now that he thought about it, the idea of being stuck in an elevator with Sophie Gift and a veritable mountain of gourmet food and wine was pretty much a wish come true. Unfortunately, he had a store to close. Lounging around on Christmas Eve while a beautiful woman in an elf suit fed him smoked salmon, although certainly appealing, wasn't exactly conducive to the successful running of one of the largest department stores in the country.

Lifting his hand halfheartedly to the console, he punched in order the buttons for the first, third, fourth and fifth floors. But none lit up, and the elevator didn't move an inch. That eerie silence seemed to snuggle more closely around them, and Mitchell couldn't shake the notion that this was all prearranged, that any effort they might make to rescue themselves was absolutely pointless.

"Don't worry," he told Sophie in spite of his conviction. "I'll have us out of here in no time."

He punched the alarm button to alert custodial that there was someone stuck in the freight elevator, but no annoying, grating bell sounded when he did. Instead, that oddly still silence settled even more resolutely. When he looked at Sophie, she was standing with her weight leveled on one stocking foot, arms crossed over her midsection.

"You were saying?" she asked.

"Okay, so the alarm doesn't work. Not to worry." He reached into his jacket pocket, withdrew a cellular phone, flipped it open, and punched a quick series of numbers. Then, with a confident smile for his companion, he cradled the receiver against his ear.

Immediately, his smile fell. Because no signal hummed from the phone. No dial tone, no ringing, no buzz of an engaged line, nothing.

"What?" Sophie asked when she noted his frown.

Mitchell snapped the phone shut and stuck it back in his pocket. "My, uh, my phone doesn't seem to be working, either."

Her head fell backward as she gazed at the elevator ceiling and expelled a soft, frustrated sigh. "This is just great. Stuck in an elevator on Christmas Eve."

He strode back to her, wanting to pull her into his arms again, a reaction he quickly squelched. As much as he would have liked to plumb the depths of Sophie Gift—so to speak—he simply did not have the time for it right now. As attractive as she was, as interesting and charming as he knew her to be, as luscious as she looked in that outfit, as hot and steamy as she made him feel, as full and red and ripe as her lips were . . .

Where was he? he wondered idly. Oh, yeah. As incredibly beautiful and arousing as Sophie Gift was, it would be against store policy to initiate any kind of romantic . . . um, thing . . . with her while she was in his employ. He conveniently forgot about how they'd already done that once, wondered if she'd be offended if he fired her on the spot, then reminded himself that they were running out of time.

"Look, it'll be fine," he assured her. "This time of year, this elevator must get used at least a few times after closing. The minute someone presses a button on another floor, we'll be jarred up or down. It's just a matter of time."

"Yeah, but how much time?" Sophie demanded. "We could suffocate in here."

He shook his head. "No, we won't. This elevator isn't air-tight. The upper half of the interior door is just a grate. We'll get a steady stream of relatively fresh air from the elevator shaft. Our biggest enemy for now is going to be boredom, should our rescue take longer than a few minutes."

He immediately wished he hadn't said that. Because the second he mentioned boredom, he began to entertain all kinds of ideas about how to relieve it. And just about every single one included Sophie Gift and some aspect of her elf suit. Specifically, the removal of some aspect of her elf suit. And caviar. For some reason, caviar played a very significant role in his fantasies. Caviar and champagne. Caviar and champagne, and bare skin and—

"I mean . . ." he tried again, hoping she couldn't detect

the train of his thoughts. "It's too bad we don't have a shipment of Trivial Pursuit or Yahtzee in here."

She said nothing in response to that, only looked around again, as if certain there must be another way out. Mitchell, too, surveyed their surroundings, but didn't see much hope of anything other than a nice, long wait. The elevator was large by elevator standards—roughly twelve by twenty feet—but there was definitely only one way out. And that way out was blocked by not one, but two sets of doors, neither of which showed any indication that they were currently in working order.

He looked around again. In addition to the shipment of gourmet foods in the corner, there were a number of cartons destined for gifts, some stereo shelf-units for electronics, what appeared to be an assortment of tablecloths for linens and—

"Hey!" Mitchell cried, noting one particular shipment stacked haphazardly toward the center. "That's the holiday china I've been looking for. How did it get in here?" He shook his head, bemused, then turned to Sophie. "You know, if one didn't know better, one might think this was all prearranged."

"What do you mean?" she asked him, clearly concerned about their predicament.

Mitchell spread his arms wide. "I mean look around. What do you see? With all that food, we certainly won't go hungry. Hell, we even have fine china and linens to eat off of. And look—" He moved to one of the smaller boxes from Williamsburg Lighting and tugged it open, then extracted a handful of long-tapered candles. "We can even enjoy our pickled herring and chardonnay by candlelight. And I'll wager that at least some of those stereo units run on batteries, which, oddly enough—especially at this time of year—are more than likely included."

A quick inspection of the electronics in question proved him right. Just to test further, Mitchell stabbed the *On* button on one, and immediately, the elevator was filled with a soft, romantic, instrumental rendition of "White Christmas."

"How terribly appropriate," he said with a smile. "And

look,'' he added, pointing toward the opposite side of the elevator. "A shipment of Dearfoams. Now your feet won't get cold. Is that a coincidence, or what?"

Sophie seemed to digest that for a moment, then said, "You aren't suggesting that someone set us up for a nice, long stay here." She swallowed visibly. "Are you?"

"Not just someone," he told her. "Mr. Krist."

"Don't be silly," she said a little anxiously. "You have to close the store. When you don't show up back at your office, someone will come looking for you, and they'll get us out."

He smiled grimly. "The only person who'd come looking for me is Hazel. And I guarantee, if I don't show up in about fifteen minutes, she'll lock the receipts in the safe, lock up the office and go home to whatever she has that resembles a family. She's not going to waste time looking for me."

Sophie eyed him warily, and he could see that she was beginning to waver in her conviction about the Mr. Krist connection. But all she said was, "Do you think it would be okay to break into some of that Godiva? I didn't get a chance to eat dinner tonight, we were so swamped."

Mitchell smiled. "I'm the store manager. I can do whatever I want." As he lifted a Neuske's carton from the top of the stack, he qualified that with, "As long as I keep a record of it somewhere. Now then. Do you prefer Chablis or chardonnay with your smoked salmon?"

Normally, the closing of Lauderdale's on Christmas Eve was his signal to depart. But then, normally, by closing time on Christmas Eve, he'd completed the task he'd set out to achieve. Mitchell and Sophie, however, had caused him no end of trouble, and although things were certainly looking up for the two of them, they were by no means . . . settled.

He sighed. Mrs. Krist would be waiting for him. He'd never missed spending Christmas with her since she'd come to the other side. And this year was even more special, because now they would have Louise to celebrate with them, and they had invited someone special over to meet their granddaughter. Nevertheless, he couldn't leave things undone. Surely Mrs. Krist and Louise would understand if he was a few hours late. After all, they were romantics at heart, too . . .

 EIGHT

Sophie licked the last of the mandarin orange truffle from her fingertips and then washed it down with a swallow of Chablis that emptied her glass. Okay, so maybe being stuck in an elevator wasn't the most traditional way to spend Christmas Eve, she conceded. At least she'd enjoyed one of the best holiday meals she'd ever had. She glanced over at Mitchell, who was tugging at the cork on another bottle of wine. And the company, she thought, had been extremely agreeable.

It certainly beat spending Christmas alone, she thought further, which would have been the fate that awaited her should things have happened the "right" way this evening.

More than six hours had passed since they'd been imprisoned in the freight elevator, and in that time, she'd learned more about her employer than she knew about herself. Mitchell had been talking constantly, though whether it was because he was nervous about their predicament, because he wanted to ease her own anxiety, or because he simply wanted, for some reason, for her to know every last detail about him, she had no idea.

Like, why had it been so important for her to know that he had been both a starter for Northwestern's football team *and* his class president two years straight? And why had he made such a point of emphasizing that he had *never* received a speeding ticket? He had also made her privy to all his favorites in the world—color: blue; number: eight; food: Mexican; song: "The Weight"; movie: *On the Waterfront*; novel: *The Big Sleep*; holiday: Arbor Day (Lauderdale's didn't have an Arbor Day Sale); Beatle: John—and she would certainly sleep easier at night with the knowledge that, if Mitchell could be any animal in the world, he would choose to be a Siberian tiger.

It had been small talk meant to keep boredom at bay, but it had provided her with an insight to him that she realized she'd never had with most people—including her ex-husband. She couldn't begin to tell which Beatle had been Evan's favorite, nor would she have known what animal he would like to be. She could pretty much identify him herself as an ass, but then, that wasn't exactly surprising.

In turn, she had answered Mitchell's questions about herself without inhibition, offering up similar snippets of her own experiences and preferences so that he could create whatever mental picture he wanted to paint of her. And now, with her belly full of fine food, finer chocolate and mellow wine, she felt amenable to conversation along just about any line of subject matter.

"So what happened to break up your marriage?"

Except that one.

At Mitchell's softly uttered question, she glanced up to find him looking not at her, but at the generous serving of wine he was pouring into her beautiful Waterford wineglass. And he kept not looking at her as he set the glass down beside her Lenox dessert plate decorated with boughs of holly, which in turn sat slightly catty-corner to his on a gold brocade tablecloth they had spread open on the elevator floor.

They each sat on opposite corners of that tablecloth, as if two boxers poised for a fight. Despite that, there was nothing to suggest animosity in their postures. Mitchell had removed his jacket some time ago, and had loosed the knot from his festive red tie, letting the length of silk hang unfettered from his open collar. Sophie had found a pair of red slippers in her size among the assortment stacked along the wall, and she wiggled her toes gratefully in the warm fur surrounding them.

To the casual observer, they might have been sharing nothing but a wonderful, expensive holiday picnic. However, the question he had just posed made her feel anything but casual.

"Why do you want to know about my marriage?" she responded. Oddly, she didn't feel defensive about replying. Just . . . curious as to why he'd be interested.

He shrugged as he topped off his own glass, then set the bottle on the floor and met her gaze. "Guess I'm just having a little trouble figuring out why a man who was fortunate enough to have you for a wife wouldn't have fought your divorce with every ounce of strength he possessed."

His comment made something effervesce inside her, bubbling up with warmth to make her smile. Her wry comment, however, was at odds with her physical reaction. "He didn't fight the divorce, because he was the one who wanted it."

Mitchell shook his head slowly. "In that case, I'm *really* confused."

"Why?"

"Because I can't fathom a man crazy enough to leave you."

He punctuated the statement with a look that was positively incandescent, and she dropped her gaze back to her glass before he could burn her to her core. "Not even for an eighteen-year-old girl who worshipped him and thought he was perfect in every way?"

Mitchell chuckled, but there wasn't an ounce of humor in the sound. "Oh, so he was an idiot, was he? Well, then. That would explain his behavior."

Sophie forced a smile, but kept her attention fixed on her glass. "Actually, I think things between Evan and me were starting to decline before his girlfriend ever entered the picture. I'm not exactly sure when it started or what specifically went wrong." She shrugged. "Maybe we were just too young when we met, I don't know."

"High school sweethearts?"

She nodded. "He was the only man I ever kissed."

"Until the other night, you mean."

She felt her face flame at the reminder, but she looked up at Mitchell levelly. He was eyeing her back as if her revelation had been Biblical in proportion. "Until the other night," she verified.

He smiled at her admission, and that smile sent a warm ripple of delight right down into the very deepest recesses of her soul. She'd never felt anything like it before. How could a man she had known for such a short time make her feel so many wonderful things she'd never experienced before? How could a man who had been a stranger less than a month ago, suddenly feel more comfortable than the husband she'd known half her life?

Then again, was that really important? she asked herself. Wasn't *what* she was feeling far more significant than how long she'd felt that way?

She shrugged again. "Maybe Evan never really loved me," she said quietly. "Not the way a man is supposed to love a woman. And," she conceded further, "maybe I never really loved him. The way a woman is supposed to love a man."

"Why do you say that?"

This time she was the one to smile. "He was remarkably easy to get over. And I'm quickly learning that he'll be easy to forget about, too."

Mitchell's smile grew, into something winsome and wistful and wonderful. "Is that the only reason you think what you felt for him wasn't love?" he asked.

How much should she confess? she wondered. Clearly, there was something very intimate going on between her and Mitchell, something neither of them could in honesty deny. And she could easily see that he felt as strongly as she did about whatever that was, and knew that he had been affected by it as quickly as she had. But things like this just didn't happen in real life. Did they?

She sighed heavily, and dropped her gaze back down to her wine. "No. That's not the only reason."

"What else then?"

Obviously, he wasn't going to let this go, she thought. So she looked up at him again and tried to explain it as best as she could. "Whatever I felt for Evan," she began slowly, "it was . . ."

"What?" Mitchell prompted softly.

When she met his gaze again, she felt herself falling, but for the life of her, she had no desire to stop her descent. "Different," she told him.

He rose from his position on the opposite side of the tablecloth, and prowled like the tiger he had pictured himself as earlier to where Sophie sat cross-legged at her own corner. He plucked the wineglass from her hand and set it down on the floor, then cupped her jaw in his palm.

"Different from what?" he asked her.

She swallowed hard. "Different from . . . from this. From what I feel for . . ."

His voice was scarcely a whisper when he asked, "For who?"

She hesitated only a moment before telling him honestly, "For you."

The fingers on her face wandered into her hair, and he bent his head to hers slowly. Sophie met him halfway, tilting her head back for his kiss, curling her own fingers around his neck to guide him in. His mouth covered hers lightly, tentatively, lovingly. And, not surprisingly, she realized they were a perfect fit. But instead of taking the kiss deeper, Mitchell pulled back, then pressed his forehead lightly to hers.

"Sophie?" he said softly.

"Hmm?"

"We can't do this."

"Why not?"

"Because you know Lauderdale's has a strict policy about employees dating, especially relationships between management and hourly help."

"Oh. That's too bad."

She threaded the fingers of her other hand through his hair, cupped his head in her palm, and pulled him down for another kiss. This time, she tilted her head more fully to the side, slanted her mouth more completely over his, and drew his tongue deep inside. He followed her unspoken directions willingly, eagerly, avidly, scooping her up from the floor to deposit her in his lap. But again, just when things began to heat up, he pulled himself away.

"Sophie?" he said again.

"Hmm?"

"You're fired."

"Okay."

Then he covered her mouth with his again and drank his fill of her. The errant hand that had been so curious before found its way up over her rib cage again, curving over her breast without hesitation and with much possession. A long, low sound of satisfaction wound up from someplace deep inside her, and she lowered her own hand to his open collar, curling her fingers into the coarse, dark hair she uncovered, along the rough, warm flesh she encountered.

At her soft touch, Mitchell tore his mouth from hers again. His breathing was ragged, the pulse at the base of his throat was racing, and his eyes . . . his eyes were so full of passion, Sophie felt herself swaying right back toward him again. But he covered her hands with his, pulled them gently from his hair and his neck, and settled all four against their thighs.

"We have to stop this right here, right now," he said roughly.

Still feeling a bit hazy, it took all the strength she had just to ask him, "Why?"

"Because there's something I need to know before we go any further."

"What?"

"I need to know if you feel about me the same way I feel about you."

Once more, she swallowed with some difficulty. This could either be very, very good, or very, very bad. Especially since they were pretty much trapped. "How . . . how do you feel about me?" she asked, hoping her voice didn't sound as weak and uncertain as it felt.

For a moment, he didn't say anything, and only continued

to stare into her eyes as if he couldn't quite remember where or who he was. Finally, he told her, "I know this sounds crazy . . . I mean, I know we haven't known each other long . . . And you're probably going to think I'm nuts, but . . ."

When he hesitated, she asked softly, urgently, "But what?"

"I think I . . . no, I'm *sure* I . . ."

"You're sure you what?"

"Sophie, I . . . I've . . ." He uttered an exasperated sound, then tried again. "Don't laugh, but somehow, somewhere along the line these past two weeks, I . . . I've fallen in love with you." Before she could comment, he rushed on, "Now that I think about it, I think I've loved you since the minute I saw you tackling Mrs. Claus." He smiled, his voice softening as he added, "And something tells me I'm going to love you for the rest of my life."

Something exploded inside Sophie at his words, carrying heat and joy and wonder to every cell in her body. Unbidden, laughter welled up from inside her, and she jerked her hands free of his to throw her arms around his neck. She trailed a line of butterfly kisses along the strong column of his throat, then murmured her own feelings against his warm, rough skin.

"What?" he asked. "What did you say?"

She pulled back and smiled at him. "What do you think I said?"

"It sounded like, 'Eyeloomoodoo.'"

She shook her head at him. "Why would I say 'Eyeloomoodoo'?"

"I don't know," he replied bemusedly. "But that's what it sounded like. And we have been drinking."

She flattened her hand gently over his jaw, loving the look in his deep brown eyes. "I didn't say, 'Eyeloomoodoo,'" she clarified. "I said, 'I love you, too.' And I do. Love you. Too."

She marveled at the relief that seemed to come over him at her assurance, wondering how he ever could have doubted her feelings. He was right. It was crazy. But there it was just the same. She loved him. He loved her. Was Christmas a great holiday, or what?

She leaned toward him, to kiss him again, but again, he pushed her gently away.

"What?" she asked. "What's wrong? If you're worried that you'll get in trouble for firing me over this, then don't. Because I quit."

"Actually," he told her. "Now that you mention it, what I had in mind for you was more of a promotion."

Her eyebrows shot up in surprise at that. "What do you mean?"

"Well, you know that Lauderdale's is and always has been a family-run operation."

"Yes."

"So anyone who moves into the upper echelons of management usually has Lauderdale for a last name."

"So?"

"So, if your name was something like, say . . . Sophie Lauderdale, you might qualify for a really primo position. I happen to know that vice-president in charge of finances is coming up for filling soon."

She laughed, and shook her head. "I don't know. I've been thinking lately that retail might not really be my thing. I never got to go to college, and I always did want to major in English."

His smile fell. "Oh."

"Does that mean I can't change my name to Sophie Lauderdale?"

His smile returned, this time with all his other facial features joining in. "Well, there is one small little requirement," he responded.

"What's that?"

"You'd have to marry me."

She pretended to think about that for a minute. "You're not just asking to keep that Christmas Day wedding tradition alive—and all that good PR along with it—are you?"

He shook his head. "Nope. I'm saying it because I love you and want you to be my wife forever and ever and ever."

She laughed. "Oh, well, if that's all . . ."

"So is that a yes?"

She nodded. "It's a yes."

She tightened her arms around his neck, and he settled his around her waist. For long moments, they joined in a kiss that nearly stopped their hearts and stole their breath. Then Mitchell seemed to remember something, because he set Sophie away again. He glanced down at his watch, then held it up for her inspection.

"It's after midnight," he pointed out.

"Christmas Day," she said with a smile.

"Merry Christmas, Sophie."

"Merry Christmas, Mitchell."

"And you know what?"

"What?"

"The idea of a Christmas Day wedding sounds kind of nice to me." He pulled her close again. "It would be a shame to ruin what has become an unofficial Lauderdale's holiday tradition."

She gaped at him. "Mitchell, we're trapped in an elevator. How are we going to get married today?"

As if her observation offered up the magic words, the big metal doors grated and groaned, and then yawned open wide. They looked at each other, then at the doors, then back at each other again. And they smiled.

Sophie glanced upward, though why she chose that direction for her gaze, she couldn't have said. Then, very quietly, she murmured, "Thanks, Mr. Krist. For making Christmas special again."

Mitchell joined her in gazing upward, and added, "Yeah, thanks, old man. For everything." Then he looked at Sophie again. "Christmas Day wedding," he stated.

She shook her head. "Everything's closed for the holiday. We couldn't get a license or minister today to save our lives."

He thought for a moment, then snapped his fingers. "Las Vegas *never* closes," he said. "And you can get anything you want there, anytime."

"A Vegas wedding?" she asked.

He nodded. "A Vegas *Christmas* wedding. If we go straight to the airport from here . . ."

She nodded back. "You know, it could work. But I have one stop to make first."

"Where?"

She smiled as she stood and raced for the elevator's entrance. "The ladies' room," she called over her shoulder.

Okay, so instead of "The Wedding March," she walked down the aisle to someone named Elvis singing, "I'll Have a Blue Christmas Without You." And okay, so instead of roses, she was carrying poinsettias, and he was wearing a holly boutonniere. And okay, so instead of a big white, frosted wedding cake and champagne, they toasted their nuptials with fruitcake and bourbon-spiked eggnog. And okay, instead of a white wedding gown, she was dressed in a coffee-stained elf suit.

It was still a Christmas Day wedding. He'd brought two people together who deserved a whole new reason to enjoy the holiday and celebrate it for the time of love that it was. And that was all that mattered.

He smiled as he watched them gaze at the diamond ring on her left finger, the one that had belonged to Mitchell's mother. And he followed them as they left the little chapel to stroll into the gaudy streets of Las Vegas, wishing he could have brought Mrs. Krist here once or twice—she would have enjoyed the shows. But now it was time to go home, back where he belonged. It was time for him to return to the people he loved and the people who loved him. Because love . . . that was what Christmas was really all about.

And he wanted to see his granddaughter's expression when she met the young man he and Mrs. Krist had invited to share Christmas with them. The boy had been admiring Louise ever since she'd come over to the other side, had been badgering him to introduce the two of them for some time now. And he knew Louise would like the boy. She always had loved his movies.

So Tyrone Power hadn't had such a good reputation in his first life. He'd been the soul of goodness since coming to the other side. And he did so have a fondness for Louise.

He smiled again at the newly united couple, feeling satisfied and happy and festive. He surely did love Christmas. And he could hardly wait for next year. . . .

THE GHOST OF
CHRISTMAS PRESENT

Jenny Lykins

ONE

For the briefest of seconds, Alane Travis thought she saw someone looking out the front window of the rented mountain cabin. As she pulled the Jeep Cherokee into what she hoped was the cabin's driveway, the headlight beams penetrated the near-blizzard storm to sweep across frosty windows and Christmas garland swagged over the porch and balcony railings.

Stress and fatigue, she told herself. And it was hard to see anything through that solid curtain of snow. Besides, the rental company had said the cleaning lady would be there the day before to decorate a little. No one should be there now.

Pulling her hood over her hair, she ducked her head, climbed out of the car, then grabbed two bags of groceries from the backseat. In a blur of white, she slogged through snow up to her knees then knocked the worst of the slush off her boots as she stomped across the porch.

The welcome warmth of the cabin engulfed her the moment she stepped across the threshold. The interior was just as she'd hoped. Rustic, homey, loaded with personality. She could already feel the knots in her muscles dissolving.

She found her way to the kitchen, dropped the groceries onto the scarred wooden table, then trudged out for another load. Returning with her suitcases, she raised her head to find the porch steps in the virtual whiteout and thought she saw a movement in the window again.

Had it been a reflection of something outside? Had the wind moved the curtain through a drafty window?

A hard knot of fear curled in her stomach and inched its way up her throat. Should she run? Should she drop her suitcases and make a dash for the safety of the car?

She reasoned with herself at the bottom of the porch steps. If someone was in there, surely they would have already shown themselves, whether they meant her harm or not. She'd made a mountain out of a molehill. Was she going to let a drafty window and fluttering curtain keep her from the much-needed vacation?

Stiffening her spine and straightening her shoulders, she tightened her grip on the suitcases and mounted the steps to the porch. She had to work on her painting, as well as use this opportunity to make a decision about herself and David. She'd chosen to spend Christmas alone so she wouldn't be distracted from either her work or her decision-making, and she'd be darned if she'd let a little gust of wind scare her away.

In the distance, a country church bell chimed eight o'clock. She sent up a little prayer, only half jokingly, that she'd live through the night.

Showing more courage than she actually felt, she kicked open the door and swung the Samsonite ahead of her into the cabin, half expecting to see some psycho in a goalie mask with a chainsaw in his hand. But if the psycho came after her, he'd have to hack his way through the luggage to get at her.

The living room couldn't have been more peaceful. Logs and kindling lay stacked in the fireplace, waiting for the touch of a match. The house didn't *feel* like someone was hiding from her. She hauled her bags over to the tiny staircase leading to the bedroom, then peered up the stairs. The dark, gaping blackness at the top of the stairs was anything but inviting, but she forced herself to lug the suitcases up the creaking steps, then fumbled in the dark until she found a light switch and flicked it on. She jumped a foot in the air, dropping her luggage, at the sight of something sprawled across the bed.

"Oh, good grief!" Her heart raced beneath the palm she'd clapped to her chest, and then a timid little giggle escaped her throat.

The creature lurking across the white eyelet bedspread was a fake bearskin rug with a cuddly teddy bear head grinning blankly up at her.

"*Way* too much imagination, Travis."

She dragged her suitcases over to the bed, then scanned her surroundings. The room took up the entire second floor of the small cabin. Roomy, bright, and airy, it still held a cozy, welcoming feel. An antique shaving stand stood in the corner, complete with china pitcher and bowl and a matching chamber pot beneath. An afghan-covered rocking chair sat in front of a set of sliding glass doors that looked out on a small balcony and the lake beyond. A telescope stood just inside the doors.

Alane flipped open her suitcases and started to unpack, but before she stored her clothes in the antique chest of drawers she decided she'd better put the groceries in the refrigerator.

A little tingle at the back of her neck kept her from moving. She turned a full circle, scouring the room with her gaze, then dropped to her knees and flipped up the bedskirt.

Not even a dust bunny stared back at her from the shiny hardwood floor under the bed.

"Yep. *Way* too much imagination."

Her knees popped as she stood, then the floorboards and stairs creaked as she made her way to the first floor.

The small kitchen held no space for someone to hide in so she tiptoed to the bathroom and peeked around the door.

Nothing.

"Looking for me?"

Alane started so violently she bounced against the wall. Her hands flew to her chest as she backed away, trying desperately not to faint at the sight of the man in front of her . . . and the sight of the kitchen table showing hazily through his body.

The last thing she remembered was the feel of her body sliding down the door frame.

Jared Elliott looked down at the unconscious woman lying in a boneless heap on the floor. He guessed he should have expected that sort of reaction, but for the life of him—or the death of him—he'd never found a gentle way to reveal himself to the living, in all his two hundred years.

The minute he'd caught a glimpse of those disturbing, dark brown eyes, he'd known he would never remain cloaked throughout her stay. And when she'd entered the house, obviously terrified, and proceeded to investigate, he'd found himself intrigued for the first time in decades. Had he ever encountered a woman so brave? He wanted to meet her, get to know her, and if she proved too afraid of him to stay, then at least he would have the cabin all to himself again.

The woman's lashes fluttered against cheeks still pink with cold. Her eyes opened and she blinked at the ceiling for a moment, causing two little vertical lines to mar the perfection of her forehead.

"I mean you no harm," he said, and sank to a kitchen chair to make himself less threatening. She shot upright, all color draining from her face, then she scrambled backward until she hit the bathroom wall. With enough force to tear it off its hinges, she slammed the door in his face.

Jared smiled and shook his head. The living could be so illogical.

"I truly mean you no harm," he said, raising his voice just a little. "And even if that door had a lock, you must know that I can walk through walls. I learned that in House Haunting 101."

The door remained closed and total silence virtually vibrated from the other side. Well, he couldn't just leave her in there cowering on the floor.

He strolled to the door and decided not to waste his limited energy in knocking.

"Hello? Are you decent?"

A faint scuffling behind the door was his only answer.

He moved around to another wall, then let his head and shoulders dissolve through the wood. She stood with her back to him, facing the door, a bathroom plunger held over her head as if it were a headsman's ax, ready to separate his head from his shoulders. Little did she know he could already do that, without the ax.

"Excuse me, but do you plan on using that—"

The woman spun, slicing the plunger through thin air. He flinched and dodged, a reaction left over from his mortal days. Remembering himself, he stepped through the wall and stood there with his arms crossed while she swung at him like a blindfolded child swinging at a piñata. Not until she began to tire did he bother to speak.

"If you hadn't overreacted, I was going to tell you that you can't—"

She threw the plunger through his head and it clattered off the wall to land in the bathtub. Yanking open the door, she raced through the kitchen, the parlor and out the front door, hesitating only a second before skidding down the steps and doing a sort of loping, wading run through the snow to the car.

Before she even climbed inside, he moved himself into the passenger seat with a mere thought. She slammed the door, hit the lock, then grabbed the steering wheel with white knuckle strength and stared at the front porch.

"If you're looking for me, I'm not—"

This time she hit her head on the door window when she jerked around. She grappled blindly for the handle, kicked open the door, then fell from the car, scrambling to her feet in the snow and running toward the darkness.

Did the woman never hang around through a complete sentence? Did she think she would get very far in this weather? He appeared before her, walking backward with ease as she struggled through the snow.

"I really do mean you no harm."

She changed directions and continued to lope away from him, her ragged breath bursting into the air in white clouds.

Before she could lose sight of the mountain cabin, as well as her bearings, he placed himself in front of her, forcing her to stop or run through him. She stopped.

"Look, have I hurt you? Have I done anything to intentionally make you fear me?"

Cowering, her arms crossed, she fought to catch a breath while fear gleamed in her eyes.

"I'm not going to hurt you. Look. I can't." He held out his hand to caress her face. A sharp stab of disappointment hit him in the chest when his hand passed right through her, even though he'd known it would.

She flinched, then shuddered.

"See? How can I hurt you if I can't touch you?" he asked logically, ignoring the tearing of his heart at the thought of never touching her.

Her breathing slowed a bit and he thought perhaps a little of the terror left her eyes. She straightened and glanced around, no doubt looking for an escape, but from the way the snow was coming down, it was going to be a while before she could get very far.

"Come back to the cottage. I'll leave you be, if you wish. But you can't set out in this weather, and you can't stay in your car. You really don't have an option."

The woman swallowed hard. Little droplets of melting snow in her hair quivered with her body as she tried to look everywhere but at him.

"All right. I'll leave you alone. But you have to admit, if I meant you any harm, I've had plenty of time to carry out my plans." He vanished then, reappearing immediately on the small, darkened balcony overlooking the lake.

What would he do if she continued on? She'd surely die in the storm, if not by falling into the lake, then certainly by freezing to death.

He sharpened his night vision, which, after two hundred years of honing, could spot a praying mantis in the middle of a garden at a hundred paces.

She stood as he'd left her, her dark eyes an incongruous contrast against the wisps of cornsilk-colored hair escaping from beneath her hood. She looked back at the house, then into the darkness. She wrung her hands and glanced back and forth again, obviously weighing the risks involved in either direction.

Damn. He shouldn't have revealed himself the way he had. But there was something about her . . . For the first time in nearly two hundred years he hadn't thought before he acted.

Finally she turned back to the house, yanking her hood tighter and ducking her head as she waded through the knee-deep snow.

He sat, perched on a step of the tiny staircase, his body cloaked in transparency as she stomped her way across the porch. He heard the twang of the screen door opening, then she pushed the front door inward. Only her head appeared as she scanned the room. When she saw no sign of his presence she inched her way in, looking back at the open door as if deciding whether or not to close it.

With exaggerated stealth, she tiptoed to the door and closed it without so much as a click. Jared grinned at her caution and noted that she didn't lock the door behind her.

After standing for a few indecisive seconds, she virtually dove toward the fireplace. With clumsy fingers she produced a match from its box—several matches, actually, most of which now littered the floor at her feet. After two unsuccessful attempts to strike the match, the tip finally flared to life. She held it to the fire-starter and kindling, and within seconds a nice, hungry fire roared in the grate.

She huddled by the fireplace and looked around, as if she expected the flames and heat to keep him away as it would a wild animal. He grinned again.

How naïve of her.

He settled back and watched, dipping every now and then into her emotions, becoming more intrigued with every passing moment.

Alane cowered against the fireplace until her legs went numb and she had a crick in her neck. Frozen food sat thawing on the table while she starved and waited for some ghost to come along, carrying his head under his arm, no doubt, with intentions of scaring the life out of her.

Her rational voice told her he would have done that by now if he was going to. Her irrational voice told her if she didn't move a muscle then maybe he wouldn't see her and she could run to safety in the morning.

Yeah, right.

She sighed. Yesterday she never would have believed in ghosts, would have laughed at the idea. But not now. Not after today.

Straightening her painfully cramped legs out one at a time, she got to her feet and pulled herself upright. While she stayed close to the fire, she fought to gather enough courage to go to the kitchen. Maybe she'd imagined him. Maybe, as Dickens suggested, he was the result of a bit of undigested beef.

From the corner of her eye she caught a movement near the stairs. The air shimmered for a moment then formed the shape of a body sitting on the steps.

"I figured it was harder on you *not* knowing where I am. This way you can keep an eye on me," the translucent ghost said apologetically.

Alane shook her head and backed up until the stone of the fireplace bit into her back. Why hadn't she listened to her mother and gone on a cruise?

"How . . ." She cleared her throat and tried not to croak again. ". . . How long have you been there?"

"Oh," he tilted his head to the ceiling and rubbed the back of his neck, "couple of hours, I guess."

Anger replaced fear at his words. The whole time! He'd been there the whole time she'd huddled by that fire, baking on one side, freezing on the other, starving to death, trying not to draw attention to herself while he no doubt had a good laugh at her expense.

Exhausted, her adrenaline now on a downward spiral, she stepped away from the jabbing stones of the fireplace and rammed her hands onto her hips.

"Look, you . . . you ectoplasmic Peeping Tom. I don't appreciate being scared out of my wits, watched like a bug under a microscope, or sharing a cabin I paid for with the likes of you. So vacate the premises, Casper. Spare me the boyish smiles and let me concentrate on my work!''

''Boyish smile? Really?'' His grin brightened by at least a hundred fifty watts.

Alane growled part of a curse before she caught herself, then marched into the kitchen to put the thawing groceries away, the ghost be damned.

As her temper faded, so did her bravado, and she found herself watching the door to the living room while she stocked the refrigerator. Maybe if she made a run for it out the back door . . . But one look out the window at the thick, snowfall blowing nearly horizontal changed her mind. Why couldn't her car have broken down before she got to the cabin?

He appeared in the doorway, then leaned against the counter and crossed one foot over the other.

''Now you won't be wondering when I'll appear.'' With his last word he widened his eyes and fluttered his hands, like the melodramatic, theatrical ghost he probably was. Her initial reaction was to narrow her eyes and glare at him.

''Oh, well, excuse me for overreacting. Coming face to face with a walking, talking dead man shouldn't have upset me so much!''

She slammed the refrigerator door shut then started putting things in cabinets. When she used up what little storage space she had on her side of the kitchen she realized she would either have to leave the rest of her things on the table or start using the cabinets he was propped against. Sucking in a deep breath, she balanced a half dozen cans of soup in her arms, marched up to him and threw open the cabinet door next to him. The door flew back through his head, bounced off the cabinet and banged shut. All six cans of soup hit the floor when Alane cringed at the thought of the door hitting his head.

When she opened her eyes he hadn't moved. His eyes— not quite brown, not quite green—very nearly twinkled with amusement when he smiled.

''Missed me.''

TWO

Alane dropped to her knees and chased rolling soup cans across the ancient, uneven floor of the cabin. She used that time to try desperately to get her heart pumping again. The door had bounced right through his head! And that smile of his had sent her heart to her feet!

She scavenged three cans from under the table, one from behind the stove and one from the farthest corner of the kitchen. The sixth lay innocently at the feet—make that *in* the feet—of the ghost. A ghost in cowboy boots.

"Oh. I would help, but . . . ," he bent and scooped his hand right through the can, ". . . I have this problem." He smiled with all the charm of a mischievous six-year-old.

Alane swallowed hard and chewed on her lower lip.

"W—Would . . . ahh . . . you mind stepping to your right?"

He continued that bone-melting smile as he slid down the counter a few inches. She snatched the can from the floor, then dumped them all in the nearest cabinet.

"Am I making you nervous?"

She merely cocked a brow at him in answer.

"I'm not so bad when you get to know me. Really. Why don't you pour yourself a glass of wine and we'll talk by the fire."

Her first impulse was a rude snort and a "Yeah, right," but she stifled them both. Instead, she found her nail cuticles infinitely interesting while she chewed on her lip again and wished fervently that he'd just disappear.

"All right. I'll tell you what. I'll go wait by the fire and if you want to talk you can join me."

He didn't wait for an answer. But at least he used the doorway when he left the kitchen.

Alane stood in the center of the floor, wringing her hands, her stomach churning. If she talked to him for a while, would he go away and leave her in peace? *Could* she talk to him without stammering incoherently? After all, he was a ghost, a ghost with the face of Michelangelo's David.

Whether she joined him or not, a glass of wine was a good idea. Good for the nerves. Strictly medicinal.

She pulled her favorite white zinfandel from the fridge with a mental tweak to all the wine snobs who would look down on her choice. It took four tries before her shaking hands managed to center the corkscrew, and by the time she separated the cork from the neck, she was ready to forego the glass and do a bottoms-up with the bottle.

She stifled that urge . . . after the first long gulp.

Rummaging in the cupboards, she unearthed a wineglass and poured the accepted amount. When she started to stopper the bottle she flicked a glance at the glass, shrugged, filled it to the rim, then jammed the cork back into the mouth.

With a few more sips she felt mellow enough to confront the lion in his den, so to speak. Or would she be a virgin sacrifice to the spirits?

She eyed the glass of wine with suspicion, wondering if she should quit while she was behind and dump what was left down the drain.

Jared watched her peer around the door then try to amble nonchalantly into the living room. She took a nervous sip of wine when she glanced at him and caught him looking at her.

Damn, she looked even more beautiful, now that she had

that overstuffed parka off. Silky, spun-gold hair kissed her shoulders; the kind of hair that falls perfectly back into place, even after a windstorm.

She started to lower herself into the leather recliner, then glanced at him and moved onto the floor closer to the fire, a good three feet farther from him. She took another sip of wine and looked at the ceiling, then at the wall, then at the fire, then finally at him. He let the silence stretch a minute.

"How's the wine?"

"Good. Good." She nodded. "Would you like . . . I mean, can you drink . . . ?"

"No, thanks. The stuff goes right through me."

She grinned at that and took another sip.

"So what do you do for a living?"

"I paint." She swirled the wine in the glass and watched the liquid climb to the rim. "Dad was an artist. I hope to be as good as him someday."

"A name I might recognize?" He was pulling teeth here.

"Xavier Travis."

Jared nodded. He did recognize the name. During his wandering years he'd seen more than one of the man's paintings.

"So, do you go by Travis? Are you here on sabbatical? Is someone joining you? Do you like dogs?" He tossed that last one in to see if she was paying attention.

She blinked at him, then leaned back against a footstool, drew her legs up, and propped her wine atop her knee.

"Ummm . . . yes, no, no, and only big ones."

A woman with a sense of humor.

"So, what's your first name, or should I keep thinking of you as that gorgeous mortal?"

He shouldn't have waited until mid-sip to ask that one. But she only choked for a second, then her eyes watered.

"I'm Alane. Travis. Alane Travis," she clarified for any idiots who might be in the room.

"Jared Elliott, at your service. I'd offer you my hand but I don't have much of a grip."

She smiled and bowed her head as she shook it.

"So, Alane Travis, you're here to work, you're working

alone, and you have a soft spot for large dogs. Got a husband? Kids?''

She cringed and took another sip.

''Can't find a man who understands the artist in me. And my only child is a mutt named van Gogh. He lost an ear in a dog fight before he landed in the pound. I rescued him from death row.''

Ah! A sense of humor *and* a soft heart.

''What about you?'' She took him by complete surprise, but he assumed the wine had loosened her tongue enough to ask. ''Your story's *got* to be more interesting than mine.''

Now it was his turn to cringe.

''Well, my name's Jared Elliott, as I said.''

''Yeah . . . ,'' she said leadingly, but he remained silent. ''How long have you been . . . ,'' she waved the hand holding the wineglass at him, sloshing some onto her fingers, ''. . . like this? What would be the politically correct term? Bodily deprived? Pulse impaired? Heartbeat challenged?''

Definitely mellowing. He'd have to encourage her to imbibe more if she clammed up on him again.

''Two hundred years.''

''Huh?''

''I've been like this,'' he gestured from head to toe, ''for two hundred years.''

''No, you haven't!''

''Yes. I have.''

''Say something to me in . . . no wait. That's not right.'' She blinked. ''You don't sound two hundred years old.''

He bit back a grin and wished he could smooth away the silken strand of hair that had flopped over her eye.

''What manner of speech would the good mistress have me speak? I vow my life has seen many. Wish you that I converse as a rebellious traitor to the crown? A damn Yankee? A really swell World War II vet? How about a real cool cat, or maybe a groovy dude? Of course I can be awesome and radical, and even bad, but you're such a def chick I can probably just be myself.''

When he finally wound down she had the goofiest, most endearing smile on her face he'd ever seen. He'd never met a woman who made him feel this way. It was unnerving.

"Point taken," she said.

Jared smiled in satisfaction.

"But you don't *look* two hundred years old, and I don't mean in age. Don't you guys walk around in shrouds or the clothes you were buried in or something?"

Jared rolled his eyes, then leaned back and sprawled his legs out toward the fire. "You can thank Hollywood for that myth, but guys like Shakespeare and Dickens started the rumor." A sudden mischievous urge overwhelmed him. "Would you believe me if I looked like this?"

Alane again choked on her wine as she stared at Jared through a blur of teary eyes. He rose from the matching recliner clad in gray, skin-tight knee breeches, hosiery, and shoes with buckles. His heretofore nineties hair was several inches longer, pulled back in a queue with a black ribbon. A vest to mid-thigh and cutaway jacket finished the picture of a man who could have signed the Constitution. With the flick of a lacy cuff, he bowed.

"I never powder my hair. Attracts bugs."

In the blink of an eye he wore a Confederate officer's uniform, then a zoot suit, then a pair of chinos and a tee shirt with a pack of cigarettes rolled in the sleeve and hair slicked into a ducktail. He faded into bell-bottoms and a tie-dyed shirt with below-the-shoulder hair, then ended in loose cut jeans, logo tee shirt and a baseball hat on backwards. Before she could breathe, he morphed back into his boot-cut jeans, oxford shirt, and cabled crewneck sweater, as devastatingly handsome in that simple attire as he'd been in all his other personas. Too handsome for her own good.

"Sorry," he shrugged with a smile that was anything but sorry. "I don't get a chance to show off much."

Alane closed her mouth, wondering vaguely how long it had been hanging open.

"Poi . . . ," she cleared her throat, ". . . point well-taken." She looked at her nearly empty wineglass, then set it aside and pushed it further away. "How did you . . . become..." she wiggled her fingers at him, at a loss for words.

"Heartbeat challenged?" he supplied.

Giving him a weak smile she cringed for letting the wine make her so dubiously witty.

"I don't need a demonstration, by the way," she hastened to add.

He lifted his head and grinned, but his smile didn't have the usual megawatts behind it. He sighed.

"Oh, another time. Young mistress must be sorely wearied from her lengthy journey. Retire to your bedchamber and sleep well this night. We shall speak again on the morrow."

Slowly, very slowly, he stretched out a hand toward her. When she forced herself not to back away he passed his hand along her cheek. Instead of the cold, clammy feeling she expected, her cheek felt as if a warm, summer breeze had kissed it.

Then he was gone.

# THREE

Jared watched her sleep. Even with the wine she'd lain awake far into the night, watching for someone who wouldn't allow himself to be seen.

Ah, but she was lovely. For the first time in more years than he'd let himself count, he gave in to the ache for the gentle touch of a woman. Just her touch. A finger on his brow to swipe his hair from his eyes. Hands on his shoulders to rub away the knots. A loving palm on the cheek to remind him to shave.

He closed his eyes, imagining it, but the mere thought hurt like a dull blade through the breast.

He moved to the bed and sank down beside her. Focusing all his will, knowing it would cost him strength, he concentrated and traced the tips of his fingers along her jaw.

Sweet Gabriel in heaven, the feel of her shot through his soul like a drug. He held the connection, savoring the moment, until his strength began to ebb.

He left part of his soul behind when he lifted his fingers from her face.

Closing his eyes, he dropped his head in denial. For nearly two centuries he had walked this earth alone, at times feeling his loneliness, at times enjoying his solitude. But during those years he'd remained constant in accepting his fate. In life, he'd been unwilling to give of himself, and because of that his wife and unborn child had died at his hands. He hadn't been able to give the ultimate gift—himself—and she had died trying to love him anyway.

He deserved the curse her mother had laid upon him as he lay, broken at the foot of the stairs, his wife's twisted body tangled with his.

And now, when no chance of love existed for him, he looked at the sleeping woman lying curled on her side and knew for the first time what selfless, all-encompassing love felt like.

He'd fallen in love, and feared it would be a process that would last throughout an eternity.

In the space of a heartbeat, he walked the frigid shores of the lake, unable to feel the cold nor smell the perfume of the trees.

He would give the earth and the moon and the stars, were it in his power, to have but one day to love Alane Travis with more than his heart, his mind, and his soul. To feel her head against his chest, her breath against his face. To smell the scent she wore and taste the sweetness of her kiss.

He would give any wealth he had, but all he had was a solitary nonexistence. A vacuum in which he'd lived with no feelings or emotions for decade upon decade.

Now, God help him, the vacuum had been broken.

Alane rolled over and came slowly awake, trying to remember exactly where she was. Oh yes. The cabin.

Her eyes flew open and she searched the room as memories of the night before returned. Surely it was a dream. Surely she hadn't spent the evening drinking wine and conversing with a ghost.

Her first impulse was to curl into a tight little ball and pull the covers over her head, but Mother Nature forced her to climb out of bed and find her way to the bathroom in her hopelessly wrinkled clothes.

The living room looked normal. No sign of shimmering air or guys she could see through. The kitchen looked just as she'd left it the night before. Groceries still on the table.

The bottle of wine sat at the edge, a testament that she hadn't dreamed the whole thing. Then again, considering how little wine was left in the bottle, she may have dreamed *part* of it.

Moving on to the bathroom, she peered around the corner, half expecting him to float through the wall. Once she determined the room was empty, she rushed through the necessary activities before brushing her teeth and dousing her face with a splash of cold water.

Feeling a little more in charge, with no sign of the resident ectoplasm, she finger-combed her hair and shuffled into the kitchen to start her morning IV drip of caffeine.

After putting away the rest of the groceries, throwing a conglomeration into the Crock-Pot for dinner, then pouring herself a fresh cup of coffee, she had convinced herself that the whole thing really had been just a result of too much wine and a long day of driving. After all, the guy really was too good-looking to be true, with all that black-brown hair and greenish, brownish eyes. Really, had anybody *that* good-looking ever really walked the earth? And if that's the way they grew them two hundred years ago, she'd been born in the wrong century. Besides, if he was real, that meant she was attracted to a dead man. And she was much too levelheaded ever to do something that foolish. Nah, she'd dreamed that one up for sure.

"No hangover?"

She jerked as if she'd been shot, this time slinging a mug full of coffee against the wall in a sort of impressionistic caffeine mural.

"Holy crap! I'm going to make you wear a bell around your neck if you don't stop that!"

He shrugged innocently and said, "It's not on purpose. Honest."

Alane snatched a wet dishcloth from the sink and started mopping the wall, blessing whoever made the decision to use glossy paint.

"What do you want anyway?" Her nerves felt like rubber bands stretched to the max. When he didn't answer she glanced at him over her shoulder.

He stood there, hurt evident in his eyes, though he tried to mask it with a careless shrug.

The coffee stains and wet dishcloth forgotten, she wanted to bite her tongue in two for snapping at him.

"I thought you might need a hangover remedy. I had my share of them before I took the ultimate cure," he muttered before disappearing.

"Irreverent. Here I am vacationing with an irreverent ghost who has a face and body to die for," Alane mumbled under her breath.

"No! I don't! And don't you ever say anything like that again!" he bellowed as he reappeared from the outside wall.

"Excuse me? What?" Alane asked, afraid the answer would be what she thought it was.

"To die for. I am *not* to die for. Have you any idea what you're saying when you use that term?" He towered—hovered—over her, his rage mingled with an underlying fear she didn't understand.

She generated more than a little rage of her own.

"I wasn't talking to you. I was mumbling to myself. Which means you've been spying on me like some kind of . . . of . . . paranormal eavesdropper! Well, I don't appreciate it, Casper, so stay the hell out of my head!" She threw the dripping cloth through his head, hitting the kitchen window with a *splat* and making one more mess to clean up.

The nerve of him! The unmitigated gall! If she could get her hands around that vaporous neck of his, she'd choke the life right out of . . . Oh!

She speared him with a glare. He looked as angry as she.

"There are very few things in life 'to die for,' Alane. And I am certainly not one of them."

"That's just a . . . Nobody ever means it when . . . Oh, for pity's sake, why am I on the defensive? You're the one in the wrong." She narrowed her eyes and searched his face. "Have you been spying on me all along?"

He snapped his mouth shut and had the decency to look at least a little uncomfortable.

"No."

"No?"

"Not exactly."

"Not exactly? What do you mean, 'Not exactly'?"

When his gaze dropped to the floor, her stomach dropped with it, "I'm waiting."

He studied the ceiling, then took a deep breath.

"I'm an empath. I can . . . feel . . . your emotions. I know how you're feeling when you're frightened, angry. Attracted."

Alane fought to keep her mind blank at this news, yet her thoughts raced to catalog the number of emotions that had danced through her since she'd arrived there. Since that first time her stomach flipped from looking at him.

"How do you do it?"

He looked her straight in the eye, but she could have sworn he tried not to cringe. "I concentrate. I see an aura around you. And then I feel what you're feeling."

If he wasn't already dead, she'd kill him.

She stomped right through him and snatched up the dish-cloth again, biting back a gasp and fighting to ignore the melting warmth she felt as her body passed through his. From the corner of her eye she saw him turn and watch her start back to work on the coffee-stained wall.

"I'm sorry about the invasion of your privacy," he said in a voice that weakened her knees.

She rinsed out the cloth and started on the floor.

"It's easy to forget one's manners when you spend so much time alone."

She worked her way halfway under the table, then around to the other side of the wall.

"Will you forgive me?"

She pulled herself to her feet, walked through him again as if he weren't there, then turned on the water to rinse the cloth. When she turned back around to finish the job, he was gone.

Alane sat, curled in the corner of the couch, wearing three pairs of socks, two sweatshirts, sweatpants, wrapped in a blanket, with a sketch pad propped against her knees. A virtual bonfire roared in the fireplace and a charcoal pencil dangled, forgotten, from her fingers.

Maybe she'd been too hard on him, ignoring his apology the way she had. He did have a point about spending so much time alone and all. And it would be awfully hard to resist divining someone else's feelings.

She wiggled into another position and kicked off the blanket.

He'd been gone since morning. All day long she'd kept expecting him to show up and shock another ten years off her life. She'd finished cleaning the kitchen, unloaded her paints and other materials from the car, as well as a forgotten bag of groceries. She'd unpacked, brought in enough firewood for the night, then spent the last several hours trying to sketch something—anything—that wasn't the face of her ghost.

She stared into the fire, wondering at the odd sense of loss she felt. What if he stayed gone?

She should be irritated that he'd interrupted her vacation, taking her mind off her work and the problem with David. But her work and her decisions seemed somehow less important the longer Jared stayed away.

Just as she started to worry if she'd see him again, an eighteenth century tricorn fluttered out of nowhere and landed in the center of the living room carpet.

Alane sat up and swung her feet to the floor. He was back!

She scanned the room, anxious for him to appear. Finally the air shimmered and he stood there, wearing jeans and an oxford shirt. Just the sight of him sent her heart to her throat, and the reaction had nothing to do with fear.

"I thought I'd throw my hat in first. If you didn't pull a gun and shoot at it, it'd be safe to come in." Though his smile had her insides doing somersaults, his eyes asked if she was still angry. How could someone with such raw sexuality have so much little-boy charm?

Alane chewed on her lower lip in an attempt not to smile.

"I won't shoot at your hat if you promise not to delve into my feelings anymore."

He screwed up his face and rolled his eyes toward the ceiling. After several seconds of melodramatic deliberation, he looked back at her and nodded.

"It's a deal. But I can't promise I won't slip now and then. Old habits die hard."

She narrowed her eyes at him.

"No loopholes allowed."

"Okay, okay. I promise." The hat melted away into nothing as he flopped into the leather recliner. "What are you working on?"

She glanced at the sketch pad, which was covered with charcoal drawings of him.

"Oh, nothing." She flipped the pad closed. "Just trying to generate some inspiration."

"Lost the spark, huh?"

Alane blinked at his perception. She didn't often meet someone who understood artistic highs and lows.

"Yes, as a matter of fact. That's why I rented this place. To try and concentrate on finding the passion."

"And I've done nothing but interrupt you. I'll go and leave you—"

"No!" She nearly jumped off the couch. When he didn't move she leaned back and tucked her legs back under the blanket. "You don't need to go. As a matter of fact, I could use some company."

"Great!" He settled back into the leather. "Do you like television?"

"Television?" Not exactly what she had in mind.

"Yeah."

"It's okay, I guess. Is there something on you'd like to watch?" She hoped he'd take the hint at her lack of enthusiasm.

His eyes lit up. "Would you mind? It's been years since anyone rented the place at Christmastime. I'd love to see a good old-fashioned Christmas special."

Alane started to ask him why he didn't just turn on the TV and watch them, but she caught herself. There was probably a good reason, and she probably didn't want to know it. She picked up the remote and flicked on the TV, then channel surfed through three cartoon specials, a Christmas in Hawaii show, and a dozen sitcom reruns.

"Looks like you're out of luck," she said as she tossed the remote onto the coffee table, not at all sorry to turn off the boob tube.

He scrunched lower in the recliner and sighed.

"Hey, I know!" She snapped her fingers and kicked off the blanket again. "I've got some Christmas CD's out in the car." She tried to cram her feet into her boots, then had to stop and take off two pairs of socks. "We'll have our own Christmas special. You'll have to imagine the tree, though. I don't do real trees. Too much of a fire hazard."

"My imagination's good. Not as good as a real tree, but good."

She headed out the door and found Jared waiting for her in the car.

"Are they old Christmas carols? I don't think I could abide anything with rap music or barking dogs."

Alane smiled at his look of horror. "Do I look like the rap music type?"

He squinted at her.

"One can never tell these days."

She pulled a handful of CD's from the car, then slipped and slid back to the house. He was pacing next to the stereo when she stomped her way through the door. She half expected him to ask her what took her so long.

"Let's see, I've got—"

"This one. Play this one first." Jared poked his finger through the first CD of mixed artists.

Alane pulled the disc from its cover and slid it into the player. She added four more, then turned on the system and adjusted the speakers. A male tenor's clear, haunting voice filled the room with "O Holy Night."

Jared smiled and closed his eyes.

"It's been a long time."

"How long?" Alane asked.

"At least ten years since I've heard a Christmas carol that wasn't part of a TV commercial. This place doesn't stay that busy this time of year."

Alane wanted to ask him how long he'd been at the cabin and why he didn't leave, but he looked too happy at the moment. She couldn't imagine ten years without celebrating Christmas. Ten years, alone on Christmas Eve. She'd struggled with the decision to spend just one alone.

While he sank back into the recliner and became one with the music, Alane kicked off her boots, put her two extra pairs of socks back on, then tossed a bag of popcorn into the microwave. All the comforts of home, she thought, in a hundred-year-old cabin. And no one for him to share it with.

She started to pour herself a glass of wine, then remembered the night before and poured a diet cola instead. When she reentered the living room with a heaping bowl of popcorn, Jared sat in the recliner, his head back and his eyes closed, looking for the world as if he were asleep.

She admired the curve of his jaw, the way his hair fell in dark waves that begged to be touched, and wondered if ghosts slept.

He opened his eyes and smiled at her.

His heart lurched at the sight of her, all warm and cuddly-looking in those awful gray sweats smeared in a rainbow of paints. He wondered if she smelled as good as she looked.

"Enjoying the music?"

He closed his eyes and pulled his thoughts away from what it would feel like to nuzzle his face in the silk of her hair.

"Mmmm. Yes. Thank you for thinking of it."

"My pleasure."

He heard her munching on popcorn and wished he could feed it to her, one plump kernel at a time.

The jangling ring of the telephone jerked him from his pleasant thoughts. The irritating sound of that contraption was a noise he would never, in a hundred lifetimes, learn to like.

Alane wiped her fingers on her sweats and thankfully picked the thing up before it could ring again.

"Hello?"

Jared fought the overwhelming urge to tune in on her

aura, especially since the look on her face suggested the other person was a male.

"No. I don't think that's a good idea . . . I came here so I could be alone and work." She flicked her gaze toward Jared. "No, I'm not lonely. Really, David. I don't mind spending Christmas alone. I *want* some time alone . . . All right . . . I'll see you then." With a hastily murmured, "Bye," she hung up and gave Jared a weak smile.

"Boyfriend?" he asked, amazed at how hard it was to keep the red-hot jealousy from creeping into his voice.

She gave a noncommittal shrug. "Sometimes."

"Is he coming up?" Jared would be damned if he'd let the man within one hundred yards of the cabin.

"No. I came here to be alone and I don't want any company." She tossed a handful of popcorn into her mouth, then her eyes widened and she swallowed fast. "Not that I want *you* to leave."

At least those words lessened the sting of a boyfriend.

"I couldn't leave even if you wanted me to." Damn. Why had he said that out loud?

She sat up a little straighter in the corner of the couch and took a sip of her soft drink.

"You can't leave? Why not?"

Jared slouched in the chair and wondered when he'd lost control of his mouth.

"I don't know."

"You don't know why you can't leave?"

He sighed. "No. I came back about twenty-five years ago and I haven't been able to leave since."

"You came back? You mean you'd been here before and managed to leave?"

Jared closed his eyes and massaged the bridge of his nose. He hadn't wanted to get into this conversation. Not yet. He raised his head and looked her in the eye.

"I died here."

FOUR

Alane couldn't believe her ears. She looked around the room and shivered.

"Here?" She hadn't actively thought of him dying.

"Not actually in this cabin. It hadn't been built yet. My home sat on this site nearly two hundred years ago, but I found that it burned to the ground shortly after my wife and I died."

Two hundred years. It sounded just as astounding as the first time she'd heard it. And he'd had a wife. Why did that knowledge cause such an emptiness in her? Had he loved her very much?

"How . . . How did you die?"

He stared into the fire as "Silent Night" played softly in the background. He stared so long, she thought perhaps he hadn't heard her question.

"It's not important now," he finally said, a seriousness in his voice she'd never heard. He continued to gaze into space, seeing something that must have brought him immense sadness.

How she wished she could touch him right now. To thread her fingers through his dark, thick hair. To smooth away the lines caused by the pain in his eyes. Without thinking, she rose, then knelt at his feet. Ever so slowly, as he turned his gaze to hers, she placed her hand through his on the armrest. She felt that warmth again. That subtle, summer's breeze warmth as her hand mingled inside his.

He looked at her, then closed his eyes, as if she'd somehow made the pain increase.

And then he vanished.

Jared plowed his fingers through his hair from forehead to crown, pacing the length and breadth of what had once been his property.

How could he continue to spend time with Alane? The very sight of her stirred an ache in his heart he'd thought never to feel. When she'd so gently placed her hand in his, he thought he would perish from the want, the need, to touch her. But to touch her, to really touch her, would take more than all his strength, and he would fade to whatever world awaited beyond this. An unknown world, without Alane. A fate, in his eyes, far worse than wandering the earth alone.

He paced throughout the night, cursing himself for caring, wanting desperately to go to her, forcing himself to stay away. Not until the morning sun had climbed high enough to burn away the fog did he finally admit he could never stay away from her now.

In the space of a heartbeat he stood inside the cabin, sensing instantly that she wasn't there. He found her digging her car out of the snow. A knot of fear lodged in his throat. Would she leave now? Would he never see her again?

He moved himself to her side, watching as she dug her tires out of a drift.

"I'm sorry about last night."

She bounced off the car and landed in a four-foot snowdrift.

"Bloody hell! Would you stop doing that?" she yelped as she struggled to her feet, snow-encrusted from head to toe.

"Okay, I'll wear a bell around my neck if you promise not to leave." He tried to keep his voice light and playful. Neither of which he felt.

She worked in a vain attempt to knock the snow from her clothes.

"Leave? I'm not leaving."

"You're not?" His day brightened as if the sun had emerged from a total eclipse. "I thought you were leaving because of the way I . . ." He let the statement trail off, not exactly anxious to put his behavior into words for her.

"No, I'm just digging the car out in case I need to go get supplies. Some of my paints froze when I left them in the car." She fished around in the snow for the shovel, which had buried itself when she dropped it. "Actually," she dragged the back of a ski-gloved hand across her forehead as she stared at the ground, "I figured I should be doing the apologizing. I shouldn't have been so nosy. I didn't really mean to pry." She straightened and looked him in the eye. "It has to be painful. I shouldn't have asked you to recall those memories."

Did she have any idea how beautiful she was? Not just the combination of hair and eyes, skin and cheekbones, lips that begged to be kissed. But beautiful from within. A goodness, a serenity within herself that radiated from her like rays from a sun.

"It wasn't the memories, Alane," he said quietly. "I left because it hurt too much not to be able to touch you back."

The apology left her eyes, replaced by an emotion he couldn't quite name. She dropped her gaze and he thought he would go mad resisting the impulse to read her aura. She shook her head, then looked back at him.

"Jared, I—"

The blare of a car horn interrupted her as a four-wheel drive pulled up the freshly plowed road.

"Damn you, David," she muttered under her breath.

Alane threw down the snow shovel and waded over to the car pulling into the drive she'd just shoveled. Ice on the driver's window distorted the handsome blond features of her on-again, off-again boyfriend.

The window came down and little sheets of ice fell into

the car. David smiled up at her with his you-can't-be-mad-at-me smile.

"Hi, sweetheart. Thought I'd surprise—"

"Don't even bother getting out, David. Just turn it around and go home." She pointed in the direction he'd just come.

"Now you don't mean—"

"I meant everything, David. I meant I don't want company. I meant I want to spend Christmas alone. I meant I want to get some serious work done, and I meant I want to be alone to think about us and whether or not there *is* an us. What part of that don't you understand?"

He shoved the door open and stepped out into the snow.

"Okay, okay, just calm down. I shouldn't have come up here against your wishes. I realize that now." He leaned against the car and pulled her to him. "But I miss you, and I hate the thought of spending Christmas Eve alone."

Alane dodged a kiss and stepped away from him. If he'd said he couldn't bear the thought of *her* spending Christmas Eve alone, she might have caved. Her thoughts went to Jared, who'd spent the last ten Christmases in a lonely cabin in the mountains by himself. Her glance searched for his hazy form, but he was nowhere to be seen. Not, she'd discovered, that that meant he wasn't still around.

"David, I need this time to myself. I've looked forward to it, I deserve it, and I'm going to have it."

"You know, I've come all this way." He tried to pull her to him again, but she turned her back on him. "Why don't I just crash here for the night and then—"

She spun around and sent him a glare that he should have been able to read by now.

"You can stay for lunch and then you're leaving. You know, this hasn't helped your case any. You keep telling me you're sensitive to my artistic needs, but when I *need* to get away, you give me barely twenty-four hours before you're following on my heels. You're smothering me, David, and I don't *need* to be smothered!"

He glared at her then with the look that always told her she was being selfish.

"I'm not trying to smother you. I'm trying to protect

you." His gaze swept the snowy landscape, the solitary cabin, the lonely, slush-covered road. "This is an isolated place here, Alane. Accidents happen. Things . . . happen." He slid back into the driver's seat and fired up the engine. "Don't bother with lunch. I'll leave you here with your solitude."

Before she could even open her mouth, he slammed the door and threw the car into reverse. Snow and slush sprayed from beneath all four tires as he spun out of the drive and fishtailed down the road.

A scant twenty-four hours earlier, his last words might have spooked her into begging him to stay. But today, if he'd meant to frighten her, he'd fallen far short of his goal.

Jared sat at his wife's grave on the very top of the mountain overlooking the Shenandoah Valley. The tombstone marking the site had long ago crumbled away under the boots of soldiers during the Civil War, but Jared could still remember the first time he'd seen the marker, just months after their deaths.

Carved in the cold stone had been the words:

KATHERINE EVANS ELLIOTT AND HER UNBORN CHILD
BORN 1781   DIED 1801
BELOVED DAUGHTER

Not, "Beloved Wife and Daughter."

Jared's existence had been ignored, as had his burial, for the grave was a solitary grave, and he'd never found what had become of his earthly body.

He stared at the flat, frozen ground that held no hint of the grave lying beneath it.

He'd been fond of Katherine. He'd grown to love her, after a fashion, and he'd treated her with as much or more respect than most husbands treated their wives in that day. But he'd married her because his parents wished to join the two families, and he'd gone into the marriage knowing he would always want something more than she could give.

And God knows, she'd given him everything she'd had

to give. Loved him to distraction, bowed to his every wish, very nearly groveled for any crumb of affection he'd cared to bestow upon her. And still he'd held part of himself back.

Now he loved someone with the kind of love Katherine had so craved, and he could not even touch her. For the first time in two centuries, he knew the full impact of his mother-in-law's curse.

May your soul know no peace, Jared Elliott, until you give up your existence in the name of love.

As the words and meaning finally rang clear in his mind, he did something he hadn't done in two hundred years.

He prayed.

Alane slid another set of CD's into the player, then tossed a couple more logs onto the fire. She settled back on the stool in front of her canvas and tried to paint while she waited for him to come.

It didn't take long.

She watched him appear by the fireplace, the very sight of him sending exquisite ripples of heat racing through her blood. When he smiled she felt as if a hundred humming-birds fluttered in her stomach.

He turned in a circle and scanned the room with a grin. She'd scattered a dozen or so candles over every surface, and they cast their soft yellow glow into the evening gloom, perfuming the air with scents of pine, cinnamon and vanilla.

"I like what you've done to the place," he said in his usual teasing tone.

"I tried to stay busy while you were gone."

He smiled and nodded but didn't say what he'd been do-ing or where he'd been.

"I thought you might need a little time alone with Dun-can." He looked around. "Where's he lurking, anyway."

Alane laughed and the knots in her stomach loosened a little.

"You're a good one to talk. And *David* went back to Roanoke."

Jared flopped into the recliner and muttered under his breath, "A good place for him."

"How do you do that?" Alane asked.

He looked up at her and arched a brow.

"How do I do what?"

"That. How do you walk through walls but manage to sit and lean on the furniture and counter and things?" She figured that was a pretty safe question to ask. It shouldn't stir up painful memories of a dead wife.

He looked at himself sitting in the recliner, then shrugged.

"Basically, I will it. It's a thing left over from my mortal days, I suppose. It doesn't take any energy. In fact, I don't even think about it."

"So, if you can lean on things, can you pick things up?"

Jared looked away from her and she had the distinct feeling she'd hit on a topic that bothered him.

"Yes and no," he said when he looked back at her. Whatever had flashed in his eyes moments earlier was gone now. "I have to really focus my energy to actually touch something. If I use all my energy, I'll cease to exist on this plain. And since I'm not sure of which direction I'm headed in the hereafter, I plan to hang around here as long as I can." His devilish grin set the hummingbirds to flapping again.

"Does it take any energy to *be* touched?" Alane walked over to him and dropped to her knees beside the chair.

A muscle in his jaw flexed before he answered.

"I can't be touched."

"No?" she said quietly. Then she raised her hand and slowly traced the air along his jaw to his chin. All her fingers encountered was that same elusive warmth. "Can you feel this?" Her words came out barely above a whisper.

He closed his eyes, as if in pain, and he swallowed hard. When he looked back at her it was as if his gaze looked into the deepest part of her soul. He curled his hand into a fist and placed it in the center of his chest.

"I feel it here."

Tears burned behind Alane's eyes and she blinked them away before they could spill over onto her cheeks.

In the silence between them the CD player whirred as it changed discs. Jared drew in a deep breath and let it out.

"Let's change the subject, shall we? For instance," he

nodded toward a speaker from which Colin Raye's latest song drifted. "I wouldn't have guessed you to be a country western fan."

Alane worked to shift from the tenderness overwhelming her at his admission, to his statement about her taste in music.

"I . . . uh . . . I'm a recent convert."

"So what converted you?"

What converted her? Would he understand if she told him?

"Well, I'm not into the 'crying in my beer' music, but some of these songs are so . . . I don't know . . . visual. They're truly poetic. The love songs are so plain-spoken they can speak to everyone. And some of the other songs just tell it like it is. Like this one, for instance."

Jared listened for a few minutes to the upbeat music and lyrics.

"So do you like the country western dances?"

She got to her feet and picked up her paintbrushes.

"How do you know about country western dances?"

He pointed at the television like a game show model displaying the latest prize.

"Meet my main source of information for the last quarter century. I had to watch whatever the people renting the place watched." He leaned toward her conspiratorially. "Some of those people had very odd tastes."

She chuckled at the thought of who all had passed through this cabin over the years, and how horrified they'd be to know they'd had a witness.

"Did you ever show yourself to anyone else?"

A look of tenderness flashed in his eyes before he replaced it with a wide-eyed look of innocence.

"Not here at the cabin. You're the first. Couldn't resist you. So, what about the dances? Do you know how to do them?"

She smiled at his efforts to stay off the previous topic.

"I like the line dances." She tossed her paintbrushes back down. "There's this new one out that I can't quite keep up with. It sort of goes . . ." She did a little step-together, step-together, kick, kick, tush push. "There's a couple extra steps but I can't seem to get them all in and keep up with the music."

"Hey, I know that one." Jared jumped to his feet and waited for the beat. "There was a couple here last month who watched nothing but that country video station. I thought I'd go mad for want of hearing the news." He looked up at her and winked. "It's amazing what idle hands will do when there's not even a devil's workshop to be had. Besides, you don't need a partner to line dance. Now watch."

He did her steps and then added the others as smoothly as a country-western Fred Astaire.

"See how I'm doing this?" he asked as he did a ninety-degree turn and repeated the steps.

She stared, a little speechless at watching a ghost line dance in the middle of the living room floor. And dance flawlessly at that.

"If you do sort of a triple step here, it all fits in. C'mon. You try."

Alane chewed on her lower lip as she moved to stand beside him, watching his feet and waiting for the music.

She followed his steps fairly easily but screwed up the triple step.

"Come on. You can do it," he told her, never missing a beat. "It's like this. One, two, one, two, onetwothree."

"Hey! I think I've got it." She managed to squeeze in all the steps, but not with Jared's finesse.

They continued to dance, side-by-side, with Jared coaching her along the way. She watched her feet and chewed on her lip until the steps felt right and she could keep up with him. Just as she started to feel comfortable, the song ended.

"Dance with me through the next one to make sure I've got it down pat, okay?"

They both waited with one ear cocked toward a speaker, their bodies poised for the music to start.

Instead of a fast song, though, the strains of a sultry, moving love song swirled around the room.

They looked at each other and smiled, then the mirth left

Jared's eyes and he peered into her soul again as the song spoke of a love that could never be.

"Will you dance with me?" he asked, his voice low and husky.

Hot tingles ripped through Alane and her heart pounded harder at his simple, knee-weakening request.

He raised his hands as if he could actually hold her for the dance.

Hesitantly, her heart climbing in her chest, she stepped up to him, mingled her hand with his, and curved her arm around his vaporous waist.

She felt the warmth again, tingling in her fingers and arm where she touched him, and the melting sensation traveled through her body like it was part of her blood.

As they swayed, as she burned from within, she gazed into Jared's eyes—eyes that reflected need, pain. Love. An aching throb started in her chest, growing with each passing moment as she returned his look, yearning to feel his arms around her, to be able to press her head against his chest. A knot of misery formed in her throat at the thought that she could never feel the warmth of his lips on hers. Never taste the sweetness of his kiss.

How she wished she could touch him, for his sake, not for hers. To wrap her arms around his neck, to caress his cheek, to trace her fingers across his lips. His thick, dark hair, falling in shiny layers begged for her fingers to sift through it, to smooth it back at his temples.

How had this happened? How could she find herself drawn to someone who'd been dead for two centuries? Misery mingled with want, denial warred with acceptance as her head spun and she wondered if there could possibly be a more hopeless situation.

She held his gaze as the song continued, so perfectly meant for them that the words brought tears to her eyes. She squeezed her eyes closed, to ward off more tears and to escape from the tortured look on Jared's face. The knot grew in her throat and she struggled to swallow around it. A hot, wrenching coil spun in her chest.

As the song drew to an end she opened her eyes and looked up at Jared.

He slowly dipped his head, and for a moment a heavenly warmth passed across her lips.

"God help me, Alane," he moaned as the warmth traveled along her neck, "but I've fallen in love with you."

Joy and agony exploded in her at his words, staggering her and nearly bringing her to her knees.

"God help us both, then," she whispered, "God help us both."

 FIVE

Jared drew in his breath and tried to calm the raging need to touch her.

He had to touch her. Just once more. Once, while she looked at him with those dark, soulful eyes, so giving, so loving.

Giving in to his need, he focused his energy, then brought his hands up to gently cradle her face. She gasped at his touch, then her eyes lit with a joy that came from the center of her soul. She nuzzled his hands as he slowly found the softness of her mouth with his.

He absorbed the feel of her, the essence that was Alane, and his mind swam at all she meant to him. He indulged in the drug of her kiss, the wonder at never having felt such euphoria. Then as his strength drained from him, weakening him, reminding him of who and what he was, an empty, gnawing ache curled in the pit of his stomach at what he would never have.

Before the encroaching blackness could engulf him, he released her and stumbled to the couch.

"Jared!" Alane ran to his side and fell to her knees. "Jared, what's wrong? I can barely see you!" She grabbed at him with frustrated cries, but her hands touched nothing but air. "This isn't funny! Stop it!"

He raised his head and looked at her, the pain in her eyes tearing at his heart.

"I'll . . . I'll be all right," he struggled to say. "I just . . . need rest."

Alane didn't try to stop the tears. For one brief, exquisite moment, when he'd touched her, when his lips set off fireworks in her blood, she'd thought she owned the world. Then reality came crashing back, more painful than before.

He leaned back against the couch and dragged his legs onto the cushions. She reached to help him, then couldn't quiet the frustrated sob at her vain attempts.

He raised a weak hand to her.

"Don't . . . worry."

She watched as he seemed to lose consciousness.

"Jared!" she yelled, then screamed his name again when he didn't answer.

"Okay, stay calm," she told herself. She sank back onto her heels and stared at the face already precious to her heart.

His weakness was evident. He had lost his strength, and a piece of his existence.

Is that how much he'd given up to touch her?

She knew now what he'd meant about using his energy. About ceasing to exist. The thought terrified her and she swore she'd forbid him to touch her like that ever again. Nothing was worth the price of his existence. She refused to be the one he would give up his existence for.

She knelt by his side, cursing her helplessness. Her mind raced for ways to help him, but all she could think of were mortal comforts. She couldn't get him a pillow or drape a blanket over him. She couldn't even hold his hand.

The fire died in the grate and the candles guttered in their holders, and still she stayed by his side. Sometime during the night she woke to find her head cradled in her arms, resting on the couch cushions. Every joint in her body ached and she finally struggled to her feet and dropped into the recliner. Moonlight fell across his body on the couch, but he looked no stronger than he had hours earlier.

She sat there and stared at him until her eyes burned. She

willed him to get better. And as she sat vigil she faced the truth that she'd fallen in love with a dead man. After knowing Jared, every other man she'd ever known, including David, especially David, paled in comparison. Jared would forever be the standard by which she measured other men, and she knew beyond a shadow of a doubt that none would ever come close.

Sometime before noon his eyes finally opened and he stared heavenward for a moment before turning his gaze straight to her, as if he'd known she was there all along.

He just looked at her, with such a love and sadness in his eyes it brought burning tears to her own.

"Thank you for staying with me," he said quietly, his voice stronger than before. "I knew you were here. I don't sleep, you know, but I'd lost the strength to speak."

Alane didn't trust her voice so she just smiled and shook her head to tell him it was nothing. When she'd swallowed back the tears, she knelt by his side, aching to be able to take his hand in hers.

"You're never to do something like that again, do you understand?"

"Do what?" he asked with a weak, innocent grin.

She couldn't even punch him in the arm.

"Touch me, smart aleck. You're never to take a chance like that again."

He lifted his hand and drew it along her cheek.

"It was worth it."

"No, it wasn't. I was scared to death!"

He dropped his hand to mingle with hers and all traces of a smile left his face.

"If I had awakened in Hell this morning, it still would have been worth it. I kissed an angel last night, and I learned the joy of what it is to love and to be loved. If I cease to exist this minute, I will go a happy man."

"And you'll leave me to mourn you for the rest of my life. Promise me you won't take that chance again." When he didn't answer she nearly screamed for wanting to shake him. "Promise me!"

When he still didn't answer, she got to her feet and glared down at him, hands on her hips. She had to know he'd be safe.

"Promise, or I'll leave right now and never come back. I won't stay here and jeopardize your existence."

He struggled to sit up, then swung his feet to the floor and sighed.

"I promise never to touch you again, unless you ask. How's that?"

A hollow victory, she thought. But at least it would keep him safe. She nodded.

"Now. Is there anything I can do to help you get your strength back?"

"A cup of coffee and a twenty-ounce steak would do wonders."

She picked up a throw pillow and hurled it at his head. He actually tried to dodge it, but it sailed through his chest and bounced off the back of the couch.

"I'm serious, Casper. I'm new at this. What do sick ghosts do to get well?"

He laughed weakly and shook his head.

"Nothing. I should be back to normal by this evening. See?" He waved his arms and legs around, like a little boy in show-and-tell. "I'm getting better already."

She eyed him, not quite certain he was telling her the truth, but what else could she do?

"Okay. You just stay there and get your strength back and I'm going to get some breakfast. Then I've got a surprise for you."

His eyes lit up and he sat up straighter.

"A surprise? I love surprises! What is it?"

She turned and gave him a long-suffering look.

"I'm not telling. And if you don't behave yourself, I'm not going to." Good grief, her mother's voice had just come out of her mouth. She needed to go dunk her head in ice water.

Jared paced in front of the window, through the wall and onto the front porch. Back and forth. Back and forth. Every time a flash of headlights swept across the snow-covered road below, he zapped himself to the edge of his land and waited to see if the car would turn up their road.

Where the devil was she? She'd taken the Jeep hours ago, with a mysterious smile and a light in her eyes, refusing to offer even a hint to her activities.

He hated surprises.

Finally! Twin beams of light sweeping onto their road. He whisked himself to his boundary, and the moment her Jeep crossed his land he melted into the car.

"What took you so long?"

Alane jerked with a gasp, and the car went fishtailing across the road. Once she steered her way out of the problem, she stopped, fell back against the seat and held her heart.

"Criminy! Would you stop that?"

He barely even heard her as he scanned the interior of the car, taking in nothing but a grocery bag and art supplies.

"Sorry. What's the surprise? What took you so long?"

She stared at him, her straight face given away by the smile in her eyes.

"The surprise is a great big, *loud,* cowbell to wear around your neck. And have you ever tried to make good time on mountain roads after a blizzard?"

She put the car in gear and continued up the road to the driveway. Jared stared at her as she drove.

She wasn't serious about a cowbell, was she?

Before he could ponder that question she climbed out of the car and grabbed the bags from the backseat. He followed her into the cabin while she dropped them on a table, then he followed her back out again.

"You aren't serious about the cowbell, are you? Because surely you realize I can't . . ."

He forgot what he was saying as she went to the back of the car and yanked on a rope dangling from the top.

"A Christmas tree!"

Alane pulled a small, lush, magnificent fir from the top of the car, then expertly grabbed the trunk and headed back to the house.

"You got this for me, didn't you? This is the surprise! I know it is because you don't do real trees. This is wonderful! You couldn't have picked a better gift."

He passed through the wall and chattered at her from the other side of the screen door. With a grimacing smile, she struggled at the door but couldn't let go of the tree to grab the knob.

He reached out his hand, focusing to push open the door for her.

"Don't even think about it," she ordered from the porch. "I can get it."

With a healthy kick to the bottom, the door slammed hard against the frame and bounced open a little. She hooked the toe of her boot in the opening, flicked it wider, then pushed it all the way back with her foot. Seconds later she'd squeezed through the doorway and stood the tree in the corner. With a satisfied nod, she dusted off her hands and smiled up at him.

"I am woman. Hear me roar."

Did she possibly know how much an impish smile like that made him want to kiss her? He hated to think what would happen if she ever turned a smoky, heated gaze on him. He'd probably enjoy his last few seconds on earth touching her in ways she'd only dreamed of, then die all over again of ecstasy.

"What?" she asked with a slightly uncomfortable look.

"I was just thinking how kissable you look right now."

Her eyebrows shot skyward and she sidestepped around him.

"In your dreams, big boy. I don't want to go through another night like last night. Now get in the Christmas spirit, no pun intended, and show me where they hide the decorations."

He must be back to normal, since he was already planning how to sap his strength again. But he'd promised her. With a sigh, he dragged his thoughts away from how nice her mouth tasted and tried to remember where the owners had stored the Christmas decorations back in . . . what? 1986?

"Gotta be in the closet," he mumbled, more to himself

than to Alane. "There's no other storage place unless it's
in the building out back."

He walked through the door and into the closet's depths,
strolling through a vacuum cleaner, lawn chairs, umbrellas,
a badminton game, and an assortment of junk collected over
the years. Scanning with his night vision, he found two
boxes of decorations in the farthest corner under two old
suitcases and a bag of old clothes.

Without bothering to go back to the door, he stuck his
head through the wall and found Alane moving furniture
around, making room for the tree.

"You want the good news or the bad news?"

She bumped a heavy table a few more feet with her hip,
then straightened and raked a silky blond strand behind her
ear.

"I don't do bad news."

"Okay. The good news is the decorations are in here."

She looked at the door, then dragged her gaze six feet
along the wall to where his head protruded.

"Let me guess," she groaned. "You're standing in the
middle of them and there's not exactly a clear path back
there."

"Give the lady a prize!"

When she walked to the closet and opened the door, he
pulled his head back in and waved at her.

"Down here, under the stairs."

Alane flicked on the light and groaned again.

"Oh well." After dragging the heavy, dark green sweater
over her head, she shoved the sleeves of her pale mint turtleneck up to her elbows and started pulling junk from the
closet. Halfway back she stopped and dragged a hand across
her cheek, leaving behind a brown smudge. His heart
melted.

"How 'bout handing me that—" She stopped pointing
at a large box of junk and thumped her head with the heel
of her hand. "Duh!" She giggled and kept plowing her way
through. "I forget sometimes that you can't . . . well, you
know. Not that it makes any difference . . ."

Alane kept talking but Jared didn't hear her words.

He couldn't even hand her something. Couldn't help ease her life in any tangible way at all. Hell, he couldn't even open a door for her when she had her hands full. What was he doing, falling in love with this woman?

"Tada!" While he'd wallowed in self pity, she'd finished working her way to the boxes. "Just let me cram all this junk back in here and then we can do the fun stuff."

Jared made himself smile at her look of triumph. She lugged the boxes out of the closet, then set to work replacing what she'd taken out.

He wandered out of the closet and flopped into a chair. This was a mistake. This whole fiasco would never have happened if he'd controlled himself and remained cloaked throughout her visit.

But he hadn't bargained on falling in love.

" 'Oh, the weather outside is frightful,' " Alane sang in the most horrendous, off-key voice, " 'but the fire is so delightful . . . ' "

Jared grimaced but couldn't help smiling. How could he *not* love her? For the first time in his life—or death—he listened to his heart. Throwing off the self pity, he stood and followed her voice into the closet.

" 'Let it snow, let it snow, let it'—GEEZ! Would you stop doing that?"

Alane propped her feet up on the coffee table and scooped up a handful of popcorn. She gestured for the third time that night toward the tree.

"Not bad, if I do say so myself."

"A work of art," Jared agreed, also for the third time.

They both looked at each other and burst out laughing. The tree was the sorriest Christmas tree she'd ever seen. The box had contained every hideous decoration that had ever been made, from silk-covered balls that had frayed to furriness, to neon-orange glass balls, to Elvis ornaments. And only one lonely little string of lights worked after she'd tested a dozen.

She smiled up at him. It felt strange to sit so close to someone and not be able to snuggle up with him.

He smiled down at her and scrunched deeper into the couch, crossing his legs at the ankles, his feet next to hers, and focusing his attention to the old movie on TV. He couldn't get enough of old movies.

She'd spent a long night the night before, watching his weak form, thinking about what an impossible situation she'd gotten herself into. Falling in love with someone she couldn't touch; who couldn't touch her back. Someone who would never grow old and die. It was as hopeless as if she'd fallen in love with an imaginary lover.

And when she'd teased him earlier and told him to behave himself, sounding exactly like her mother. She'd ignored the voice in her head at first. The voice whispering about babies and motherhood. But she'd finally had to give in and listen. And think about never having babies. Would she never have the opportunity to put to use all that her mother had taught her? She'd had to ask herself which would be worse? Never having something she'd never had, or spending the rest of her life thinking about Jared. Loving and missing him, wondering about him and wanting to be with him so badly she would ache.

She'd finally accepted the fact that there would be no easy answer to this situation. She would just live her life one day at a time, make decisions as they were presented to her, and pray whatever decision she made would be the best for both of them.

"Oh! Now, how insulting! Was that their idea of romantic back then?"

Alane pulled her dark, gloomy thoughts back to the cheery room lit by sparse Christmas tree lights and a cozy fire.

"What? What was insulting?"

"In this movie." Jared flicked a disdainful hand toward the TV. "These people are on their honeymoon, and Fred MacMurray asks his new wife—oh, what's her name? Claudette Colbert! He asks Claudette Colbert, 'Is your dress you're wearing to dinner very pretty?' and she says, 'Well, yes, I think so,' and he says, 'Because I want you to be the prettiest woman at dinner tonight.' And she melts all over him! Now I ask you, what kind of compliment is that?"

Before she could even absorb the question, let alone attempt an answer, he turned to her, his fierce gaze raking the length of her, taking in her scraggly ponytail, her turtleneck smudged with ten-year-old dust, her jeans, her feet clad in three pairs of jogging socks.

"You could walk into any room in the world right now and be the most beautiful woman there. Without," his voice gentled as he traced his hand along her cheek, "even washing the dirt from your face."

Talk about melting. Alane could have trickled right off the couch just from his look.

"You're so sweet," she told him with a grin, "but you must be mentally disturbed."

His only answer was a grunt as he settled back to finish the movie.

"Tell me about yourself, Jared." She could almost feel him tense up at her question, but she forged on. "I don't want to dredge up painful memories, but I feel like this is something I need to know now. All I know about you is that you died two hundred years ago and that you had a wife. Did you have any children?" He continued to stare at the television, but she could tell he was no longer watching. After a while he blinked and a muscle flexed in his jaw.

"She was pregnant."

She swallowed back the first words of sympathy and fought the nauseating pitch of her stomach at the thought of another woman carrying his child. Even centuries ago.

"Did . . . she die in childbirth?"

He continued to stare at the happy couple on the television screen. His jaw flexed some more.

"Leave it be, Alane. You don't want to know the story."

"Yes. I do. What could possibly be so bad?" she questioned, then added jokingly, "Unless, of course, *you* killed her."

His features never changed, but he turned his head slowly and nailed her with dead, emotionless eyes. Tingles of icy spiders crawled up her spine and into her scalp. He couldn't have! Not Jared!

"Don't even try to convince me of that! I'll never believe you could murder anyone, especially a woman you loved."

He turned his gaze away, back to the TV. She picked up the remote and switched off the television, but he didn't seem to notice.

"Talk to me, damn it! The truth can't be as bad as what I could imagine." She'd give up everything she owned to be able to shake him right now. "Nothing will convince me you murdered your wife!"

"I didn't murder her, but I killed her. Her and our unborn babe."

Alane wanted to scream.

"Jared, look at me," she said in the calmest voice she could muster.

His head didn't turn, but he slid his gaze to her.

"You've got to tell me now. You can't drop something like that in my lap and then not explain. What happened? Tell me how she died. Start at the beginning. Hell, start anywhere, just tell me what happened."

Jared studied her face with cold, hopeless eyes. Finally, defeat shadowed his features and he drew in a deep, resigned breath.

"I didn't love her."

Alane was horrified with herself at the wave of relief she felt. She swept it away and prodded him to go on.

"Our parents wanted a union of families. She was the only daughter, and I was the only son. There was never any question. Back then children married who their parents told them to marry."

Alane only nodded, not wanting to interrupt him.

"She was in her seventeenth year. We married on my twenty-fifth birthday. I was fond enough of her. And I was gentle with her. I suppose I even grew to love her in time, but like a sister. I felt no passion for her, no matter how hard I searched my soul for it.

"She'd tried from our wedding night to conceive. But it took three years. She was nearly hysterical with worry, until it actually happened. By that time she'd changed from a sweet, gentle child to a possessive, clutching harridan."

He stopped for a moment, as if searching his soul. Alane was afraid to breathe. Afraid to break the spell and send him back into himself.

"One night I was going upstairs to dress. By that time I usually spent my evenings out, looking for . . . something . . . missing in my life. I'd tried to find it at home, but though Katherine had been a good wife, I could never give all of myself to her, nor accept everything she offered to give."

Katherine. Her name had been Katherine.

"She wanted me to stay home that night. Her parents were visiting, to celebrate the announcement of the child, but they'd been there a month and I desperately needed to get away. Katherine followed me up the stairs, begging me to stay. She grabbed my arm to stop me and I yanked it back." He jerked his arm, as if reliving the moment. "She lost her balance and fell backward. I tried to grab her," he reached out, trancelike, "but she pulled me with her. We fell. All I could hear through the pain was the thump of our bodies and the crunch of breaking bones, until we landed on the floor at the bottom of the stairs.

"When I opened my eyes, Katherine was dead. I knew it. I don't know how long I was unconscious, how long her parents and the servants stood over us. I looked up at her mother, standing there, sobbing. The last thing I remember was the pure venom in her voice as she cursed me. 'May your soul know no peace, Jared Elliott, until you give up your existence in the name of love.' I have wandered the earth ever since."

 SIX

Jared finally dragged his gaze back to hers, braced for the disgust, the revulsion he knew would be in her eyes. But all her eyes held were shimmering tears. And love. Understanding, *healing* love.

"The curse," she whispered. "The curse is why you're a ghost." Then two lines creased her brow. "But, that means you have to cease existing for someone you love, in order to find peace."

He nodded. He'd had two hundred years to think about finding a loophole. There wasn't one.

"Oh, Jared," she began, but he stopped her with an upraised hand.

"No pity. I won't have it."

"But it was an accident! It's not fair—"

"It wasn't fair that Katherine died when she was twenty years old. Or that the baby she wanted so desperately never grew to even swell her belly." He draped one arm behind her on the sofa and traced her face with his other hand. "It hasn't been such a bad existence." *Until now,* the words burned in his mind. *Now, when I've found you, and all I can think about is touching you, holding you, what it would be like if things were different.*

319

But he said none of these things, knowing they would leave her as raw and wounded as he.

She leaned her head back on the sofa, back into his arm. He closed his eyes and imagined he could feel her nestled against him.

"But to be so alone," she went on.

"Alane, I spent a hundred and seventy-five years roaming all four corners of the earth. I watched the Civil War, from both sides. I was in Washington when Lincoln was shot and I watched as the doctors worked to save him. I was in England at Queen Elizabeth's coronation. I witnessed both World Wars from every country involved. I've wandered in and out of the Oval Office during top-secret discussions. I've seen the telephone, lightbulb, radio, and television born. I've seen the Wright brothers fly and watched a man walk on the moon." He stopped, took a breath, then gave her his best mischievous grin. "And I've contributed my share to all the ghost stories floating around this country."

Alane smiled a sad, unconvinced smile, but she didn't pursue the conversation. Her eyes drooped heavily, and for the first time he realized she looked exhausted.

"Whatever you say, Jared." She yawned an enormous yawn, then relaxed into the couch and closed her eyes. "I'm so tired."

Jared had forgotten how easily mortals tire, and she'd been awake most of the night before, worrying at his side. He watched her face relax into sleep; watched as shadows from the moon passed over her precious features. Then his breath caught in his throat and his heart lurched when she shifted, leaning into him so that he surrounded her. If he tried, he could imagine he was holding her.

He sat there, unmoving, savoring her presence, weaving a dream in his mind while she slept. And in the dream he was whole, and Alane came to him, loved him, touched him.

But no matter how hard he tried, he couldn't remember how it felt to be touched.

Alane snuggled deeper into the heavenly, melting warmth and tried to hold on to the misty dream of Jared kissing her, but brilliant sunlight prodded her awake. She felt for the covers to pull over her head.

She didn't remember climbing the stairs to go to bed last night. And where were the covers?

She pried one reluctant eye open and peered at the living room through a blur. The fire had burned down to nothing more than a few glowing red coals, and she was lying on the couch without so much as a blanket to cover her.

Then why was she so warm?

Blinding sunlight bounced off the snow and burst through the eastern windows, bathing everything in a white light. It turned the lake into a giant, silvery reflecting pool.

She opened her other eye, then massaged them with the heels of her hands. Everything was still a blur.

"Good morning, sleepyhead."

The voice seemed to come from within her.

No. It came from around her.

Alane elbowed her way to a sitting position, feeling the chill of the room as she rose. Her vision cleared and she looked around.

Jared leaned into the very corner of the couch she'd just vacated. His grin was all little boy, but his eyes held the pain of a man who wanted something so badly he ached.

She should have been flustered when she realized she'd lain *inside* him. But instead she felt closer to him than ever. Connected somehow. When he sat up and swung his legs off the couch, it was as if he whisked away a warm summer breeze and replaced it with the chill air of the arctic.

"Do I have you to thank for keeping me warm all night?" she asked as she plucked her sweater from the end of the coffee table, shaken at the sense of loss she'd felt when he'd moved.

He wiggled his dark eyebrows at her in answer.

"Should I thank you for that dream I was trying not to wake up from, too?" Even as she asked, elusive remnants evaporated like wisps of fog in the sun.

"Not guilty on that count, counselor, but I could oblige you if you'd let me. If you'll remember, you banned me from your brain."

It occurred to her that she might consider lifting the ban for another dream like the one so rapidly fading from her mind.

The frigid air in the cabin raised goose bumps on her arms and turned her thoughts to building the fire and turning up the oil heater. With more than a little reluctance she rose from the couch, then knelt by the fireplace and stacked kindling and wood over the glowing coals.

"I really do appreciate you keeping me warm. I don't even remember falling asleep."

"Believe me, it was my pleasure," he said from behind her in a voice as smooth as old bourbon. "When I tried, I could almost believe we were holding each other."

Tears, hot and choking and unexpected, surged to her eyes at his words. She blinked them back and swallowed past the tightness in her throat.

"It almost felt like you were holding me," she agreed quietly, thinking of the warm, comforting feeling she'd awakened with. She gave the fire one more jab, then turned on the balls of her feet and looked at him with a moist smile. "We're a pair, aren't we?"

Jared studied her, looking as miserable as she felt.

"Yeah. A regular Romeo and Juliet."

He jumped up from the couch and started prowling the living room. It still unnerved her to watch him pace through solid objects, but he didn't even seem aware he was pacing.

He followed her into the kitchen and prowled while she made coffee. He followed her into the bathroom, then did an about-face and left her alone when she turned and quirked an eyebrow at him.

Once alone, Alane took care of the necessities, brushed her teeth, dunked her face in icy water, then decided to draw a nice hot bath and soak for a while to try and get her mind off the storm of emotions buffeting her.

While hot water filled the tub and scented steam fogged the mirror, she flopped her hair atop her head and peeled off the clothes she'd been wearing for twenty-four hours. She stepped gingerly into the tub, then sank with a sigh until the steaming water lapped at her shoulders.

With eyes closed and muscles relaxed, she leaned back and tried to clear her mind of all the worries that had plagued her from the moment she'd realized she was falling in love. Ridiculous. Impossible. Heartbreaking. Wonderful.

The mere thought of Jared brought a smile to her lips. A short-lived smile.

She loved a man who was no more tangible than a dream. A man bound to his property—a property she had rented for only five more days. Five days of ecstasy and torture. Five days of trying to outwit fate. Five days before she had to leave and Jared had to stay.

"Alane, we have a problem."

She jerked so hard, water erupted over the sides of the clawfoot tub. She splashed more over in her attempt to cover herself with a pitifully small washcloth.

Jared finished melting through the wall, apparently taking no notice that she was in the middle of bathing, a frown drawing his eyebrows into one straight line. He paced the length of the room once, then perched on the edge of the clothes hamper.

"I've been thinking," he went on, as though he made it a habit to chat with her while she bathed. "How long have you rented the cabin?"

She sank a little deeper into the tub and narrowed her eyes at him.

"I've rented it through the twenty-sixth."

His face mirrored her own overwhelming dread as the date sank in.

"Five days," he stated, barely above a whisper. "You're leaving the day after Christmas."

Alane swallowed hard, searching for words to ease the pain in his eyes, in his voice. She found none.

"I was just thinking," she said, knowing the offering would be feeble, "that I could call the rental company and rent it longer. I know it's never booked up this time of year." She knew renting longer would be like putting a Band-Aid on a broken bone, but at least it would give them time to think of something else.

He perked up a little at her suggestion and launched himself to his feet.

"Excellent! Make the call now." He towered over her, as if he expected her to bound from the tub and run, dripping, to the phone. She scrunched lower in the water and batted her eyes up at him.

"Oh," he said as realization dawned on his face. And then, for the first time since walking into the bathroom, he seemed to see her as she was—the woman he loved enjoying a nice hot bath. A lecherous little gleam sparked in his eyes, and when Alane sank until the water lapped at her chin, he rolled his eyes and threw up his hands. "Oh, very well. I'll leave you alone."

Before she could blink, he vanished into thin air, but his voice filtered in from nowhere.

"Party pooper."

He didn't like the sound of the one-sided conversation, nor the sickly look creeping over Alane's features.

"A buyer?" Her face paled. "I didn't realize it was for sale."

For sale? It couldn't be for sale. The same people had owned the place for fifty years.

"Today? I'm afraid not. They'll have to wait until I've left to come and measure." She glanced up at Jared with a look of panic.

His stomach churned, and for the first time in two centuries he felt queasy.

"I'm sorry, but I'm working. They'll have to wait until after the twenty-sixth. No, I know you wouldn't have asked. Yes. Well, thanks anyway."

Alane dropped the receiver from her ear and let it dangle from her fingers, forgotten.

"They're selling the cabin," she said as she brought her eyes up to meet his. "The owner died last summer and the heirs have a buyer for it." She shook her head, denying the words. "And the buyers had the nerve to want to come out here today and measure for curtains and carpet and to see if their big screen TV will fit through the door."

A muted, obnoxious beep sounded from the telephone receiver and Alane blindly fumbled it into its cradle. She rose from the couch and roamed aimlessly around the living room, touching things, stopping and staring out a window.

"What do we do now?" She turned and met his gaze.

He cursed himself and Katherine's mother for not being able to wrap her in his arms and comfort her.

But he could. For her, he could. He lifted his arms and focused, willing to give up everything in order to soothe her.

"Don't you dare!" She stepped back and blinked teary eyes when she realized his intent. "Yes, I want to be held. I want to feel your touch so badly I ache for it. But I'd never forgive myself if I caused your death."

He started to point out that he was already dead, but levity would only make things worse right now. He dropped his hands and shook his head before he spoke.

"I'll tell you what we're going to do. We're going to take one day at a time. One minute at a time. And we're not going to waste even a split second mourning the future."

"But there is no future! If they sell this cabin, how will we be able to see each other again?"

Jared stepped up to her and traced his hands along the length of her arms. When she shivered he brought his lips to brush across hers.

"We'll not mourn the future," he repeated. "We'll live a lifetime in these next five days, and when they're over, we'll worry about the future."

She stared up at him with shimmery beads of tears hovering on her lower lashes. He wanted to rail against the fates for giving him what he could never have, like a man dying of thirst with a lake of cool, fresh water just beyond his reach. Instead he forced his best boyish grin and tried to make his voice sound light.

"Starting now. Let's see. What shall we do?" He paced the floor, then spun back around to point at her. "I know! I want to see you paint. That's what you came here for, isn't it? Yes. That's it. Can I watch you paint?"

She sniffed and rubbed the tip of her nose with the back of her hand.

"That should be about as interesting as watching someone fish."

He forced another grin and ushered her toward her paints and the canvas by the window.

"Let me be the judge of that. Now, what have you been working on?"

Alane picked up a tube of paint and fumbled with the palette.

"Nothing, really. I . . . I can't seem to find the passion. I just feel stale."

He draped himself across the leather recliner.

"Then paint me."

Alane blinked and cocked an ear toward him.

"Do what?"

"Why not? I'm better than a bowl of fruit."

She studied him for a minute, then shrugged with a smile.

"All right. Get comfortable. This could take a while."

Jared shifted to a slightly more dignified position and watched quietly as she prepared her paints.

"Do you talk while you work, or do I have to keep my mouth shut?"

She didn't even look up from her preparations.

"Absolute silence. I don't even play music."

"Okay. I can deal with that. I mean, I've gone years at a time without talking, so a few hours here and there will seem like nothing. Unless, of course, you want to try something different, which, in that case—"

"Ahem!"

He snapped his mouth shut and grinned as her brow furrowed in concentration.

She worked quietly for hours while Jared tried to behave himself. It was harder than he'd imagined, keeping his mouth shut and sitting still.

He watched her face change from concentration to frustration. She chewed on her lower lip, squinted first at him, then the canvas, frowned, sighed. When she pinched the bridge of her nose and shook her head, he decided to break his silence.

"You want to know what I think?"

She raised her head and looked around as though she'd forgotten she wasn't alone. "I think you're trying too hard."

"How can someone try too hard at something?" She frowned and dabbed the brush against the canvas.

"When you suck all the enjoyment and spontaneity out of something, you're trying too hard." He got up and circled around behind her as she continued to make improvements on her work.

What she'd done was good. Very good. But Xavier Travis's daughter could do better. She'd painted a very good, two dimensional portrait, but Jared knew she had the talent to make him come to life on the canvas.

"If you'll allow me to, maybe I can help."

She turned and gave him a suspicious look.

"Oh, come on. What do you have to lose?"

She chewed on the end of her brush for a minute, crinkled up her nose and sighed.

"Why not? At this point I'm ready to try anything." She sat back on her stool and looked up at him. "What do I have to do?"

"Nothing," he said as he melted into her. He heard her gasp, then felt her tense up.

Relax, he told her silently. *Relax and trust me.*

She loosened up a little. "This is so weird. I heard you and you didn't even speak."

I can hear you, too. Now open your mind.

He felt her open to him, and he nudged his thoughts into her consciousness. He fed her some of his memories. Happy, carefree, funny memories. He sent them swirling through her like an ever-changing kaleidoscope. She giggled at some of the bits and pieces. He felt her heart tug when he remembered seeing her father's work.

All right. You've relaxed a little. Now pick up the brush and paint what you feel. Don't try to make it perfect. There's no such thing.

She dabbed the brush against the palette, then hesitantly applied it to the canvas.

Stop trying so hard.

She took a deep breath and rocked her head back and forth on her shoulders, popping her neck and loosening her muscles. He cringed at the sound, so reminiscent of those he'd heard while falling down the steps behind Katherine.

This time she approached the canvas without hesitation. She applied the strokes with confidence, and each sweep of the brush was pure genius.

Beautiful! That's exactly what I mean!

Alane was in her own world, focused on her painting as Jared focused when he touched something. He slipped from her body, fighting the emptiness he felt when he did, then watched in awe as she brought him to life on canvas. She spoke only once, to order him back into the chair. He obliged her and managed to sit quietly while he drank in the sight of her.

Did she have any hint as to how irresistible she looked, with a pale blue smudge on her cheek and her hair still flopped atop her head in a wobbly ponytail?

He closed his eyes and fought the pain. No mourning. Not yet. He had an eternity to mourn when she was gone.

Her deep sigh and the creak of the stool as she sat back caught his attention. He opened his eyes to the sight of Alane staring at the painting.

At her side in an instant, he too could only stare at the life she'd breathed into the portrait.

"Magnificent. Perfect," he said, his voice almost reverent.

She turned her head and looked at him, then looked back at the painting.

"You said there's no such thing as perfect," she stated, her awe equaling his.

"I lied."

They stared at the portrait, then at each other. Jared's world shifted as she thanked him with her eyes. He studied her face, so full of want and need, love and pain, and he contemplated touching her again. As he raised his hand, the sound of a car's tires crunching in the snow drew his attention to the window.

He dropped his hand with a curse.

SEVEN

A silver Mercedes rolled to a stop behind Alane's car. Jared groaned at the sight of the two people getting out.

"What is it? Do you know these people?" Alane pulled the curtain farther back and peered out the window at the couple getting out of the car.

"Chuck and Dot Hamlin, if memory serves." He watched Chuck haul his girth from the car, looking like a whale in his gray suede overcoat. Dot emerged from the other side in Spandex pants, cowboy boots, and a mink stole. A cigarette dangled from fuchsia lips, her helmetlike titian curls wreathed in smoke.

"They stayed here a couple of years ago and I thought I would go mad. They watched twenty-four hours of professional wrestling. And when they weren't cheering on Mad Monster Max, they were bickering about everything from which log to put on the fire to who closed the curtains last."

The couple slipped and slid their way onto the porch. When they knocked, Jared cloaked himself so he wouldn't be seen.

Alane opened the door and a gust of cigarette smoke wafted across her face.

"Can I help you?" she asked after a delicate cough that got her point across. Dot took one last drag, blew it out the

side of her mouth, then flicked the cigarette into the snow
with the tip of a gold, dagger-length fingernail.

"Dot and Chuck Hamlin. We're here to measure the
cabin for curtains and carpets."

Alane cocked her head and tapped her fingers irritatedly
against the door.

"You're the buyers?"

"Yep," Chuck spoke up.

Jared moaned. The odd couple's eyes widened and they
craned their necks to look past Alane into the living room.

"I specifically told the rental agency that today wasn't
convenient. I'm sorry but you'll—"

"We just knew you wouldn't mind, since we were out
here anyway. It'll only take us a sec." The screen door
whined as Dot pulled it open and marched past Alane into
the living room.

Chuck waddled in behind her, wheezing with each labored breath.

"Dot, I don't think this lady wants to be bothered. I told
you—"

"Hush. It'll only take a second. You don't mind, do you,
sweetie?" She rummaged around in a gold lamé purse the
size of a suitcase and finally fished out a tape measure, ignoring any answer Alane might have given.

Jared hovered behind Alane and whispered in her ear.

"Have you any idea how long I had to wander the limits
of my boundaries when these two started making up from
one of their arguments? In front of the fireplace, no less?"

Alane's laugh sounded more like a strangled choke.

"Hurry up, Dot. We're bothering the lady." Chuck
turned to Alane. "Hey, you don't mind if I turn on the
match, do you?"

Before she could answer, the TV flared on and an an-
nouncer screamed about the body slam just delivered.

"Jared, get these people out of here," Alane whispered
through clenched teeth. "We can't let them buy this place!
You'll be figuring out a way to kill yourself all over again!"

As if to drive her words home, Chuck bellowed at the
television, belched, then threw his hands in the air and

dropped to the couch. The unfortunate furniture creaked and popped as he bounced to the edge.

"I'll see what I can do. Play along."

Rumbling from deep within his chest, Jared gave forth with his best bloodcurdling moan. Dot and Chuck both froze, their wide eyes turned to Alane.

"What was that?" Dot barked.

"What was what?"

"You didn't hear that gawdawful sound?"

Alane shrugged and shook her head. "No. It was probably the house settling. It does that a lot."

They both studied her for a moment, then Chuck grunted and turned his attention back to yelling at the TV. Dot shrugged and went back to her measuring. Jared walked over in front of Dot, focused his energy, then grabbed a window blind, pulled it down and let it fly back up to rattle at the top of the window. Dot yelped and jumped away, and Chuck cowered in the corner of the couch.

The clock on the wall chimed three o'clock, and Jared moved the hand backward, groaning while the Hamlins gaped at the clock suddenly running counterclockwise.

"Hey! What's going on here?" Dot rasped when she finally found her voice.

Alane looked at the clock and pursed her lips.

"Might be the resident ghost."

"Ghost?" Chuck squeaked. Dot suddenly developed a hacking cough.

"Yes. Sometimes he misbehaves. Takes a dislike to some people and just—"

The floor upstairs creaked and groaned as Jared stomped across it.

"Is someone else staying here?" he heard Dot ask with panic in her voice.

"No. Just me. Why do you ask?"

"You don't hear that racket upstairs?"

"Why, no. I don't hear any—"

For the *coup de grâce,* Jared made himself visible, removed his head from his shoulders and tossed it down the tiny, narrow stairway. As his head bounced down the steps,

Dot went rigid, screaming, and Chuck nearly stuffed himself inside the couch. Alane's eyes widened momentarily before she fixed a look of inquisitive confusion on her face.

Jared followed his head down, trying not to stagger from the vertigo of having one's head bounce down the stairs. This was not his favorite trick.

Dot's scream at the sight of his headless body would have done a horror movie proud.

Chuck scrambled over the arm of the couch, grabbed his rigid wife and shoved her toward the door.

"Is there a problem?" Alane asked with a straight face.

The couple ignored her as they fought to get the door open, Dot still screaming and Chuck puffing with exertion, whining like a puppy.

The door flew open and they shot out, one after the other, onto the porch, down the steps, then loped across the snow to their car. Before the doors were even shut, Chuck had the car in reverse and backing out of the drive.

While Alane watched them flee, Jared recovered his head, tucked it under his arm and joined her at the door. She watched, laughing and holding her side, as the car fishtailed down the road.

"Oh, my," she breathed as she closed the door and turned. "Do you think we've seen the last—Oh, Jared, put your head back on."

Alane hummed along with the Christmas carol on the radio as she turned onto the road leading to the cabin. She braced herself for Jared's arrival, and the moment the car passed over his ancient property line, he appeared in the passenger seat.

Ha! She didn't even flinch that time.

"Do you have any idea how long you were gone?"

She could almost hear his foot tapping, like a father whose daughter stayed out past curfew. She looked at her watch.

"Three hours and thirty-seven minutes. Give or take a few seconds."

He almost growled. "Well, I hope it was important."

She just smiled mysteriously and thought about what his reaction would be when she gave him the gift she'd been working on all afternoon.

"So what did you do while I was gone?"

"I sulked."

She threw her head back and laughed as she pulled into the drive and turned off the car. At least he was honest.

"Poor baby. I'll make it up to you this evening. What would you like to do? Just name it."

The scowl left his face and his brow quirked as he clearly contemplated the possibilities. He followed her into the cabin, and she could almost hear the gears turning to come up with something she wouldn't normally agree to.

"Hmm," he teased. "This is a very interesting proposition. I certainly don't want to waste the opportunity."

Alane smiled indulgently as she shrugged out of her coat and set her bag of art supplies on the end table. How much could he come up with, considering how sorely limited his options were? She headed for the kitchen, poured herself a glass of wine, then stirred up the fire and laid a few logs on. With a playful grimace, she plugged in the lights to the Christmas tree.

"A work of art," she reassured herself under her breath, then she stretched out on the rug in front of the fire and let her muscles relax, one by one. She hadn't realized how tense she'd been all day. But she'd achieved what she set out to do, and now she could just sit back and enjoy Jared's reaction.

Tomorrow, Christmas Eve, she'd give him his gift.

"I know how you can make it up to me," Jared interrupted her musings with a low voice near her ear.

Alane raised her head, surprised to see him stretched out beside her.

"I think I'm afraid to ask."

"Let me in your head again."

Just his saying the words caused her to go all warm and tingly. His persuasive smile didn't hide the raw need in his eyes. She swallowed and bit her lower lip.

"All right," she whispered, scared of opening up that

much; wanting to open up desperately. Then a thought occurred to her. "This won't hurt you will it? Like when you touched me?"

A sadness flashed in his eyes and he looked away, but when he looked back it was gone.

"No." He shook his head. "It'll be like when you painted. Since I'm not touching you, it won't take much energy."

"What are you going to do?"

Almost before she finished her question, he rolled over, melting into her, turning her blood to warm, heady brandy. She sighed, then gasped when a swirl of . . . feelings . . . touched her in ways words could never describe. Tenderness assaulted her senses. Love—his love—coiled in a tingling spiral in her chest. Visions of him making love to her floated through her mind and she felt as if it were real. Her bones turned to putty and sensations intoxicated her, heightening her senses, smoldering in her blood.

"Oh, Jared, do you feel it too?" She wanted to share this with him. Wanted to give back to him what he was giving to her.

She felt as if strong arms cradled her against a hard, warm chest; as if her head nestled broad shoulders.

She had no idea how long he bombarded her with one dizzying sensation after another. It could have been minutes. It could have been hours.

Finally, reluctantly, the sensations ebbed, and the warmth of him glided from her body, leaving her with her mind spinning and her body aching for more.

She turned to him and wanted to hold him so badly she could cry.

"Crying won't help," he responded to her unspoken thought.

He reached out his hand and touched her again, and suddenly she felt his torment. His agonizing torment to want. To love. Torment at being nothing more on this earth than a sigh of wind through the trees.

"Oh, Jared." She willed away the burning in her eyes. He wouldn't want her pity or her sympathy. He'd delved into her thoughts, her mind, and instead of taking, he'd given of himself, opened himself to her and let her feel his joy, his wonder, and his agony.

And neither of them would ever be the same.

EIGHT

The distant church bell tolled as Jared walked along the lake in the predawn hours of Christmas Eve. A thin layer of ice crusted the water along a shore as black and as cold as his mood.

He had to let her go. He'd known all along that this was just a brief moment in time for him to enjoy now and savor for decades to come. A keepsake of a precious memory. But he'd managed to tell himself that it didn't have to end.

Now he knew it must, for her sake, not for his.

Two days left together and then she would leave. And if she ever came back, he would not appear to her. Not ever. And eventually she would give up, go away, and live a normal life.

Perhaps she would marry David and have the children she denied wanting. He cared for her, Jared knew that for sure. He'd dipped far enough into David's thoughts that day to know that the man really did love Alane, even if he didn't understand her.

The thought of her leaving tore at Jared's chest, but the thought of what might happen if she didn't leave tore at him more.

He sensed her waking and was at her side in the space of a breath. He found her as he had left her, curled on her side, buried under a mound of blankets. He lay down beside her, watching, memorizing, as her eyes slowly opened and a soft, lazy grin curved her lips.

"You weren't watching me sleep, were you?" she asked, her voice husky.

"One of my favorite pastimes."

She faked a yawn that turned into a real one. "That's as bad as watching somebody fish."

He forced a grin. "That's what you said about painting, and look what it got you."

"Mmmm," she purred. "You do have a way of changing reality."

He only wished.

She rolled over, rolled into him, and he gasped at her unexpected move.

"I love it when you hold me," she murmured in a voice as soft and smooth as a kitten. He closed his eyes and willed the wrenching pain in the center of his soul to go away. How could he live without her? How could he continue to exist with her?

He lay there, holding her the only way he could as she dozed. When he could bear no more he rose and moved himself to the porch, staring out at the lake until he heard her moving around upstairs. She'd just come down the stairs when he entered the living room.

"Hey, you deserted me."

He shrugged and kept his tone light. "You were snoring."

She snatched a throw pillow and flung it at him. "I don't snore!"

"No, and I don't walk through walls."

She "hrmphed," tossed her head, then prissed into the kitchen.

Faith, every move she made, every breath she took made him love her even more.

He wandered into the kitchen and she playfully ignored him until he stepped in her way one too many times. With a giggle, she conceded defeat.

"But I still don't snore."

Her mood remained high—downright perky—all day long, while he fought to live up to his words and not mourn the future. In truth, it dented his ego that she so easily staved off her dread of their parting.

By evening he was misery incarnate, and Alane was all smiles and sparkling eyes. He'd had the devil's own time of keeping on a cheerful face, and the task became harder and harder as he watched the clock tick away the minutes.

"Do you want to watch another movie? *It's a Wonderful Life* is coming on."

"No," he sighed. "I think I've had all the Christmas spirit I need. Haven't you?"

She smiled mischievously and leaned into him.

"On the contrary. I can't seem to get enough Christmas spirit."

Her double meaning only depressed him further. They had such little time to get enough of each other.

"Oh, come on, sourpuss. You've been down in the dumps all evening."

"I have not."

"No? And I don't snore."

He smiled at that. She could always make him smile.

"I bet I know something that'll cheer you up."

He doubted it very seriously.

"What?"

He watched as she dropped to her knees and rummaged under the hideous Christmas tree. From within the folds of the sheet that was the "snow" beneath the tree, she pulled a small, flat box. She'd wrapped it in red foil with little silver bells in the ribbons. She jingled them at him.

"I'm going to figure out a way to put these around your neck when we're done."

He tried hard to keep an expectant smile on his face as she scooted back next to him on the floor.

A gift. What could she possibly give him that she could wrap in a box? What could he ever hope to give her in return?

"Merry Christmas. Open it. Oh, you want me to? Okay." She grinned up at him and tore into the foil with as much

excitement as if it were for her. When the wrapping fell
away, she stopped before taking off the lid.

"Wanna guess?"

He arched a brow at her and scanned the gift.

"A tie."

"Nope. Half right. It's a tie box. But . . ." She lifted the
top and folded back the tissue paper, one layer at a time,
". . . it's big enough to hold a cabin."

The last of the tissue paper fell away to reveal a long,
folded legal document that was obviously a deed.

Oh, sweet Gabriel, what had she done?

"I bought it this afternoon." She pulled the deed from
its bed of tissue paper and flipped it open with a flick of her
wrist. "I don't have to leave day after tomorrow. The
cabin's ours and nobody can make me leave."

His split second of pure elation died with the agonizing
sensation of being torn in two.

He couldn't allow her to stay.

"Alane . . . I . . ."

"I know. You're speechless. But it's okay. I took the
money Dad left me and paid for it. Even the bank doesn't
have a claim on it."

Her brilliant smile didn't start to fade until she realized
he didn't mirror her enthusiasm.

"What's wrong? We're supposed to be doing the dance
of joy right about now."

He closed his eyes and rammed splayed fingers through
his hair.

"Alane, you can't stay here."

"Of course, I can. I own—"

"No. Don't you see? It's impossible. As much as I love
you, I could never spend the rest of your life with you and
not touch you. Not go further than we did the night we
danced. Last night was one-sided, Alane. I felt images of
emotions, but that was all. I'd touch you again, even without
your permission, and I'd cease existing with the taste of you
on my lips, the feel of you lingering in my arms. And I'd
go happily because I've loved and been loved.

"But you would never forgive yourself. Ever. I've known

enough of your soul to know that you would blame yourself. You'd mourn me for the rest of your life and grow to hate yourself in the process."

He rose and paced the floor, shoving his hand through his hair and making a fist at the crown.

"You need children, Alane, and a husband who can touch you, pull you into his arms and comfort you when you've had a bad day. One who can make love to you. Hell, you need a husband who can open a door for you when your hands are full or help you decorate a Christmas tree. And you need one you can touch as well. It's a painful, empty feeling to never hold another human being in your arms." He pinned her with his gaze as he paced. "If you don't believe anything else I've ever told you, believe that."

He stopped his pacing and turned to her. He didn't bother to hide his tortured pain. He wanted her to know he loved her and to know that what he was about to do did not come easy.

She looked up at him. Her amazing brown eyes swam in tears while glistening drops fell from her lashes and etched silvery trails down her cheeks.

Wordlessly, she reached for him, but her hands grasped nothing but empty air.

He swallowed and closed his eyes.

"See?"

As he vanished, he heard her cry, "Jared, don't!"

Alane saw him in the distance, his ghostly figure paled by the moonlight that filtered through him. She knew she would find him here. Whenever he was deep in thought, he stared at the lake. It made sense that he would go there when he was troubled.

She had to make him listen; had to convince him that somehow they could make this work. The closer she got, the faster she walked. Her breath exploded in white clouds as she hurried to catch up with him.

She got within a few feet before he raised his head and spun around.

"Jared, I—"

Suddenly the snowbank fell away and she felt herself slipping toward the water. Her hands flailed as her body slammed into the bank and slid down, breaking the thin crust of ice and sliding into the freezing water.

Within seconds her heavy clothing absorbed the frigid waters and pulled her down, sucking her deeper into the numbing lake.

Jared bellowed her name and scrambled to the edge on his hands and knees, reaching for her hand that grasped at the slippery bank. His hand passed through hers once, twice, then solid fingers gripped her wrist and pulled.

"Jared, don't! I can—"

"Shut up and help me! Can you get a footing?"

She struggled to find solid ground beneath her, but her feet slid down the steep slope under the water.

"No. My clothes are pulling me down! Let go! Let me try to get my jacket off!"

"If I let you go, you'll die!"

"If you don't let me go, we'll both die!"

He held onto her, his fingers steel bands around her wrist. He heaved and she rose a couple of inches, then sank back deeper than ever. Her legs were going numb from the cold and her teeth chattered so hard they hurt.

"Jared, let go!"

He pulled again, yanking her higher this time. But his grip started to fade. His solid fingers took on a vapory look.

"Oh, please! Let go before you die!"

Another yank pulled her out of the water, then the iron-clad grip came back for a split second as he heaved her up to safety.

His fingers faded from her arm, and she rolled over to see him fall back against the snow, his body nothing more than a faint shadow against the silvery white.

"Jared, no! Don't go!" She reached for him. Tried to crawl to him, but her legs refused to move.

He rolled his head to hers, gave her a weak smile and stretched out his hand.

"I love you, Alane." As his words faded, so did his body.

She watched in agony as the shadow of him turned to mist and swirled away on a gust of wind.

She buried her face in the snow and screamed, her body shivering, her mind denying his death.

In the distance, the muffled sound of a church bell began its midnight toll.

She lay there, racked with violent shivers, drowning in guilt and misery.

Why had she come looking for him? If she had stayed in the cabin, he would have come back. Sooner or later he would have come back to her. And even if he hadn't, at least he would still be in this world. It tore at her heart and battered her soul to think that she was the one for whom he'd given up his existence. Damn his wife! Damn his mother-in-law! And damn herself for causing this.

The toll of the church bell rang for the twelfth time. Christmas morning.

She looked up at the midnight sky, at the millions of stars all blurred together through her tears.

"Good-bye, Jared." Her voice caught on a sob. "I love you."

Then a warmth surrounded her as she felt a jacket being wrapped around her. Her gaze flew to the man kneeling above her, his face a black silhouette against the moon.

"Who . . ." she managed to croak through chattering teeth and a throat thick with tears.

"Shut up and help me."

Jared! He moved to wrap his sweater around her legs, a sweater still warm from the heat of his body. Moonlight fell across his face, revealing solid features, warm and already red from exposure to the cold.

"Jared!" she cried, and staggered upright into his arms. "You're alive!" Her frozen fingers touched his face, encountered solid, warm cheeks, smiling lips. "How?"

He worked to wrap her in his dry things. "I don't know. I felt myself fade, and just as everything went black, an angel appeared out of the darkness. He said the curse had been broken. That Katherine knew I'd tried to love her. It wasn't her mother's words that kept me from peace, but my own guilt." He finished wrapping her in his warm clothes, then a look of awe spread across his face. "He reached out and touched me here," Jared held Alane's hand to his heart, "then he whispered, 'Never forget the greatest gift.' Then all of a sudden I felt cold and wet. And whole." He seared her with a smile.

She did what she'd ached to do since the moment they'd met. She sifted shaking fingers through his soft, luxurious hair, cupped the back of his head, and covered his mouth with hers.

He picked her up and cradled her against the warmth of his chest, his lips never leaving hers. By the time the kiss ended, they were halfway back to the cabin, the ice in her blood melting but the drum of her heart still crashing in her chest.

He grinned down at her, a solid, beautiful, Christmas miracle grin.

"I love you, Jared," she whispered with elation.

"I love you, too," he whispered back. Then he raised his face to the sky and yelled, "I love her, too!"

"You were right." She nuzzled her face against his neck as the warmth of him radiated into her very soul. "I do need to touch and to be touched."

He looked down at her, pulled her closer to him and murmured in her ear. "You've got a husband to marry today, and then I'm going to touch you in ways you've never even dreamed of."

"Mmmm," she sighed against his neck.

"And I've had two hundred years to dream."